CONFESSIONS OF A MARRANO ROCKETEER

DANIEL SCHENKER

Black Rose Writing | Texas

ISBN: 978-1-68433-856-6
PUBLISHED BY BLACK ROSE WRITING
www.blackrosewriting.com

Printed in the United States of America
Suggested Retail Price (SRP) $21.95

Confessions of a Marrano Rocketeer is printed in Book

*As a planet-friendly publisher, Black Rose Writing does its best to eliminate unnecessary waste to reduce paper usage and energy costs, while never compromising the reading experience. As a result, the final word count vs. page count may not meet common expectations.

In memoriam

Tracy Leverton

hope you found the gimmick

CONFESSIONS OF A MARRANO ROCKETEER

"All I maintain is that on this earth there are pestilences and there are victims, and it's up to us, so far as possible, not to join forces with the pestilences."

–Albert Camus, *The Plague*

EDITOR'S NOTE

I came to know Dr. Waldmann during the months of protracted litigation over the Technical Director's will. The more established firms would not come near the case, of course, but as I had only recently moved to town and had distant relatives who perished in the Holocaust, I was passionate--and foolish--enough to accept his retainer. After the local situation became untenable for him and he decided to leave town, he designated me as executor of his own will, but only several years later did he send me the following narrative with instructions that it not be published until twenty years after his death, which occurred on August 10th, 2000, at the age of 88. Composed on a typewriter, the manuscript copy was very clean and seemed the result of much polishing. I have made no changes except to correct a few minor factual errors and render into better English the occasional teutonism.

It goes without saying that certain episodes described herein will necessitate a major revision in our current understanding of the early history of space exploration.

Alan Fleming, Esq.
10 August 2020

PROLOGUE:
WHEN WE HEARD THE LEARNED ASTRONOMER

I knew the drill, having been on the inside for more than twenty years, almost half a century if you count my history with the Technical Director. Although I was leaving town the next day, indeed, leaving the country, I hoped forever, and wished to be well rested for the exhausting trans-Atlantic flight (but then, all flights exhaust me), I could not resist the temptation of attending that evening's public lecture.

Of course, the Cosmocrator, as we began calling him many years after the Technical Director's death, in both awe and derision of the fame he had acquired from his popular books and television shows, invariably entitled with variations on that numinous Greek word that signifies both order and beauty—the Cosmocrator would not simply get off a plane at 6:00 p.m. and begin discoursing an hour later. No, he would be met at our bucolic middle-American airport by a delegation from the hosting academic, corporate, and government elites in the early afternoon and given the VIP tour of the community's accomplishments from statehood through the space age, culminating in a visit to the Center for Space Exploration and Technology, a Smithsonian-affiliated museum.

Here he would have the opportunity to crawl through a mock-up of the International Space Station's living quarters, contemplate the vastness of the now empty neutral buoyancy tank where astronauts of our heroic age used to train, and take a ride in a virtual reality Mars Rover, a popular attraction not included in the regular admission price. Before participating in these activities he and the rest of his handlers would repair to the Space Camp locker room to change into NASA blue jumpsuits, a bit of ersatz realism that I will modestly take credit for having introduced during the Shah of Iran's visit. While there were some awkward moments with the Shah, not so the Cosmocrator. The exchange of custom-tailored $1,000 business suit for powder-blue $100 jumpsuit, with the appropriate banter distracting from the obvious imperfections of the middle-aged male body, is a natural action for a man who likes to play pick-up basketball with his graduate students those rare weeks he is actually resident on his home campus.

After bouncing around in the Rover and viewing rare archival footage of the Technical Director explaining the operation of the V-2 to the Reichsführer-SS (recently acquired at considerable expense from an anonymous donor in Surinam), he will take a stroll through Tranquility Base Plaza where Redstone, Jupiter, Atlas, and Saturn rockets are displayed in their launch positions, along with the Pathfinder, the original dummy prototype of the Space Shuttle. He will try hard not to be impressed with this display of hardware, styling himself today a Jonah in the land of Nineveh, but he will fail because like all highly accomplished persons he cannot mortify himself to the aura of seven and a half million pounds of thrust that still clings to the long silent motors of the Saturn V. He might perhaps regain moral equilibrium when he passes by the SR-71, Mach 3 successor to the infamous U-2, which has precious little to do to with space exploration, but is nonetheless extremely popular with tourists. The plane is black and dagger-like, and makes no bones about its connection to the military, a candor that makes it easier for him to resist its undeniable aerodynamic charms.

It's now coming up on four o'clock, and the current iteration of my middle manager former self, to whom the vaguely demeaning task has been delegated, escorts the Cosmocrator across the vast parking lot between the Space Center and his hotel, the only one in town to have earned a coveted four diamond rating in the AAA Tour Book. "Very tasteful," he says politely and unconvincingly as he crosses the atrium of potted palms and edgeless waterfalls he has seen a hundred times before, from Fresno to Dubuque, from Macon to Boise. His handler checks him in at the front desk, and at the hushed mention of his name, the Cosmocrator is ready with a self-deprecating smile and a Groucho Marx joke ("You know why the astronomer couldn't book a room on the moon? Because it was full!"), but the young woman at the desk, a second-year nursing student at the university, gives him no sign of recognition, and hands over a key while telling him about the hours of the breakfast buffet.

Associate Professor Flumdum, who cannot help feeling like a pipsqueak white dwarf in the presence of this mighty supernova, is happy to have discharged his formal obligation to the event as he perfunctorily asks if there is anything else he can do, and without missing a beat the Cosmocrator pulls a cashmere sweater vest from his partly unzipped overnight bag and indicates a dark splotch. "We hit turbulence over Virginia and the coffee popped right out of my hand. Do you think you could run this by one of those one-hour dry cleaners?" Flumdum, who hasn't patronized a dry cleaner since the Ford Administration, thinks he remembers a shop that offered one-hour service in a strip mall somewhere, but he will turn out to be wrong, and the rest of his afternoon will be consumed with a futile search to find a cleaner who can remove the stain from the distinguished astronomer's garment.

At around 5:30, a little early perhaps, but for a $10,000 lecture fee one is willing to make concessions, his hosts, the University Provost and the NASA Field Center Director, come by the hotel to take him to dinner. The Provost's late model Iridium Silver Mercedes carries them like a magic carpet over the interstate spur that leads from the technology zone on the west side of the city to the vestigial downtown area. Restored nineteenth-century shops and warehouses, now mostly law offices and artisanal microbreweries, ring the town square, facing the monstrous black cube in the middle that looks more like a replica of the Kaaba than a provincial courthouse, and which occasions an empathetic sigh of regret from the Cosmocrator as the Provost tells him about the beautiful Italianate structure that was unthinkingly torn down to make way for it. Continuing in this sentimental vein as they pass the now vacant Loew's Theater, the Provost recalls the day back in July 1969 when they switched off the projector in the middle of *True Grit* so that people could join the pre-arranged spontaneous celebration of the moon landing out in the streets. The Technical Director was carried around the square for nearly an hour on the shoulders of the ecstatic citizenry before his colleagues and the police could pull him back down to Earth.

Just past the theater is the French Quarter-style façade of the Founders Club, a recent venture of old real estate money and new high tech money. The Cosmocrator remarks on the name Grunwald carved in stone above the second story, and the Provost tells him that the building had once been a dry goods store owned by a Jewish family. In fact, the Jewish community in town went back to before the — . But here the Cosmocrator, who is rather touchy and secretive about the cultural Judaism that commands his lukewarm allegiance, changes the subject to the elaborate filigree of the Club's wrought-iron gate.

The dinner party now steps inside a foyer illuminated by gilt torch-bearing cupidons and carpeted by oriental rugs that look so authentic the Cosmocrator comes close to asking his companions if they would mind stopping for a moment so he could peel back a corner and look for labels in Farsi, but just knowing that the magnitude of his eminence would preemptively excuse even the most vulgar acts of gaucherie is reason enough to suppress this petty impulse. Moving on to the private dining room, the dentist's office décor cries out "white people!" to him. Thinking back to the late Mr. Grunwald, he wonders how many actual Jews have ever been inside this club, not that he would recognize a kosher lamb chop if it jumped off his plate and bit him on the nose.

After dinner, the Provost's Mercedes joins a convoy of corporate and academic vice presidents for the short drive to the university, whose campus blends seamlessly with the office park across Admiral Alan B. Shepard Boulevard. Indeed, the venue for this evening's lecture is the glass-walled trapezoidal McDonnell Douglas Gymnasium.

While the platform party enters by a rear door, I stand with the crowd out front, wearing tinted glasses and a houndstooth fedora like the ones favored by the late Paul "Bear" Bryant, legendary football coach of the Crimson Tide. The glasses and hat are probably an unnecessary, and perhaps even ineffective, precaution. During my working life I never came into clearer focus locally than as "one" in the phrase "one of the German rocket scientists," a pudgy-faced foreigner with a simple enough German name whose spelling and pronunciation the natives found relentlessly opaque. But what I see as we surge toward the entrance vindicates my extra efforts toward anonymity. Handing out flyers at the door is Dr. Nathan B. Royal, a professor in the school's history department, noted for his revisionist theories of both the American Civil and Second World Wars. Over the years Royal had served as a kind of informal advocate for the interests of the rocket community, though one whose tendency to go rogue would often cause as much consternation as comfort. During the firestorm over the contested addendum to the Technical Director's will, Royal had written a series of letters to the paper, exposing certain facts about interested parties to the dispute (one of them a notorious Francophile), and proving conclusively that their behavior in the affair had been motivated by "a deep-seated ethnic anxiety" with regard to the Nordic races.

I briefly review the flyer, a Xerox of a *USA Today* article about the Cosmocrator's messy divorce (female graduate student, Hawaiian "research" trips) from his third wife several years ago.

Inside, a standing-room-only crowd fills the gymnasium. Its bare concrete walls have been decorated with a dozen silkscreen images of the Technical Director, extending from floor to ceiling, that hang like medieval tapestries rippling in the air currents of the building's internal climate. In the 1960s, a local schoolteacher gained national recognition by writing a children's book that taught the Twelve Virtues using many of these same pictures. One wall displays "Imagination," in which a contemplative Technical Director in profile gazes at the model of a rocket he designed for a Walt Disney program; opposite hangs "Determination," which shows a younger version of himself seated at his desk in Peenemünde, eyes locked on to the viewer as he holds pen in hand, ready to sign some important document.

Just before the house lights dim, a side door below the stage opens and a line of balding, white-haired men enter the building. They move toward a roped-off section of empty seats directly in front of the speaker's podium. Most are in shirt sleeves, a few wear dark jackets and narrow ties. They move as if trudging through the heavy snows of a Pomeranian winter. When seated, they fold their hands and stare down into their laps. These are my former colleagues whom I haven't spoken with in the past ten years. If I could feel hatred, I would probably hate them, but I am cursed with a promiscuous empathy that leads inexorably toward forgiveness of almost any form of human behavior, except perhaps when it comes to my own. As I look at them from my remote bleacher, I find myself sharing their reluctance to gaze up at the iconic images of the Technical Director, which only serve to remind us of his untimely departure. He was only sixty-five! Without him we would have been a collection of brilliant nonentities, and when he abandoned us (since even the most natural of deaths contains an element of personal choice), we sank back into the historical oblivion from which he briefly raised us.

Although no formal announcement has been made, enough members of the audience recognize the former rocket team members to begin a round of applause, but before this builds to an ovation, the hall darkens, and in the space above center court materializes the image of a one-stage rocket, painted in harlequin lozenges, sitting on its launching pad. The surrounding countryside is heavily wooded, not with the familiar palm and palmetto of Cape Canaveral, but rather with the tall spruce of northern Europe. The colors are peculiar, too, recalling the preternatural richness of gladiator films from the 1950s. A man's voice, flat but booming, now fills the gym: "fünf, vier, drei, zwei," only to be lost inside the roar of ignition. Technicolor pink flames billow out from around the base of the rocket as it lifts from the pad and begins a lazy counter-clockwise roll. I recognize this as a holographic re-mastering of the film I shot, under the Technical Director's direction, of a successful A-4 test in 1943 using color stock so rare that it entailed a personal appeal to the Reichsführer-SS to obtain it. The rocket ascends toward one of the basketball hoops where, after a few seconds, it disappears into a virtual cloud bank just like the one over the Baltic that world-historical morning half a century ago.

The clouds now coalesce into holographic nebulae and stars, and floating beneath them materializes an eerie but recognizable landscape: scattered boulders in high resolution, the pink sky of a Martian sunrise. Everyone knows this scenery from the photographs sent back by Viking, the unmanned probe perhaps closest to the heart of this evening's distinguished speaker. But we are not alone. Spacecraft are parked all around, their names stenciled on their sides: Oberth, Ley, Goddard, Tsiolkovsky, Armstrong. Astronauts bustle about, setting up equipment. Their silvery visors reflect the landscape and one another, until slowly one of the visors clears, revealing the face of the Technical Director, in the prime of life. Then another clears, and it, too, is the Technical Director. Then another, and another, until there are three dozen Technical Directors going about their business on Mars, marking, measuring, collecting. The audience signals its approval with a standing ovation. At its climax, the vision melts under a blaze of spotlights that illuminate both the podium and the learned astronomer himself. For a moment everyone is surprised to see someone who isn't the Technical Director, but goes on applauding anyway.

The Cosmocrator appears taller now than he did on television, an illusion produced by a manipulation of light and shadow that conforms his body with the El Greco-esque images of the Technical Director around the hall. He lowers his outstretched arms, signaling for the crowd to be seated. The noise in the hall is turned off like a faucet, and the well-behaved audience is as attentive as the freshmen in the professor's introductory astronomy course on the four days during the semester when he and not one of his doctoral candidates delivers the lecture. He smiles broadly and gestures toward a line of chairs on the stage behind him, where sits a gathering of local dignitaries, anchored by the ubiquitous Provost and his stony-faced team of vice presidents.

Also on stage, separated from his colleagues by a couple of empty chairs, and indeed, almost in the shadows, is the university president, Dr. Frank "Fritz" Vohles. His responsibilities as a lobbyist and fundraiser dictate that he rarely comes to campus, leaving day-to-day operations to the Provost. From many years of huddling with legislators and wealthy donors, Dr. Vohles's head seems to hang a little distance in front of his stooped shoulders, like the lanterns carried by the Negro jockeys that once decorated the lawns of many rocket engineers' homes, in imitation of the town's elites. In contrast to the vaguely disapproving frown of the Provost, the President's owlish face beams at an audience he is genuinely delighted to see, never imagining that ordinary townspeople would show up at a university-sponsored public event in such impressive numbers.

The Cosmocrator begins his address with the obligatory expressions of gratitude to the Trustees of the Saturn Program Memorial Lecture Fund, and his hosts, the NASA Field Center Director, the Provost, and the University President. Dr. Vohles bobs his head and waves meekly at the audience, pleased to have been recognized.

"How long has it been, Fritz," muses the Cosmocrator aloud, "since we stood on that lonely runway at Goddard watching as the Technical Director brought his lovingly restored Storch to a landing? Fifteen years? Sixteen? We gave it our best shot at trying to save Saturn for unmanned interplanetary missions, and although we failed, I still treasure the note the Technical Director sent afterwards, assuring me that we had done nothing to be ashamed of."

Without looking in their direction, the Cosmocrator now extends his left hand toward the old men seated directly beneath him. "Let me acknowledge, too, the work of the collaborators whom the Technical Director loved like brothers, and whom we are honored to have with us tonight as our special guests. Your careers began in what were not the best of times, and like your youthful leader, you had to make difficult choices. Squeezed in the same vise of history, any one of us might have done the same. Or differently. Who am I to judge?" The Cosmocrator shrugs like Herman Weinstein, an old Jewish tailor I patronized in the early years, whenever I asked him if a new suit made me look fat. "But from that miasma of moral ambiguity arose technological marvels that would inspire a boy on Long Island who knew, like another boy in Upper Silesia a generation earlier, that his destiny lay in the heavens."

None of the former rocketeers looks up at the Cosmocrator. They contribute polite applause to the general din before hunkering back down into their seats like prisoners awaiting the next truncheon blow of a sadistic interrogator.

The Cosmocrator continues: "Today our scientists and engineers face the same dread ambiguity. Will the modern rocket lead us to mass annihilation, or will it carry us to the planets and the stars? Recently the President of the United States proposed a space-based anti-ballistic missile system which he claims would render America invulnerable to Soviet attack. Could we develop such a shield? Soon after the Apollo landings in 1969, a young space enthusiast asked the Technical Director, 'What is the most important thing a man needs when he wants to build a spaceship and travel to the Moon?' and without missing a beat he replied, 'The will to do it!' But can a triumphant will alone guarantee security?"

"As most of you know, I have long been a proponent of unmanned rather than manned exploration of space because I believe that from an ethical perspective no datum of scientific knowledge is worth the cost of a human life." Scattered booing can be heard throughout the auditorium. The Cosmocrator allows this to continue for a few moments before proceeding.

"But the world moves on. Let me tell you, once at a conference on planetary exploration I heard the Technical Director admit that his advocacy of nuclear bomb rocket propulsion had been misguided, and then quoting, I think, the Bible, he continued, 'the man who never changes his opinion is like standing water and breeds reptiles of the mind.'"

The Cosmocrator draws close to the microphone while turning his face toward the image hanging nearest the podium. It reproduces not a photograph but rather a mural executed in the American primitive style of Grandma Moses that once decorated the foyer of a popular restaurant in town known for its unique synthesis of German and Appalachian cuisine. The head-and-shoulders portrait of the Technical Director shows him almost breaking into a smile (an admittedly crude allusion to the Mona Lisa) as he fixes the observer in his gaze. Above him the various missiles whose development he oversaw trace arcs in a cloudless robin-egg blue sky; beneath are scenes of old houses, horses and buggies, dancing farm laborers (both black and white), bales of cotton, and other mementos of the town's bucolic past.

The Cosmocrator seems lost in contemplation and then, speaking in barely above a whisper, says, "And so in the shadow of his greatness and his humility before you tonight, let me make my confession: I was wrong." I note that the final word is punctuated with the vocalized "g" of his native Long Island dialect, indicating the sincerity of his contrition. No Marrano hauled up before the Holy Office of the Inquisition for spitting out a mouthful of pork on the Feast Day of St. James, and begging the magistrates at his auto-de-fé for the relaxation of a sentence of burning at the stake to one of simple garroting and decapitation, could have presented himself as more thoroughly penitent.

The crowd is electrified. Riding the wave, the Cosmocrator goes on. "I used to think that science and politics were of two houses, nothing kin, but the Technical Director knew better. As a young engineering student he accepted the world-historical burden genius imposed upon him and dutifully went to work for the German army. After the Führer came to power, hours that he would rather have spent at his beloved test stands were passed haunting ministerial offices in Berlin, persuading the barbarians and thugs to believe whatever tickled their fancies about the military uses of his rockets as long as they gave him the money to pursue his not so secret dream of space travel. Even the success of his wonder weapon against civilian targets in Paris and London, which he personally deplored, he used as an argument for a multi-staged winged version that could reach New York, knowing that it might serve as a test vehicle for a manned mission."

"And so tonight I present to you my humble proposal. Where your departed leader made politics work for space, I want to make space work for politics." The Cosmocrator draws himself up to his full height, like a boy about to recite the Pledge of Allegiance before a school assembly. "I believe that the President of the United States and the General Secretary of the Soviet Communist Party should commit their nations to a joint venture of landing men and women on Mars by the year 2019, the fiftieth anniversary of that one giant leap for mankind. The risks will be enormous and the financial cost considerable, but when one views the world today with the same ruthless toughness that the Technical Director and his colleagues brought to an understanding of their own times, it's clear that this may be our last best chance to achieve peace and guarantee the survival of the human species."

The Cosmocrator cringes as he speaks these final words, but the audience responds with unexpected warmth and enthusiasm. Is it the proposed 30-year life of the project which would keep every engineer in town busy through retirement? Or has his statesmanlike rhetoric achieved ethical contact with these people and awakened the better angels of their nature? Whatever the reason, his relief is palpable, and he moves toward the peroration.

"Years ago at the Cape over his favorite breakfast of bacon and grits before the launch of Surveyor 6, I asked the Technical Director what he considered the strongest argument for space exploration. He turned pensive and, looking more like the man who wrote poetry than the manager of the most complex technical enterprise in history, said, 'Life is a bitter fruit that we digest into sweet knowledge. But now the old Earth is filling up with these wondrous turds of civilization and the time has come to begin dropping them on other worlds. This is the vision that calls me forth as a scientist.' "

"So what will it be, my friends, Star Wars or Mars, science fiction or science fact? I know what he would have chosen," and here the Cosmocrator turns a complete circle as he extends his outstretched arm toward each of the larger-than-life portraits, "and I think you do, too."

When the applause dies down, the Cosmocrator announces that he will be happy to take a few questions. A dozen student ambassadors in red blazers stationed throughout the auditorium wave wireless microphones over their heads. Hands go up and the Cosmocrator takes his first question, an obvious softball, from a teenager who asks whether the Mars expedition would use nuclear or chemical propellants. Next, an older gentleman with a jet black pompadour asks how America can cooperate with a slave state whose space program has abandoned dozens of cosmonauts to circle the Earth forever in their ghost Vostoks. Another questioner, a woman in a lime green pants suit, brings up the Trilateral Commission.

Turning now to the opposite side of the hall, the Cosmocrator points to a man in his sixties wearing an off-white linen suit with wide crimson tie just a few rows below me. A smattering of applause erupts as some people recognize him as the distributor of the scurrilous flyer at the door. Professor Royal can hardly believe his good fortune. He stands up, arms akimbo, holding back the sides of his jacket. His mouth opens, and at first no words come out, but after a few seconds he finds his voice.

"First, the Technical Director and his colleagues have nothing to apologize for. Moral ambiguity? I don't think so. The decision in 1932 was between Judeo-Christian free enterprise and atheistic communism, and I think they chose well. The tragedy of war might have been averted if the Anglo-Saxon race had presented a united front to the world, but Britain and America were held hostage by the same Zionist cabal that had declared war on Germany and planned the genocide of its people. Der Führer, the popularly elected legal head of the German Reich, was backed into a corner and had no choice but to negotiate with Stalin in the hope that it would buy time for at least Churchill to come around.

"Second, let me propose an analogy. A man points a gun at you. You can stand there unprotected and wait for him to fire, or you can put on a bullet-proof vest to defend yourself. What do you do? Or do you think this is a matter for situational ethics to resolve? So my question to you is, where do you stand on world government gun control, or what you liberals call the nuclear freeze? Or for that matter, on gun control, period."

The Cosmocrator, having loosened his tie and stepped in front of the podium, listens carefully to Royal, nodding at points of emphasis. As his questioner finishes, he smiles brightly and opens the left side of his jacket to reveal a stainless steel Luger in a leather holster. He reaches over with his right hand, unfastens the snap, and against all expectation, fires straight up in the air. Simultaneous with the report of the gun there is a loud hollow popping sound as the bullet takes out one of the spotlights suspended from the ceiling. A small shower of debris falls upon the Provost and his vice presidents.

Royal topples over backward, howling in pain, though it's obvious to everyone that the Cosmocrator has merely let off a warning shot. Above the buzz of the crowd, the Cosmocrator announces, "I support the right of every American citizen to bear arms, within the confines of the law, as guaranteed under the Second Amendment. You would be amazed at the number of crank calls and death threats I receive each week." As he returns the Luger to its holster, my former colleagues spring preternaturally to life. They stand up and cheer at the top of their wheezy old-man lungs, many of them waving handkerchiefs above their heads. A few sectors of the audience join in, but most of us sit in stunned silence, unsure whether to be impressed at the learned astronomer's bravado or shocked by his bad manners. The President, however, seems to enjoy the moment, laughing and making funny faces, as his head snaps back and forth between the Cosmocrator and the audience with a kinesis that reminds me of Harpo Marx in *Duck Soup*. The Provost, on other hand, struggles to maintain dignity, furtively shaking bits of glass and metal from the cuffs of his trousers.

A questioner's voice comes over the sound system, but it is immediately swallowed up in a new commotion. Off to my right, men in short-sleeved shirts with pocket protectors have taken up a chant. Their passion reminds me of the Civil Rights demonstrations of the 1960s our town was mostly spared. Soon Royal is back on his feet, picking up the chant which can now be understood as "Star Wars! Star Wars! Star Wars!" In his low-country planter white suit he is an unlikely protester, but he embraces his role with zeal, clapping with hands held high and gesturing for others to join in. Many do, but across the gymnasium another group has taken up a different call: "Mars! Mars! Mars!" They, too, wear the same standard livery of the local engineer.

The Cosmocrator has been trying to ignore the disruption, but it's clear that rational discourse has come to an end. He looks nervously back at the President. Dr. Vohles is still smiling, thinking about how an annual controversial speaker's series might help to make up for the lack of seasonal excitement on a campus without a football team, and wondering how many notches tonight's event might lift the school in the next *U.S. News & World Report* college rankings. The Provost, however, senses real trouble. He orders the Cosmocrator back from the podium. Royal and his Star Wars partisans can now be seen throwing small objects at the Mars faction. These are plastic replicas of the Hermes, Nike, Saturn, and other missiles designed by the Technical Director which were being sold as souvenirs in the lobby before the lecture. Soon the air is filled with missiles being thrown back and forth, and when the supply of these is exhausted, bigger objects, like folding chairs and pieces of bleacher seats, become airborne. The whole auditorium has been sucked into the vortex of a street brawl the likes of which I haven't seen since the last days of the Weimar Republic.

By now the Provost and his Vice President for Faculty Management have drawn their own concealed weapons, and with the professional aplomb of Secret Service agents, shield the Cosmocrator from the bombardment aimed at the stage, although from their manner of pinning him to the floor, it's unclear to me whether their goal is to protect him from bodily harm or prevent him from slipping away. Only now does the President realize that he's in the midst of an old-style putsch, and he stands there like a one-man chorus in a Greek tragedy, too deeply in shock to fend off the occasional Hermes or Nike that comes his way.

With cries of "Chancellorsville! Chickamauga! Let's get 'em boys!" Royal leads his band hop-scotching down the bleachers toward the nearest Mars cadre. Within a couple of minutes, a whole scrum of bodies rolls onto the gymnasium floor. Amid the confusion, someone has inadvertently hit the switch to start the laser light show again, and the first V-2 on film renews its holographic path across the Baltic sky of a long lost world. The campus police at last arrive and immediately deploy themselves to create a cordon sanitaire between the VIP section and the nearest door so that my former colleagues can leave safely. They hardly need the assistance. Invigorated by the evening's events, they have already formed themselves into a line of march, four abreast with arms linked, which rolls over bodies and debris as it forces its way to the exit.

CHAPTER 1
ESCAPE VELOCITY

I confess that for a moment I wanted to elbow my way down to the gymnasium floor and join the phalanx of old men in their triumphant march from the building. The evening's events had been an unexpected reversal of fortune, a last minute snatching of victory from the jaws of defeat, as if Stalingrad or Bastogne had gone the other way. I had expected chastisement from the celebrity astronomer, and there it was in the form of his platitudes about moral ambiguity. Of course, as even a non-practicing member of a once persecuted religious sect, he had the right to inflict this public humiliation on us, but to his credit that wing-nut Royal saw right through the Cosmocrator's hypocrisy. The revelation of the Luger was a complete vindication of what we had done, although that solace was now denied to me personally, estranged as I was from my former sodality. To put it bluntly, Royal had shown that even ethnically privileged superstar liberal intellectuals need guns. Honestly, how much difference is there between that and a sovereign nation building the world's first ballistic missiles?

It was chaos out in the parking lot, a lurid automotive Gotterdämmerung bathed in the strobing blue, red, and yellow lights of emergency vehicles, and it took me almost an hour to return home, but as soon as I arrived, I went right to the sliding door of the master bedroom closet and felt around inside for the wooden holster, with its resident Luger, that I had installed there several years ago when the State Department stripped our Production Chief of his citizenship and deported him back to Europe under threat of prosecution for war crimes. Guilty or not, I wasn't going to be taken without a symbolic display of resistance. As it turned out, the Rosenthals and Leventhals in the State Department were satisfied with their one sacrificial lamb and never again sniffed around in these parts, but by that time I had come to appreciate the instinctual sense of empowerment, so obviously native to this region of my adopted (and soon to be disowned) homeland, that I could see no reason to dismantle my handiwork. Once I made the decision to move away, I also took pleasure imagining the puzzlement of successive owners discovering this odd little wooden pocket on the inside of the door, and their idle speculation about the rationale behind it.

Well, that's enough excitement for a while. I hope the reader appreciates this dramatic beginning, because what follows will be largely conventional autobiographical apologia, though there are some truly spectacular episodes in the second half of the narrative. I also promise to deal with the matter that I know is on the mind of everyone (at least, everyone beyond the city limits here) who has enough interest to dip into the memoirs of a mid-level operative of the Third Reich, what contemporary Holocaust scholarship has labeled "The Speer Questions": What did I know about the murder of the Jews, and when did I know it, and for good measure, how much guilt do I carry around? Etc., etc.

But before transporting us back to my peculiar youth in pre-war Germany, let me describe the thoughtfully choreographed movements of my final Rocket City leave-taking.

Because of my personal (but not principled) revulsion against air travel, I would be driving to the Atlanta airport in a rented car instead of taking the short connecting flight. The drive takes about four hours, and navigating the maze of interchanges, exit-only lanes, service roads, and construction zones over there is an absolute nightmare, while the flight on the Delta puddle jumper is only about twenty minutes, take-off to touchdown, but I'll take four hours of misery over twenty minutes of hell any day. While I'm well aware that the odds of dying in a commercial airliner crash are approximately twenty-nine million to one, the odds were about three in four for the unfortunate souls in a DC-9 that went down on that very same route in 1977, and to those of you who would say that lightning never strikes twice, it's one of the commonplaces of television meteorologists' visits to fifth-grade classrooms that in fact it does, hundreds, if not thousands of times a day. So my plan was to leave early enough in the afternoon to arrive before dark, but late enough to miss the peak of the rush hour, and then to spend the night in an airport motel steeling myself for the eight hours of airborne hell the following day.

One collateral benefit of this late day departure was having just enough hours for a reflective but not excessively sentimental farewell tour of the sites that bore the residue of personal mythology that accumulate when you have lived in a place for a long (or even short) time.

Having already sold my Mercedes 220 diesel sedan, I took a taxi to the rental agency near the airport where, in keeping with my preference for anonymity, I had reserved the vehicle that I thought least likely to be driven by a retired foreign-born rocket scientist: a red Pontiac Catalina Safari station wagon. The thing feels as big as a school bus and guzzles almost as much gas as a Tiger tank, but since I would be throwing away my driver's license when I dropped off the car in Atlanta, I figured that I might as well go out in the best big shoddy American style.

I headed back toward town and turned onto Memorial Parkway, the city's main north-south artery, whose original design I had overseen at the Technical Director's behest back in the early 1950s. At the time the only connection to the river some ten miles to the south was a narrow two-lane road which, before our arrival, wasn't even completely paved, despite its designation as a U.S. highway. This was clearly inadequate for the transport by tractor-trailer of the large rocket boosters that we planned to load onto barges at a proposed river terminal for shipment down to the Cape. The solution was obvious — an American Autobahn — and I put together a committee using several of our people who had come to us from the Todt Organization, Germany's wartime public works administration. We came up with a perfectly serviceable design that met all of our work-related requirements, but before vetting it to the state highway department, the Technical Director modified it in light of his conviction that the Autobahn would become the focus of the town's commercial and residential development.

"Who the hell will build a department store out in the middle of a cotton field?" I objected.

"People who have no memory of trolleys and streetcars," replied the Technical Director. "Trust me, twenty years from now people will think nothing of driving ten miles to buy a cheap toaster."

He was correct, naturally, and today it's strip malls and subdivisions all the way down to the river. The road looks like commercial thoroughfares in a thousand other places, with one notable exception: Most intersections feature surplus hardware from the Army missile programs that our group managed during the early years. (Missiles from our later NASA period are exhibited at the Center for Space Exploration and Technology.)

Since there was not time to pay my respects to every one of these elegant weapons systems, I drove the Safari to a personal favorite of mine that is representative of the whole class of these civic installations, located at the anomalously named Airport Road, which hasn't been home to the regional airport in over half a century.

Surrounded by chevrons of colorful tulips, daylilies, asters, chrysanthemums, and other seasonally appropriate blooms maintained by a men's garden club stands a Hermes anti-aircraft missile. Hermes was an American version of the Wasserfall missile whose guidance system I had been working on in the winter of 1944-45, when the Technical Director reassigned me to a special project. Wasserfall itself was a scaled-down version of the V-2, and while both the Technical Director and I were always skeptical of the difference that our exotic weapons might have made in the war's outcome, Speer in his memoirs muses that a combination of Wasserfalls and jet fighters might have stalled the Allied bombing campaign and turned the tide: Thus, the missile here is an unwitting monument to our counterfactual victory in World War II, and my never having come to America in the first place.

As I walk the cobblestone labyrinth adjacent to the Wasserfall, I'm struck by how it both dominates and harmonizes with the surrounding landscape of flowerbeds, loblolly pines, and open green spaces (a nine-hole golf course sits directly behind the site). There will be time later to satisfy the reader's ineluctable curiosity about the psycho-sexual aspect of rocket development, but for now let me note the exoskeleton's graceful arc from exhaust nozzle to nosecone, the reassuring stolidity of its square-tabbed base, and contrasted with this, the almost whimsical ethereality of its trapezoidal midsection fins. The time traveler from an earlier century who had absolutely no knowledge of aeronautical machines would think the Hermes an example of inspired tribal art, a henge stone in polished iron.

Indeed, when equally effective means of meeting program requirements were presented to him, the question of aesthetics moved to the fore of the Technical Director's deliberations. I remember one meeting in the late summer of 1943 when the wind tunnel people reported out two tailfin configurations for the V-2. I had expected a tedious hashing out of their respective capabilities, but the Technical Director announced his decision immediately, noting that one created a cleaner visual line where the fins joined the body. Our Production Chief then chimed in about the limited welding skills of the assembly line workers, who were increasingly drawn from the ranks of forced labor levies in occupied countries.

"I understand the concern," replied the Technical Director, "but the rocket must not only lift a payload of dynamite, nerve gas, or whatever, but also the spirits of all the lives it touches in its tragically brief existence. The Polish welder in the tunnels might find it difficult to render seamless the junction of the two-dimensional fin with the spheroid body, but imagine his sense of personal satisfaction in contemplating the successful result. Think also what it will mean to the soldier in the field who fires the missile, or the civilian lucky enough to catch a fleeting glimpse of it as it screams across the skies of Lower Saxony and Westphalia on its way to the coast. Regardless of the war's outcome, our people will know that our weapons are not only more powerful but also more beautiful than those of our enemies. Consider, too, that rare victim who catches sight of the rocket on its supersonic descent in the fraction of a second before their conjoined annihilation. Although he will not fully comprehend the means of his death (but who among us does?), his last thought will be of its unique character such that only the Reich could provide."

Colonel D., who always began to fidget at about this point in the Technical Director's rhetorical flights, then added, "The competition for scarce resources is becoming intense. Of course the Führer wants a weapon with annihilating effect but elegant design will also speak to the artist in him." The Colonel, a career artillerist, had little appreciation for art himself, but was resigned to the fact that the exploitation of exceptional talents was inseparable from the management of artistic temperaments, even ones as diverse as the Technical Director's and the Führer's. He had always suspected that the latter's indifferent response to his visit to Kummersdorf some years earlier was because a rocket engine on a test stand that might look beautiful to a mechanical engineer would appear to a former Austrian art student as an expensive pile of junk. Here was another reason that the Colonel had objected so robustly when Todt complained about architects' fees for the vernacular-style laboratory buildings at Peenemünde. There was no way the Colonel would allow the Führer to leave at the end of an official visit (which never did take place, as it turned out) thinking that he had spent the day at a glorified machine shop.

At all events, Wasserfall was the first of these public erections in town but by no means the last. After the Soviets detonated their hydrogen bomb in 1953, the pressure on us to develop ever more powerful and accurate delivery systems for nuclear payloads was unrelenting, which meant that within just a few years every missile became obsolete, surplus, and available for public display. Driving a few more miles down the Parkway, then executing a sloppy U-turn (my big, boxy American car being as responsive as an oil tanker) I called the roll of projects that had consumed my waking hours: Major, Honest John, Little John, Nike, Lacrosse. As it became more generally known that the Army had dozens of missiles awaiting consignment to the scrap yard, businesses and nonprofit organizations entered into keen competition to acquire one. You can see them today at supermarkets, building supply stores, the botanical garden, the Red Cross; there's even a well-maintained Hawk at a veterinary clinic that specializes in the care of birds. Homebuilders also acquired them, and the entrances to most residential subdivisions feature a missile or two.

While obviously none of them were operational, their ubiquity contributed to the atmosphere of relative calm that prevailed here, in contrast to the rest of the country, during moments of heightened Cold War tensions, like the Cuban Missile Crisis.

Having bid my fond adieus to the ordnance along the Parkway, I headed toward the downtown historic district which, despite the absence of significant commercial activity, remains home to most of our town's public buildings. By 1960 not only had actual missiles become a feature of the urban landscape but local architecture had come to incorporate quotations of missile design. I-beams protruding from the corners of the Kaaba-like courthouse (an amateurish homage to the Bauhaus style that most of us never liked to begin with) attenuate into nosecones with bas-relief steel fins. The Civic Center, named for the Technical Director, and opened two years before his untimely death, looks nothing like a missile per se, but was closely modeled on his gargantuan space wheel, a proposed Earth-orbiting space station, that was featured in both popular magazine articles and television programs in the mid-1950s. Like the space wheel, the Center measures some 250 feet across, and although stationary, its smaller glass-enclosed upper deck houses a cocktail lounge that rotates about one revolution every three minutes, affording panoramic views of the surrounding hills.

Within a couple of minutes, the Safari and I have bounced through downtown and plunged back into the neighborhoods. The houses here are mostly ranchers and split-levels, but you can often spot the home of an engineer by the gantry-like structures of tubular steel and corrugated metal that replace the more conventional garages, carports, and backyard workshops. In Twelve Points, an area now home to the city's gay and lesbian community but once a working-class mill village, "Four B's" — Big Bob's Burger Bunker — still does a substantial lunch business. It's the last surviving example of several locally-owned meat-and-three restaurants that were built to look like the concrete igloos of rocket test observation blockhouses.

But the most dramatic manifestations of the Missile Style have to be seen in the more than sixty churches that were built during the boom times of the mid-fifties through the mid-sixties. When our team arrived in 1950 there was an Episcopal church, a handful of Presbyterian and Methodist churches, dozens of Baptist churches (distinguished from one another theologically by a variety of dour adjectives), and a plethora of other denominations that were unknown to us in Germany. Perhaps unsurprisingly, there was no Lutheran church in town, but hardly had the moving vans been unloaded when the Technical Director initiated the process of establishing a mission, and within the next year all but the Catholic minority among us celebrated the first worship service in our own sanctuary, a converted funeral home. Curiously, while our goal in the remodeling process was a building that blended with the relatively unadorned style of local church architecture — plain brick walls, a modest spire — other churches in town moved ever more boldly into the Missile Style. A spin-off Methodist congregation rejected the traditional white clapboards in favor of prefabricated metal siding, some of it salvaged from an obsolete test stand; a new Episcopal church featured a lofty planetarium-like nave with side chapels whose conic ceilings tapered into actual surplus Jupiter-C exhaust nozzles.

The culmination of this phenomenon, however, must be the First Baptist Church, which relocated from a grumpy nineteenth-century brick pile downtown to a spacious new campus on the Parkway. Its ranks had grown by leaps and bounds with the influx of hundreds of young engineers and their families in the run-up to the Apollo program, and they were determined to spare no expense in their desire to make a statement that the religion of the substitutionary sacrifice and the technology of space exploration were perfectly compatible. By this time, too, many of us original Germans had drifted away from the Lutheran church with its Old World fustiness and toward the Baptists whose barely restrained triumphalism seemed more in keeping with the unbroken successes of the American space program. The Technical Director was among these. While he remained a member in good standing of the Lutheran group, he spent most Sunday mornings in the pews of the Baptist church, which now became the object of a financial largesse made possible by the royalties from his many books. Certainly there was grumbling about this in our own group. Many felt that his motivations were political, alignment with the Baptists giving him better access to local movers and shakers; some defended him on precisely these same grounds.

Whatever our differences, I believed in his sincerity. Sunday mornings just for show? Perhaps, but he certainly wasn't getting a lot of visibility out of his regular attendance at Wednesday night Bible study. Rather, unlike most of us as we grow older, the Technical Director remained a seeker. God in the mainline churches wasn't acting much like God anymore. He made mistakes, He couldn't do this or that, we were supposed to feel sad or sorry for Him. The Technical Director wanted — needed — a God who could zap fire down onto a water-logged altar and vaporize the bad guys, a God with a voice that could shake the ground like a Saturn V test firing. Of course, you could always find that God in the holy roller and other off-brand churches, but obviously those could never be the spiritual home of a cultivated European who had studied the cello with Paul Hindemith and could recite from memory Part I of Goethe's *Faust*, so the First Baptist church was the next best thing.

I pulled the Safari into a spot at the back of the empty church parking lot from where I could take in the whole view, and turned off my engine.

The resemblance to the Vehicle Assembly Building at the Cape is subtle but nonetheless uncanny. (Several members of the church building committee were engineers who used to travel down there on a regular basis.) The exterior of the sanctuary is a five-story concrete box whose main façade is covered by a mural of a stylized crucifix. A crown floats above the head of Jesus, but except for the head and upturned hands, the rest of the image is nonrepresentational. In place of his body is an orb of concentric red, orange, yellow, and white circles upon which is superimposed an elongated cross bearing the Greek letters alpha and omega. Some people in town think that lines paralleling the base of the cross make it look like an eggbeater, but I see the shockwaves radiating outward from a rocket ignition sequence. Blue and green circles further out, along with several yellow orbs, suggest either the solar system or a spiral galaxy. The whole scene is framed by a series of seven Romanesque arches, the central arch focusing the viewer's attention on the seemingly oscillating crucifix. All that's missing is the thunderous roar and the smell of burning hydrazine.

A few years after the completion of the sanctuary, an anonymous donation of half a million dollars made possible the addition of a free-standing steeple whose tripartite division from top to bottom is so obviously an aerospace allusion that everyone refers to it as the "Rocket Steeple." Since a city ordinance requires that no structure in town (except television antennas) be taller that the Saturn V mock-up at the Center for Space Exploration and Technology, the Rocket Steeple is exactly three hundred sixty two feet, eleven inches.

From the church I headed west again toward the university. It's a generic sort of institution with a bi-directional modifier before our state's name, but every few years some retired general or millionaire defense contractor proposes that it be renamed for the Technical Director, who was almost wholly responsible for its establishment. (Why has that never happened? See "Rosenthals" and "Leventhals," above.) When we arrived in 1950, there was already a university in town but its mission was to train black people to be farmers and mechanics, while we needed bulk quantities of mechanical and electrical engineers. I was a member of the delegation that the Technical Director led to the state capital to request the creation of a College of Engineering at the existing university, but we were told, no, that was impossible because blacks and whites could not attend the same schools, the exigencies of the Cold War notwithstanding.

Of course, we knew as early as our surrender to the Americans in Bavaria that blacks and whites were not equal when we observed that the many black soldiers in the unit were all enlisted men who performed menial tasks, like cleaning our toilets. The black soldiers didn't seem any less intelligent than the white ones, but we figured that all nations have their caste systems, established at some point in their histories by right of force: The Americans had their Negroes, we Germans had our Slavs (or did until that spring of 1945). When our request was turned down, the Technical Director smiled and gently slapped his outstretched palm onto the table and said, "Well then, gentlemen, let's found a brand new university up there!" He had, of course, come prepared for any eventuality, and before the stunned state officials, he removed a map from his briefcase showing a three-hundred-acre tract of abandoned cotton land that was currently available, along with written pledges from local civic and business leaders to assist with funding. Within six months, construction had begun on two buildings at opposite ends of the property, one for classrooms and administration, the other called simply Research Institute. Fifty years later, the space in between is filled with state-of-the-art facilities for five colleges and eight thousand students, more proof, if any were needed, of the Technical Director's visionary powers.

Although I still hold the title Research Professor Emeritus, my affiliation with the university ended some years ago during the dispute over the will. Frankly, I had never wanted to be a professor in the first place. I had no academic ambitions, and no desire (or training) to be a teacher. All I ever wanted was to work half the day in the lab and the other half outdoors at the test stand or the firing range. But once the university was set up, it needed to attract top quality faculty and students, and the Technical Director twisted the arms of a lot of us old-timers to accept faculty appointments. Even if hardly any students could work with the Technical Director himself, whose leadership positions with the Army and later NASA virtually precluded his advising doctoral candidates, much less teaching undergraduate courses, they could still work with one of his original team members. Plus, there was the mild frisson of the Nazi thing: Where else could you sit at the feet of brilliant men who had once sat down to lunch with Führers and Reichsführers-SS?

In the end, the Technical Director persuaded me to join by drawing the analogy to the SS, which I had also been reluctant to become involved with. "It's what we have to do to grease the wheels, Arthur, but at least this time there's no ugly black uniform to put on, just the regulation shirt and tie."

And so I did. While there were some good days, and I occasionally liked my students, I mostly hated my time on campus. When you step before a group of strangers, you become a performing monkey in their eyes, and I was a monkey who had a funny accent and a body that became both more comical and more pitiable to my youthful charges with each passing year. Even now as I cross the last intersection before the entrance to campus, I feel the old tightening of the chest and exuding of the gastric juices. I don't know why I stayed on as long as I did, but I do know that one of the first thoughts that passed through my mind when I heard news of the Technical Director's death was, now I can leave that hellhole.

Having had no reason to come to this part of town, it's probably been three or four years since I've been on campus (until last night in the dark), and I note with a twinge of grudging pride new buildings and landscaping projects. The original administration and classroom building, now home to a rump College of Arts, Humanities, and Social Sciences, looks more out of place than ever, with its mock Corinthian columns. The President, Provost, and their ranks of vice presidents moved out of there about ten years ago and into a twelve-story steel and glass tower, considered the apotheosis of the Missile Style, that occupies a quadrangle (known as the "Launch Pad") in the geographic center of campus, providing senior administrators with panoptical views of their entire domain.

I continue around the loop road to the other end of campus to say good-bye to the Research Institute, whose propulsion lab with its static rocket motors and blast walls was my one place of refuge, but as I approach it, I see instead a massive hole in the ground from which arise concrete pillars with protruding tufts of rebar.

I pull the Safari off to the side of the road. A sign announces this as the future site of a much enlarged Research Institute, now to be named in honor of the Technical Director. The Technical Director has been dead for over a decade, and I have come to see my unexpected longevity as recompense for whatever deprivations I endured in the shadow of his genius, and yet I still can't help feeling a moment of irritation—I won't go so far as to call it resentment—when I see his name up on the sign. It's not that I think it should be called the Arthur Waldmann Research Institute—my name on a laboratory or conference room inside the building would more than flatter my vanity—but rather I mourn the loss of the transcendent functionality implied by the original generic designation.

As I am imagining the Technical Director's posthumous disapproval of this superfluous honor, I notice a white BMW sedan approaching from the other direction. As it passes by, the driver's head turns to look in my direction, and I find myself staring into a familiar face with a familiar look of utter contempt. It belongs to the Aviatrix.

The Aviatrix, the Technical Director, and I have a long and intimate history, but let me clear the decks right at the outset and say that romance never entered into it as far as she and I were concerned, and probably not when it came to the Technical Director, with the possible exception of their early days at Grunau. There will come a point in this narrative where I'll tell the story of how we once competed for the trust and confidence of the Technical Director, but that moment was long in the past and in another country.

Today the Aviatrix holds the title of Distinguished University Professor of Aeronautics, Philosophy, and Culture. There is no Emerita after her name because, although we are now both in our seventies, she has never retired and continues to teach, conduct research, and fill various administrative roles. Indeed, she is both a former Dean of Engineering and a former Provost.

After those of us in the original group of scientists became U. S. citizens, the Technical Director worked tirelessly to bring over other former friends and associates whom he thought might be valuable to our work but who for reasons of obscurity or ideology had not been vetted by our American handlers. The Aviatrix was the first on his list. Born just a few days apart, they had met while attending glider school at Grunau back in the early 1930s. Later, they were also in the same SS equestrian unit. She was a small, wiry person, never more than fifty kilos, but every bit of that bone and muscle. She would have been pretty in a china doll sort of way were it not for a thin, angular nose that gave her face a rodent-like aspect that hinted at vast resources of quick wit and intelligence. The Technical Director would go on to learn to fly almost every civilian or military aircraft in the German arsenal (with the significant exception of Zeppelins), but he was the first to admit that the Aviatrix was a better pilot of every single one of those machines. During the war, she flew combat missions in every theater, from England to Azerbaijan, and Speer used to joke that there was enough metal in all the Iron Crosses she had won to make a whole Panzer division.

She was one of the last people to see the Führer alive and still make it out of Berlin before the Russians took the city. In the years immediately following the war, she dressed only in black and called herself the Widow of the Fatherland, which obviously did not endear her to the Allied authorities, but she returned to something like a normal life after German citizens were allowed to fly airplanes again. By 1955, worries about a resurgent Nazi movement had been pushed aside by the Cold War, and the Technical Director, making the case that nobody understood the "human factors" dimension of manned flight better than the Aviatrix, managed to obtain a visa for her.

When she arrived as a visiting professor at the new university, she was the only woman on the engineering faculty, a situation that would continue for almost twenty years. This caused her to become more brusque and uncompromising—more Teutonic, as it seemed to her American students and colleagues—than she was already, and while well respected, she was not very much liked, a fact that toughened her up even more. Her outlets were her horses and her airplanes, both of which she had in abundance on a three-hundred-acre farm about a forty-minute commute from campus. Even when she was Dean and I had to suffer through her bullet-pointed lists of "areas of concern" during my annual reviews (non-compliant syllabi, inadequate assessment metrics), I always felt a bit sorry for her, and I think she sensed my compassion and respected me for it. Or maybe it was that she felt sorry for me, a man who had never come close to winning Iron Crosses or honorary doctorates, but who had spent a lifetime walking dutifully behind those who had.

During our last annual review meeting just weeks before the Technical Director died, she went so far as to tell me that she had always valued my opinions even when diametrically opposed to her own. (We had just been discussing one of my doctoral students: She had drawn little circles all over a piece of paper to show how unfocused his research was, while I had countered that his scattershot approach had led to several original insights.) "Perhaps Swedenborg was right about opposition being true friendship," she said with a rare smile.

But there were no smiles during the battle over the will. When she called me into her office a few weeks before that fall semester, she acknowledged her lack of authority over my extramural activities, but hoped she could prevail upon my instincts for loyalty. It wasn't just the legacy of the Technical Director that was at stake, but the reputation of everything he had created, or helped to create, from the space program to the local symphony to the university itself. "Think about all the students who have earned degrees from this institution," she pleaded with me. "The first thing prospective employers will say when they glance at their resumes is, isn't that the place founded by the German rocket scientist who shocked the world when it came out in his will that—etc., etc? Even if this is an act of conscience on your part, as you tell me, isn't it also an act of self-immolation that hurts others?"

She asked me to go home and think about it. For the next few days I did nothing else. Finally, unable to sleep at three o'clock in the morning, I sat down at my old manual typewriter and composed a short letter. "The last thing I want is to bring embarrassment or shame to my students and colleagues," I wrote, "and therefore I have decided to resign my faculty appointment."

I could have just mailed the letter or dropped it off with her staff assistant, but despite being rather diffident in most social situations, I never shy away from personal confrontation when I think there are moral or ethical issues involved, so instead I called to make an appointment and walked into her office promptly at 10:00 a.m. the next day. She greeted me warmly; I'm sure my physical presence was a sign to her that I was coming back into the fold. But immediately after the pleasantries, I told her I was resigning, orally conveyed my reasons, and handed her the letter. As her eyes passed over the lines, her shock turned to anger and then rage. When she looked up at me I could see more clearly than ever before the dark place in her soul from where this petite woman had forged the acts of will to fly a glider into a thunderstorm or fire the 20 mm cannons of her Focke-Wulf at survivors of the B-17s she had just shot down as they parachuted helplessly to Earth. She crumpled the paper in her hand, threw it at my face and yelled, in German, "Traitor! Get out!"

That was ten years ago, and we hadn't laid eyes on one another since then. My ostracism was so thorough, and my embrace of it so absolute, that I wondered for a moment if she had thought I had died, and her contorted features were more the shock of seeing someone risen from the dead than an expression of simple hatred. Perhaps she was already back at her office gossiping about me on the phone with some of the old-timers. When you have spent all or part of your formative years in a police state, encounters like this one automatically start you thinking about who your friends are and where you can hide. I had none, of course, and although the fear quickly passed because I knew I was not, in fact, living in a dictatorship, I took this chance meeting as a sign that impending self-exile was the right decision.

The final stop on my itinerary was Mont Vert (both "t"s pronounced), a long flat-topped ridge that rises semi-dramatically to an elevation of 1,500 feet just east of town. The name derives from a crusty group of pioneers who left the Green Mountains of western New England in the late eighteenth century when Congress dashed their hopes of remaining part of New York state and instead created the new state of Vermont. Out of spite they embraced every aspect of Southern culture, especially slaveholding, and this contrarian spirit continued through the Civil War when they voted to secede from the Confederacy and welcomed with much fanfare the invading Union Army led by Brigadier General Ormsby "Old Stars" Mitchel in 1862.

Local legend has it that within a day or two of our arrival, the Technical Director organized a hike to the top of Mont Vert where, from an outcropping of limestone overlooking the then tiny town best known for its watercress, he spread out his arms and declared, in German and English, "This is the place!" The story is true, though only much later did we find out that the Technical Director, who was already preparing for his citizenship exam by reading deeply in American history, had borrowed this line from Brigham Young, who is reputed to have said this as he led his Mormon followers into the Great Salt Lake Valley.

What's not true is that we thought our new home was just like Germany. Yes, unlike the deserts of Texas and New Mexico where we had been living, it was green, and the Prussians and Upper Silesians among us (including the Technical Director) were, I think, comforted by the view of the verdant plains extending out toward the western horizon, but as far as I was concerned, this was my worst nightmare of North America. As a boy studying English at my boarding school in Koblenz back in the twenties, I'd once had to memorize a poem by Oliver Goldsmith entitled "The Deserted Village." It tells of poor Englishmen who get kicked out of their homes by wealthy landowners and are forced to emigrate to the New World:

> Far different there from all that charm'd before,
> The various terrors of that horrid shore;
> Those blazing suns that dart a downward ray,
> And fiercely shed intolerable day;
> Those matted woods where birds forget to sing,
> But silent bats in drowsy clusters cling;
> Those poisonous fields with rank luxuriance crowned,
> Where the dark scorpion gathers death around;
> Where at each step the stranger fears to wake
> The rattling terrors of the vengeful snake.

There were no bats or scorpions that day in June, but the temperature and humidity were both in the nineties, and Max Jenke was nearly bitten by a copperhead as he stepped off the trail to relieve himself. The superficial resemblance of these wooded hills to my native Trier only worsened my homesickness. The wastes of El Paso were so alien to me that it was like living on another planet. (Indeed, NASA trained astronauts there for moon missions.) All of my mental energies were consumed dealing with that hostile environment; there was nothing left over for nostalgia. Here, however, the greenery raised expectations of a world and a past recovered, perhaps even redeemed. When I looked at the steep slopes, I could almost imagine them covered with row upon row of the Riesling grape arbors where I used to play hide-and-seek as a child, but no grape worthy of being pressed into wine could possibly grow in this climate that was too muggy in summer and too frigid in winter. (Trust me, I tried when I lived up there.)

The road from town to the top of Mont Vert ascends by a series of switchbacks and hairpin turns that were no problem for my old Mercedes but presented a serious challenge to the Safari's poorly engineered V-6 engine which knocked so badly that I had to downshift to first gear every few hundred feet. After a twenty minute drive that should have taken ten, I arrived at the top. Most of the land here is now incorporated into a 6,000 acre state park, whose original core was a 1,200 acre donation by the Technical Director. It had once been the private hunting club he had started with our more avid outdoorsmen. I drove past the unmanned gate house, electing for the first time ever to ignore the "honor system" request for a three-dollar donation. From the parking lot I walked down the short gravel path to Apollo Point, where an historical marker commemorates our group's initial visit and the Technical Director's momentous declaration. Through the haze I can see the plains spreading out before me with a silvery bend of river off in the distance. Roads, highways, and buildings have filled in what were cotton fields fifty years ago, but the most notable features are, of course, the missiles and test stands that shimmer dully in the afternoon heat.

I take a last look at this impressive view that encompasses the geography of my long decline since the *anni mirabili* of the war years, and a wave of sadness breaks over me, but then life is full of last looks, we just don't recognize them as such. I try to focus on how my determination to never lay eyes on these sights again was a sign of self-mastery and thus an occasion for rejoicing, but the melancholy state persists and I let it ride. Eventually I turn back toward the parking lot, cross it, and walk a quarter mile to the bald on the highest point of the ridge where stands the astronomical observatory, now named in honor of, well, you can guess. That same day back in 1950 that the Technical Director looked out from Apollo Point, he also led a small expeditionary force equipped with topographic maps, compasses, and an altimeter to scope out possible sites for an observatory. Indeed, it struck us as bizarre that no one had thought to place an instrument on such easily accessible high ground. The following spring we began work on the building. It was constructed by hand out of native limestone, and although none of us were masons, the apprenticeship of German engineers in the prewar era always began with the grinding and shaping of blocks of metal to exacting specifications, so we quickly mastered the techniques.

I walk around the building several times — seven times, to be honest, whistling an improvised tune, on the billion-to-one chance that a personal God sends me a little going away present, but the walls just sit there as I know they will for the next thousand years. Although I dressed blocks and trowelled mortar those many weekend afternoons, my main contribution to the project lay inside. We knew that we wanted a large instrument, but because commercially available models are both expensive and of uneven quality, it was always a given that we would build our own.

There are two general types of telescopes, reflectors and refractors. Reflectors, which use mirrors to gather light, are easier to build, but more difficult to maintain in a non-climate-controlled environment, where changes in temperature can nudge components out of alignment. Refractors use lenses which must be ground to more exacting specifications than mirrors but, when fixed into place, are less subject to the stresses of climate in an unheated structure built for only occasional use like our planned observatory. Arguments can be made for both types, but what tipped the balance toward the refractor was the presence in our group of an accomplished lens grinder: myself.

The story of the Technical Director's receipt of a telescope as a confirmation present is well known, but I, too, have a long history with telescopes, and while the Technical Director and I were both interested in what the instrument could do, I also became fascinated with its mechanics, so that I had taken up lens grinding as a serious hobby even before I had met him. I had developed a philosophy that only the maker of an artifact could fully exploit its potential. Thus it was no accident that Galileo, while not the inventor of the telescope, had made the most momentous discoveries in the history of astronomy, if not the history of science, with telescopes that he had made himself. If I had thought music a worthwhile pursuit for me, I would have insisted on making my own flutes or violins. In retrospect, of course, this idea was the product of youthful hubris. Galileo was perhaps the world's greatest astronomer, but nobody thinks Stradivarius was the world's greatest musician. Nor for that matter did Herschel or Hubble build the telescopes at Greenwich and Palomar. As it turned out, while I spent many happy hours looking at the heavens through my instruments, I never achieved any results of scientific significance. The Technical Director, on the other hand, while never touching a grinding stone, discovered no less than five comets, the last one in the early 1960s from this very same Mont Vert observatory.

It's fitting that my farewell tour ended here with this symbol of estrangement and unfulfilled promise in what even I must admit now is a lovely setting. I return to my car and head back down the mountain to my house, a short but nerve-racking drive, given the combination of excessive play in the Safari's steering wheel and the sluggish reaction times of a man in his mid-seventies. Although part of me could live with, as it were, a fatal crash at a missed hairpin turn ("Original Rocket Team Member Plunges Off Mountain"), I manage to guide the car back to the driveway of my craftsman-style bungalow on the edge of the Twelve Points neighborhood. Directly across the street from me is a flagpole adjacent to the entrance to our town's most historic cemetery, Catalpa Hill, final resting place of mayors, magnates, and even a couple of state governors (but not the Technical Director).

When I came to this place in 1950, I occupied bachelor quarters for a few years on the Army base, but like most of my colleagues, I eventually bought an acre of land on the shoulder of Mont Vert where, with the help of the best carpenter in town (when he was sober), I built a small house in the style of a Mosel farmstead winery. I also made most of the furniture that went inside. I was content in my little kingdom with its summer greenery and winter views along the ridgeline when about ten years ago a multimillionaire defense contractor offered me more than twice its market value. Although he spoke admiringly of the skill that went into its construction, I knew perfectly well that he was only interested in the land, and that upon taking possession he would tear down the house and replace it with an ugly nouveau riche monstrosity more appropriate to such a prime piece of real estate, which is precisely what he did. But I didn't care. I was already more than a year into my internal exile by then, and the house had become a reminder of times that, if not happier, were at least less painful.

I banked half of my windfall profit and with the other half bought this bungalow. It's been a place to hang my hat (I still wear one, Old World gentleman that I am), brood, and more recently, compose the bulk of the following memoir. While the house has an abundance of character with its multiple fireplaces and backyard solarium, the only thing that mattered to me was its location. The cemetery was a no-brainer, but what really fixed it was the flagpole which my front door perfectly frames as you exit the house. At one point I actually contacted the city to see if I could volunteer to raise and lower the flag. Like the speck of dust that enables the formation of the surrounding raindrop, I figured that this simple dawn and dusk task would provide just enough formal structure to a day that contained no other obligations or responsibilities, beyond keeping myself groomed and fed. I could see myself consulting the *Old Farmer's Almanac* each night before retiring, and then carrying out my official duties at the exact times of sunrise and sunset listed in the tables, rain or shine, popping in and out of my bungalow like a carved figurine on a mechanical clock. But I received a very polite letter from the Director of Public Works explaining that liability considerations precluded anyone other than city employees performing this operation. What? The flag was going to fall on my head and kill me? Or I would accidently hang myself with the rope? Perhaps he was right. Given the odds against my having survived into old age after a life governed by war and rocket research, it would only be fitting to meet my end in some such mundane yet freakish manner.

Underneath the dogwood in my front yard is a realtor's sign with a "Sale Pending!" sticker slapped rakishly across the front. In the interest of making an absolutely clean break when I drive out of town today, I have turned my power of attorney over to a lawyer who will represent me at the closing in two weeks. A few days before then all of my furniture and most of my household goods will be offered to the public at an estate sale (as if I'm already deceased), with any unsold items being donated to charity. I pick up my two suitcases (1960-era Samsonite warhorses that accompanied me on many a trip to Washington, White Sands, or the Cape), pull the door closed behind me, and load myself and my luggage into the Safari. Just like checking out of a motel.

The highway east heads over a modest ridge (once wooded, now converted to subdivisions) from where I have a final inadvertent glimpse in my rearview mirror of the city in its saucer of haze. Then it follows the bends of the river until it ascends the southern sputterings of the mountains which form the watershed divide between the pygmy rivers of the coastal plains and the mighty Mississippi. Along the way I pass signs advertising caves, a minor tourist attraction of the region, some named for their presumed discoverers (DeSoto, Nelson), others for some notable aspect (Ice Cold, Bat Hell). There are, of course, many hundreds of smaller caves, and the Technical Director, never missing an opportunity for adventure, no matter epic or petty, used to lead weekend expeditions to explore them, even founding our local chapter of the National Speleological Society. Since my large portfolio of anxieties and fears did not include claustrophobia, I'd sometimes accompany him on these treks. I mention this because about an hour into my trip I leave the highway for a gravel road that leads to a tract of several hundred acres surrounding an abandoned nuclear power plant by the river. I park at a trailhead, grab a flashlight and a small fanny pack, and walk several minutes to the unmarked entrance of a cave, just big enough for a smallish grown man to squeeze through. Fifty yards along I feel for a crevice that extends downward beyond the reach of my flashlight.

I now unzip my fanny pack and remove the Luger that used to inhabit the wooden holster built into my bedroom closet door. (For the record, I left behind the remainder of my arsenal to be sold at the estate sale.) Am I dropping it into this miniature abyss to hide the evidence of some gruesome crime I've coyly refrained from telling you about until now? No. Rather, I decided that with a few small modifications the Luger could serve as a time capsule, and after coating the insides of the bullet chambers and barrel with special waxes, I've inserted microfiche of a number of important documents relevant to my case, including at least one item of correspondence from a world-historical figure.

I now release the Luger without hesitation and hear a few clinks as it tumbles down the crevice. Then nothing. I doubt that anyone will find it soon, but since, like the Technical Director, I, too, believe that in the fullness of time the turds of human civilization will penetrate to every nook and cranny of the physical universe, some fool or genius will eventually stumble across it. After seven decades on this planet, the only thing I can say for sure is that no matter how far away it seems, your future will always arrive.

CHAPTER 2
THE LAST MARRANA

In later years I've wondered how many other children in Lutheran families had been put to bed with stories from the Zohar. I don't recall exactly when this practice began, but it was no later than the evening of November 10, 1918, when I was eight. My grandmother and I were re-enacting the story of Eliezar at Laban's Well, using a stuffed camel that she had given me for my birthday, when my father came bounding up the stairs into my room. Out of breath and still wearing a fedora lightly dusted with snow, he announced that the war would be ending at eleven o'clock the next morning. Although I had heard my parents talking about the effect of the war on my father's business, the only guns I ever saw during those years were those of the occasional quail hunter we'd pass on walks in the country. I have no memories of the war at all, except this one of being annoyed at my father's uncharacteristic interruption. My grandmother had just reached the point where Eliezar utters the *Shem Tov*, the signal for me to begin pulling on the string that she had threaded over a ceiling fixture. This would elevate the attached stuffed camel to the amazement of the Nahorites below, represented by an assemblage of other toy creatures. Seeing that he was unwelcome, my father grumbled something under his breath, and retreated through the door. Moments later, the Good Name spoken, I drew the camel up into the air.

At first it was just the stories. Later, she added her own commentaries.

Several stories alluded to the belief that when people dream, the soul leaves the body and ascends toward Heaven, from which it returns before morning, but only through God's plea with the Angel of Death. This seemed to her (and to me) a reasonable proposition. The dreams that we awakened from didn't follow the logic of this world, so where could they come from but the next? Other times, she would pause in her reading, and look up at me, shaking her head. It said in the Zohar that when King David grew old, he was so intent on clinging to life that he appointed one of his servants to awaken him at the first sign of a dream, since he feared the Angel of Death might prevent a return from his nightly ascent. "A pious fabrication," she announced flatly. "If your grandfather got less than eight hours of sleep, he was good for nothing. Worthless. He ran a factory that made stinking cigars. David was the king of Israel. They expect us to believe that he ruled a country without a decent night's rest?"

My own dreams were impoverished and unmemorable, and I assumed that my skills as a dreamer would develop as I grew older, like athletic or artistic ability. When this failed to happen, I formed the idea that I might better direct the movement of my soul by studying the night sky through which it would pass, as a traveler might stand on a high plateau and view the plains stretching before him. Although this did nothing to enrich my dreams, I learned to identify all the major stars and constellations, and how to follow the motion of the planets. My grandmother, whose extensive rock collection indicated her curiosity about the natural as well as the spiritual world, encouraged this interest in astronomy. Together we persuaded my father to buy me a telescope, even though he had lately refused the purchase of a radio, calling it an expensive toy for the leisure classes.

The telescope arrived one day in a wooden box that looked like a child's casket. Opening it, I was dismayed to find dozens of unassembled components accompanied by a sheet of badly printed instructions. I went to my father, whose approach to technical problems was to call his shop foreman, Otto Schultz. For forty years, old Schultzie had fiddled with the machinery that had allowed my father and grandfather to prosper, but whose workings it was almost a point of family honor not to understand. Bony and arthritic for as long as I'd know him, Schultzie had once spent a rainy Sunday morning alone in our garage putting together my first bicycle, but the telescope, which wasn't mobile and produced nothing, left him baffled. He placed the tube into its felt-lined cradle and pointed it toward a distant estate set among the vineyards overlooking our town, but no matter what combination of lenses he tried, he could not get the house to stand right side up. "I'm licked," he told my father, as he returned parts to their padded niches, handling them like sticks of dynamite.

That afternoon, when my grandmother came downstairs, she found me at the kitchen table, tracing star charts onto sheets of onion skin. "Where's the telescope?" she asked. I explained about Schultzie's failure and how my father was already talking about sending it back for a refund.

My grandmother slapped her forehead in mock exasperation. "The men in this family don't have enough sense to know how to blow their own noses," she said.

Ten minutes later she had all the parts arrayed on the ottomans in the living room. She examined each lens, bracket, and thumbscrew, comparing them to their depiction in the schematic diagram. She held parts up against one another and tested their fits before attempting to connect them. Within the hour we had the telescope re-assembled, and again pointed toward the estate. The house was still inverted, but my grandmother read in the instructions that for reasons of optical efficiency, images in telescopes were reversed and upside down. I was bothered by having to accept this distorted view of the heavens, and it occurred to me that the dramatic photographs I had seen in astronomy books might themselves be equally unreliable.

At sunset we carried the telescope to a field beyond the Porta Nigra. We picked out the dozen brightest stars (all of which I could name) before it was dark enough to locate Polaris. I soon became frustrated trying to orient the polar and declination axes, but these were eventually calibrated, thanks to my grandmother's patience, and we were thus able to follow the progress of heavenly bodies across the night sky by using two flexible handcranks that bobbed about like a pair of giant antennae. We looked at the rings of Saturn and counted the stars in the Pleiades; I sketched the outlines of the faint blur I thought might be the Crab Nebula, because I had read that even amateur observers could make important contributions to knowledge.

Still, my excitement at seeing these mysterious objects I had known only from books was already tinged with disappointment over the telescope's considerable limits. The more magnification, the more the stars and planets became just colorful smudges. I could hardly go home and ask my father for a bigger telescope, but I had read about people who had built their own, and wondered aloud to my grandmother if perhaps she and I could make one someday.

She was standing next to me wrapped in an old horsehair blanket, studying the sky in the vicinity of Castor and Pollux. I expected a noncommittal answer, but she said, "Before I married your grandfather, I thought about going to Antwerp to see if they'd let a woman learn to cut diamonds. How different could it be cutting glass?" She went on with her stargazing, and quietly chanted some verses from the Zohar. I recognized them as the passage which explains that because the world is sustained by both Jacob and Esau — by thinkers and doers — God spoke to Moses under the sign of Gemini.

We folded up the tripod and walked home around midnight. On the way back, I talked excitedly of how I was going to become an astronomer. She nodded her approval and said that she wished she had had more time to learn about the stars so that she would not lose her way. I was puzzled by the response and told her that she knew the constellations as well as I did.

"I know them from here," she replied

I was confused. The arrangement of stars in a constellation would always look the same, though familiar constellations would disappear and new ones come into view as you traveled north or south.

So I asked if she meant how the stars looked different from Spain. A few years before, within months of my grandfather's death, she had traveled there on her own, announcing that she wanted to sit beneath the orange trees that had shaded her Graetz ancestors before the Expulsion, when the family name was still Garcia, and their conversion to Christianity and later move to the Rhineland were the catastrophes of a future that no astrologer could have predicted. My mother said that it was unseemly for a woman of her social standing to travel unescorted, and threw the postcards of ruined synagogues and mosques into the trash after determining that they contained no desperate cries for assistance. (I secretly recovered them and added them to my scrapbook.) When she returned several weeks later, her life continued to revolve around such domestic activities as baking bread and weeding the garden, but there were also indications of renewed self-assurance, signaled by the occasional Mediterranean flourishes, like the gypsy scarves she began wearing in her hair. She also began spending the hours between two and five in the afternoon alone in her room, studying what she called her "old books," the four leather-bound folios of the Zohar that she had purchased from an antique dealer in Toledo.

"No, not from Spain," she said. We walked the rest of the way home in silence.

As we turned onto our street, I noticed that a light was still on in the living room. Someone was waiting up for us. My grandmother put her hand on my shoulder, and we stood there together at the end of the walkway leading to the house. "Not from Spain," she continued, as if there had been no break in the conversation, "but let me tell you what happened to me while I was in Spain." We stepped a few paces off the path and into the shadow of an evergreen which blocked the light from the late-risen moon. She spoke just above a whisper.

"I had arrived in Córdoba on Christmas Eve. When I arose the next morning, the air was crisp and the streets nearly deserted. My thoughts wandered back to the winter of 711 when a handful Jews patrolled the city after its abandonment by Christians, fleeing the invincible armies of Tariq ibn Ziyad, who now pursued the idolaters into the parched deserts of La Mancha. I put the map away and let my senses guide me through the maze of alleyways. Within minutes I arrived at the Sinagoga. It was smaller than I imagined, but infinitely more splendid, the stone inscriptions and intricate geometric filigrees looking as though the masons had put down their chisels only yesterday. With my poor, belated knowledge of the Hebrew alphabet, I began piecing together words. It must have taken me an hour to read a single line, but the hours flew like minutes, and there was no one to hurry me along. To the left of the holy ark I read the opening lines of Psalm 19: 'The heavens declare the glory of God, the sky proclaims His handiwork.' The writing on the other side commemorated the generosity of the man who had paid for the synagogue's construction. His name was Efraim Garcia. Could this have been a Garcia from whom the Graetzes were descended? There was no way to know, yet I felt utterly homesick as I spoke the syllables of his name: Gar-ci-a. It was nearly dusk when I left there. I took a brief stroll through the Patio de los Naranjos, and picked up a couple of oranges that had fallen beneath the trees. As there were no restaurants open that day, I let these become my supper, along with some bread and olive oil I had bought the day before in Baeza.

"That night as I lay in bed going over the day's events, an odd thing happened: My body drifted off to sleep while my mind stayed nimble. I had felt this once before, when I was a young army nurse at Sedan. I was thinking then about a young French prisoner whose leg we had had to amputate, wondering if he would survive the night, when suddenly I realized I couldn't move even a finger. I was totally paralyzed. I panicked and felt like a drowning person desperate to swim back to the surface. Several minutes passed. Finally, I was jolted back awake by an awful groan I dragged up from somewhere deep inside me, more like the sound of a crocodile than a human being.

"This time, however, I did not panic. To be honest, I thought it must be death, and I was ready for it. That morning in the *judería* God had granted me a vision, which is all anyone can reasonably ask for in life. Besides, after months of doing all sorts of things that your grandfather would have hated — staying up past midnight, eating lots of garlic, traveling outside of Germany — I was starting to miss the old stick-in-the-mud. He had always been such a gentleman, his manners so . . . elegant, his clothes always well put together. (I can't stand a badly dressed man!) So I let the paralysis break over me like a wave, and the walls of the room dropped down like the petals of a flower. I flew upward at what must have been incredible speed, yet had no sense of motion. Soon I was surrounded by stars.

"Despite the fact that I would have the words for it only much later when I found the passage in the Zohar, I knew with absolute certainty that my final destination was the Sanhedrin of the Immortals, though why I was allowed to be conscious during the journey, and what exactly I was going to do when I arrived remained (and still remains) a mystery to me. At first I felt happy and confident about my route, like a girl walking home from school. But the farther I went along, the more unusual became my surroundings. Slowly but unmistakably the stars were migrating out of their familiar constellations. The belt of Orion was unloosed, and Castor and Pollux found themselves new companions. It then occurred to me that for someone hurtling through space, knowledge of how the heavens looked from Earth would be utterly useless. Just thinking about this was exhausting, and I now fought to hold my eyes open. Before giving in to sleep, however, I determined to memorize the exact location of the brightest stars, thinking that I could use them as a landmark to begin the next stage of the journey, should I ever return this way. Then it was morning, and I awakened to the street sounds of everyday Córdoba.

"By trial and error I found that by chanting certain variations of the *Shem Tov* I could return to the exact place in the heavens from which I had awakened the night before, and that from there I could travel another vast distance until I wearied from the strain of navigation. This is how I pass most nights, pressing on toward a well-known destination through unknown territory, like the ships with their Marrano crews which Prince Henry sent down the coast of Africa to discover the route to India."

Two or three times as I listened to the story, I noticed the curtains on the window being parted and my mother's face peering out into the moonlight. When we walked in, my mother was sitting with her back to the door, noisily flipping the pages of a magazine. She turned around and asked with feigned indifference how the evening had gone. I told her about seeing Saturn's rings and sketching the Crab Nebula, but said nothing about what I had heard from my grandmother, who was already halfway up the stairs.

Naturally, the instant I climbed into bed I closed my eyes and began reciting tidbits from the Zohar. Nothing happened. In the weeks that followed, I adjusted every factor that I thought might influence my prospects of success: the words I spoke, the position of my body, the time of night, the consumption of various foods and beverages. I was able to achieve a high degree of concentration by focusing on certain letters of the Hebrew alphabet, but this did nothing to lower the partition between the chambers of consciousness in my soul. Around dawn, frustrated and exhausted, I would fall into a dreamless sleep from which I would awake a few hours later more refreshed than if I had slept the whole night.

I said nothing to my grandmother or anyone else about my efforts.

After several months I concluded that it must be my limited experience with death that made me a poor candidate to explore the region between this life and the next. I had lost my grandfather, but he had died when I was so small that I could hardly distinguish between what I actually remembered of him and what people had told me. I secretly longed for some limited exposure to grief that would propel me across the divide: the death of one of my father's estranged brothers, or maybe of a neighbor's infant child. But happily for them, everyone remained in perfect health.

I finally resigned myself to failure, but at the same time decided that although my soul had proven inadequate, I might be able to use my brain to help others. I conceived the project of creating a series of maps that would show the changing positions of the stars, not as seen from Earth, but from the viewpoint of a traveler moving through space. The obstacles in the way of completing such a task were considerable. The ideal map would have to incorporate four dimensions; I had no idea how to produce one in two, much less three. I also lacked information about the precise locale of the Heavenly Sanhedrin, or even grounds to believe that such a mystical establishment occupied a point in real space, despite my grandmother's word that her travels took her past many recognizable astronomical objects. The only solace was my extreme youth and the decades I would have to complete the project, though I knew that time was running out for my grandmother, who I prayed might be my work's first beneficiary.

For the next year, I doggedly read every astronomy book I could get my hands on. I started with works written for a popular audience, many of them large format, with slick paper and lots of artists' conceptions of the surface of this planet or that moon. From there I moved on to more technical studies which motivated me to excel in mathematics classes at school. At the age of twelve when other boys in the neighborhood played kickball in the street before dusk, I went to bed right after dinner, and awakened at two or three in the morning to pore over my books undisturbed, or step out onto the small porch off my bedroom seeking renewed inspiration from the stars. Sometimes toward the dawn of nights when I had accomplished little, I found myself carrying on imaginary conversations with the Arab astronomers who had given those stars their names: Deneb, Rigel, Arghol, Aldeberan, and many more.

Because I had to start somewhere, I decided to begin with a set of maps that would show the sky as it appeared from a planet orbiting each of the dozen brightest stars that my grandmother mentioned passing. Whenever I sat down to work at my desk, I imagined the day I would hand her a sumptuously bound volume of folio-sized pages, replete with quaint, medieval-looking devices, depicting the heavens above remote galaxies, so that her nightly ascents might be undertaken with more assurance. I reasoned that such maps might one day facilitate everyone's final journey into the afterlife, mitigating the fear of death.

My plans were interrupted around the time of the Easter holidays when my parents announced that they would be sending me away to boarding school. For some weeks prior to then, I had been aware of their muffled arguments about me behind closed kitchen and bedroom doors. My mother was increasingly worried about my "moleish" behavior, which she traced to her mother-in-law's influence. I would turn fourteen in the fall, an age, she said, when young gentlemen should begin "socializing," by which she meant show an interest in girls. If I stayed up in that room all the time, I would never learn to socialize. My father acknowledged my grandmother's eccentric behavior, but said that it was good for a boy to be close to a grandparent, and that my shyness was a phase I would outgrow. Besides, the expense of sending me away to school would be considerable, and although business had improved of late, the onerous terms of the Versailles Treaty still clouded the economic outlook for Germany.

In the end, my mother prevailed, as she did in most things. To her credit she had chosen a school in the Hermann Lietz system, whose progressive founder advocated a curriculum that allowed students unusual latitude in exploring their own talents. Lietz schools had a reputation for fostering exceptional ability, and while I resented this enforced departure from home, I was also flattered that I had been accepted for admission. My mother's vicarious excitement about my upcoming matriculation soon became infectious. Not a day passed without a conversation about the school's outstanding teachers, well-bred students, or many fine opportunities for socializing.

To be honest, even I had begun to wonder about my grandmother. She had become difficult to communicate with of late, claiming that she was forgetting German, and could converse now only in Ladino, whose basic grammar and vocabulary she had taught me. When alone in her room, she kept up a constant patter. Asked about this, she said that from all the hours she had spent studying the Zohar, she was now able to talk directly to Moses de Leon, the thirteenth-century Spanish rabbi who probably forged most of the work.

But the biggest source of tension in the family was her insistence that I have a bar mitzvah, which was about as likely as my parents agreeing to let me enter a Buddhist monastery. Even I thought the idea was absurd. The last practicing Jew in my family had been my great-grandfather, who had accepted baptism on Pentecost in 1817 along with Heinrich Marx (yes, Karl's father), and half the town's other Jews. I had never set foot inside a synagogue, and despite my acquaintance with the synthetic Aramaic Moses de Leon had invented for the Zohar, I knew only a few words of Hebrew.

By mid-summer I, too, was excited at the prospect of going away, though out of respect for my grandmother, I rarely spoke of my leaving. While every night this old woman traversed unimaginable distances between galaxies, I had never even crossed the border into France. I became convinced that boarding school was an adventure offered me in compensation for my failings as a mental traveler. Still, I spent many long afternoons with her reading the ancient sources, until shortly before dinner when my father would bring up an hors d'oeuvre of black bread and butter. Never did I waver in the conviction that I would one day produce a set of universal star charts.

By September, my grandmother had accepted the inevitable and began echoing my mother's line about how going away would make me a more well-rounded young man. She found several occasions during our studies to reference the optimism of Don Isaac Abrabanal who, forced to watch Ferdinand affix his seal to the Edict of Expulsion, turned to Torquemada and said, "The Holy One, Blessed be He, does not exile His people unless He has already foreseen their return." She encouraged my continued study of the Zohar, but warned me to be circumspect about sharing my knowledge. Withdrawing from between the mattress and box springs a large poster board on which she had sketched an elaborate Garcia / Graetz family tree, she pointed out the names of several Marrano ancestors who had maintained some form of Jewish practice while rising to prominent positions in Christian society. "Trust your instincts," she told me. "You have secrecy in your blood."

Talk about the proposed bar mitzvah was quietly dropped as a subject of family discussion.

The evening before I left for school we took out the telescope one last time to look at some nebulae in Scorpio, which snaked along our southern horizon. Antares, the variable red star that dominates the constellation, was at its brightest, and my grandmother remarked that the Hebrew term for a scorpion was an anagram of the words "essential house," which according to the Zohar prophesied the building of the Third Temple. I had become so captive to my own private researches that when I looked at Antares I no longer saw it as part of Scorpio, but as a place from which one could observe a brilliant constellation, invisible from Earth, that I had named The Temple because it resembled an illustration in one of my grandmother's books. But not wanting to reveal anything of my work until I had brought it nearer to completion, I said nothing about this amazing coincidence.

Later, when we finished disassembling the telescope and returning it to its box, my grandmother closed her eyes and kissed me on the forehead. "Because every departure is a little death, I will not see you off in the morning," she said, "but I will lie awake listening to the sounds of the house, putting them in reverse order, imagining that they announce your return." The next morning, as my father loaded the suitcases into the car, I glanced up at my grandmother's window. She was not lying in bed but rather sitting up in stark profile, staring blankly into space, or, I thought jealously, reviewing the splendor of the previous night's travels.

CHAPTER 3
LOVE AND THE ZOHAR

Four years at boarding school in Koblenz had turned me into the well-rounded young man of my parents' expectations. I was no longer the little introvert who would go to bed right after dinner so that I could rise after midnight to study my astronomy books and the night sky without interruption. I had also given up my attempt to map the route between our house in western Germany and the Heavenly Academy of Hillel and Akiba. At school I had received a solid foundation in mathematics, physics, and chemistry, and I was grateful now for this training in the sciences which disabused me of my grandmother's superstitious beliefs. But like my Marrano forebears, the spurned convictions still lurked in forgotten chambers of the heart. It would require another Inquisition to dislodge them. For every heretic the burning stake takes its own special form.

During the summer before my last year at school, the subject of dinner table conversation was my future. My father wanted his only son to take over the family tobacco importing business, despite the fact that I had shown no more inclination toward commerce than any other Waldmann male, himself included. My mother would hear nothing of it, and said that I should be a doctor or a lawyer. She also thought I would make a brilliant architect, and recalled, to my dismay, the drawings I had made of the planets as seen through the small telescope I had once begged them to give me.

We talked about where I would attend university. My father hoped I would stay close to home, perhaps in Trier itself, where the faculty's progressive reputation appealed to his liberal sympathies. My mother, though she cried every time I went back to boarding school, wanted me to take full advantage of both my evident intelligence and our family's comfortable social position. She declared that it would be a loss to myself and to the world if I did not attend the most prestigious institution in Germany, the Friedrich-Wilhelm University in Berlin.

My mother had neither attended a university nor spent time in Berlin, but her conviction on the matter was unshakeable. Within weeks she had become thoroughly versed in the traditions of the school. "You can study the philosophy of Hegel in the classroom where Hegel taught," she said one morning over breakfast. My father slowly lowered his *Mosel Morgenpost* to look in amazement at a woman who had never once before let the name Hegel pass her lips.

I had no ambition to be famous. I only wanted to be obscure on my own terms.

Perhaps I feared that when I entered the aura of Hegel's ghost, people would see Hegel and not me. I might no longer even see myself. The Zohar teaches that each person is assigned a unique destiny, and I did not want to be separated from what was rightfully mine.

True, my grandmother's state of mind was not the best advertisement for adopting her as a role model: She had passed beyond thinking that she could commune directly with Moses de Leon to the point of believing she was one of that pseudepigraphist's chief collaborators, and now conversed mostly in Ladino, or worse, the Zohar's synthetic Aramaic, which even I could hardly understand. And yet between spending her conscious hours in medieval Spain, and travelling billions of miles in her dreams to the Academy of Hillel and Akiba, I knew no one more at peace with herself. While I did not foresee a future bounded by small rooms and voluminous texts, I thought my chances of finding happiness would be greater watching the hours slip by among the crates of cigars in my father's tobacco warehouse than in savoring the pygmy recognition that would come from a successful legal or medical practice.

The other force that would conspire to keep me home was Greta Marx, the daughter of Julius Marx, my father's accountant.

When home for vacations, I would sometimes accompany my father to the Marx household, where after lighting up a couple of my father's most pungent Havanas, he and Herr Marx would spend the afternoon tracing the mysterious flow of marks and pfennigs across reams of paper. Occasionally I joined my father for these sessions, but more often than not, I sat in the kitchen talking with Herr Marx's wife and seventeen-year-old daughter, Greta. Greta was slightly taller than I, slender without being thin, and had blue-gray eyes that embraced rather than fixed the object of their attention. Her mother, an attractive woman in her early forties, was so youthful in appearance that she could pass as her daughter's eldest sister. Frau Marx worked part-time in the town library, and had interests that were both refined and catholic. At least once a year since Greta had turned twelve, the two of them went abroad to visit museums, attend concerts, and breathe in the atmosphere of sophisticated Europe.

One late spring afternoon they were telling me about their recent trip to London which included a visit to the Royal Observatory, and the opportunity to look through the 24-inch reflector that Lassell had used to discover the moons of Neptune.

"A most remarkable occasion," said Frau Marx.

"Not a cloud in the sky," said Greta. "The guide, a nice young man from Cambridge, told us that days like that came once or twice a year. He was doing some research on solar flares and invited me to observe them through the telescope. They looked like so many orange serpents uncoiling from a fiery den. He whispered that those were bursts of hydrogen gas streaming millions of miles out into space, but I thought, how can miniscule creatures like ourselves even begin to comprehend such vast distances? The image in the eye piece was tiny, more like a cell in my own body than a firestorm in an immense heavenly body. There was something almost intimate about it; it felt so close."

"Almost as close as that handsome young astronomer was getting to you," added Frau Marx, and although Greta blushed, they both had a good laugh over it.

I laughed, too, but only to cover a pang of jealousy. Of course, without beauty there could not have been love, but it was really her brilliant intuition that had just captured my heart. Although Herr Neumann, my chemistry teacher, would have heaped scorn upon such a notion, the belief that every star was a cell in the body of a celestial Adam Kadmon was a commonplace for students of the Zohar. There now came back suppressed memories of stargazing with my grandmother, her head wrapped in gypsy scarves against the night air, as we looked up at galaxies that were for us not distant lights, but the pale auras of multitudinous personalities. When I next opened my mouth, out spilled a jumble of facts about radiation, light years, gas clouds, and spectroscopy, but only because I was insufficiently bold to utter the words I longed to speak: *Tzim'tzum, Olam ha-bah, Sephirah, Ein Sof.*

My three-inch refractor was still in its wooden casket in the attic where I had left it before going to boarding school. That same weekend, the three of us, at Frau Marx's suggestion, had gone out to look at what several years later one of my Rocket Center colleagues would call "the tourist traps" of amateur astronomy: Saturn's rings, the Pleiades, the variable star Arghol. A dense fog came rolling up the Mosel around eleven and made further viewing impossible. We resolved to continue our session the following Friday when we might catch a glimpse of the elusive Mercury, which would then be moving out of retrograde.

When I went by their house on Friday, however, I found Frau Marx wrapped in blankets on the sofa reading an English murder mystery. She was blowing her nose and drinking from a mug of hot tea with an exotic, smoky aroma. She had taken a cold from being out the earlier evening, but insisted that her incapacitation not prevent Greta and me from stargazing.

We headed out through the narrow streets of town, past the imposing mass of the Roman Gate, with the box swinging gently between us, until we reached the open countryside where we took the path that led up the hill opposite the Dominican Retreat House. The early June evening looked forward to summer, as the day's heat now lingered after dark. After setting up the telescope, we looked at some globular clusters and dark nebulae whose visual appeal was more subtle and mysterious than that of the planets. Sometimes as she searched for these faint images in the eyepiece, she would steady herself by holding onto my arm, but I dared not attach any significance to these casual contacts.

As it neared eleven and we began packing up, Greta remarked that the sky was indeed full of curious objects, but added, "Can we honestly say that we know these things? A luminous smudge in a lens isn't a galaxy, is it? It's only the light from the galaxy which could have gone extinct centuries ago. The whole universe could have blinked out yesterday." How rarely is beauty conjoined with skepticism, but when the combination occurs, it's irresistible.

We walked back through the empty streets of Trier. I chattered on nervously about boarding school, cigars, a tetrahedral kite I had once made out of tissue paper and soda straws, and how there were times when you felt yourself expanding in all directions like a supernova. I may or may not have let slip the word Zohar. She kept pace beside me, rarely looking in my direction, but nodding in response to my overly dramatic gestures. As we turned onto her street, I realized that I had become my own ventriloquist, the words coming out of my mouth but the mind engaged elsewhere. I was acutely aware of the few remaining hints of warmth in the early June air, the aureoles of light above our heads where the gas lamps disappeared into the trees, and the overwhelming sense that while the stars had all the time in the world to tease us with the possibility of their existence, I had only this moment, which was now, just before Greta stepped out from the shadow of a linden tree, and into the glare of light from a fixture by her front door. We said good night. I leaned close to kiss her cheek, but she turned her face squarely toward mine. She looked at me for a moment with a frank expression, eyes wide open, and then closed them smoothly as she brought her lips to mine.

As our relationship deepened through the following weeks, I instinctively kept the romance a secret from my family, though my father was probably too busy, and my grandmother too withdrawn into her Zoharic studies, to have taken much notice anyway. My mother, however, was on to me from the beginning: She was too smart to believe that my frequent visits to the Marx household were simply a function of Frau Marx's new-found passion for astronomy.

By the end of June I had resolved to attend university in Trier. I entertained fantasies of settling down here with Greta and inheriting my father's (or even her father's) business. I knew that would mean studying law or accounting instead of physics or philosophy, but this seemed a necessary concession to love. Besides, I would then be assured of sufficient wealth to pursue my private researches in the tradition of the gentlemanly amateur.

My mother's charade of indifference finally broke down in July. I had come home around midnight from what was ostensibly an outing "with the Marxes" to observe a meteor shower. By now I had become somewhat cavalier about the romance and hadn't bothered to erase the signs of having spent the last few hours lying with Greta in a damp field. My mother surprised me when she stepped around the wingback chair where she had been waiting up for me, and at that moment I felt as though the grass stains on my clothes might as well have been circled in red and annotated. After a perfunctory exchange about the meteors, I started upstairs, at which point my mother announced that she wanted to talk to me. One didn't have to be the rocket scientist I was destined to become to know that this was the conversation I had vainly hoped to avoid.

"You're very fond of Greta, aren't you, Arthur?" she said. I was already in trouble: "Fond" was the most erotically charged word in the Waldmann family vocabulary.

"Greta and I have become very good friends; and the Marxes have been more than kind to me."

"That's exactly what I wanted to talk with you about," she said, visibly relieved that I had given her this opening. "I know you've developed a strong attachment, and that's normal in a young man, but I don't want you to do anything that will cause you to get hurt. There's something you need to keep in mind about the Marxes. I wouldn't be a good mother if I didn't mention it, so I'm willing to take the risk that you'll think less of me." She paused and looked down at the carpet for a moment, shaking her head. "It's this: The Marxes, you know, are Jewish."

I was dumbfounded. "I can't believe I'm hearing this," I said.

"It's not that I have anything at all against Jews. I've never told you this before, but when I was engaged to your father, your aunt Magdelena took me aside and told me the whole story of your great-grandfather's conversion to Christianity after Napoleon's defeat at Waterloo. She asked me to reconsider my decision, but I snapped right back that I knew all about the Waldmann family history, which was a bald-faced lie, and that I didn't care if your father was descended from orangutans. He was a loving and kind-hearted man, and I was going to marry him. The issue never arose again, and not long before Aunt Magdelena died, she told me that she loved your father as much as any of her nephews. Still, everyone knows that the Jews can be a clannish people — just look how withdrawn your grandmother has become since she got interested in all that medieval hocus-pocus, and she's just a nutty old woman who thinks she's Jewish. Do you know what they do when a man marries a non-Jewish woman? They hold a funeral for him as if he were dead. They don't do that for a woman, and you know why? Because it's in their law that a woman who marries outside the faith must be stoned to death. Of course, they don't really do that anymore, but it tells you something about how their minds work."

As my mother went on, I relaxed, thinking how easy it was to refute her. Without exploring the religious ironies that haunted both the Marx and the Waldmann families, I pointed out that Greta knew less about Judaism than I did. She had never been inside a synagogue, I was certain, couldn't tell you the difference between the Torah and the Talmud, and ate bacon for breakfast every other morning.

"It's not what a person knows or eats," she replied, "but what they are. The Marxes are Jewish. A hundred years ago Greta's ancestors could have decided not to be Jews, and all the Jewishness would have been washed out of them by now. Maybe in a hundred years it won't matter whether someone is Jewish or Christian or Hindu, or bows down before a block of Limburger cheese. But nowadays, it matters. You're still young," she said, shifting to the world-weary mode of a minor Hohenzollern baroness, an attitude I found irritating beyond all reason. "Eventually you'll see that you can't be something just because you say you are."

The effect of this conversation was to convert a serious and sentimental adolescent romance into one that was serious, sentimental, passionate, and reckless. At the very least, her admonition had a profound effect on the erotic fantasies that dominated my mental life. Greta's Jewishness now became a potent aphrodisiac. Despite blue eyes and a fair complexion that could have belonged to any Mosellander, I searched her features for signs of exotic Near Eastern origins, and found them in the slight convex bend of her nose and the gentle depression beneath her high cheekbones. I turned then to the Song of Solomon, which I had once studied with my grandmother, and immediately discovered that Greta's breasts were the two towers referred to in the text. "I am my beloved's, and his desire is toward me" —I pictured Greta dressed in translucent veils speaking these words against a backdrop of date palms and camel herds. A light breeze parted the veil around one of her ankles, revealing a finely wrought silver chain, each link a letter of the Hebrew alphabet. Brilliant, six-pointed stars shone down from the heavens. "Come, my beloved, let us go forth into the field. Let us get up early to the vineyard; let us see if the vine flourish, whether the tender grape appear, and the pomegranates bud forth. There I will give thee my love," she said with a look that told me she knew exactly what was meant by the words "grape" and "pomegranate."

During the ensuing weeks of turmoil and excitement, I continued to work in my father's business. My clerical duties were monotonous, though I never wearied of the intoxicating tobacco smell that permeated every corner of the building. One day when I was searching for an invoice among the papers stuffed into the cubbyholes of a massive roll-top desk, I happened across an old note to my parents from the headmaster of my school. Underlined, in bold script at the bottom of a memo about the upcoming year's calendar, he had written: "Your Arthur is a scientific genius. He will make you proud. A glorious destiny awaits him!"

My father was usually scrupulous in keeping family matters separate from business affairs, and in later years, I questioned just how accidental was my finding of this note. Yet I recognized the handwriting as the headmaster's, and its authenticity blinded me to any consideration of its rhetorical intent. I saw my name connected to the words "genius" and "destiny," and it now struck me that perhaps life in Trier might be too confining after all. Why not study Hegel in the room where Hegel had taught? Who could know? I might be the next Hegel!

Toward the end of August, there was to be a spectacular display of planets in the evening sky. An hour after sunset, a brilliant crescent Venus would be high in the west, while Mars, on one of its closest approaches to Earth this century, would be a glowing orange beacon in the east. As the Zohar identifies Mars with the divine emanation of *Tiferet* (beauty) which governs the heart, and Venus with *Yesod* (foundation) which governs the genitals, I knew that this was destined to be a special occasion for Greta and me.

We stepped out that evening with star charts, flashlights, a canteen of watered-down Liebfraumilch, and of course, the telescope. Upon arrival opposite the Dominican Retreat House, we set up the instrument, knowing full well that even if we had intended to do astronomy, this was an event to be seen with the naked eye, not through the medium of a lens. In the last light of day I screwed in the eyepieces and adjusted the setting circles. A light southerly breeze carried over the voices of the priests at vespers. We lay down on the grass in front of the tripod and held each other, picking out Venus and then Mars. So ended our stargazing. Minutes later, half undressed, I feared that some casual stroller would discover our bower. She kissed my eyelids closed and told me not to worry.

As we walked back into town, I thought that the rabbis and church fathers had been absolutely right to superimpose upon those erotic verses in the Song of Solomon a mystical significance. Later, drifting off to sleep and savoring a scent not quite my own, I watched as the ceiling above my bed dissolved to once again reveal the night sky. I floated upward at an impossible speed; Venus, Mars, and the other planets whizzed by me. Soon I was passing stars that were familiar to me from both my grandmother's visions and the charts I had constructed on the basis of them. Moments later I was approaching a dark nebula in the tail of the Scorpion. I heard a chorus of men's voices, intoning what sounded like aphorisms in a language I could not quite understand but suspected was Aramaic. I tried to make sense out of what I was hearing, but the effort was exhausting. The next thing I knew I was awake lying on sheets soaked in cold sweat. I looked at the clock. No more than two minutes had passed. I turned over and didn't awaken till noon.

Before parting that night, Greta and I had made a date to meet secretly two days later at the warehouse. My father would be away on business, and we could easily lose ourselves in the maze of cigar crates. The thirty-six-hour separation had been almost unbearable, and when I heard her call my name as she came tip-toeing past a shipment of Sumatra Golds, my heart was racing with desire. I took her in my arms, and pulled her down on the floor next to me. But as I began to unloosen clothing, she said to me between kisses, "I think we need to be more careful."

"Careful? My father's in Dortmund and not even the Spanish Inquisition could find us in this labyrinth."

"That's not what I meant by careful."

I was not so naive a teenager as to be blind to the connection between sex and pregnancy, but I had assumed, like generations of Romeos before me, that even if this was not exclusively a women's problem, it was one that women knew how to manage. Surely Greta would not have allowed things to get this far if there had been a chance of her becoming pregnant. Besides, what could I have possibly done about it? While medically effective condoms existed in Weimar Germany, they could be legitimately obtained only with a doctor's prescription by married men, or illegitimately through the black market of a demimonde that respectable adolescents like Greta and myself would not dream of entering, even if we had known how.

"You don't think you're pregnant, do you?" I asked as if this were the most preposterous thing since the notion that long-dead sages were meeting every night in a distant galaxy to discuss arcane points of Jewish law.

"I don't think so. I hope not. I'll know for certain in a week. I'm usually as dependable as the town clock."

"And what will we do if you are?" I asked, instantly embarrassed by the undertone of panic.

"There was a girl in my class last year who dropped out in the middle of the term. The rumor was that she had gotten pregnant, and that her parents had sent her to a convent hospital in Karlsruhe to have the baby. She never came back, though." Greta propped herself up on an elbow and looked down into my eyes. "Of course, they could make us get married."

"I can't imagine being married," I said truthfully.

"Neither can I, but you know my mother was married when she was only a year older than we are now."

We parted that afternoon with a kiss that seemed more fraternal than romantic.

I spent the rest of the day checking invoices in the office, tedious work that provided little mental distraction. At first I was surprised at Greta's relative calm about our situation, but as the hours wore on, I felt increasing anger and resentment. It was simple for her to look at marriage as a solution. How significant an impact would it have on her life? If our paths had never crossed, she would have gotten married in a few more years anyway, and so the domestic career for which the bourgeois Marxes had trained her would merely begin sooner rather than later. As for myself, however . . . . I removed from the cubbyhole in my father's desk (where I had been careful to replace it exactly as I had found it, down to the creasings) the note from my headmaster identifying me as a genius destined to do great things. While I might look forward to settling down with Greta some day, I couldn't see pursuing my studies in Berlin, Trier, or any place else for that matter with the responsibility of a wife and child. Why didn't she see this? Indeed, even to entertain marriage at this time was rather selfish on her part. There were other alternatives to this beside the convent. She and her mother could go abroad a few months before her time (the Marxes could afford such things), and the baby could be adopted by some doting childless couple overseas.

The next morning I was seized with a new fear that in a moment of distraction Greta would confess to her mother the true character of our relations, and that even if she were not pregnant, I would never be able to live down the shame. I decided right then and there to make a pre-emptive strike, and so at breakfast I announced to my mother that I would study physics and philosophy at Friedrich-Wilhelm. Although she said she only wanted me to make the best decision for myself, I could sense the joy behind her outward reserve, and within minutes we were conspiring how to break the news to my father. I figured that once I had made the commitment to Berlin, my mother would become the staunchest defender of my remaining unencumbered, no matter how much pressure the Marxes might exert against me to do the honorable thing by their daughter.

But the actions of which I'm still most ashamed involved the invisible operations of my soul. For the first time since I was nine or ten years old, when my grandmother's tutelage in the mysteries of the Zohar had led me to question the dogmas of the Lutheranism to which my parents and I outwardly adhered, I found myself praying to, and actually trying to make bargains with, God. Not the God in which I thought I had come to believe — the pervasive mystical essence that Moses de Leon called *Ein Sof* — but the overblown caricature that had been written into Genesis and Exodus for the benefit of the simple-minded, and which the opportunistic Paul had reduced to the figure of another run-of-the-mill Hellenistic man-god for the sake of his idol-worshipping patrons. I promised Him that if Greta were not pregnant I would stop dabbling in the pseudo-science of the Zohar, abandon all further attempts to commune with dead sages who existed only in legend, and confine my study of astronomy exclusively to the kind of hard facts that would meet the approval of Herr Neumann. Needless to say, I also promised henceforth to remain chaste until that time I should marry, if I ever did.

As the crescent moon appeared in the sky the evening before my next meeting with Greta, I walked across town to an unfamiliar neighborhood and slipped into an empty church. I knelt down behind the altar at the foot of a cross on which hung a disturbingly life-like effigy of the dying Nazarene, and for over an hour repeated these promises, interspersed with whatever snatches of Christian dogma and liturgy I remembered — the Apostles' Creed, the Nicene Creed, the Lord's Prayer, the Lutheran catechism, and the first verses of a number of hymns and Christmas carols. Throughout this whole confession I felt myself to be the fraud and hypocrite that I knew I was, but rationalized that desperate circumstances call for desperate measures.

Greta and I had arranged to meet a week later at noon in front of the Roman Gate. Overwhelmed by impatience, I arrived almost half an hour early, and was surprised to find her already there, feeding the doves from a bag of breadcrumbs. When she saw me standing next to one of the blackened columns, she ran toward me and threw her arms around my neck. "We're safe," she whispered in my ear, and then bent her head around to gaze knowingly at the clock tower. At that point I began sobbing uncontrollably, and she walked me to a place away from the lunchtime crowds. "It's just the joy of relief, isn't it?" she said anxiously, as if half-expecting to hear that I was now pregnant. "That's all," I replied. It was relief, but also mourning for the loss of both love and faith, which I now recognized as the price of having my prayers answered. It was beyond my capacity to explain this to Greta at the time, and fortunately, there was no need to do so, as she told me that in a few days she and her mother would be leaving on a three-month trip to the United States. "We have cousins who live on a farm in one of those 'I' states—Iowa, Illinois, I forget which. My mother has wanted to go see them for some time, but I was reluctant to be away from home for that long. But now . . ." She smiled and added, "When I find out what the stars look like from Iowa, I'll write and tell you all about it."

That night as I drifted off to sleep I had, not a vision or a dream exactly, but a mental picture of a comet coalescing in the outer reaches of the solar system. As it approached the sun, it glowed brighter and brighter, until it came so close that it was lost in the sun's glare and I thought that it had been swallowed up. But moments later, it emerged on the other side, and began its long journey back to the remote void from which it had come. Since the Zohar never mentions comets, I felt free to allegorize: I was the comet, Greta the sun; although our rendezvous had almost consumed me, it had also hurled me into a trajectory that I could not have attained on my own. Henceforth my study of the heavens would be purely scientific, and my attempts to reach them, purely mechanical.

CHAPTER 4
KORVO

In the weeks after the Greta fiasco I wavered between depression and lust, and filled a notebook with poetry that might have been read as passable juvenilia by some future doctoral student if the impulse to write rather than engineer had persisted beyond my immediate emotional crisis and carried me on toward a distinguished career in literature. It did not. I mention this because as I was throwing out my possessions before leaving town I actually found the notebook in a box of school papers that hadn't been unsealed since before the war. Here's a sample:

Remember? Those furtive evenings watched
me claw at the pungent tailings
of your exotic bloodline. From my loins
would spring picket fences or golden railings
to immure dreams of white comets blazing
and white-haired children and white horses grazing.

There's nothing especially poignant about the intensity and after-effects of first loves. It makes perfect psychological sense. While I cannot say that I have thought about Greta every day of my life since our last good-byes at the Porta Nigra in Trier, I have probably thought about her every week, or at least, every couple of weeks. It occurred to me, however, as I was re-reading these lines born from fantasies of boundless sex and dynastic triumph, that in these fortnightly visitations Greta remained the glowing young woman of 1929, whereas I had evolved into the sort of flabby, bony old creature who should have dismissed all thoughts of amorous connection decades ago. Even in the presence of my ghostly Greta simulacrum, I should be ashamed of myself. But what about the real Greta of today, circa 1986? She would be 74 if she were still alive. I knew that some years before the war she had married a promising young lawyer, doubtless unencumbered by kabbalistic longings, and started a family. Maybe he had received a promotion, moved to a fine house in Dresden, and all of them been incinerated by the RAF's genocidal attack in February 1945. Alternatively, perhaps they spent a relatively peaceful Nazi Gotterdämmerung at their farmstead along the banks of the Mosel. (I refuse to imagine that she was carted off with Trier's other Jews in cattle cars to Dachau.) I consulted actuarial tables and learned that her odds of survival were better than even, while those of her husband were not. Maybe he had grown too fond of Bratwurst and beer and died of a massive heart attack. So Greta was now a widow, tending a small garden and baking Lebkuchen with her grandchildren in Baden-Württemberg. It occurred to me that I could write her a letter, or even come up with a phone number and call her. But to what end? To be reunited in childhood love after a lifetime of harsh separation? (A fairytale ending you read about a few times a year in the newspaper.) To find the perfect audience for my life story? (There is never a perfect audience, which is why, dear reader, whoever you are, you will do just as well as another.) I therefore elected to do nothing.

•   •   •

I began my studies in Berlin in the fall of 1929. Like most undergraduates I attended lectures in the mornings and returned to my lodgings to study during the afternoon. I had little to do with the other tenants of my building, most of whom I was more likely to hear through the paper-thin walls than to see in passing, with one exception. This was a fellow about my height but more durably constructed without being stout or stocky. Apart from his nose, which was bony and curved downward like a tapir's, he was doughfaced, almost unfinished looking, wanting someone to come along and pinch a bit of excess flesh off the chin or from under the eyelids. His hands were similarly meaty. I later learned that he had run track and field in school and could move with grace, though I would have predicted the opposite, because for a long time I never saw him in motion. Indeed, he was the only tenant I ever observed using the downstairs sitting room for its intended purpose, legs crossed, bent forward, intently studying some book balanced on his lap, sometimes smoking a pipe of cherry-flavored tobacco which I recognized as one of my father's downmarket wares. My passing by the entrance to the sitting room never distracted him one iota; indeed, the unbroken focus on his text positively irradiated a warning of *noli me tangere*. His most striking feature was his hair, black and frizzy, which if it were stretched out probably would have reached down below his shoulders, but otherwise accumulated in a black mass that had been barbered in such a way to give it the appearance of a tricorne hat permanently affixed to the top of his head.

Coming home from campus one afternoon I noticed that the sitting room was empty but that on the table next to his usual chair was an open book turned upside down. Pausing for a moment to listen for footsteps and hearing none, I walked over to have a look and was taken aback to see Hermann Oberth's *Rocket into Interplanetary Space*. I had first learned of the book when I was at boarding school but at the age of fourteen or fifteen could make little sense of the many equations embedded in the text. This served to motivate my study of higher mathematics, however, and when I re-read the book within the past year, not only did I understand the math, I could also recognize errors in calculations related to payload capacities and engine performance.

"The numbers on isentropic flow though the exhaust nozzle just don't add up, do they?" a voice behind me said, and knowing that this was indeed the case, I replied, "No, they most certainly do not," before realizing that this conversation was not unfolding in the echo chamber of my own thoughts but in real space and time with another person. I looked up from the book and into a face that was smiling, perhaps in unanticipated pleasure at the interruption. He held out his hand. "My name is Korvo. Jakob Korvo."

"Hello. I'm—"

"Waldmann. A. Waldmann." He paused for my inevitable reaction. "Don't worry, I'm not a police spy or anything. It's just that when you embrace stasis, sitting in that chair several hours a day, as

I'm sure you've noticed, you become attuned to things, like the creak of the little brass hinges on our assigned mailboxes which our fellow tenants check incessantly it seems, for God knows what, letters from home I suppose, as if those would help. Despite my best efforts, even I sometimes succumbed to curiosity and kinesis, and after I watched one of our resident scholars ascend the stairs, I'd tiptoe to the mailboxes and by peeking through the decorative apertures and comparing the presence or absence of mail with my previous mental notes, deduce a match between receptacle and owner. After the first week I knew everyone's name by the creak of their little hinges, kinesis no longer required."

"And curiosity?" I asked, wanting to show that I could play this game, too.

"Perhaps. I tend to let the world seek me out, not the other way around."

"Me, too," I said, unguardedly.

"So we have at least something in common," said Korvo.

The conversation turned to the mundane: leaky plumbing, the music student in 2B, drunks in the alleyway. But all I could think about was the book I had picked up and was still holding awkwardly in my hand. I wasn't so naïve to think that I belonged to a tiny cabal of cognoscenti who were familiar with, or even aware of, the arcana of *Raumschiffahrt* (or in English, space travel, though on account of the almost mystical resonance of the word in the original, I will retain the German throughout this narrative). Oberth's book was obviously in the public domain—it's not like it had been circulated in manuscript, after all—but I considered it likely that of the several hundred people in Germany who had read the book, only a few understood it, and that among that miniscule subset I would likely be about the youngest, which is to say, the only person with enough years ahead of me to actually realize the possibility of going into space myself.

" —Christian name?" The words came out of Korvo's mouth. I had become lost in my thoughts. Why was I now being asked for my religion. "Am I a Christian?" I said rather defensively.

"Your Christian name," said Korvo. "I'm clever but not clairvoyant. What's the "A." stand for?"

"Arthur."

"Like Schopenhauer!" Korvo responded excitedly. "My favorite dead philosopher!"My heart leapt up. He was a philosophy student, and like most students of the so-called humanities, probably had the technical ability of the average kindergartener. So what if he understood the math? He would never use it to bend metal. The psychological cocktail of the spiritual and the technological that had yielded me up was one in a million.

"So you also like astronomy?" I asked off-handedly.

"Only tangentially. It's rockets I'm concerned with. I know it sounds crazy but I want to go into space one day to see if Schopenhauer was right. While it's pretty obvious by now that there's no God down here, we can't be sure about what's up there." He raised an index finger and I gazed vacantly at the ceiling. "It's probably fair to assume that the heavens are as much dead matter as the Earth, but I don't want to be caught flatfooted one day by the discovery that we're enveloped a hundred or a thousand miles high by some cloud of spiritual gas where Moses and Jesus and my great-grandmother from Sub-Carpathian Ruthenia are all floating around, making fun of the whole Rise of Science gestalt. If that turns out to be the case, I want to be the one who knows about it first, because I'm by nature a skeptic, and I'll never be satisfied with secondhand knowledge of such a momentous truth."

"So you're really a divinity student here?" I asked, still hopeful.

Korvo let out a massive guffaw. "How I wish!" he said, "but I don't think there are many openings in the Lutheran clergy for deracinated Jews. I'm in the Faculty of Physical Sciences, actually. It's the price I had to pay to be in a place where I could best pursue my real obsessions. My father is a hotshot chemist at IG Farben—he invented some kind of insecticide—and wants me to follow in his footsteps. Bourgeois poltroon horseshit. But since only physics and chemistry will get us into space, it fulfills my theological imperatives while keeping the old man off my back." He turned wistful for a moment. "I dream about penetrating the nothingness of space, the non-stuff stuff out of which a non-existent God could never have created matter."

Then he dropped his bombshell "I'm actually tinkering with some things right now."

"Tinkering?" I squeaked out.

"Well, they're only powder rockets, not much more than firecrackers. Of course Oberth is right on about developing liquid fuels for space travel, but it's like any business, I want to learn it from the ground up, and this way I'll be able to gather some basic data on fluid dynamics and drag coefficients that I can apply to real rockets if I ever get the chance. Come on up, I'll show you."

Opening the door to Korvo's room was like entering the Bedouin tent that turns out to be a sultan's palace, if the sultan in question were a highly accomplished amateur aeronautical engineer. In place of the usual student furnishings of wash stand, writing table, etc., were sturdy workbenches covered with tools and pieces of sheet metal cut into various polygonal shapes. There were soldering irons and metal punches, and in one corner a bookshelf that contained two or three thick volumes that looked like shop references, but was mostly filled with brown glass bottles, many with skull and crossbones labels. Leaning against one wall were several small metal tubes. A vaguely sinister vinegar-like odor filled the air.

"Be it ever so humble," said Korvo as I looked around, trying to suppress astonishment.

"I can see why you do your reading downstairs," I said. There was no obvious place to sit down. "Where do you sleep?"

He pointed to a ratty-looking sleeping bag under the one window in the room. At its foot was a cardboard box containing a small pile of clothes. "My wardrobe," he said with obvious pride.

We talked some more about the shortcomings of Oberth's book. I certainly did not want to reveal anything of my own theological motivations for my interests at this point, and thought it wise to present myself as just another adolescent male infatuated with the gee-whiz dimension of space travel.

We made plans the following Sunday to head out to Korvo's "proving grounds" in a remote suburb about half an hour outside the city.

When I returned to my room, I was overwhelmed by a sense of just how prissy and unimaginative it was. Where Korvo had two workbenches, I had a neatly made bed with clean sheets and pillowcases. I found it almost impossible to undertake any of my day's tasks until I made my bed, right down to the perfectly tucked hospital corners. In the time it took me to do that every morning, who knows what possibly revolutionary technical insights Korvo might have already come up with. Maybe I was really just one of those people who subconsciously accepts orderliness as a consolation for their lack of creativity. From there it was a short step to the thought that my status as the chosen one in the world-historical movement from Earth to Heaven was a monstrous self-delusion; that if such epochal events really were on the horizon, surely an eccentric genius like Korvo would be leading the way.

Of course, on the other hand, the thrust of Korvo's techno-theological objective was radically unlike my own. Quite the opposite in fact. He wanted to penetrate the heavens to confirm his belief that there was absolutely nothing up there beyond the emptiness he already found on Earth. I wanted to demonstrate that the anagogically saturated environment we inhabited here, as described, for example, in the Zohar, extended without limit into the heavens. So perhaps my self-conceived status as the chosen one remained intact. Or maybe we were both chosen to pursue symbiotically related quests, though assuming that the term "chosen" requires a chooser, it was hard for me to imagine that Korvo's project could be anything more than a brilliant foil designed to enhance the ultimate glory of my own.

I knocked on Korvo's door Saturday at 4:30 a.m. as instructed. (Although I'm often up at dawn myself, when I asked him about the early hour, he replied "to limit exposure and thus reduce suspicion.") He was dressed in exactly the same outfit that I'd seen him in the other day — indeed, the only clothes I'd seen him wear before, or would ever see him wear: white linen shirt, black pants, braided hemp rope belt, and heavy hobnailed boots. When I stepped in he asked me with great solicitousness if I would like some breakfast. As I'd only had time for a quick cup of tea in my room, I said yes, and he gestured me over to what he called his larder, a small table in one corner piled high with tins of sardines, and a paper bag splotchy with grease stains.

"Sardines or honey cakes?" he asked, and then added emphatically, as if embarrassed at his lack of hospitality, "or both!" I opted for the honey cake, and he handed me one from the bag using a pair of tongs. "Between the amino acids and monosaturated fats in the fish and the complex carbohydrates in the honey cakes, plus an occasional glass of milk, you could live on this diet indefinitely. My current streak is 421 days. A Mars mission, by Hohmann transfer orbit, and allowing for time on the ground there (not that I would require more than a couple of minutes) would take 630 days. Something to think about."

I made a mental note to find out what a "Hohmann transfer orbit" was. How could I not know about these things?

There were two canvas duffel bags on the floor. "This one is mostly test equipment and notebooks," he said, handing it to me. "The actual rockets are in here," he added, taking the other. "Black powder isn't particularly volatile, but let's try to not bump into each other."

At around 5:00 a.m. we boarded the first train of the day from Oranienburger Strasse. At this hour on a Saturday we were the only passengers in our coach. We rode to the end of the line in the direction of Frankfurt-am-Oder, and began walking. Tidy suburban houses gave way to farmsteads and then open fields. We trudged on for another half hour or so, talking more or less continuously, filling in the outlines of our previous lives for one another's consumption with (for me at least) the guarded sense of excitement that characterizes what I would later think of as the boost phase of any given relationship's trajectory. Korvo, it turned out, was a year older than I, as unlike myself, he had graduated from his *Gymnasium* later than usual at the age of nineteen. (I took more than a little solace in this.) His father was now a middle manager at the IG Farben ammonia factory in Merseburg, though a generation earlier his ancestors had been dry goods merchants in little towns throughout Lower Silesia. On this occasion he elected not to bring up religion, but it was obvious from this account that he was the scion of first generation nouveau-riche *Ostjuden*. Though perhaps a bit unrefined in his personal habits, Korvo possessed a formidable intellect. It turned out that in addition to his interests in science and engineering, he was also a passionate student of ancient and medieval history, and having mastered Latin in high school, was now enrolled in courses in Greek and Old Norse.

At around 6:30 a.m. we turned down a gravel road at the end of which was a landscape quite unlike anything I'd ever seen before. In the foreground of an area the size of several soccer fields were a dozen or so perfectly conic mounds of coal-black ashes, probably twenty or thirty feet high. Farther back were a small number of taller mounds of what looked like garbage and debris; these were smoldering, with a few spots glowing orange or actually on fire.

Choosing a location behind one of the mounds not visible from the road, Korvo set down his bag and directed me to do the same with mine. He looked around at the literal wasteland with an air of satisfaction and proprietorship. "Ever wonder what happened to those magazines I saw you stuffing in the trash one day last week when you thought no one was looking?" he asked, with a sweeping gesture toward one of the burning piles. "This is the toilet at the end of the mechanical peristalsis that is modern industrial culture. Weekdays there's an endless flow of garbage trucks, but on the Lord's Sabbath it's as deserted as Petra. Who in their right mind visits a dump on their day off?" — as if we ourselves would be the last people on the planet to do such a thing.

As we began unpacking, there was a muffled thud and then a plume of smoke rising from one of the nearby trash piles. "Be mindful to keep your distance from those things," he advised. "People throw out all kinds of toxic and combustible artifacts, and you never know when something is going to blow. Excellent smokescreen for our activities, however."

Korvo removed a dozen rockets from his bag. Of course, now when someone says "rocket," most people will think in terms of something like the mighty Saturn V, hundreds of feet long, millions of pounds of thrust, deafening roars, etc., etc. But these devices were mere fingerlings, metal tubes barely an inch in diameter and less than a foot long, lashed to thin wooden sticks that served as miniature launch gantries. What would have been notable to even the untrained eye was how finely wrought they were: perfectly folded seams, smoothly trimmed edges, faultless symmetries throughout. Each of the rockets had a unique configuration of fins and subtly different nosecones. All were painted in harlequin patterns of black and white for better visibility. He removed the nosecones to check on their fueling, and seeing the need to make some last minute adjustments, unstoppered bottles of sulfur, charcoal, and potassium nitrate to mix up a fresh batch of propellant.

"You've got the important stuff over there," he said to me as he carefully tamped some additional powder into one of the tubes. "Anyone can shoot off a rocket. It's what you make of it that really matters." In front of me I had spread out notebooks containing both ruled and graph paper, pens, pencils, a protractor, a slide-rule, a Leica camera, two telescoping tripods, and most amazingly to me, a Siemens Model C 16 millimeter portable movie camera. I had never seen such a sophisticated camera before, much less held one. It wasn't the sort of thing I would expect normal people to have, and I figured it most have cost a fortune. "How did you ever come by something like this?" I asked. Roughly the size of a tissue box, it was made of textured black metal with silver trim. It wasn't heavy yet possessed a heft and a solidity that was emotionally satisfying. I resisted the immense temptation to adjust dials and switches.

"I don't even like thinking about how much that cost, but my father gives me a generous allowance, and when you eat sardines and buy your clothes at second-hand stores, you have money for such essentials. Speaking of which, would you help me set up those theodolites?" By quick process of elimination, I figured he must be referring to the two sextant-like instruments lying on the ground in front of me.

Korvo affixed the theodolites to the mounts on the tripods and positioned them about twenty meters apart. Then he handed me the movie camera and give me a brief tutorial in its use. "Get some footage of me sticking the rockets in the ground. I never know what's going to turn out to be the critical variable in a test, and the camera is gloriously unprejudiced in what it elects to see. Besides, if we become famous some day, it will be neat to have documented how we began working in a dump, literally."

After another quick tutorial in setting f-stops and camera speeds, I took some footage of Korvo kneeling down by his rockets and unspooling the fuses out to a safe distance. "That's enough for now," he said standing up. I was happy before when he used the first-person plural in alluding to the possibility of our future fame, but I wondered if I would always be the one to hold the camera, and so remain invisible to posterity (thus the only photographic record of Neil Armstrong on the moon being his tiny reflection in Buzz Aldrin's visor).

Next, Korvo walked me over to one of the theodolites and showed me its basic operations. ("I've been waiting for what seems like hundreds of years to have someone else out here so I could use these things," he said.) He then went over to the other tripod and, after a countdown from ten (just like in the film, *Woman in the Moon*), lit the fuse. When it reached the rocket, there was a sound like schnitzel sizzling in hot oil and a sudden puff of smoke. It was all over before I even had a chance to lean into the theodolite, and the next thing I knew Korvo was coming back with the spent device that his more practiced eye had tracked through its whole trajectory. He dismissed my efforts at an apology. "It's going to take a while to get the hang of this procedure," he said. "That's why I brought so many devices. If we get a decent reading from even one launch, I'll consider our day a big success."

As it happened, we managed to collect good data from the fourth launch onward. Korvo was brimming with enthusiasm as he graphed trajectories in his notebooks and annotated them with field observations. I also shot quite a lot of additional footage. Korvo never asked for the camera—his absorption in the mechanics of launching and tracking the rockets was total and absolutely genuine, I'm convinced—but the more I filmed, the less I cared about this. After all, controlling what's seen is more important than being seen. Who would you rather be, the renowned director, Fritz Lang, or one of the actors in *Woman in the Moon* whose names are now mostly forgotten?

Besides, why would I of all people really want everyone to know what I looked like?

It turned out that Korvo and I were enrolled in a few of the same physics and chemistry lectures, though I had never seen him there. "I read the books, show up for exams, and pass with high marks. Why waste time going to classes? The university works hard to constrain knowledge more than to advance it. Every minute I spend behind those walls is one less minute for discovery and innovation." I, too, had excellent marks but with perfect attendance. While I didn't attribute my success to conscientiousness — going to class was more just an ingrained habit, like brushing your teeth before bedtime — it did undermine self-confidence in achieving my world-historical ambitions. After all, weren't Edison and Einstein also both resistant to the stultifying protocols of formal education?

While I didn't own a movie camera or theodolites, one piece of equipment I had brought from home not in Korvo's inventory was a three-inch refracting telescope. For a long time the wooden box sat in a corner of my room as a makeshift table covered with an old tea towel, but toward the end of that year, there was to be a lunar eclipse visible in eastern Germany shortly after moonrise. While these are not usually thought of as telescopic events — you can see the eclipse fine without one — it's also the case that physical features on a full moon absent the sun's glare stand out in heightened relief. Mountains and craters whose dimensions you can only fully appreciate on successive nights during waxing or waning crescent phases can be observed as a complete ensemble, albeit in coppery hues.

When I mentioned the upcoming eclipse to Korvo, he expressed enthusiasm in joining me to view it. "I love the moon," he said. "The more we learn about it, the more we realize how utterly dead it is. If only we could be so confident about the rest of the galaxy."

On the appointed evening, we walked the several blocks to the edge of the Tiergarten, carrying the refractor in its casket-like box between us. After setting up, we observed the moon for about half an hour. Ultimately, the eclipse did function as a kind of pretext, for both observation of more distant objects and speculation on their significance. Thinking about what makes for interesting viewing in the autumn sky, I suggested Arghol, the winking double "demon star" (the meaning of its Arabic name, I believe). I pointed the telescope toward the constellation Perseus and quickly located our target, as it was near the peak of its brightness. After watching it fade over the next hour or so, Korvo remarked, "Jacob and Esau, Cicero and Cataline, Jesus and John. Hmmm. I wonder if there's a reference to this phenomenon in Origen."

"*Der Ursprung*?" I asked, thinking that Korvo for no doubt good reasons of his own had employed the English instead of the German word. I assumed he must be referencing some ancient or medieval astronomical treatise.

"No, Origen, the third-century Church father. He's very, very dead but still someone we have to pay attention to because he asserts with formidable authority that the sun and the moon and the stars are actually personalities whose existence preceded the creation. They supposedly spend all their time praying to God (and thus don't merit worship from ourselves), but binaries like Arghol suggest petty conflicts and jealousies even among these superior beings, if they exist, which of course I hope that Raumschiffahrt will disprove, once and for all."

"Was he an astronomer? Or at least, an astrologer?"

"No, purely a theologian. Lately in my spare time I've been burrowing through his works in the original Greek, along with the Latin translations, and I can't find any evidence that he even looked at the sky. No matter. His testimony is not easily dismissed."

"But why?"

"Number one, despite being the first real theologian in history and the most brilliant mind of the decadent era to which he was assigned, the Church to this day refuses to canonize him because of the preexistent souls doctrine, that and his belief that at the end of time everyone and everything, both good and evil, would be folded back into the divine essence, thus effectively denying existence of Hell."

"I can see where that would cause difficulties," I said. This notion — apokatastasis — is near and dear to students of the Zohar.

"Number two, he castrated himself."

"That's a good thing?"

"Well, it would certainly solve a lot of problems. But to speak impersonally, you have to admire the man's conviction. He read in the Gospels that while some are lucky enough to be eunuchs by accident of birth or the cruelty of their fellow man, others make themselves eunuchs for the Kingdom of Heaven's sake. Augustine would hem and haw for years before accepting a painless baptism, but I can see Origen encountering those words in Scripture one day, coming to a sudden realization of their shocking import, and racing into his kitchen for a paring knife. You can't trifle with someone like that, no matter how cockamamie his world view."

Barring occasional excursions to a dump to assist Korvo with his testing program, and still less frequent outings with my telescope to observe notable celestial events, my life as a university student was essentially unremarkable. If I wasn't attending lectures, I was studying in the library or completing assigned exercises in the chemistry or physics lab. Normal student relationships would develop through chance meetings on campus, or by sharing a meal at one of the many cheap cafes in the neighborhood, but since Korvo rarely went to campus and ate alone in his room, such opportunities were unavailable. He did go for walks several times a week, however, and if I happened to pass him on the way out of our building, or run into him somewhere on the street, he would always invite me to join him with an unexpected outburst of bonhommie.

I soon came to think of these walks as essentially peripatetic dialogues and even fantasized about writing them up and publishing them one day with appropriate geographical designations, depending on our route or perhaps the location associated with a particularly noteworthy insight. Despite Korvo's characteristic trenchancy, he was quite a good listener, and our conversations were just that, a genuine exchange of thoughts and feelings. This was reassuring to me since it suggested, if not an equality in the relationship, at least a present indeterminacy with regard to our future status vis à vis one another;

or to be more blunt, it wasn't yet obvious who was the chosen one and who was not. Rocketry and the basic sciences that supported it were naturally high on the agenda, but since we both (Korvo explicitly, I tacitly) understood this as means to an end, philosophy, cosmology, and theology were equally important topics of discussion.

While I was content to wander the streets more or less aimlessly, Korvo usually preferred a specific destination, especially monuments to the glories of Prussian militarism which, without evident irony, he claimed to admire. One cold gray winter afternoon (we shared an intense dislike of cold sunny days), we found ourselves near Victory Column where we passed a double line of Brownshirts carrying Nazi flags and shouting anti-Communist and anti-Semitic slogans. We paused to watch them. Perhaps around a third of the bystanders along the street gave them the Nazi salute, but in 1930, especially in "Red" Berlin, it was safe to stand there mutely, or even continue going about one's business. Still, I felt a strange mixture of embarrassment and fear, thinking about the composition books filled with my notes on the Zohar that were sitting in a bottom dresser drawer back in my room. Of course, like most Germans of the more liberal persuasion at that time, I viewed the Nazis mainly as a form of street theater and never considered them as serious contenders for political power. Since the war other extremist movements with funny hats and lots of leather had come and gone, and I assumed the same would hold for these characters.

As Korvo and I stood, there a ruckus broke out toward the end of the line. A couple of Brownshirts had gotten into a shoving match with some men in greasy overalls who looked like they had just come from work, no doubt Communists. To their credit, other Brownshirts came over and pulled their guys away. As the line of march re-formed, one of these impromptu marshals pointed at Korvo and called out, "Hey, Jack, how's it going?" When Korvo acknowledged him, he started to come over, but as his comrades were now a block down the street, said, "Sorry—have to go, obviously. See you in the morning," and raced to catch up.

I cocked my head to one side and gave Korvo a look, but immediately felt bad about putting him in a possibly embarrassing situation. As someone with a lot of secrets, I was passionately committed to protecting the privacy of others. I need not have worried. Korvo said, "Well that was lucky. I'd almost forgotten. Axe practice tomorrow at 6 a.m."

"Axe practice?"

"*Mens sana in corpore sano*," said Korvo. "Walking is good exercise but immobile as I am for so many hours a day I found I needed something a little more robust, so I joined this Nazi Equestrian Club that's more into Nordic martial arts than horses. Next question. 'Aren't you Jewish?' Answer: yes, in fact so savagely Semitic that I know people would never accept me as a Christian even if the College of Cardinals voted me in tomorrow as Pope. So I was perfectly up front about it with them and they appreciated my honesty, along with my demonstrably encyclopedic knowledge of ancient Germanic and Scandinavian military practices. I may not be the most fearsome wielder of the double-headed axe, but what I lack in strength I make up for in style points, as anyone who knows the Sagas can see."

Despite my squeamishness about even saying the word I asked, "So you're really telling me that it's not a problem being Jewish?"

Korvo looked at his watch. "Come on," he said, "we can make it if we step lively."

We continued down Oranienburger Strasse in the direction of home, but a few blocks before reaching our alley, Korvo suddenly turned to walk through the iron gates fronting the New Synagogue.

It was, of course, impossible to ignore this massive edifice, the outstanding architectural landmark of our immediate neighborhood. Built in the middle of the last century in an ostentatiously Moorish style that evoked the Alhambra Palace, its huge central dome somehow always reminded me of the Montgolfier's hot air balloon, the first machine to free mankind from the prison of Earth's gravity. I had been curious about it but never worked up the courage to go inside, not having been in a synagogue before, even back in Trier. Some weeks ago I had seen a sign outside advertising a violin concert for charity given by Albert Einstein that was open to the public, and as superficially tempting as it was to be in the presence of THE GREAT MAN, I couldn't see that it would offer any practical benefit toward advancing either my technological or theological ambitions. In fact, I took it that Einstein's devoting this much effort to his musical hobby was an indication that his creative life as a scientist was probably behind him. The experience would be more pathetic than inspiring.

I hesitated to follow Korvo through the doors, but resolving to just bite the head off the snake, propelled myself inward, expecting the worst, whatever that might be. (Being conducted to a private room for circumcision inspection?) To my immense relief, the interior looked for all the world to me like an ornate baroque church—gothic arches, stained glass windows, the nave, apses, side galleries, and so on. Decorated six-pointed stars instead of crosses or crucifixes, but the organ music in the background could have been Bach or Buxtehude for all I could tell. The main sanctuary was huge and must have held over a thousand, which made the few hundred people who were there in the front pews seem more like a few dozen. Korvo and I took seats about six rows back next to the center aisle just as the rabbi ascended the bima and began the service. It was very church-like and mechanical, lots of sitting and standing, with rote recitation of prayers in German and occasional Hebrew snippets. (I could puzzle out the Hebrew text but maintained the stranger's respectful silence the whole time.) To my surprise at the point in the service where the ark is opened, the rabbi invited Korvo up by name to be the Torah bearer. The subsequent sermon on a passage from Exodus was learned and mildly interesting, and wouldn't have sounded strange coming from the mouth of a liberal Lutheran pastor. There were no references to the *Ein Sof, Sephirot, Shekinah*, or celestial rabbinic academies. I felt that the complete absence of mystical content vindicated my heretofore ignorance of actual Jewish religious practice.

As we exited the building about an hour and a half later, I expected Korvo to ask me something about what I thought of the service, but instead he returned to tomorrow morning's axe practice and the need to oil and polish his weapon when he returned to his room. But I couldn't quite let it go. "So not only are you a Jew who goes to Nazi axe practice, you're an observant Jew."

"What do you mean by "'observant?'" he responded drily.

"Well," I said, suddenly recognizing that the question might not admit a simple response. "You participate in institutionally sanctioned group religious worship."

"On an irregular basis, yes. And not only that, I observe the traditional dietary restrictions at home. While I could buy my sardines and honey cakes just about anywhere, I limit my food purchases to a strictly kosher grocery store. You Christians have ten commandments, but for Jews there are 613, both positive and negative. At last check I was in compliance with 471, though quite a few are more or less by default, and most anyone who's not an outright monster or pervert is probably above 300."

"I also presume being observant means that you believe in God, though perhaps not in the literal sense."

"Don't be ridiculous, Waldmann. There is only the literal sense. If an anthropomorphic supernatural being didn't actually divide the Red Sea or zap the prophets of Baal with lightning bolts from a cloudless sky, what's the point? One may as well read novels. And so far as I'm concerned, that's exactly what the Bible is, a very long novel of uneven quality. It's obvious to any person with half a brain that most of that stuff could never have happened, so to return to your question, no, I don't believe in God."

"But there you were holding the Torah," I objected. "Doesn't that make you a hypocrite?"

"To the simpleminded, yes, but a very old religion like Judaism, and unlike Christianity, is less about God than about the history of a people believing in God. I certainly believe that people believed in God, and that it meant something to them, but at least since Spinoza, it's also about people not believing. That's where I come in."

"Isn't it possible that non-belief is part of a divinely willed dialectic intended to sharpen belief?" I was going out on a limb here, risking self-exposure of my own researches into mystical doctrines.

"*Touché*," said Korvo. "I don't believe in God, but I'll also confess to you here and now that I might be wrong. But don't get the idea that going to the synagogue is some kind of Pascalian hedging of my bets. At the end of the day, it's more out of a sense of ineluctability."

We had now reached the front door of our building. "Listen," said Korvo. "You know how I ended up in this place? It wasn't by design. In fact, when I moved to Berlin back in '28, given where I was from and how I knew that not everybody at the university was in love with *Ostjuden* like myself, I went to some lengths to stay away from this neighborhood, with its big famous synagogue and long history as a Jewish enclave. I found a nice place across the river, but literally at the last minute it fell through—the landlord's nephew returned unexpectedly from Sweden or some such nonsense. Maybe that was the real reason, maybe not. Anyway, I scrambled to find even a hole in the wall, and this was it. Strange, isn't it? Could almost make you a believer."

That this was a Jewish enclave was news to me. I knew about the synagogue, of course, but even after living here for eight or nine months, I was unaware of its historical significance to the Jewish community.

"You see," continued Korvo, as he selected a book from the stack next to his reading chair, "what I cannot escape I might as well embrace. The Nazis say there's something about us Jews that makes us inherently aberrant and inassimilable. I'm okay with that. In fact, that's exactly the point that the Zionists make for wanting to set up a Jewish state in Palestine. So ironically, I fit in perfectly with the guys at axe practice."

CHAPTER 5
TYCHO AND THE FREIHERR

Although I didn't fully appreciate it at first, Korvo's involvement with the synagogue and the SS provided a measure of reassurance that I was not self-deluded in my ambitions. Korvo was obviously far ahead of me in terms of practical knowledge about space travel. Once every couple of weeks or so I would accompany him out to the ash heaps for testing, but always in the subsidiary role—Wagner to his Dr. Faustus. His rockets' performance improved with every test, achieving remarkable levels of arrow stability and responsiveness to ground-based commands via radio control. He also possessed the kind of outward passion and force of personality that one would expect of a pathfinder through a new technological landscape. While I believed in the intensity of my commitment to the enterprise, I could never quite translate my inward feelings into expressive words and gestures, whereas when Korvo made the tiniest adjustment to a fin or nozzle, you sensed that every cell in his body was subordinated to the task.

On the other hand, as I came to know him better, I decided that his stubborn eccentricities were not only signs of his genius but also obstacles to the realization of its potential. At the physical level there was the problem of diet. Observing him over a period of several months, it was obvious that his assertion one could live on sardines, honey cakes, and milk was simply wishful thinking. Despite his vigorous exercise program of long walks and regular axe practice, he often complained of feeling tired and out of sorts, along with miscellaneous other issues, including joint pain, sore gums, and odd discolorations of the skin. (Years later when the Technical Director had me combing through the journals of Captain James Cook's voyages across the Pacific for possible insights on how to handle the monotony and deprivations of a two-year Mars mission, it occurred to me that Korvo was probably suffering from scurvy.)

Both Korvo and I also recognized that Raumschiffahrt was an inherently collective enterprise. When we looked to the future, we spoke in the first person plural. One man alone could never construct machines weighing thousands of tons, much less possess the knowledge to design the dozens of systems and sub-systems — propulsion, guidance, life support, communications, etc. — that a successful spacecraft would require. Raumschiffahrt would be a team effort. Yet Korvo was an incorrigible loner. While he was perfectly companionable during his rocket tests, and even open to my suggestions for improvements, he never invited me to join him up in his room where the real work of development took place. At first I thought this an unwillingness to share potential glory, but glory presupposes the valuing of other people's opinions, and with the possible exception of his reputation as an axe wielder among his SS colleagues, Korvo either didn't care what others thought of him, or simply assumed they thought the worst. He was, in sum, a misanthrope, though no doubt being Jewish in that time and place didn't help.

As I began my second year at the university, I continued to apply myself diligently to both my academic studies and my private researches, though I did allow myself certain small indulgences. Like most students I lived on a very tight budget, but unlike them, when it came time to cut loose, instead of repairing to the nearest raucous tavern on a Friday or Saturday night, I went to the Tea Room on the sixth-floor of Wertheim's Department Store on occasional weekday afternoons. There I would drink herbal tea and nibble a selection of Pfannkuchen (a kind of jelly-filled doughnut) under the high pseudo-Baroque ceiling where cavorted fat, ruddy-faced cherubs who looked like they would grow up to become full professors. I was the only younger person, and often the only man, among a clientele of matronly women dressed in cloth coats and fur hats, regardless of season. My one rule for Wertheim's was that I would not read anything having to do with science or religion while I was there, so on this particular occasion I pulled out a translation of *Njal's Saga* that I had borrowed from Korvo's small personal library:

Kol thrust at him with his spear. Kolskegg had just slain a man and had his hands full, and so he could not throw his shield before the blow, and the thrust came upon his thigh, on the outside of the limb and went through it.

Kolskegg turned sharp round, and strode towards him, and smote him with his short sword on the thigh, and cut off his leg, and said, "Did it touch you or not?"

"Now," says Kol, "I pay for being bare of my shield."

So he stood a while on his other leg and looked at the stump.

"You don't need to look," said Kolskegg. "The leg is off."

Then Kol fell down dead.

I could see Korvo's point. Here were a people who refused all blandishments and mitigations — strict empiricists. Kolskegg chops off Kol's leg. Kol acknowledges the tactical mistake of losing his shield and accepts the price without complaint. He looks at the stump where his leg used to be. Is he sentimental about his formerly unmutilated body? Instead of sympathy Kolskegg offers Kol facts: Your leg is gone, you're bleeding to death. Yes, Kolskegg is correct, and without more fuss, Kol drops dead.

I lingered at Wertheim's for the remainder of the afternoon, indulging my typical German vice for sweets with more Pfannkuchen than I cared to admit, while somewhat compensating for this diminishment of personal virtue by reading about dozens of castrations, decapitations, disembowelings, dismemberments, ementulations, eviscerations, and general mutilations in the text of *Njal*. It was quite bracing, actually, and by the time I returned home, was feeling clear-headed and ready for an intensive study session into the wee hours of the morning. Before hitting the books, however, I took a moment to look at my mail, which never amounted to much beyond regular letters from my parents and the occasional bit of correspondence from the university Registrar, but today included the latest issue of the only periodical I subscribed to, *The Rocket*, published on an irregular basis by the Society for Space Travel. Its half dozen mimeographed pages evinced a vulgar fascination with the sensational aspects of the enterprise as one would expect from the group of young amateur enthusiasts who mainly constituted the organization's membership, as near as I could tell from the brief contributor notes at the ends of the articles. Solid information about technical developments was rare and light years behind what Korvo and I were doing in the ash heaps. Needless to say, no attention was given to the theological or metaphysical dimension of space travel, unless you wanted to count one article I had seen about the loneliness of astronauts travelling at the speed of light who would return to an Earth where everyone they had once known would have been dead for thousands of years. In fact, the only reason I laid out money for a subscription was so that after reading each issue I could be confident in my practice of utterly dismissing it.

While the current issue was as worthless as I expected, it did contain a notice of an upcoming lecture at the Technical University of Berlin by none other than Dr. Hermann Oberth, the Transylvanian rocket scientist manqué whose book had been the occasion of my first conversation with Korvo. When I saw Korvo the next morning ensconced in his reading chair, I mentioned this to him in a glib, off-handed way, but no doubt sensing my suppressed curiosity about the affair, he immediately responded, "God damned waste of time. I'm surprised Count Dracula has the nerve even to show his face back in Berlin after the *Woman in the Moon* fiasco."

"The *Woman in the Moon* fiasco?" Of course, I had seen the Fritz Lang movie back in Trier.

"You knew he was the technical advisor on the film, didn't you? Well, he was also going to build a working rocket and shoot it into the stratosphere to help publicize the movie's premiere. It turned out to be a lot harder than he thought. Though not the worst theoretician on the planet, he had no talent for engineering. Never bent a piece of metal in his life. I heard through the grapevine that he was looking for assistants, and so found my way to his shop. It was a mess, plus most of the others who had answered the call were charlatans, people who just wanted to have some connection with the movies. I left after a few weeks. When the rocket was finally tested at some Army base, it blew up on ignition. The Count suffered a nervous breakdown and returned to Transylvania for a rest cure, but I did hear recently that he was working again on some dipshit little motor. Maybe that's why he's here."

Korvo's words initially confirmed my intention to skip Oberth's lecture, but as this was also the time that I began embracing the theory of Korvo as a flawed genius, I decided to hedge my bets. The second worst thing that could happen would be that I would learn nothing and simply have wasted my time. The worst thing would be discovering that Oberth knew something about space travel that I didn't know. Still, in the long run, a known unknown was always preferable to an unknown unknown, and so I went.

Across town in the Charlottenburg District, the Technical University of Berlin was a vocational institution founded by Kaiser Wilhelm II to mass produce the engineers who would help Germany beat England in the race for dreadnoughts and empire. Inquiring for directions when I arrived on campus, I was directed to a cold, shabby lecture hall, illuminated by bare light bulbs that dangled down on long wires from a high, flat ceiling. While the venue could probably hold a couple hundred, there were no more than three dozen young men scattered among the first few rows.

Oberth approached the podium to enthusiastic applause. At first it was hard to understand him through his thick Transylvanian accent. Not once did he attempt eye contact with his audience. Every few minutes he would pause, as though mentally drained, and release through his pursed lips an audible sigh that rippled the hairs of a thick mustache which stood out like a push broom in the middle of his face. When he stopped to take a drink of water, allowing a view of his profile, the rationale behind the comical mustache became clear: it was a pathetic attempt to distract from a nose so humongous that it made him look destined for the title role in the Propaganda Minister's film version of *Jew Süss*.

Oberth's subject was the small rocket motor he had built called the Kegeldüse, which to the Anglophone ear might sound like another diabetes-inducing pastry but in fact was an utterly utilitarian neologism meaning "cone nozzle." He proceeded with all possible pedantry through discussions of ignition timing and propellant valve apertures. Initially, everyone in the audience (except myself) was bent over his notebook scribbling like mad. After nearly two hours, however, no one was writing anything, and several in the audience were slouched down in their chairs, heads flung back, snoring audibly.

As he finally wrapped up his presentation to a smattering of applause, a wave of relief passed over me. I had learned nothing new and had caught not the slightest whiff of genius. I bolted toward the exit, but as I did so, I noticed someone shadowing my retreat and gesturing for my attention. *"Un instant! Un instant s'il vous plaît!"* he called in French. It was impossible to ignore him without being rude, and being a genius, especially the self-effacing kind, did not excuse one from being a gentleman.

My pursuer extended a hand and introduced himself as the Society's corresponding secretary. "I don't believe I've made the pleasure of your acquaintance," he said with genuine graciousness. He was at least two inches taller than I and solidly built without seeming stocky. His bright blue eyes were set in a face that retained the pudginess of childhood, and the wavy blonde hair that he wore longer than most students further exaggerated his youth. Indeed, despite an adult-sized body, his head seemed disproportionately large. He wore a nicely tailored wool jacket and tie, but what I would remember most were the knickers.

We exchanged names, and when I told him that I was a student at Friedrich-Wilhelm (without telling him of my interest in rocketry per se), he nodded approvingly. "One can't do physics without metaphysics, as I'm always telling them here. It's more than just how much gas you can squeeze through a nozzle. Any old fart can figure that out," he said, rolling his eyes back toward the hall. I was surprised at this display of sarcasm toward Oberth, who had, after all, made a credible contribution to knowledge for a *Gymnasium* teacher from the orphaned islets of the German Fatherland in remote Transylvania.

But before I could offer anything in Oberth's defense, the foyer doors flew open and in marched a squad of crew-cut engineering students. One of them boxed the corresponding secretary on the ear as he went by and said, "Time to put the Count to bed, Sunny Boy!" Sunny Boy blew them a kiss along with an obscene gesture, and turned to me saying, "I have to drive Oberth to his hotel in my roadster. He refuses to take public transportation."

Back in my room later that evening, I ran a finger over the raised lettering of the card that had been pressed into my hand, along with an emphatic request that I call the number printed on it. I had never known anyone my own age to carry business cards, much less anyone whose multiple names included the aristocratic title Freiherr. I had always thought of barons as old men in dinner jackets and cummerbunds, but here was a young baron still dressed in knickers. The surname sounded familiar, too. I looked through some week-old newspapers in my room and eventually found the article that had caught my attention about the German Association of Agricultural Cooperative's efforts to discourage unscientific practices among farmers, including the planting of crops according to the phases of the moon or its passage through the Zodiac.

"It's mythology," declared the association's middle-aged vice president. "There's no physical reason why the moon's different phases would affect soil properties, soil temperature, moisture content, and precipitation." (My grandmother would have demurred.) In addition to sharing a name, the accompanying photograph of the vice president showed the same bright eyes and over-sized head.

The combination of the Freiherr's pedigree and his casual remark that the penetration of space would have both physical and metaphysical consequences frankly unnerved me. Had I dodged one bullet in that dingy lecture hall only to find myself in the path of another?

Two days later I made the call, and though I tried to pretend otherwise, was secretly excited at the prospect of knowing such a well-connected person. As soon as the Freiherr picked up the phone, I began with an explanation of who I was and the circumstances of our meeting, assuming as I do that I'm not likely to make a strong first impression, but I was interrupted after only a couple of phrases: "Arthur Waldmann! Of course!" Although there was a lot of background noise, including what sounded like verses from "The Merry Heathen," a popular cabaret tune, the Freiherr seemed neither distracted nor impatient. We arranged to meet the very next day.

I expected that the Charlottenburg address he gave me would lead to one of the Technical University's functional brick residence halls that made my shabby flat seem positively romantic by comparison, but instead it brought me to the gated courtyard of a sumptuous baroque mansion. A butler came out to meet me when I rang the bell. After passing through multiple vestibules, drawing rooms, and galleries decorated with oil portraits of determined-looking men in either military uniforms or aristocratic formal wear, he led me to the Freiherr's room, or rather suite of rooms. He greeted me with a fraternal clap on the shoulder, and drew me in to a sort of den furnished with oriental carpets, overstuffed chairs, and mahogany bookcases that extended from floor to ceiling. In one corner of the room a cello sat on its stand; in another there was a six-inch reflecting telescope fitted with polished brass knobs and setting circles. The whole place had a smell that, because of my grandmother and the Zohar, I associated with old people and forgotten texts.

I commented on the telescope, which he told me had been a confirmation present.

I then asked about the framed woodcut on the wall above it, showing a corpulent man with a full beard, dressed in thick robes, and seated behind a table on which were displayed sextants, astrolabes, and miniature orreries. Except for a missing piece of his nose that seemed to have been replaced by a metal prosthesis, he bore a certain resemblance to a picture in my grandmother's study of Isaac ibn Yashush, called "The Blunderer" by his contemporaries in eleventh-century Spain for suggesting that it was not Moses but the *Shekinah* that had inscribed the names of Edomite kings near the end of Genesis who lived long after Moses had died. "Kepler?" I asked tentatively.

"Good try, old chap," said the Freiherr. "No, it's the forerunner. Tycho Brahe."

Tycho. The last great astronomer before the telescope. History had done him the honor of remembering him by his first name, like his younger contemporary, Galileo, though he lacked the same courage of conviction when it came to the theological implications of his research. Unwilling to alienate his royal patron, Friedrich II, he devised a compromise system in which all the planets revolved around the sun, except Earth, which remained the unmoved center of the universe. This bastard offspring of Ptolemy and Copernicus never gained wide acceptance.

"An odd choice of mentor for a rocket society," I said.

"He's not the Society's mentor," said the Freiherr. He reached into a jacket pocket, and removing a silver case embossed with a family crest, offered me a cigarette, which I politely declined. "He's mine."

The Freiherr took a long drag and exhaled the smoke in a neat jet toward the ceiling. "One could do much worse with the scant fifty-six years allotted him," he continued. "He was the first to observe a nova and know what he was looking at. He built Uraniborg, his own private observatory, complete with printing press and paper mill, on an island in the Baltic where he carried out the most advanced scientific research of his day. He constructed automata. And he developed a cosmology that elegantly resolved the competing claims of physics and metaphysics."

"Although it was all wrong," I said with renewed confidence. Perhaps the Freiherr was just a dilettante after all, more Sunny Boy than genius.

"Wrong in a complicated and interesting way," he replied. "I'm convinced that Tycho deliberately built an error into his system because he understood that the heavens were more than any rational philosophy could comprehend. Do you know what filled his library shelves?" The Freiherr stepped over to the mahogany bookcase and pulled down a leather-bound folio which he handed to me after opening to the first page. I ran my finger over the soft, skin-like surface: vellum. In a series of lines that ignored word endings and diminished in size as they ran down the page I read: *Artis Cabbalisticae Scriptores Johannes Pistorius Basel 1587.* Nearly filling the blank page opposite in florid script was the Latin autograph of Tycho himself. It seemed unfair that any private person could own such ancient and priceless originals.

"How did you come by this?" I said, barely able to suppress my astonishment.

The Freiherr masked a proprietary air with his boyish grin. "As much as I would hate for my father to hear this, family background affords certain . . . advantages. The two upper floors of his estate in East Prussia house every heirloom bauble going back to the Black Death. My mother's people were Danes from Scania, Vikings, really, and Tycho a great-great-great-great-great-great uncle. 'You have the stars in your blood,' she tells me whenever my father isn't around. Here, look at this."

He turned the page to a fanciful map of the heavens, framed by angels and devils, which depicted the stars as radiant faces expressing the whole range of human emotions. I had seen medieval star maps, but while the names were familiar, the constellations were highly unorthodox, unlike any I had ever seen before.

Ever seen before from Earth.

For I now recalled a map I had once drawn, based on my grandmother's spiritual travels, of how the sky would appear to an observer on Aldebaran. I saw, too, a network of faint lines connecting ten illuminated nodes in diverse constellations which nearly matched Moses de Leon's scheme of the *Ein Sof's* emanations in the Zohar. A wave of nausea passed through me. Forcing it down, I whispered that the page was both curious and beautiful.

"Precisely!" said the Freiherr, poking me in the chest with his finger. "There's a lesson in my ancestor's mystical studies that probably no one at the Oberth lecture except you and I could begin to understand. Tycho built Uraniborg, but knew that the goal of science was to exalt the human mind from earthly to heavenly things. That's why he ended up at the court of Emperor Rudolf. His friends thought him a fool to move to a backwater like Prague, but Tycho was impressed by Rudolf's dream of establishing a 'Heavenly Academy' that would bring together the best of the new and the old learning. He even had some rabbi there."

Judah ben Bezalel. He wrote the *Shem Tov*, the holy name of God, on a scrap of parchment, and inserted it into the mouth of the Golem which would come alive to protect the Jews of Prague when the

Emperor could not. As a small boy under my grandmother's tutelage, I had many times dramatized the exploits of this wonder-rabbi with the help of my toy stuffed animals.

As he brought his panegyric on Tycho to a close, the Freiherr removed an envelope from inside the back cover. "Nor is it just the great men of the past who believed this," he said, handing me the letter. It began in stilted German by thanking the Freiherr for a copy of his essay entitled, "Journey to the Moon: Its Astronomical and Metaphysical Aspects." His correspondent noted that space travel would be more than just another technical challenge, and said that "while I can conceive of a God who cares nothing for scientists, I cannot imagine a scientist who would dare to ignore God. Besides, who really knows what we will find up there?" In closing he wrote, "I envy you your youth." It was signed "Edwin Hubble."

Here was the commission of an emperor. Here was a contemporary of mine actually corresponding with the man. How unfair, I thought, as it never even occurred to a petit bourgeois like myself that one could write to famous people.

I now took solace in the perverse thought that the extraterrestrial dreams of young Germans like Korvo and myself and even this over-privileged Freiherr were nothing more than an escape from the personal frustrations of young manhood and the unhappy realities of the Weimar Republic (or what little was left of it), and that Raumschiffahrt might never happen anyway. "Well," I said, in a lame gesture toward sarcasm, "not much worry we'll be bumping into God anytime soon with Oberth's Kegeldüse!"

The Freiherr fixed me in his sights like a gunner. "Arthur, this isn't about you or me alone, but about the survival of the species. Human beings are like migratory birds who devour the fruit of an island until they foul it with their turds and move on. Man, too, must escape this tiny cosmic atoll called Earth, or die. Count Dracula is a pompous ass, and his Kegeldüse a tinker toy, but we must begin somewhere." He spoke with real authority, not the vacuous hyperbole that suffused the pages of *The Rocket*.

"So you really believe that men will go into space?" As soon as the words were out of my mouth, I felt ashamed of my own lack of faith, but perhaps for once I was being honest with myself. Maybe my fascination with Raumschiffahrt had always been predicated upon its impossibility.

"Truly I tell you there are those of us here today who will not taste death until they see the first man walk on the moon," said the Freiherr, as if he had already watched the newsreel footage. "I myself fully expect to be freed one day from the brutal tyranny of the Earth's gravity."

He stepped over to an armoire from which removed an oversized notebook with arabesqued covers. "I've already made sketches of the kind of machines that we could build today if we just had the money." The pages were filled with exploded diagrams of a strange tadpole-shaped vehicle designed for travel outside Earth's atmosphere. The level of detail was staggering: motorized gyroscopes, attitudinal thrusters, a magnesium-based signaling system, anti-glare window coatings of various intensities. It even included a compact septic system that recycled the pilot's bodily wastes back into potable water. I asked him what the "rock box" was for and the Freiherr, without missing a beat, said, "For the pilot to bring back samples of any passing asteroids." Another drawing showed the Freiherr's cosmic spermatozoa slicing through a field of six-pointed stars that would have been unfamiliar to anyone—except a student of the Zohar. "And what's this?" I asked, my heart pounding.

"Just a doodle. I think that's how the night sky would look to someone orbiting Alpha Centauri."

Yes, to the spiritual traveler passing by Alpha Centauri on her way to the Heavenly Academy, that's exactly how it would look. The last twist of the knife.

I continued glancing at the pages as the Freiherr turned them, nodding at his explanations, raising an eyebrow occasionally to indicate judicious skepticism. It was no more than a sorry effort to hide the Tychonian revolution unfolding deep in my soul. Despite the kind words of my provincial headmaster—"your son is a genius!"—here was the genuine article. I had once spent six months working out the appearance of the heavens from our sun's nearest neighbor, and here the Freiherr had "doodled" it into the margins of his Raumschiffahrt plans. Scientific value aside, the artistry of the Freiherr's drawings rivaled that of Da Vinci's notebooks. I was tempted to ask him for a random page, thinking that when I was old and impoverished I could sell it to the Louvre for a million marks.

I did not need to look. The leg was off, and it was now only a question of bleeding to death with a minimum of fuss. The satchel I had brought with my own notebooks had become a source of monstrous embarrassment, and I tried to push it out of sight with my foot. As the Freiherr snapped open his case for another cigarette, he told me how much he'd value a man of my intelligence and sensibility in the Raumschiffahrt society. With my last tatter of pride, I demurred. "What you need are helping hands, not helping brains, and I'm much more a thinker than a doer." This was, of course, a lie. I aspired to be both, for why else would I be spending Saturdays in the ash heaps with Korvo? I also made some noises about how busy I was with school right now. The Freiherr cut me off with a scowl that at first seemed mock serious but actually wasn't. "Let's keep our priorities straight. Formal education is for people who would rather follow rules than make them. You don't want to end up teaching geometry to high school students in — you're from around the Rhineland, right? — Mainz or Speyer, do you? Really, now." He took a long pull on his cigarette, and then returning to his former humor added, "Besides, there's too much glory for just one man."

· · ·

Since it was a warm day and time now seemed abundant, I elected to walk home. I passed through the Zoological Garden and wondered if I might be lucky enough to get eaten by an escaped tiger. In the Tiergarten I considered telling a group of picnicking Brownshirts that I was sort of one-quarter Jewish so that they might pummel me to death.

An hour later I was back at my usual table in Wertheim's Tea Room. I looked up at the fat, happy cherubs on the ceiling. I nibbled Pfannkuchen and read *Njal's Saga*. When I reached the end of a chapter, I thought to pay my bill and leave until I recalled that I was no longer under the obligation to learn everything about astrophysics in the next three years, so I kept reading. Medieval Icelanders never moped. For them life was a simple matter of being strong or weak. If strong, lead; if weak, follow. Otherwise, die.

When a waiter finally interrupted my reading to tell me it was closing time, I felt surprisingly jaunty for a young man whose life had just been emptied of purpose. I had begun to consider the putative advantages of discipleship: freedom, obscurity. Let others occupy seats at the head of the table. I would find happiness in the second cohort, down there with James son of Alphaeus and Simon the Canaean, names nobody remembers and about whom nothing is known.

CHAPTER 6
ROCKET CENTER BERLIN

I awoke the next morning to a state of euphoric release when I remembered that the long-term physical survival and spiritual fulfillment of the human species no longer depended on me. That was now the Freiherr's responsibility, whether he fully realized it or not. If he did not realize it, then he would not suffer under its crushing burden as I had; if he did realize it, the calmness of his outward demeanor was further proof of his fitness for the task. This supercession did not mean, however, that I was completely off the hook.

From a practical standpoint, I now had to consider how to finesse my transition from Korvo to the Freiherr. I dithered for a few days, avoiding him on my comings and goings for fear that he might ask me what happened at the Oberth lecture. Then came a Saturday for which I had previously agreed to help him with some test launches. Because I find it difficult to be convincingly duplicitous, I had composed a little speech about how I had joined the organization only to be polite. I never had the chance to deliver it, however, because as we were waiting for the train to take us out into the suburbs, Korvo said, "So you've met the Freiherr? Quite a personality, isn't he?" He spoke without a hint of sarcasm or derision.

"You know him?"

"I met him back during those few weeks I worked on that bogus rocket launch for *Woman in the Moon*. He was still in high school but knew more about what he was doing there than anyone, including the Count. I suspect the only reason it ever got off the pad before it blew up was because of him. The Count knew it, too. Though he looked more like fifteen than seventeen, the Count hung on his every word, like the RCA Victor dog looking into the Victrola horn. Of course, being a Freiherr didn't hurt. I lost track of him after that, but this past spring when I was leaving axe practice one day, I passed him coming in. He had signed up for the SS equestrian class that starts right after us berserkers leave. Tweed jacket, knickers. Still looks wet behind the ears but he told me that he graduated from his Lietz School a year early and was about to start an engineering course at the Technical University. I think his parents have a house in Berlin. Smart guy, no getting around it. You could do worse than to hang around with someone like him."

I waited for him to continue since I was dying to know what exactly the Freiherr had told him about our relationship. Did he know that I had actually visited the Freiherr at home? That I had agreed to participate in the current Society for Space Travel rocket project? But Korvo fell silent. In an effort to draw him out I asked, "Well if that's true, why aren't you – we – collaborating with him?"

"Good question, two part answer. One: I can't get past the tweed and knickers. *Junkers* just aren't my cup of tea. Two: Related to that I don't just want to be the first man in space. I want the first man in space to be a Jew, and since I'm the only Jewish rocketeer that I know, I want that Jew to be me. Moreover, I want to get into space the Jewish way, not the Christian way, by which I mean a path that involves irony, absurdity, and unlikelihood. If you were to ask me right now, I'd say that the Freiherr is way more likely to achieve Raumschiffahrt than I am, through a straight line methodology of brilliance and brute force. But who knows, maybe that's not how the story will end. Stuff happens. Anyway, your meeting him has the definite stink of the absurd, and so rather cheers me up. He told me he twisted your arm into joining his group. Good. To be honest, there's probably a thing or two I could learn from them, but I'm just not going there. You, on the other hand, are at least a *goy* and can probably stand the son of a bitch."

This was the first time I had ever heard Korvo utter a word of Yiddish, and I'm sure it slipped out by accident, but it stung in ways Korvo never could have imagined. A *goy*? Someone who had been inducted into the mysteries of the Kabbalah since childhood, who could read with facility the Zohar's synthetic Aramaic and, with more difficulty, the Hebrew of later commentators? Of course, he knew nothing of this, and despite the impulse to recite verbatim a whole tractate of the Zohar as proof that I was, in fact, more profoundly Jewish than he could ever be, I kept my own counsel.

One Saturday morning a few weeks later, I found myself in the passenger seat of an Aston-Martin 1.5 Litre International driven north out of Berlin by the Freiherr at speeds approaching 80 miles per hour. I don't know that I'd ever travelled in a car going half that fast and I was, of course, terrified, clutching the small knapsack that contained my lunch and a light jacket to my chest as if it were an airbag that would protect me against the force of an inevitable impact. (Needless to say, sports cars of the 1930s did not come with airbags, seat belts, roll bars, or any other modern safety equipment.) The Freiherr drove with one hand on the wheel, the other holding a cigarette, or occasionally using both hands to light a cigarette while bracing the wheel with his knees. Here was a man whose natural element was machines moving at high rates of speed. He talked almost continuously, but it was not the compulsive monotonic chatter of the garden-variety extrovert, rather a sequence of cogent discourses, ranging from the personal through the technical, whose rhetorical style mirrored precisely the contours of his subject matter, despite the frequent and abrupt transitions.

"So let me tell you about Foggy," said the Freiherr, inclining toward me while keeping his eyes on the obstacle course ahead. "We call him that for two reasons. First, we don't have the foggiest idea who he really is. He claims that he was a Fokker tri-plane pilot one kill away from becoming an ace when the war ended and that he later earned an engineering degree somewhere, but when my father's people looked into it, all they could find was service in an artillery unit on the Alsatian front and two terms at a provincial technical institute. Second, he doesn't have the foggiest idea about aerodynamics or propulsion. Whatever he did at that technical institute, it didn't have much to do with rockets."

"So how did he end up as the leader of a bunch of rocket enthusiasts?" I asked.

"You just answered your own question," said the Freiherr. "Enthusiasm. Or rather, enthusiasm channeled into organizational ability. He knows the lingo, and he knows how to get things out of people, both resources and results. One time I went with him on one of his 'scavenger hunts.' He had an in, don't ask me how, with a manager at Siemens. He waxed poetic about the future: 'Berlin to New York in one hour! Giant sun reflectors in space that could incinerate whole cities on Earth! Mining colonies on the Moon and Mars!' The Siemens guy didn't know whether Foggy was a genius or a joke, but you could tell he was impressed with his brashness, so he gave us a trunk full of welding wires. These were useless to us, but we took them to a welding shop in town and worked out a deal where in exchange for the wires one of their most skilled workers would weld our tanks and rocket motors, all on a cash-free basis. Then he goes out the very next day and tries to work another angle. He's shameless. His persistence is amazing, and instructive."

The road passed through a landscape of muddy fields and stunted fir trees. After a mile or two the trees disappeared, the ground firmed up, and we arrived at an expanse of gravel and broken asphalt. Concrete bunkers perhaps ten meters wide and twice that long protruded one or two stories out of the ground, mostly enclosed on three sides with earthen walls of approximately equal height. Scattered about were piles of rusted military equipment—trucks, cranes, shell casings, tank treads, gun barrels. The Freiherr noted that this was an ammunition dump abandoned under the terms of the Versailles Treaty. "Foggy is under the impression that he obtained the three-year lease through his connections in the Reich Defense Ministry, but I happen to know his request was rejected out of hand. Only when word of this reached my father's people was I able to pull a few strings myself and secure it for the group. Foggy considers it his baby and today is christening it "Rocket Center Berlin," as if spacecraft loaded with passengers for Mars, Jupiter, and Saturn are leaving every hour on the hour."

About two dozen people were gathered in front of an impromptu podium that had been set up next to one of the bunkers. They were mostly young men, seemingly the same crowd from the Oberth lecture, though there were also a few middle-aged women, who I later learned were mothers of the rocket enthusiasts. A balding man in his mid-forties with a long, horsey face was talking with the best dressed and most attractive rocket mother, but as soon as he noticed the Freiherr, he excused himself and headed in our direction.

"Here's the new man I was—" but the Freiherr's attempt to formally introduce me was mooted by the anxious chatter that rolled ahead of Foggy, like the hiss of waves fizzling out on shore.

" —got some decent weather, finally. Good sized crowd, too, better than I expected, what do you think? I tell you, this is big, big! Hope it wasn't a mistake snubbing the Count, not that anybody knows who he is anyway. Well, at least there's one representative of the press here, *Die Wochenzeitung Nord-Berlin* sent a man. I'm sure the story will get picked up by the major papers, don't you think?" He brusquely pulled back his sleeve to check his watch. "10:02. Keep 'em waiting a few more minutes."

At that moment a Mercedes sedan pulled up. Two men in belted trench coats and fedoras emerged, but instead of joining the small crowd, they took up positions at opposite ends of the car, expressionless. Foggy looked over at them and then back at us, eyebrows arched. "Well," he said, "time to get this new age in human history underway."

Although at the time both the Freiherr and I anticipated the advent of a new age, albeit, I believed, from contrasting secular and sacred perspectives, we involuntarily rolled our eyes at one another as Foggy returned to take his place at the podium, certain that historical epochs did not take their cues from blowhards like him. Indeed, the ensuing short speech was little more than an exercise in self promotion. He had put together the team that built the Kegeldüse (with no mention of Oberth's name); he had come up with ideas that were the inspiration for the technical details in Fritz Lang's movie; and he was now establishing a facility that by 1950 would launch astronauts on the first lunar expedition. At that point he pulled a bottle of cheap champagne from a paper bag, walked over to the nearest bunker, and smashed it against the concrete, announcing, "On this day, September 27th, 1930, I hereby christen this place Rocket Center Berlin and announce the Birth of the Space Age!"

I looked back at the Mercedes and noticed that one of the men was taking pictures with a telephoto lens. As the smattering of applause died down, both men got back in the car and quickly departed.

"Do you know who those guys were?" I asked the Freiherr. He hesitated for a moment and then pulled me back a few paces. "Foggy thinks they're artillery officers from the Defense Ministry, but they're actually Prussian State Security, at least for now. Mums the word," and he added in Italian, "*capiche*?"

When the ceremony was over most of the group adjourned to a long table covered with homemade delicacies brought by the rocket mothers, but the Freiherr led me in the opposite direction. "Let me give you a little tour of the operation." He took me over to one of the bunkers and pushed open a thick steel door which then slammed shut behind us. Illumination was provided by two brilliant white bare light bulbs hanging down from the ceiling. Sheet metal and tubing of various lengths and dimensions sat on work benches, though nothing that would have been recognizable as a rocket or even a projectile. The smell of the place was as complex as the most expensive French perfume, if not as aromatic: a combination of dirt, mold, alcohol, acetylene, and gasoline, with notes of stale sweat. There was the most absolute silence I had ever experienced. For all it mattered, we could have been a thousand feet underground. I remarked to the Freiherr on the irony of developing the means to reach the heavens in such an earthbound, even infernal place. "I had the exact same thought when I first saw it," he said. "It's an ongoing crime against humanity the conditions under which we inventors have to work, have always had to work, at least in the early stages. One day rocket men like ourselves will work in buildings the size of sports stadiums with transparent or retractable domes that will afford us intimate emotional and spiritual contact with the world of our dreams. I've already sketched out rough plans for such a facility which ideally would be built in some semitropical location with a much more temperate climate than we have here in Germany. But that will take time and money — lots and lots of money. Trust me, we'll get there."

•   •   •

In my second year at the Friedrich-Wilhelm University, I continued the routine of intensive study during the week, with rocket work on the weekends. The difference now was that I spent most Saturdays and Sundays at the Rocket Center, and only the occasional Saturday morning accompanying Korvo out to the ash heaps. I sometimes wondered if this is how it would be to have both a wife and a mistress. I had known Korvo almost since the beginning of my time in Berlin, and he had been a salve for the usual vagaries of self-doubt that afflict the young man from the country who goes off to the big city and that might otherwise have sent me running back to Trier. Though Korvo was a certifiable eccentric, he was also sessile (except for trips to the ash heaps), predictable, and then there was the Jewish connection, which of course he was oblivious to, as I scrupulously avoided all references to religion, especially Judaism, but which gave me the sense of being somehow on track, pulled along, as it were, by an undercurrent of destiny. I always felt comfortable around Korvo, and this I also attributed to ethnicity, the characteristic Jewish trait of empathy for others, forged out of centuries of collective and individual suffering. Yet for all these reasons Korvo was also a little boring, even annoying, in the Gallic sense of the word. I had grown weary of his obsessive quest for command and control at the expense of the other elements of rocket development, chiefly propulsion. He wanted his puny black powder devices to obey every little whim of trajectory that might pop into his head, and whenever I suggested that it might be time to consider scaling up or thinking about liquid fuels, he would sententiously quote Bismarck's response to the question of when the bombardment of Paris would begin after the Prussians had surrounded the city during the Franco-Prussian War: "I'm waiting for the psychological moment!"

By contrast, at the Rocket Center the emphasis in the autumn of 1930 was on building a device that looked and acted like the rockets of popular imagination. There was sublimity in size, Foggy used to say. The rocket should make a lot of noise and its launch should frighten the mass of spectators. It should vanish into the stratosphere. Where it went afterwards or how it got there was not a matter of concern, at least, not yet. The Freiherr acknowledged the utter vulgarity of such a program but conceded that Foggy was right in believing that this was the only way to attract attention, and ultimately, financial support. He even admitted to me that he had been complicit in a misleading photograph that had been circulated to the press on the day that Kegeldüse' s thrust output had been certified by the Reich Bureau of Standards: The impressive six-foot tall rocket at which Oberth stares with both paternal pride and concern was in fact a dummy used in the advertising campaign for *Woman in the Moon*. The actual Kegeldeüse was the tinker-toy contraption barely visible in the hands of the Freiherr who was standing off to the side.

• • •

I came to know the Freiherr more intimately toward the end of that academic year when he invited me to join him on holiday at his family's country estate in Silesia. The highlight of that visit was the day we went to Wolf Hirth's sailplane school in nearby Grunau, where for the past several months the Freiherr had been enrolled in the glider training course. This was the beginning of what would become an impressive career as an amateur aviator, eventually leading to certification for multi-engine jet aircraft around the time that the Boeing 707 came into service. He considered these lessons a birthday present to himself (he had just turned 19) since he was paying the substantial fees out money that he had earned writing about rockets for various newspapers and magazines. These included not only the typical "gee-whiz" articles aimed at young enthusiasts like himself but also works of short fiction, including one about an orbiting space station and a rocket plane that rescues stranded explorers in the Arctic.

The Freiherr that very afternoon completed the requirements for his "D" level license, soaring above the still snow-covered peaks of the Reisengebirge for nearly a quarter of an hour. From what he had told me beforehand about wrestling with the manual levers of the various control surfaces, I would have thought him physically and mentally exhausted at this point, but in fact the flight had energized him, another reminder to me that he and I were fundamentally different orders of being. As soon as the Freiherr climbed out of the cockpit, he ran over to Wolf Hirth, who was grinning broadly and giving him the thumbs up sign, and after a brief confab with his teacher, he headed toward me.

"Now that I have the 'D' license I can take the two-seater up. Wolf is having it readied now. Let's go!" he called out and ran toward a nearby hanger.

The last thing I had expected that day, or any day, was going up in a flying machine. My unwillingness to join the Freiherr was rooted mainly, of course, in fear. From Otto Lilienthal to Sir John Alcock to Lothar von Richthofen, the honor roll of aviation pioneers who had died in the pursuit of flight was long, and in a few years would include the renowned Wiley Post and Amelia Earhart. And these were the masters of the skies, not a young man barely out of adolescence who had been certified to take up passengers in just the past two minutes. In 1931, as far as I was concerned, the jury was still out on the Wright Brothers' accomplishment at Kitty Hawk in 1903. While the odds of dying in a plane crash today are calculated at twenty-nine million to one, back then crashes were as common as summer thunderstorms, which is why it was only around that time that a few foolhardy souls began buying tickets on the earliest commercial airlines. Although I understood perfectly well the physics of flight—the vacuum created by air passing over the curved upper surface of a wing, etc., etc.—the idea of machines weighing hundreds or thousands of pounds suspended up in the air by a delicate balance of speed and lift seemed inherently counterintuitive. Had not Galileo and Newton proven that at the end of the day, heavy objects fall to the ground as a function of their mass and Earth's gravity?

My other objection was that it was irrelevant to my goal of Raumschiffahrt by mechanical means. Theodore von Kármán had conclusively shown just the preceding year that Earth's atmosphere petered out around 300,000 feet, at which point there was not enough air to provide lift; in effect, aeronautics gave way to astronautics. Propellers (later, jet engines) and wings were never going to get us into space, so really, what was the point? Development of anything less than a self-contained rocket propulsion system was a waste of time, and as for the aerodynamic issues of an object moving through the atmosphere on its way to space, those could be studied in a well-designed wind tunnel. Of course, I could see the possible social and economic utility of air travel, but given my concerns about heavier-than-air machines noted above, I wanted nothing to do with this project.

In fairness to myself, however, I should tell you that there was one mode of air travel I did embrace: the Zeppelin. Before you laugh, please remember that while airplanes into the 1930s were mostly dangerous and unreliable (see Post and Earhart, above), Zeppelins by then had carried thousands of paying passengers around Germany without a single fatality, and would have carried thousands more had not DELAG (the *Deutsche Luftschiffahrts-Aktiengesellschaft*, or German Airship Transportation Corporation) been forced to turn over to the Allies its two newest and most technologically advanced airships in late 1920 under the terms of the Versailles Treaty.

Indeed, I had actually flown on one of these, the *Bodensee*, soon after my twelfth birthday. My grandmother and I had accompanied my father on a trip to Berlin with the idea that while he was conducting his business, she and I would visit some of the capital's attractions, including the zoo and the aquarium. It was while strolling past the lion cages that I looked up and saw the preternaturally humongous silver-gray cylinder, laterally ribbed and tapered at both ends, just hanging there in the sky, its four propeller engines attached by spindly pylons to its underside looking like giant arthropods out of Sir Arthur Conan Doyle's *The Lost World*. But even more than its size, what fascinated the both of us was its complete tranquility. It seemed motionless at first, but watching it for a few moments, we could see it moving across the sky with the same kind of nearly imperceptible progress that I later identified with the ribbons of the Northern Lights the first time I saw them at Peenemünde. "So that's a Zeppelin," my grandmother said calmly, who then went on to explain something of their history to her still mesmerized grandchild.

Two days later my grandmother and I were standing in line at the Tempelhof airfield waiting to board the *Bodensee*. "This is the closest we can come as bodies to being weightless like our souls," she had said to my father, adding that if he and my mother were serious about opening up their son to new experiences (they believed I was almost pathologically introverted at the time), here was an opportunity not to be missed. My father naturally resisted at first, saying that if she wanted to make the trip herself that would be fine, but that he wasn't going to commit the life of his only child to a giant gas bag. My grandmother parried with the fact that the Zeppelin fatality rate was zero, and what locomotive could match that? To be honest, I think my father was secretly intrigued by the idea of being lighter than air, and he eventually gave in, agreeing to meet us in Wiesbaden, the *Bodensee's* intermediate stop on its route to Friedrichshaven.

Zeppelin travel was more akin to steamships than to even the most opulent first class cabins of modern jetliners. The *Bodensee's* mahogany-paneled interior was furnished with small sofas and comfortable wicker chairs. (There was obviously no need for seat belts.) Light meals were served from a galley on tables set with crystal and fine china. When the captain called out the order, "*Schiff hoch!*" there was no sudden burst of motor noise or increase of G-forces. There was nothing perceptible at all; only a few minutes later did you notice that people on the ground had become much smaller. The diesel engines kicked on when we were a few hundred feet above ground, and while they weren't exactly quiet, there was no sense of them straining to keep us from crashing back to earth, since their main function was to provide forward motion. One could relax with the knowledge that if for some reason all four engines were to fail, we would simply hang up there until the captain vented sufficient gas to bring us down to a safe landing. And the views! While for reasons of engine efficiency airplane cruising altitudes became ever higher, Zeppelins operated below the clouds at between 500 and 1,000 feet, from which height one still felt connected to the Earth and could discern picturesque details in the landscapes below, like the half-timbered cottages we passed over in the Harz Mountains.

While after the first half hour or so most of the other passengers settled into their seats with a book or newspaper, or chatted quietly over their tea service, my grandmother never stepped away from the windows, dividing her gaze almost equally between earth and sky, and nodding contentedly as if finding herself in a familiar place.

Sadly, within weeks of our trip the *Bodensee* and all remaining Zeppelins were taken out of service and it was not until several years later that Germany re-entered the airship business with the 1928 launch of the *Graf Zeppelin*, whose epic journeys over the Arctic and around the world I followed with acute interest. Indeed, still today I would make the argument that after flying over a million miles and carrying thousands of passengers and hundreds of thousands of pounds of freight and mail without a single fatality, the *Graf Zeppelin* was incontestably the most successful single aircraft of the pre-World War II period, and perhaps of all time.

The Freiherr, however, had never mentioned Zeppelins in any of our conversations up till then, and would always refer to them derisively as "fart bombs" whenever the subject did come up. (Admittedly, he had some reason to feel justified in this view after the *Hindenburg* disaster, though this is not the place for me to explain why that event should have been viewed as an anomaly rather than as the death knell for such a promising technology.) While I saw the rocket as *sui generis* because it was designed to take us beyond Earth, the Freiherr viewed it part of a continuum whose intermediate steps could not be skipped over. He thus felt compelled to familiarize himself with every flying machine leading up to the rocket, which brings me back to the moment he called me to join him for a glider flight.

As the tandem two-seater was being pulled from the hangar, the Freiherr again called me over. I considered my options. I could stand my ground and emphatically wave him off, but knowing his determination, I figured he would come over and try to persuade me otherwise. In that case I might as well walk over there, which would also give me time to come up with possible excuses: an inner ear condition that disposed me to motion sickness and vertigo? But it would strike him as odd that in our discussions of space travel I had never mentioned this and I knew he would see right through it. Alternatively, I could simply tell him the truth, that when it came to high places I was scared shitless. But as resigned as I now was to playing a subsidiary role in another man's heroic narrative, I still had enough pride to make it hard to admit raw fear, especially with all his fellow glider school comrades crowded around. Or, I could agree to go up with him precisely because of my subsidiary role. A successful flight, by which I mean coming back to earth alive and in one piece, would further cement his status as the chosen one in the quest for Raumschiffahrt.

In the end I said nothing and made no choice, since as soon as I reached the hangar someone pulled a leather helmet onto my head and then others lifted me up, seated me in the cockpit, and buckled me in. As the glider was pulled into position, the Freiherr called back, "Just relax, Arthur. But don't touch anything! You're in the instructor's seat and all your controls override mine." Of course, I had no intention of touching the controls but now knowing that I might inadvertently bring about disaster only made me more anxious.

The Freiherr had earlier explained that the Reisengebirge was perfect glider country as the mix of fields and woods radiated the sun's warmth back at different intensities creating thermal updrafts that then climbed the sides of the opposing ridges. If one knew what he was doing, it was possible to stay aloft for hours. The actual launch site was a little back from the top of a ridge that sloped gently downward and overlooked a broad green valley, almost a moor, dotted with farms and woodlots, and delimited some miles beyond by another low ridge of forested peaks. Launching a glider required a crew of around a dozen — four men holding the wings and fuselage level, and four each on the two bungees that angled out at forty-five degrees from the nose.

"Holding team?" called out the Freiherr.

"Ready!"

"Take-off team?"

"Ready!"

"Stretch bungees!"

"Check!"

"Then run, you bloody bastards, run!"

The bungee pullers ran down the slope and the holders released the plane as we reached the edge. The Freiherr unloosed the nose cable, and in an instant we were airborne, several hundred feet above the valley floor. "Almighty God!" he shouted back to me.

I remember thinking before we launched that at least the glider would be quiet since there was no engine, but as soon as we were aloft I was almost deafened by the sound of the sixty knot wind (our airspeed as called out by the Freiherr) rushing past the cockpit. Beyond the noise my experience of the flight was far worse than I could possibly have imagined. My heart pounded like a sledgehammer in my chest, and I had shooting pains in my intestines. Previously the expression "going out of one's mind" had been nothing more than a cliché to me, but now I felt an acute sense of dissociation and loss of control, as if my brain was dying to escape entrapment in its doomed cranium. Although it may be medically impossible, I swear my nerves ached. Every now and then the Freiherr would helpfully point out some interesting building or landscape feature on the ground, but the last thing I was going to do was look down, and I spent the entire flight locked in a modified fetal position with my head braced between my knees, a contortion never achieved before or since.

After fifteen or twenty minutes of the closest I had ever come to sheer hell, the Freiherr brought us to a perfect landing back atop the ridge. As I climbed out of the cockpit, I could take some solace in the fact that my stomach had fought back the overwhelming urge to vomit, and while my large intestine had done its part to make sure I was not literally scared shitless, my urethral sphincter was the Nervous Nellie of the operation and not up to snuff: My pants were soaking wet. Fortunately, everyone was so busy slapping the Freiherr on the back for his perfect flight that no one paid me much attention, and I was able to slip back into the light trench coat I had been wearing that covered me down to the knees.

The crowd thinned, and as these uniformly tall and, for lack of a better term, Aryan youths went their separate ways, there was revealed standing almost at attention with eyes fixed upon us a petite young woman dressed in a brown aviator's jump suit. As soon as the Freiherr noticed her, he took me by the arm and pulled me over. "Arthur, let me introduce you to the Aviatrix," he said, using this exact term, "the most incredibly courageous and fearless girl I have ever met."

"Most fearless girl?" she said, shaking my hand while pouting coquettishly at the Freiherr.

"Most courageous and fearless man or woman in the Reich. Let me stand corrected."

"Now you don't have to go that far, do you?"

"Arthur, a few weeks after earning her 'D' license, she was piloting one of Wolf's newest planes when this thunderstorm came up out of nowhere. Well, most of us would have pissed in our pants and hightailed it back down, but not the Aviatrix. She sees the chance for some serious updrafts and flies right into it and starts climbing, up, up, up — nine thousand, ten thousand feet —"

"Well, nine thousand seven hundred fifty before my instruments froze solid."

"A world's record it would have been if the flight were sanctioned, and then she brings it down to a pinpoint landing right next to the ski lodge on the Schneekoppe."

"And that, my friends, was the truly scary part, when I finally got through to Wolf on the hotel phone, and he told me that the Schneekoppe was in the neutral zone on the Czech border, and landing there would probably cost me my pilot's license and maybe the impounding of the plane. But half an hour later Wolf was overhead and dropped a bungee kit, and the hotel guests were so helpful. I organized them into two teams of ten and we did a couple of practice runs before they gave me a near perfect launch. I don't think the Czechs ever found us out."

After a few more minutes of shop talk the Freiherr suggested that we continue the conversation in a tavern down below in the village.

Of course, I was naturally curious to know if there was a romantic connection between the two of them. Despite her tomboyish proclivities, the Aviatrix's small stature (she was barely five feet), sparkling blue eyes, and graceful movements gave her a thoroughly feminine aspect. On paper, you might say, she was very attractive, yet there was a cool, almost porcelain quality to her manner that quashed any nascent erotic interest that I might have taken in her. She was a goddess, yes, but less in the lineage of Aphrodite than Athena — Athena Nike, equipped with bronze helmet and javelin. These heroic attributes would have made her a good match with the Freiherr, and I think he was genuinely enamored of her, but more as a statue on a pedestal than as a flesh-and-blood woman to be enfolded in his arms. Indeed, I think the reason none of the other students accompanied us to the watering-hole was because they were afraid of her. And here was yet another sign of the Freiherr's exceptionalism: He was not.

Over multiple pints of Silesian Pils, our conversation moved from aircraft to technological innovation to how technology opened up the world to exploration. The Freiherr observed that without the caravel, the astrolabe, the compass, and the sextant we'd still believe there was nothing but ocean beyond the Azores.

"But it wasn't all technology," I said. "Economics played a role, too. If the Muslims hadn't blocked European access to the trade routes to India and China, Ferdinand and Isabella never would have bankrolled Columbus's obviously crackpot scheme to get to the East by going west."

"Interesting point," said the Freiherr. "So from the standpoint of modern civilization, it's a good thing that the Crusades were a bust."

"Well, that's one way to think about it," I said, "though as far as I'm concerned it would have been better for all parties concerned if the Crusades had never happened in the first place. The deaths of thousands of innocent people and nothing to show for it, except accelerating the eventual demise of two of the most genuinely advanced civilizations of the Middle Ages, Byzantium and al-Andalus in Spain."

"I grant that the military objective of securing the Holy Land for Christianity in the long term was not achieved," countered the Aviatrix, "but how could anyone be so foolish as to think that Europe ever would have exited the Middle Ages were it not for the mobilization of the spiritual and intellectual energies unleashed by the

Crusades?" Her smile barely distracted from what was starting to feel like an *ad hominem* argument.

"What spiritual energies were released when the thousands of young people hoodwinked into the Children's Crusade ended up being sold in the slave markets of the Levant?" I said.

"I guess I'm just an idealist," she replied. "The greater the number of people committed to a particular cause with the greater intensity of passion, and the more tragically heroic the outcome, the larger the quantity of spiritual capital passed on to succeeding generations. Absolute dedication to an absolute yields art, culture, science, truth. It's what makes some nations great and other nations flops. The Crusades have made Europeans, and especially Germans and Anglo-Saxons, masters of the world. Think about the alternative. If we had caved in to the Muslims in 1099, Germans today would be as culturally and spiritually bankrupt as the Jews. Name one great Jewish artist or scientist of the past 2,000 years."

"Einstein?" replied the Freiherr diffidently, looking off into space.

"Relativity. Right, there's an idea you can dedicate yourself to and die for. The next thing you'll be telling me is that Karl Marx was a brilliant philosopher. Between the Jewish Communists and Jewish Socialists cavorting in the Reichstag, it's a wonder we still even have a viable German nation. Relativity and Communism. These are not contributions to knowledge."

I had earlier regretted my allusion to al-Andalus, and now that the conversation had come around to the Jews I was feeling somewhat vulnerable, but I still wasn't prepared to let the Aviatrix have the last word. Before I could open my mouth, however, the Freiherr put a close to this line of discussion.

"Point well taken," he said, "but no doubt it will only be our grandchildren or great-great-great-great grandchildren who will be in a position to say whether any of these ideas will have withstood the test of time."

•   •   •   •

The remaining weekends that spring I spent at the Rocket Center working on a skinny torpedo-looking device called the *Minimum*

Rakete (Minimum Rocket) or "Mirak," because we just wanted to make something that would go fast and high, and we were told to do it without any fancy bells or whistles. It was mostly trial and error, a lot of mixing of chemicals and tinkering with combustion chambers. (Guidance still tended to be the step-child of the project.) Korvo was certainly right about one thing: No one worked harder or was more willing to expose himself to risk than the Freiherr. His was the dirtiest lab coat in the shop. It even caught fire once when he was attempting a manual ignition, but he managed to wriggle out of it like Houdini with no more injury than a few singed hairs. Finally in May we achieved a successful launch—the rocket went up and came down without killing anybody. Foggy used the occasion to reiterate his grandiose vision of the future of space travel and, not incidentally, to take most of the credit for our limited technical accomplishments. I found this personally insulting, a sign of how much I now felt invested in the enterprise, but the Freiherr brushed the issue aside.

"He's just another hack promoter or politician, a fool who will go the way of all fools," he said. "The machine itself is what matters."

Yet the Freiherr did lobby successfully to have the name of our rocket changed to "Repulsor," after the spacecraft in a popular science-fiction novel he had been reading.

In May as I completed my second year at the university, Korvo completed his fourth and was awarded his degree. I had made no further trips to the ash heaps with him since visiting the Freiherr in Silesia and now saw him only in passing, affixed in his reading chair. He still wore exactly the same uniform of black pants and white shirt that I had first seen him in two years earlier, but he was paler than ever (probably a symptom of scurvy) and the diameter of his helmet of accumulated hair had increased by a couple of inches. He would occasionally ask me about how things were going at the Rocket Center, but he never brought up his own work and since I had stopped assisting him, it seemed embarrassing for me to inquire. He told me that he was having trouble finding a job and, for that reason only, had reluctantly accepted an offer to do some kind of technical grunt work at the chemical plant his father managed back in Upper Silesia. Then one day when I went back to my room, the chair in the parlor was empty. He was gone.

Shortly afterwards I returned to Trier for the summer. To earn some extra money, I would be doing odd jobs around my father's cigar warehouse. Despite the economic crisis, business was booming: "Nothing loves a Depression like the movies, liquor and tobacco," my father used to say. I also spent time with my grandmother in her upstairs room, where the volumes on kabbalah in Hebrew, Aramaic, Ladino, and German filled not only bookshelves but were stacked so high on the floor that my grandmother at her desk almost seemed like a space traveler shoehorned into her capsule. My parents still dismissed her as crazy, but I never wavered from a belief in her fundamental sanity, though in her more rhapsodic moments she had now moved from channeling Moses de Leon to the original Moses, and spoke to me as if I were a Joshua destined to lead the people into a promised land she would never see. She listened attentively as I told her in detail about my work in the ash heaps with Korvo, and with the Freiherr at the Rocket Center.

Of course, I was frustrated that I could do no practical rocket work while at home. I was also more than a little envious of the Freiherr, who instead of puttering around at his parents' house, had enrolled as a visiting student for the summer term at the *Eidgenössische Technische Hochschule* in Zurich, one of the best engineering colleges in Europe, if not the best. He then undertook a long road trip through Italy, the kind of thing that took real money—money of *Junker* caliber. I participated vicariously through the dozen or so letters I received from him over the summer, and it was around that time that I secretly decided to become Boswell to his Johnson, intuiting that, chosen leader or not, he might still become a person of world-historical consequence. Not only did I carefully preserve all the correspondence we exchanged through nearly four decades, a world war, and emigration to a foreign country, I also began filling notebook after notebook with logs of his daily activities and transcriptions, as best I could remember them, of our private conversations. (Note to archivists and thesis writers: Out of respect for my subject's privacy, I destroyed all of these documents the moment I completed this narrative or, at least, the bulk of it.)

I returned to Berlin in the fall of 1931. I was now feeling quite positive about my work at the Rocket Center and had become less diffident about speaking up. Although guidance continued to remain on the back burner, some of my suggestions had been incorporated into the latest designs with notable results; at least, only the occasional rogue rocket now sent us scurrying back into our bunkers for cover. Maybe my new-found confidence also had something to do with the passing of Korvo from the scene. For better and worse, he had functioned as . . . I wouldn't say a conscience exactly but as a vantage point in a reality that stood a little bit apart from the one I now inhabited with the Freiherr, if only in purely technical matters, and so injected into my life an element of self-doubt, not a personal quality to be valued in the undertaking of audacious enterprises, like building rockets to the moon and beyond. At the conclusion of the Greta sequence I had imagined her as the sun and myself as a comet that was flung back into deep space by the warp of her gravitational pull. I now realized that in the course of a lifetime one might pass by multiple high mass objects that could hurl one in myriad possible trajectories. Clearly, Korvo had been another such object.

As for our collective enterprise at the Rocket Center, Foggy remained convinced that charging admission to our launches was the high road to success. A few such demonstrations enriched our coffers by several hundred marks, but ultimately provided no long-term improvement in our financial situation. Unbeknownst to most of us (except the Freiherr and later myself), Foggy was also aggressively pursuing other sources of funding. Since 1930 when the Nazi Party came to prominence after the elections that year, Foggy had been writing letters to all the Nazi bigwigs, to no avail. He redoubled his efforts after their electoral gains in the spring of 1932, this time highlighting not only the military uses of the rocket, but also its aesthetic elements ("clean lines" and "pure force") that he reasoned would dovetail nicely with Nazi racial ideology. Nothing ever came of this attempt either, except that the letter was intercepted by Prussian State Security and, since it referenced a group that the Freiherr belonged to, eventually found its way to the desk of the Freiherr's father, who was about to take over the agricultural portfolio in the "Cabinet of Barons." While Freiherr Senior had always been skeptical of his son's interest in rocketry, doubting that engineering was an appropriate career for a *Junker* scion, he had also done nothing to discourage his activities, and was now bothered at the prospect of his son's possible involvement with Nazi lowlifes. So he initiated a series of contacts within the military that eventually resulted in a clandestine visit to the Rocket Center by Captain D., an artillery officer on the Reichswehr's Ballistics Council and a degreed mechanical engineer.

One day I would see Captain D. in uniform, but that would be years down the road. On his visits to the Rocket Center, he always dressed in civilian clothes, a trench coat and a fedora. I'm sure he must have been briefed about Foggy, but it was obvious from his expression of mild impatience that from the get-go he recognized Foggy as a man of all flash and no substance. Still, Captain D. listened dutifully to all the nonsense about intercontinental missiles and giant mirrors in space that spewed out of our fearless leader, as if having learned from painful past experience that every now and then even idiots speak the truth. It was equally obvious to Captain D. that the real rocket work there was being done by young men like the Freiherr and myself.

"And you must be Herr Waldmann," he said, extending his hand to me. "Your special area of interest is guidance, if I understand correctly?" Clearly Captain D. had done his homework before the visit. His questions to us showed an understanding of rocketry that was both broad and deep, and yet he never came across as condescending. I was struck by the way that he received new information with surprise rather than defensiveness. It was like talking to an uncle, your father's younger brother, who precisely because he wasn't your father could be supportive without seeming insincere, critical while not threatening. I was 21 at the time, and from the lines in his face and the thinning hair combed over his balding head, I guessed Captain D. to be a man approaching 50. I was quite shocked to learn later that on this occasion he was only 36. I have since realized that most people unconsciously specialize in behaving and appearing a certain age, regardless of chronology. I, for example, have always been an old man; Captain D. was disposed to permanent middle age, and the Freiherr, of course, existed in the perpetual full bloom of youth.

Late that spring Foggy summoned us to a meeting which was held not in the outdoor pavilion where we usually met but in one of the laboratory bunkers. After taking roll and asking someone to make sure the door was locked, he made us swear an oath of secrecy regarding what was to follow. He then told us that Captain D.'s superiors had signed off on an invitation for us to conduct a demonstration launch of our latest version of Mirak at the Reichswehr weapons range in Kummersdorf, about 25 miles southwest of Berlin. The terms were as follows: The rocket must ascend to a minimum altitude of 3.5 kilometers where it was to release a red flare and then parachute safely back to within half a kilometer of the launch site. If all of these requirements were met, the Rocket Center would be paid 1,367 marks; if any was not met, we would get nothing. Also, the launch and all the preparations leading up to it must be conducted in absolute secrecy. Any leaks would preemptively, or retroactively, void the contract. The date had been set for June 22nd, just a few weeks away.

We went to work at a frenetic pace. My spring semester at Friedrich-Wilhelm wrapped up a few weeks before the test and so I was able to devote myself to the project without jeopardizing my academic standing. The actual rocket was essentially the latest iteration of our standard Mirak, a skinny metal tube about a dozen feet long and not quite three inches in diameter. The engine was in the nose (still the only way we could maintain a stable trajectory), followed by the fuel tank, and a compartment for the parachute and flare in the rear. The little tail fins were hardly more than decoration.

Because of the requirement for secrecy, we were supposed to arrive at Kummersdorf before dawn at 4:00 a.m. This meant leaving the Rocket Center no later than 2:00 a.m. I showed up after snatching a few hours of sleep, but the Freiherr never turned in before midnight and so decided just to pull an all-nighter. We lashed the rocket to an aluminum rack affixed to an old jalopy that Foggy had dragooned from God knows where, and made the two-hour drive through the pitch-dark countryside over roads full of potholes, every jolt degrading our delicate little machine and decreasing the likelihood of success.

When we arrived at Kummersdorf, it was immediately clear that the Army was serious about holding us to the terms of the agreement. To measure the rocket's performance, the launch site was arrayed with theodolites which were vastly more sophisticated than the simple surveyor's tools Korvo had slightly modified for his research in the ash heaps, and which we had never bothered with at the Rocket Center. Seeing those theodolites, I now pictured Korvo, whom I hadn't thought about in weeks, standing off to one side, laughing to himself about the utter amateurishness of our whole operation.

Just after dawn we counted down the ignition sequence. It was all over in less than a minute. The rocket wobbled slowly upward from its pad, penetrated a low cloud deck at about 600 meters, then rolled over into a horizontal trajectory, crashing about a kilometer and a half away. The flare and parachute never deployed. Captain D. walked over to us from where he was standing with his superiors and politely but firmly told us that the test was a failure and that we needed to pack up our equipment and be out of there within the hour.

CHAPTER 7
WALDMANN IN THE WILDERNESS

For years afterward, whenever the Technical Director was confronted with some insurmountable obstacle in the bureaucracy, he would invoke Foggy's name as he set out for the umpteenth time to break down the resistance of whatever lowly supply clerk or exalted Reichsführer stood in his way. While in the end tenacity could not make up for Foggy's deficiencies in native intelligence or communication skills, his willingness to bang his head against the wall over and over again was a lesson not lost upon his brilliant younger colleague.

Within days of the failed test, Foggy had finagled another meeting with Captain D., bringing with him the Freiherr, whose father had recently been appointed as Germany's Minister of Nutrition and Agriculture, and also myself, to make his exploitation of the Freiherr's social and political position seem less brazen that it obviously was.

First, he tried to argue that our contract with the Army had been fulfilled in spirit, if not letter, because the rocket had launched vertically, flown horizontally, and been recovered essentially in one piece. (Captain D. politely responded that his theodolites were designed to measure altitude and azimuth, not spirit.) Next, he claimed that the test had not been entirely fair because the two-hour drive over rough roads to the proving ground had probably damaged the rocket. (Captain D.: What good to the Army is a rocket that can't take a few potholes?) Finally, he gestured toward the two living props he had brought along, saying it would be a shame to cause the dissolution of a group of bright young engineers who held such promise for the future of the Fatherland.

Here Captain D. pounced.

"Exactly!" he said, "my superiors and I couldn't agree more, and so today I am authorized to offer you the full technical and material support of the Army, on the condition that your group works behind the gates of a military installation, and in accordance with the requirements of national security. Do you realize, sir, how your public demonstrations may be jeopardizing the future of the Fatherland? That Swedish woman who sang at your show last year — do you know that she has made numerous trips to the Soviet Union? Of course, you don't. I wish I could tell you more, and I will when you gain your security clearances, but suffice it to say that whether you realize it or not, Germany today is once again in a race against the other world powers, and the stakes could not be higher."

Captain D. then outlined the terms of the agreement, which would make us contract employees of the Army with stipends and daily allowances for meals and travel expenses that far exceeded what any of us were currently making, with the probable exception of the Freiherr. He also told us that ours ought to be a collective decision, hinting that at some point in the not too distant future the Army would probably enforce a complete monopoly on rocket development within the Reich.

I sometimes wonder what Foggy would have done with the offer if he had spoken with Captain D. alone and in private, but since the Freiherr and I had been party to the conversation, he had little choice but to take the proposal back to whole group. Despite his strong nationalist sympathies and resentment toward what he, like so many others, considered the shameful indignities of the Versailles Treaty, Foggy had a visceral dislike of bureaucracy, and especially of military bureaucracy, which he believed had cheated him out of being credited as an ace during the Great War. After outlining Captain D.'s proposal, he immediately denounced it, saying that it was tantamount to "turning our brain-child over to ignorant people who would only stunt its development. They see the rocket as a nothing more than a self-propelled artillery shell," he continued, "so you can just forget about your dreams of walking on the moon in 1960."

"But the money!" someone then called out, and there were murmurs of assent all around. By the summer of 1932, there were something like five million Germans out of work and even university graduates were joining the ranks of the unemployed. Here was a chance not to starve and at least be on a track parallel to one that would take us to the moon.

But now it was Foggy's turn to pull a rabbit out of his hat. "Money? How about 35,000 marks?"

There was stunned silence in the dank, sealed bunker. I shot a glance at the Freiherr and even he looked surprised; this was something apparently his father's people didn't know about. Foggy then opened a briefcase and removed a sheaf of papers.

"I have here a proposed contract from the city of Magdeburg for us to develop and launch a rocket with a 750 kilogram thrust engine during next year's Pentecost celebrations. A manned rocket."

"There's no way," said the Freiherr. "We've never done anything bigger than 50 kilograms."

"It's negotiable," replied Foggy. "I think we can jew them down to maybe half that size which should be enough to get someone up to parachute height."

Foggy explained that one day a few weeks ago when he was at the Rocket Center working by himself a civil engineer employed by the city of Magdeburg named Franz Mengering had shown up out of the blue at the front gate. He said he was on the planning committee for the city's annual Pentecost Festival, and that since the day commemorated the vertical movement of the Holy Spirit between Heaven and Earth, he had suggested the idea of a rocket launch to give the ancient miracle a kind of modern valence. Mengering had read about our launches in the newspaper and so it was natural that he would turn to us for assistance.

Pentecost would fall on the following June 4th, which gave us about nine months. Given the fact that we had to deliver a vehicle six or seven times more powerful than anything we'd built up to that point, this was a very short time frame indeed, especially when one considers that there would have to be some kind of testing program for unmanned prototypes, since we couldn't very well expect a sane person to climb aboard a rocket that had never been tried before. The upcoming start of the new academic year would also limit the time that several key players, including the Freiherr and myself, could devote to the project. Despite these formidable challenges, we saw the Magdeburg Rocket as our last best hope and threw ourselves into the task with renewed zeal.

The Freiherr, though a solid team player who continued to put in long hours, remained skeptical, and so I wasn't surprised when he declined Foggy's request that he and I accompany him to Magdeburg for a meeting with the planning commission. But he encouraged me to go, if only to keep Foggy "halfway honest," and since it was now mid-September and I still had a couple of weeks before school started, I agreed.

Once again, my youth and intelligence were being used as props, because after the initial exchange of pleasantries in the ornate reception room of Magdeburg's old town hall, Foggy took the briefcase that I had been carrying for him and encouraged me to take in the sights of the town while he met with the committee. Before I had the chance to leave, however, Herr Mengering suggested that I might like to meet the "Cavanaut" who had been selected from numerous applicants to fly the rocket, and who was now being lodged at town expense in a small cell in the basement. "He's a young man about your age, very knowledgeable about rockets, and refreshingly open-minded." I said I would be delighted to meet him, and headed down the stairway toward which he then gestured.

It turned out that the simple, elegant floor plan of the late Renaissance building above ground was mirrored by a labyrinthine system of passageways, tunnels, cul-de-sacs, and multiple levels and half-levels below ground. (I was later told that these represented defensive measures undertaken during the Thirty Years' War toward the end of which the original medieval structure had been destroyed.) Every one of the clerks and maintenance workers down there responded excitedly when I asked directions to the room of the "Cavanaut," but there were so many instructions of the sort, "two rights, a left, up a half flight, then a left, go past the cul-de-sac, then two more rights," that it took me almost twenty minutes to find the place. When I did, the door was open to a room simply furnished with a bed, dresser, desk, floor lamp, and a wing-back chair pointed away from me at a slight angle. From where I stood, I could see an arm holding a book, a pipe sticking out of a mouth, and the top of a thick pile of black wiry hair. There was no mistaking him. I was stunned.

"Korvo!"

"Dr. Livingstone, I presume? Or is that supposed to be your line?" Korvo marked the place in his book and slowly rose to greet me.

"I can't believe it," I said.

"I can. After I got this job, I learned that they were working with you guys at the Rocket Center, and assuming that you hadn't blown yourself up since we last talked, I figured that we'd cross paths sooner or later."

"You know this whole thing is one of our fearless leader's scams," I said. "There's no way we can build a rocket big enough to lift you off the ground, much less lift you to a point high enough from where you can parachute safely back to Earth, and sure as hell not by next June."

Korvo shrugged. "When I applied I couldn't know that for certain. I thought maybe they knew something I didn't, that somewhere out there someone was building big rockets already, maybe in Russia. When I found out it was you guys, I was more doubtful, but you still have the Freiherr on your team, don't you? I'd be a fool to underestimate him. And you're no lightweight yourself, Arthur."

"You could get killed doing this."

"That would have been true of anyone they chose for this stunt, yet here you are today in Magdeburg advancing the project. No, I don't hold that against you. We all have to make compromises to get what we want, and I've told you, I want to be the first man in space, so on principle, I couldn't pass this up. Either this will never come off, or if it does, it's all so absurd and unlikely that maybe my ironical God will see to it that I live to tell the tale. Besides, I was bored out of my mind at the chemical factory and quit after the first month. My indulgent parents would have let me live in their basement, but this basement comes with a small stipend and better food — they've never even heard of gefilte fish here. Socrates says in the *Apology* that the goal of every philosopher should be room and board at public expense. Instead, he got a death sentence. But look at me! I'm a roaring success! Yipee!"

He did a little two-step jig and then gestured for me to pull out the chair at his desk and have a seat.

"Any further questions?" he asked, taking up his pipe again.

"What's this 'cavanaut' business all about?"

Seeing that the pipe had gone out, he struck a match to relight it. He took a few puffs—he was still smoking his favorite cheap, cherry-flavored tobacco—and then gazed pensively up at the low ceiling of his room. "So what do you think of this guy Mengering?"

"I was introduced to him at the Rocket Center a few weeks ago, so this is only the second time I've seen him. Strikes me as kind of an odd duck for an engineer. There's a spooky light that comes into his eyes when he talks to us. Foggy says he has some odd ideas."

"Odd is an understatement," said Korvo. "You know what a Flat-Earther is, right? Well, Mengering is a Hollow-Earther, or rather, a Hollow-universer."

"He thinks the Earth is hollow?"

"He thinks we're living on the inside of a hollow sphere with the sun and all the stars suspended in the middle. The sphere itself is one of many such structures dispersed across a gelatinous 'spiritual matter' which I can only envision as a block of Swiss cheese of infinite extension filled with an infinite number of holes. Seems he got the idea from some German science fiction writer who in turn got it from some quack doctor in America. The guy attracted a following over there and even established a community of devotees in Florida. They thought he was the Messiah. Anyway, Mengering believes that if you aimed a rocket at the zenith it would pass through the center of the sphere and come down at the antipodes, which for us would be New Zealand. How big this sphere is remains a hotly debated question among the Hollow-Earthers. Like Columbus, some reckon the distance in miles; others, in light years. Mengering falls into the former camp. He knows it's more than a kilometer but sees this as a first step in getting high enough—or more accurately, low enough—to find some telltale evidence that would confirm the theory."

"So that's why you're a 'cavanaut,'" I said.

"Bingo," said Korvo. "This is Raumschiffahrt as spelunking. I'm down here in the basement because this is where the city had space for me, but Mengering secretly thinks of this as appropriate training for the mission."

"Secretly?"

"Well, not totally secret. He's smart enough not to make a big thing out of what he calls the 'scientific' component of the project when he's talking to anyone except me. Instead, he likes to push the rocket-Holy Ghost analogy, which in his mind is perfect, because like the Holy Ghost, the rocket is actually descending, not ascending."

I remembered that Korvo wanted not only to be the first man in space, but wanted that man to be a Jew. "I don't mean to insult your intelligence, but you know of course that Pentecost is a Christian holiday."

"Which is based on Shavuot, the giving of the Law to Moses on Mt. Sinai, a holiday unknown to probably nine out of ten German Jews. But as far as I'm concerned, the Pentecost connection is entirely satisfactory. It's a win-win-win situation for me. If by some statistical marvel I discover evidence that Mengering is correct, and that outer space turns out to be inner space, then I will have achieved my objective of Raumschiffahrt. If I live to tell about it, then it will be a Jew who becomes famous for overturning the whole Copernican system, and with it, the last vestiges of Christian cosmology. If I die, then I will be remembered as a sacrificial lamb in the quest for outer space (or inner space, if that's the case), a sort of astronaut- (or cavanaut-) Jesus, fulfilling the role as only a member of my persecuted race could."

"Stupid question: Do they know you're Jewish?"

"I could tell during the interview that the good burghers of Magdeburg were unsettled by my name and nose, but too polite to ask, so I circumcised the Mosaic knot, as it were, and just flat out told them. They were a little embarrassed at my candor but soon there were nods all around the table when I pointed out that most of those in attendance at the first Pentecost were Jews and thus my involvement would lend the event another layer of historical accuracy. What I didn't say, but I suspect was in the backs of their minds, is that if the whole thing turns out to be a fiasco, they can blame it on the fact that their rocket pilot was a Jew. Ditto if I come back with data that invalidates Christianity. What do I care? They already hate us anyway.

I returned to Berlin with renewed dedication to the project despite my awareness that it was basically a scam for Foggy to keep the Rocket Center going until something better came along. It was no longer just a matter of sending someone up in a rocket, but of someone I actually knew and had once accounted my closest friend. The Zohar states that "the death of one man is the death of a whole universe" (whether that universe be a block of Swiss cheese of infinite extension it does not say), and whatever my obvious moral failings throughout the ensuing years, I was always the one to argue against any decision that might jeopardize, much less sacrifice, any living being in the conquest of space. (To this day I'll never forgive the Soviets for sending the dog, Laika, into orbit before they had figured out a way to bring her back.) I burned a lot of midnight oil that week continually adjusting parameters of weight and thrust, and running the numbers over and over again until I calculated that an engine of 390 kilograms, given the right atmospheric conditions and a little good luck, would be just enough to lift a man of Korvo's weight (a very lean 160 pounds) high enough for a parachute to pop out, deploy, and waft him back to Earth at a potentially survivable velocity. So it turned out that Foggy was right for once. An engine of about half the size stipulated in the contract might do the trick. So he went back to Magdeburg to re-negotiate and the rest of us immediately set to work on a power plant of 200 kilograms that would be the centerpiece of our testing program.

Teamwork was now more critical than ever, but one Saturday in October I was surprised when the noon hour passed and the Freiherr had still not come through the heavy blast door of our bunker laboratory. He never did show up, and when I returned to my room that night, there was a note asking if I could meet him at a certain cabaret later that evening. I was annoyed because he generally respected my dislike of late hours and noisy bars, but I sensed that something was up and headed out to meet him at the appointed time.

Close to midnight I descended a flight of stairs from street level and entered a highly dubious establishment blue with cigarette smoke and redolent of the distinctive smell of American whiskey. There were a few people, mostly couples, seated at the tables toward the back, while a hushed crowd standing five or six deep was pressed up against a stage, transfixed by the performance of a dancer dressed only in translucent veils, heavy eye make-up, and hierophantic headgear that made her look like the Amazon Queen of a planet in a Kurd Lasswitz novel. Three small circles of rhinestone-encrusted silver lamé barely covered her breasts and her privates. The rotations of her hips surpassed my most depraved fantasies, and like everyone else, I stood there mouth agape until I could no longer ignore the insistent tap on my shoulder.

"A bit more than what you're accustomed to in the provinces perhaps?"

The Freiherr put his arm around my waist as if I were an invalid and led me to one of the tables in the back where two young women were seated before an array of empty highball glasses. The Freiherr struck an heroic pose: "The words of Mercury are harsh after the songs of Apollo," he announced. The women lustily protested, but the Freiherr continued, "Sorry, ladies, duty calls," and gallantly bent down to give each a quick peck on the cheek.

I followed the Freiherr up the stairs and out onto the deserted street. "The night air should help take the buzz off," he said. "Look, there's Orion rising." We walked without saying a word for a couple of blocks and then he gently pushed me into an entryway from where he cautiously surveyed the street in both directions.

"Sorry for robbing you of your beauty sleep, old bean. Officially, this isn't even happening right now, but I felt like I couldn't just disappear without giving you some kind of an explanation."

I was still struggling to banish the gyrations of the Amazon Queen from my brain and wondered how the Freiherr could be so immune. It occurred to me that maybe the two women were prostitutes with whom he had spent the earlier part of the evening in a protracted debauch.

"Explanation for what?" I asked, slowly emerging from the depths of my oversexed fog.

"For leaving the Rocket Center. And for my decision to go with the Army."

"You're joining the Army?"

"Not joining, but I will be working for them. Last week I got a message through channels that Captain D. wanted to meet with me. Turns out that they know all about Magdeburg. You know, he's a really thoughtful guy for a career Army officer. I shared my concerns with him about trying to send someone up in a rocket now, and from there we got into the ethics and morality of using human beings as guinea pigs in scientific experiments. While I might be willing to put my own life on the line, I'm not ready to have the death of some other poor schnook on my conscience."

"Neither am I," I said, my mind finally engaging the subject at hand. "I've done my homework. The numbers add up. It's tight but doable, and when it isn't, I'll be the first to put a stop to it. As for Korvo, I know he's an odd guy, but he's not someone with a death wish. Besides, you're the one always talking about successful failures. Even if this thing turns out to be an abortion, think of all the knowledge and experience we'll gain, knowledge that will be completely our own."

"Completely our own? Really, Arthur, who among us springs right from an oak or a stone? We come from a people, the German people, and I think those of us with unique talents have a responsibility to them. I could be shot for telling you this, but I've now seen intelligence about technical advances in England, Russia, and the United States that scares me to death. If we don't get moving on this, in five years, maybe ten at the outside, Germany might just as well bend over, pull down its collective pants, and get ready to take it in — well, I know your delicate sensibilities, Arthur, so I'll stop there — but you get the idea. I believe that we positively owe it to the German people to build the best, most powerful rockets on the planet. There's our real ethical imperative."

"I understand," I said, "and the way to do that is to work on real rockets, not some glorified artillery shell like they want in the Army."

"Stop parroting Foggy," replied the Freiherr, almost scolding me now. "Maybe some of the Great War veterans in the upper ranks think that way, but trust me, men like Captain D. are playing the long game. Even from a purely military standpoint, they understand that the real value of rockets will not be tossing a few tons of TNT around on a battlefield, but of moving us into space where we can control any battlefield on Earth. Plus, Arthur, I no longer have to waste a minute of my precious time doing ridiculous stunts to scrape up a little spare change. I hate to pull rank on you here, but one of the advantages of coming from money is that I know better than most people what money can do, and I mean big money. There's no way we're ever going to get from those pipsqueak Miraks and Repulsors to the behemoths that will take us to the moon and Mars without marks in the billions, and right now the only source of that within our reach is the German Reichswehr."

The hour was late, I was cold and tired, and even if the Freiherr were not someone who outranked me in all the areas of life that actually mattered, I knew that he was right about the need for billions of marks. Selling tickets to our dog and pony shows was not going to get us into space.

"I surrender," I said, raising my hands over my head. "You're right about the money. But I'm not going to bail on Magdeburg, if only for selfish reasons. What other option do I have right now to practice my craft? Maybe we can at least meet for lunch occasionally and compare notes."

The Freiherr shook his head and again scanned the area. "Out of the question. Security. In fact, the other reason I wanted to talk is to explain that if you ever see me, you can expect a nod and a wave, but no more. I'm to have nothing to do henceforth with any amateur rocket people."

"Well, that shouldn't be a problem. Subtract yourself and I will have no reason to darken the doorways of Charlottenburg."

"Me neither. You see, I'm leaving Technical University. The Army has arranged for me to be granted an undergraduate degree on the basis of the relevant work I've already done for them. Come November I'll be starting a doctoral program over at your shop, so we may occasionally cross paths. I just wanted to give you a heads up about why it won't amount to any more than that."

Almost immediately upon his death in 1977, the hagiographers at the Center for Space Exploration and Technology began the onerous task of organizing the collected papers which filled 108 linear feet of shelf space in their archives. A public exhibition of highlights from the collection a few years later included the Freiherr's grade report from his final semester at the Technical University, dated 3 November 1932. It showed the equivalent of "B's" in Electrical and Mechanical Engineering, and "C's" in Geometry, Higher Mathematics, and Thermodynamics. There was not a single "*sehr gut*" ("A") to be seen. Even the grade in Economics of this young man who had "pulled rank" on me because he knew about big money and I didn't was merely mediocre. The only "B" on my grade report, not that this means a damn thing to me now, was in the required Foreign Language course (I had chosen English) during my first semester.

Naturally I felt a twinge of jealousy and resentment upon hearing the news that the Freiherr, who was two years younger than I, would be leaping one year ahead of me academically, but these emotions passed quickly when I considered that he was, after all, a well-connected *Junker* for whom such privileges were a birthright within the current social and political arrangement. While for this reason I could accept the relative injustice of his advancement—if he were suddenly made a doctoral student, I should be a junior professor!—I still had to assume that he was at least at the very top of his class at his less prestigious institution.

And assume that I did until that exhibition in the early 1980s. Yet reflecting further upon his ostensibly undeserved advancement, I now see it as proof that he was an individual whom world-historical imperatives were pushing to transcend the standard categorical valuations of his time. Had it been up to Herr Dr. Schlumpfer or whoever taught him Mechanical Engineering, there might have been no V-2, no Titan, no Saturn 5, no Neil Armstrong in that grainy footage stepping down from the LEM. I also have a greater appreciation for the managerial talents of Captain D. who obviously was aware of these mediocre grades but could see the genius that was obscure to the hacks in the lumpen professoriate.

At around two in the morning we shook hands and parted ways. For the next three years the Freiherr went completely dark. (I never did see him on campus during my last term at Friedrich Wilhelm.) For all that it mattered, he might as well have been on the far side of the moon.

The Freiherr's evident acceptance of the Army's view that we were a bunch of hopeless clowns only stiffened my determination to make the Magdeburg project succeed, or at least to enter it into the annals of memorable heroic failures: the Spartans at Thermopylae, the Charge of the Light Brigade, the Scott Expedition to the South Pole, and of course my own personal favorite, Count Ferdinand Zeppelin, who after almost twenty years of labor was ready to throw in the towel after his most technologically advanced airship, the *LZ 4*, was destroyed in a fire in 1908, only to rise phoenix-like from its ashes when, unsolicited, ordinary German citizens contributed over six million marks to enable him to continue his research.

I now added the occasional weeknight to my fourteen-hour Saturdays and Sundays at the Rocket Center, often falling asleep at my workbench after everyone else had left and awakening at odd hours in the windowless bunker. What we would now call my Circadian rhythms fell increasingly out of synch with the orderly procession of days and nights, and the quality of my academic performance began to decline, though in my case it was only a matter of dropping from "As" to "Bs," a sacrifice I was willing to make for the advancement of science, the vindication of personal honor, and the preservation of the life of an eccentric friend.

Indeed, while I never made it back to Magdeburg those ensuing months, Korvo and I kept up a lively correspondence. (For anyone interested, the text of his portion is included on the microfiche placed inside the Luger that I dropped into the cave at the end of Chapter 1.) Looking back I see that we unconsciously came to exemplify, respectively, the modes of the active and contemplative life. My letters were filled with accounts of what we were doing to solve the myriad technical problems involved in building a manned missile, since that's what I would want to have heard about if I were in Korvo's position. His were more concerned with philosophical reflection on what he now recognized as a dominant pattern in his life: a commitment to voluntary confinement in small spaces. He was devoting several hours a day to reading deeply in the works of Arthur Schopenhauer and finding in them not only solace but mirth. "The typical bourgeois poltroon dismisses Schopenhauer as a 'pessimist,' but I find the absence of intelligent design in the universe positively liberating," he wrote me from his basement apartment in the Magdeburg Town Hall. "The poltroon mentally exhausts himself in a search for meaning that doesn't exist. I, on the other hand, waste no mental energy worrying about whether or not God has a plan for me, and so enjoy a tropically lush spiritual and intellectual life."

Korvo also sent newspaper clippings of interviews that he gave as word of the upcoming rocket launch got around. I could recognize in these stories expressions of his Schopenhauerian "mirth" in the increasingly outlandish historico-theological claims he would make to interviewers. My personal favorite among these rodomontades was his claim that Paul's three years in the deserts of Arabia immediately following his conversion (see Galatians 7:15-18) were spent under the tutelage of Nabatean astronomers who believed that access to the heavens would one day be achieved by mechanical means, and that therefore the story of Jesus's resurrection, while technically unscientific, was a kind of necessary collective thought experiment that would eventually make possible man's journey to the stars and thus affirm the underlying truth of Christian doctrine.

•   •   •

My work on the subscale test rocket continued on through the winter and spring. As absorbed as I was in the minutiae of propulsion and guidance issues, neither was I unaware of the seismic shifts taking place in German politics at the time, and so I want to pause here briefly to begin my engagement with the Speer Questions as I promised back in Chapter 1.

There were three parliamentary elections in 1932 and perhaps surprisingly, I voted in each of them. It wasn't so much that I was passionate about the issues. Like most people I just wanted the government to do something to improve the economy, and so my votes for Socialist candidates mainly reflected the liberal traditions of my native Palatinate, and not any in-depth analysis of these matters. I had also turned twenty-one a few months earlier and was still adolescent enough to take pride in the performance of a civic duty that established my credentials as a full-fledged adult. The fact that I had actually met one of the ministers in von Papen's cabinet—the Freiherr's father—further added to my casual interest in recent events.

Although those elections were inconclusive, in retrospect it's easy to see that the political maneuvering attendant upon each of them brought the Führer closer and closer to power. While I was not oblivious to the Führer's popular appeal, I was convinced that he would never make it to the top, and that his bullying tactics and general violation of civilized norms would inevitably cause the people to turn against him, as I wrote in a letter to Korvo after the election of November 1932 when the Nazis actually lost a few seats in the Reichstag. Korvo replied that for exactly those reasons the Führer's rise to power was, as far as he was concerned, a foregone conclusion. "The Führer is an everyman," he wrote, "and since the average everyman wants to be a bully but doesn't have the talent to pull it off, he does the next best thing, attaching himself to an everyman who does." Korvo predicted that the Führer would be absolute ruler of Germany by the end of 1933 and later took himself to task for not foreseeing that the work of dismantling the last vestiges of the Weimar Republic would already be completed by late March.

One of the first measures promulgated by the new regime to affect me, albeit tangentially, was the Civil Service Restoration Act, which called for the removal from government service of any teacher, professor, or judge who had either a Jewish parent or grandparent. I immediately thought about the law's impact on Korvo, who despite his atheism had adopted a strategy of wearing his Semitism on his sleeve. Although he was living in the basement of the Magdeburg Town Hall as a Pentecost "Cavanaut" he was not by any stretch of the imagination a professional civil servant, and so I didn't expect that the new law would throw a monkey wrench into the project. Still, I felt a little annoyed with him for so insistently identifying with a religion he otherwise rejected and began to think that a martyr complex should be added to the inventory of his personal eccentricities.

I also had a bit of a scare when I realized that while I did not have a Jewish grandparent, it was possible that my father did. The ambiguity resulted from the fact that my great-grandfather, who was born a Jew, had converted to Lutheranism in 1815 after the repeal of Jewish emancipation and civil rights that had come into force under Napoleon. My grandfather, the next to last of eight children, was born two years later in 1817. When I described this situation to an acquaintance of mine who was finishing his degree in the Faculty of Law, he told me that as long as there was some record of my great-grandfather's conversion before my grandfather's birth (like the baptismal certificate I had seen in my father's strongbox), he should have no problems. (The status of his older siblings born before 1815, as well as their descendants, was less certain.)

Then there was the problem of my grandmother, Elena Graetz, the self-described Last Marrana. When she married my father's father in 1877 she hadn't the slightest inkling of her descent from Sephardic Jews who had been expelled from Spain in 1492, been converted by fiat to Catholicism in Portugal in 1497, and had finally become Protestants in Holland in the seventeenth century (while possibly retaining certain Jewish practices) before filtering into Germany by the end of the eighteenth. Indeed, had she married some garden-variety Lutheran instead of my grandfather, I'm certain religion would have played no more than a perfunctory role in her life. But some aura of vestigial ethnicity in my grandfather must have awakened long dormant ancestral memories in her, and by middle age she had become a passionate, if highly unorthodox, Jew. While she seemed content to live a sort of monastic existence up in her room, she would go out occasionally to make small purchases (mostly books and paper), and so some people in town were aware of her religious persuasions. She also insisted on following certain Jewish holiday rituals, like placing the Hanukkah menorah in the window or building a sukkah in the back yard, that our neighbors could not fail to notice. Still, it seemed that the Nazi preoccupation was more blood than belief, so I figured she was safe for the time being.

In sum, the new law did not much affect me, and I honestly believed that the Führer, who wanted to be a popular leader, had simply thrown a bone to his base supporters and would now move on to other things. As for the Jews who lost their jobs, when you figured how many were within a few years of retirement and then added those who were probably incompetent anyway, the absolute number suffering real injustice was probably quite small, and while I couldn't speak to judges and school teachers, the really good professors at German universities would likely be snatched up by institutions in Austria and elsewhere in Europe. (The Civil Service Law brought about Einstein's emigration to the United States, arguably the best career move of his life.)

Besides, I was a twenty-three-year-old not-quite university graduate. What was I supposed to do? Singlehandedly bend the moral arc of history away from the coming Dark Age?

The mass book burning in Opera Square on the night of May 10th was admittedly harder to rationalize. Because of early morning classes on Thursdays, I usually spent Wednesdays back in Berlin studying. It was a balmy spring night with a full moon, and well after dark through my open window I could hear shouts coming from the direction of campus, so I decided to investigate. When I got down there, I saw several trucks filled with books sitting in front of the old Faculty of Law library. Men in uniforms atop the loads were handing out armfuls to people waiting in lines to transfer them to a huge pile in the middle of the square. I recognized some of my professors and fellow students in the crowd, a few of whom gestured for me to join their lines. I signaled back as if I had just forgotten something important but would return shortly. I then retreated into the shadows on the portico of St. Hedwig's Cathedral to watch the proceedings from a little distance.

Soon the pile was set afire, and as it burned the Propaganda Minister gave a speech which I could not hear over the roar of the flames but read in the newspapers the next day. He spoke about the end of Jewish intellectualism and how the task of the younger generation, which obviously included me, was to overcome the fear of death and regain a new respect for death. Of course, I couldn't help reflecting on the irony that one of the heroes of this new order, if only the Propaganda Minister had known about him, would have to be the young man sitting in the basement in Magdeburg waiting to be shot skyward in a rocket. Korvo, as it turned out, was broadly sympathetic with the motivation behind the book burning, complaining only that it had not gone far enough. "Zweig, Feuchtwanger, Mann, Marx, Freud—why stop there?" he wrote. "With the exception of Schopenhauer and perhaps Nordau, there hasn't been intellectual clarity in Europe since the end of the eighteenth century. You could junk the whole last hundred years as far as I'm concerned."

Not long afterwards I received my undergraduate degree in physics and the offer of a scholarship to continue my studies at the graduate level in the fall. Because we were nearing the deadline for completion of the Magdeburg Project and I could now devote myself single-mindedly to work at the Rocket Center, I decided not to participate in the formal graduation ceremonies. I knew that if my parents came to Berlin for the event, it would eat up several days of my precious time. They were naturally disappointed, but I tried to mollify them by saying that these days a degree was no big deal and that there would really be something to celebrate just a few years down the read when I received my doctorate.

As for Magdeburg, the game was now just about up in terms of building a manned rocket by Pentecost, but the half-scale model would be ready in time, and Foggy had promised that if that launch were a success, the manned version would absolutely, positively be ready by Christmas, when the accompanying publicity would do more for local businesses anyway.

During the last couple weeks of May for all intents and purposes I lived at the Rocket Center. I can hardly express now the satisfaction I felt in seeing the 200-kilogram rocket take shape. Thirty feet tall and weighing several hundred pounds, this was the first device I (or anyone else) had ever worked on that could never be mistaken for a toy. Later rockets, from the V-2 through the Saturn 5, were massive in comparison and tremendously more powerful, but were fundamentally just more of the same. It was with the Magdeburg test rocket that we made the qualitative leap from mere enthusiasts to skilled professionals.

We somehow managed to keep to our schedule and were ready to launch our half-scale test model in early June. The first three attempts from a field outside of Magdeburg failed to clear the gantry, but the fourth on June 29th travelled over three hundred yards, albeit horizontally, because one of the fins, whose design and fabrication I had overseen, snagged on the tower at the very last instant. Our activities had generated a fair amount of local newspaper coverage, but I guess that the civil engineer, Mengering, who had always been the impetus behind the project, decided that flying the length of a soccer field was never going to answer the question of whether the universe was hollow, and so the very next day they thanked us for our efforts, gave us a final payment of 3,200 marks, and wished us luck in our future endeavors.

As usual Foggy wanted to wheedle and cajole his way back into their good graces, but when we went to the Town Hall, an assistant to the mayor politely but firmly told us that the committee had been disbanded and that there was no one to discuss the matter with. When I asked about the "Cavanaut" living in the basement, he seemed not to know what I was talking about, but my description of a stocky young man with an accumulation of dark wiry hair jogged his memory. He had been gone for over a week now, he told us, affirming my suspicion that the good burghers had concluded some time ago to cut their losses with the launch of our subscale vehicle, regardless of outcome.

Despite the obvious setback, our goose wasn't quite yet cooked. We continued working through the summer and even managed a few more launches, but by September we were just about broke. At this point, unbeknownst to us, Foggy pursued his most outrageous stratagem. He sent letters to rocket enthusiasts in England with whom he had been in contact over the years and asked them for financial assistance in exchange for access to our ongoing research. He then casually mentioned what he had done to an acquaintance of his who was a civilian employee in the Reich Air Ministry, knowing that the information would eventually percolate through layers of interservice bureaucracy until it reached Army Ordnance and the office of Captain D.

This clumsy attempt at blackmail backfired spectacularly in mid-October when the Gestapo raided the Rocket Center, confiscating all of our equipment and documentation, and hauling the few members unlucky enough to be there off to jail. Everyone was released without charges later the same day, but the action had its intended effect of making sure none of us ever came within ten miles of Reinickendorf again. A few weeks later the Society for Space Travel was officially disbanded.

Fortunately, the end came about the time that I began my doctoral studies at Friedrich-Wilhelm. If I had learned anything from my undergraduate classes, it was that I had barely scratched the surface of my intended field. I was as hungry for knowledge of the physical universe as I had ever been, and as a graduate student at the best university in Germany, I felt like I had just been invited to a sumptuous Roman banquet, and I devoured whatever was set before me. This served as a useful distraction from thinking about how for the first time since meeting Korvo four years earlier, I had nothing to do with rockets, that is to say, nothing to do with the practical means for reaching the heavens, which was the underlying motivation for my academic studies in the first place.

But as the novelty of graduate study began to wear off—the seminars in paneled rooms, the informal chats with senior professors—my irrepressible sense that all this scientific work no longer served any higher purpose began to erode my mental and spiritual foundations. This process was mostly opaque to me; indeed, I wasn't even aware of a process. Until mid-December 1933 I felt much as I always did—contentment, excitement, fear, boredom, curiosity, desire, hopefulness, and all the other states of being in the proportions that passed as my version of "normal." There were, of course, the more garden variety disappointments. I fell in love with a brilliant young Polish woman finishing a degree in Art History who despite her mere twenty-one years possessed the most stunning tresses of steel-gray hair I would ever lay eyes upon, but who was far less enchanted with my modest endowments as I discovered when she grasped my wrists the one time I tried to fondle her breasts.

By the end of the fall term I could feel myself sinking into despair. I filled out the paperwork to arrange for a temporary withdrawal from the university, and bought a one-way ticket to Trier.

Back home, resigned to not doing much with my mind, I decided to focus on my body, knowing from the Zohar that mind and body are really two sides of the same coin, the visible universe being in fact a physical manifestation of the divine brain. I had never been one much for team sports, but I loved the outdoors and before I had gone to Berlin I had always been an avid hiker, swimmer, and skater. As the frigid weather had persisted for some time that winter, the conditions for skating were excellent. As it flowed through the city of Trier, the long arc of the Mosel was frozen in both directions, stranding numerous small ships and barges along its course, which made for interesting destinations. I was often accompanied on these outings by my grandmother, despite my mother's warnings that a woman in her mid-seventies was too old for such strenuous activity. "It's not even as strenuous as walking," she replied. "It's the closest thing on two feet to flying, in fact."

Skating for miles up or down the river after going in circles at the municipal ice rink in Berlin was like being released from prison, which was also how I felt now that I was no longer spending my waking hours thinking about rockets. Whether it represented an effort on her part to minister to my particular needs at that time, or it was the result of an ongoing evolution in her own spiritual development, I can't say for certain, but my grandmother's interests now embraced a much wider range of matters both spiritual and secular than had been the case when I last lived at home. I was particularly struck by her astuteness in matters of politics. The unraveling of Versailles had always been one of the Führer's major themes, and in the winter of 1934 there were rumblings that he planned to remilitarize the Rhineland in violation of the Treaty. The issue was of intense interest in Trier which was not only a mere forty kilometers from the French border but had been occupied by French troops as late as June 1930. Conventional wisdom held that the French would never permit such a move, and would use it as a pretext to fulfill their original postwar goal of annexing the region, as they had done with Alsace-Lorraine. My grandmother disagreed, pointing out that because most of the physical devastation of the Great War had taken place on French rather than German soil, France would employ every possible rationalization to discount the danger of aggressive German moves until it was too late. Indeed, she confided to me that "as a Jew" she might eventually have to leave Germany and was already looking into the mechanics of a removal to Spain, which she considered her spiritual home.

As winter turned to spring, my mental state continued to improve, and I was again able to read beyond my father's daily newspapers. Naturally, one of the first books I returned to was the Zohar, whose careful study I had somewhat neglected since going off to university. Using the ancient technique of cleromancy to determine where to enter the text, I was directed to a tractate in the Prologue to Bereshit, the Zohar's lengthy commentary on the Book of Genesis.

According to this section, when God decided to create the universe, each letter of the alphabet came before Him requesting that it be the instrument by which the world would come into being. The letter Tav came first, making the case that since it anchored the word *emet* or "truth," and that God was called by the name of truth, it should be granted this honor. But while God responded that Tav was worthy and deserving, He pointed out that Tav was also the last letter of the word *mavet* or "death," and so would not be suitable for the work of creation.

Other letters appear and each is found wanting until the letter Bet entered the divine presence:

"May it please You to create the world with me, because by me You are blessed in the upper and lower worlds." This is because the letter Bet is the first letter of the word *brachah* ("blessing"). The Holy One, blessed be He, replied: "But of course, I shall certainly create the world with you. And you shall appear in the beginning of the Creation of the world."

And so the first letter of the Bible is a Bet in the word *Bereshit* ("in the beginning"). The sudden award of this honor might seem a bit arbitrary—why is "blessing" more powerful than "truth" or any of the strengths appertaining to the other letters—but then, why did God decide to make the sun yellow and not green?

There still remains one letter not accounted for: Aleph. It is crestfallen when it appears before God because the greatest prize has already been given to Bet. God feels sorry for Aleph and as a sort of consolation prize says that it will be the first or "head" of all the letters, and that because Hebrew letters also served as numbers, "all calculations shall commence with you."

In the world of the Zohar, there are no accidents, and so it could not be by chance that I had been led to the "Procession of the Letters," as this section is known, at this particular juncture in my life. As often obscure as the Zohar can be, kabbalistic hermeneutics are actually quite simple: The *peshat* ("surface" or "straight") interpretation is always to be preferred, or at least should be the foundation upon which other meanings are erected. The obvious meaning here is that it is better to be second than first. While he who is first gains more recognition because all "calculations" derive from him, he who comes second represents the true creative force. The relevance of my encounter with this passage was equally plain. In man's quest to reach the heavens by mechanical means, I had endeavored to be first, yet I had been superseded by another who was now making the necessary calculations. But was it not possible that somehow I and not he was the truly creative one, and that the creative force might be expressed through activities neither obviously nor immediately relevant, like living a quiet and unassuming life in Trier?

The passage reminded me of an essay by the Danish philosopher Søren Kierkegaard that I had read in a required philosophy course during my first year at the university. Kierkegaard believed that the silence of Abraham throughout his near sacrifice of Isaac in the Book of Genesis was the mark of true spiritual heroism. By accepting the impossibility of his not killing Isaac on the sacrificial altar, and thus entering a state of infinite resignation, Abraham acknowledged the fundamental absurdity of the finite world, which is itself an ironic affirmation that with God all things are possible even, as it turned out, his son's survival. Moreover, once you know that the world is absurd, you realize that there is little advantage in trying to guide your life in one direction over another, and that you might as well embrace whatever mundane circumstances you find yourself in. Or to put this in the Zohar's terms, why struggle to be Aleph when you might really be better off as Bet?

Although I remain skeptical of Buddha-like moments of personal enlightenment, I have to admit that I felt a change come over me after reflecting upon the Zohar's story of the Bet and the Aleph. It wasn't just an overwhelming sense of relief, though there was that, but more positively an attunement to the order and rituals of bourgeois life, which I had previously rejected as mere convention. Since going away to university, for example, I had given up observing family birthdays, Christmas, and other holidays by sending home presents or even greeting cards. At first I had felt somewhat guilty about this, but after a couple of years, I justified it on the grounds that someone doing work as important as mine was simply too busy to keep track of when the Prince of Peace was born, much less ordinary mortals, even close relatives. Now back at home, however, I spent an entire morning developing a list of possible gifts for my parents on their next anniversary, an expenditure of hours that a few months earlier I would have considered an utter waste of time.

I also realized that I could now enjoy things. In Berlin my student life had been more than typically Spartan, books and the occasional visit to Wertheim's Tea Room for Pfannkuchen being my only material indulgences. But in fact I liked good clothes, phonograph records, quality ice skates, Swiss watches. Why shouldn't I have them now that I didn't have to worry about rockets all the time?

While my parents were initially happy to provide me with a small allowance, I knew that money was tight, and so in late March I placed an ad in the local paper advertising myself as a tutor in mathematics and the sciences. Graduates of the nation's elite universities were rare in Trier and within a week I had several clients. Although many years later in the United States I would quickly come to dislike classroom teaching, I found one-on-one tutoring quite rewarding, and by summer's end I began seriously considering whether to abandon my doctoral studies at Friedrich-Wilhelm, which no longer served any meaningful purpose, and instead cobble together a life in my home town that in the grand scheme of things would be no worse than any other. Indeed, I saw it as a charade that next October when I filed for a twelve-month extension of my leave of absence, since in my heart of hearts I already knew that I was never going back.

I continued to dip into the Zohar, though mostly on my own, as my grandmother had become increasingly preoccupied with the political situation and the consequences "for Jews like myself." Given what I viewed as my conversion from an Aleph to a Bet Kabbalist, I no longer worried much about where my soul travelled or did not travel while I slept, and began to wonder why I ever wanted to journey thousands of light years to a conclave of wizened immortals in the first place when there was so much to enrich the soul here on Earth, once you allowed yourself to see it. Isn't that why in boarding school we read selections from Dante's *Inferno* but not his *Paradiso*, because as our teacher told us, Heaven is always boring?

Over the following months, there was only one time when I wavered in my conviction to live a quiet life in Trier as a reasonably well-paid private tutor and local flaneur, and that was when I read in the newspaper the birth announcement of Greta Kuyler's (neé Marx's) second child, born to her and her husband, Alexander, a lawyer in the picturesque village of Schweich, a few miles downriver. Why did he get to enrich his soul going to bed with her every night while I was supposed to be sustained remarking the beauty of bird songs and cloud formations? Throw in the production of offspring and it was obvious that he was living the life of Bet and that I was further down the alphabet with Pei (rejected because it suggests a bent over head hiding from sin) or Kof (the first letter in the word "*klayah,*" or destruction). If Bet was already taken, at least as far as the lower Mosel Valley was concerned, maybe this was a sign I should return to the Aleph track and strive for the Heavenly Academy as just compensation for my inferior status.

I was still wrestling with this conundrum on a day in early June when my mother called me to the phone. I figured it was one of my students needing to reschedule a tutoring session and expected to hear "Professor Waldmann," a title I didn't actually deserve but had given up trying to correct. "Hello," I said, and in response came a voice calling out my given name as if I were someone the speaker half-believed had perished in an earthquake or other natural disaster: "Arthur!" And all the nonsense about Alephs and Bets went up like a puff of smoke even before my rational mind was able to form the two syllable word: Freiherr.

CHAPTER 8
NEW ATLANTIS ON THE BALTIC

"Your technical skills, Arthur, your native intelligence, familiarity with the relevant science, and all-around good judgment. I need you. We need you!" His transparent flattery satisfied a deep and long-suppressed appetite for validation, but if he had spent twenty minutes reading the Koblenz phone book and then asked me to come to Berlin to wash his Aston-Martin, I would have done it. Thus a week after receiving the telephone call that I came to think of as "The Great Commission," I found myself working in a laboratory at the Kummersdorf Weapons Development Center south of Berlin. The area of the base devoted to our top secret rocket work, generically designated Experimental Center West, had been an old artillery range, but was now undergoing a dramatic transformation thanks to an infusion of nearly half a million marks. The obvious highlight was a brand new test stand large enough to accommodate the 1,500-kilogram-thrust motor of our prototype vehicle. From an engineering standpoint, it was incontestably a thing of beauty, two inverted "V"s fabricated from I-beams set on a steel-deck base about 15 feet apart, and joined at the top by another steel plate with a hole cut in the center to allow the protrusion of a missile nose cone. The entire structure was about 25 feet tall and completely surrounded by a concrete blast wall with openings for a locomotive "tug" to tow in and out our various rockets and test rigs. It was a quantum leap beyond the erector set apparatus that we had used back at Reineckendorf for the Magdeburg rocket.

I could now admit that for the past two years I had tried to rationalize a Biedermeier existence of inconsequence and failed. Henceforth I would be contributing to both a technologically and spiritually significant episode in human history. In addition, thanks to

Captain D.'s—now Colonel D.'s—advocacy of strong science-based military research, I would be continuing my doctoral studies at Friedrich-Wilhelm, although with altered focus. Instead of studying galaxies and the birth of stars, I would be measuring the microgravity conditions attendant upon a body moving at extreme speeds and how this would affect mechanisms designed to control its attitude. Neither Colonel D. nor the Freiherr ever ordered me to pursue this narrowly constrained line of research—they didn't have to. While I was encouraged to choose any dissertation topic in physics that seemed "promising," I fully understood that I was working for the Army and what they wanted was a missile as accurate as a big artillery shell. The circumstances were imperfect, but what of it? It wasn't all sweetness and light back in thirteenth century Spain when Moses de Leon spent years channeling or counterfeiting the Zohar, a work which could only imagine for the Holy Elect the kind of travel through interstellar space and time that our machines would make possible for more ordinary mortals like myself. I would also be squarely in the position of second fiddle again—the forerunner who has been superseded, or the false messiah who could never cut it in the first place—but I was determined this time around not to obsess over it.

Over the next couple of years I worked in the lab primarily on guidance issues, attained my doctoral degree before the age of thirty (obviously not as impressive as the Freiherr's at twenty-three but still nothing to sneeze at), and attended innumerable meetings with fellow engineers and military attachés. I knew pretty much everything that was going on in the rocket program and felt the satisfaction of being an insider for the first time in my life.

Attendance at one of these meeting which included a number of Luftwaffe personnel also led to what I still consider my most daring and original line of inquiry, and one that was spiritually satisfying as well. In a session devoted to improving our aerodynamic testing protocols, we learned that the Luftwaffe had a longstanding contract with the Zeppelin Company to conduct wind tunnel experiments at their facility near Munich. I hadn't thought much about airships lately, but the trip that my grandmother and I made from Berlin to Wiesbaden on the *Bodensee* when I was twelve remained one of my fondest childhood memories. While I understood that it was technically impossible for Zeppelins to travel into outer space, I still couldn't help the feeling that its unique form of movement, which was nearly imperceptible, was the purest form of locomotion, akin to what must be the experience of the spiritual traveler en route to the Heavenly Academy. As that particular meeting concluded, I got into a conversation with a young Luftwaffe captain whose father had served on Zeppelins during the First World War and was hoping to fly Zeppelins himself now that the Air Ministry had recently entered into a consortium with the Zeppelin Company and Lufthansa Airlines to resurrect the German airship industry. Word had it that a personal rivalry between the Führer's chief lieutenants accounted for the current largesse of government funding, as both were excited by, respectively, the military and propaganda applications. As to the former, the captain noted that for several years the Americans had been working to develop Zeppelins as flying aircraft carriers, employing a trapeze system to launch and recover planes. Unfortunately, their two German-built airships fitted with such a system, the *Akron* and the *Macon*, had both met with unfortunate ends, but this had nothing to do with their roles as aircraft carriers, and besides, Germany's record with Zeppelins was unblemished, no doubt due to our long history with them and to superior crew training. Indeed, a larger and more technologically advanced successor to the legendary *Graf Zeppelin* was currently under construction and expected to enter service early the following year.

This new Zeppelin was a true behemoth at over 800 feet, twice the length of the *Bodensee*, and three times longer than a late twentieth-century jumbo jet. It was designed to carry 90 passengers and crew, plus baggage, mail, and freight, for a total payload of around 10,000 kilograms. That was equal to around ten of the small prototype rockets we were now working on, and perhaps one of our proposed big rockets. But those vehicles had to be as large as they were to overcome Earth's gravity at sea level from a dead stop. If they could be launched from a height of 20,000 feet, the ceiling of a commercial Zeppelin, the amount of fuel needed to achieve operational speed and altitude would be dramatically reduced, as would the amount of aerodynamic stress, allowing for the use of lighter weight materials. Using Zeppelins as launch platforms struck me as so obvious I could hardly believe that no one had thought of it before, at least, no one in the German rocket community.

That same evening I went back to my room and stayed up late making notebook sketches and working out some of the basic equations. I knew, of course, that it wouldn't just be a matter of loading a bunch of rockets onto a Zeppelin and dropping them out of a cargo bay. Some kind of trapeze-style infrastructure would have to be developed to correctly position the rockets for launch, and this weight, in addition to that of a crew of around a dozen men, would have to be subtracted from the payload. Still, the technical and financial advantages of launching from an airborne platform could be considerable.

Scribbling away into the wee hours, I couldn't remember the last time I had felt such pure astonishment about rocket work, maybe not since the Freiherr had shown me his notebooks at his parents' home in Berlin and I realized that I was in the presence of world-historical genius. Never myself a night owl, I was amazed when I looked out the window and noticed that it was getting light. I had filled some thirty pages with tentative specifications for a launch system that might well cut the Gordian knot of problems we were currently wrestling with in the areas of propulsion, aerodynamics, and guidance. For a time I tried to resist the thought that maybe I was the chosen one after all, and that the Freiherr, with his fixation on big rocket motors, was the forerunner. I had become content with my status as handmaiden to, and perhaps chronicler of, genius, and wasn't anxious to get entangled once again in the Moebius-like mental feedback loops of wondering whether my successes were really failures, or my failures successes. But in the end exhilaration swept the demurs of irony aside, and when I finally crawled into bed at dawn for an abbreviated sleep, I fell into dreams of triumph where, seated in the control car of a 1,000 foot Zeppelin named the *Zohar* (it was my dream, why not?), I gave the order for the launch of our first moon probe, while the Freiherr was relegated to filming the event from his Typhoon chase plane, buzzing around my massive airship like a mosquito.

Of course, I didn't go rushing over to the Freiherr's office when I got up later that morning with news of my revelation. While I was a little concerned about someone else, maybe even the Freiherr, beating me to the punch with the idea, I also knew that the likelihood of its realization depended on being introduced at (to reiterate Bismarck's brilliant phrase) "the psychological moment," which by my nature I would be more than patient enough to wait for. I was sure that one day within the next few weeks or months there would be an engine explosion on the test stand (with or without fatalities), or my colleagues would finally admit that there was no way to stabilize a gyro against the dynamic forces of a ground-based lift-off, and at that moment a gentle smile would spread across my delicate features, and I would say, "I think I've come up with the solution. . . " Not a solution; *the* solution. For the time being, however, I left my notebook in a drawer and continued with my daily routines of attending meetings at Kummersdorf and classes at Friedrich-Wilhelm.

As had been the case during my previous residence in Berlin, my communications with my family were relatively infrequent, consisting of a letter exchanged, usually between me and my father, every few weeks. They knew that I was doing something with rockets but even if they could have understood the technical issues that engaged my waking hours, I was prohibited by strict secrecy protocols from sharing any of this with them, and frankly, there wasn't much else going on in my life to talk about. On their side I think they were happy that I seemed to have both "found" myself and obtained a secure government job with excellent future prospects. Accordingly, our correspondence consisted mostly of perfunctory expressions of concern for health and hopes for continued well being.

This rather banal sequence was interrupted in late 1935 with a letter from my mother regarding renewed concerns about my grandmother. Its tone was both panicky and peevish, but given the broader historical context, wholly understandable. The domestic crisis back in Trier resulted from the promulgation that autumn of the so-called Nuremburg Laws which consisted of The Law for the Protection of German Blood and German Honor, and the Reich Citizenship Law. The former defined in very specific terms who was German and who was Jewish, and the latter resolved the legal status vis-à-vis citizenship of Germans, Jews, and those of mixed background. It seems that on November 15th, the day after both laws came into force, the *Moselander Beobachter*, along with all major German newspapers, published Chart #387 issued by the Reich Board for People's Health, which for the first time depicted graphically who was and was not Jewish. When my grandmother saw this, she announced that the handwriting was on the wall and that you didn't have to be a Daniel to read it. She was therefore moving ahead with her plan to emigrate to Spain which she had been laying the groundwork for over the past several months, having already obtained a temporary visa from the Spanish consulate in Cologne.

Though they had had their differences over the years, my mother genuinely cared about her mother-in-law, and enumerated all the reasons why it made no sense for a woman in her seventies to begin life over again in a foreign country where she knew no one and didn't speak the language (my grandmother's Ladino being a dialect of Spanish not spoken there since 1492), aside from the fact that, according to the chart, she wasn't Jewish anyway and had nothing to fear. But having laid out her arguments, neither did my mother remonstrate when my grandmother insisted that she was Jewish because she had chosen to be so, and no Nazi was going to take that away from her. In the end I think my mother figured that since my grandmother lived like a hermit in a book-filled garret in a remote corner of our house in Trier, she'd hardly be much worse off in similar circumstances in Toledo or Seville.

What really upset my mother was my father's reaction to the new laws. The situation was complicated. After the fall of Napoleon in 1815 and the rollback of civil rights for Jews in the German lands he had conquered, the Waldmanns, like many Jews, made the decision to convert to Lutheranism. My great-grandfather's baptism certificate, dated September 19, 1817, had come down to us and my father kept it in a strong box with other important papers. (The date, by the way, as

I learned when I looked it up recently, was that of Yom Kippur on the secular calendar, which I'm sure was no accident. The Marranos of late medieval Spain also went out of their way to apostatize, gorging on pork and scrubbing their stoops on the Sabbath.) The problem was that my grandfather was born on February 10th, 1815 before my great-grandfather's conversion, and while we always assumed that all the members of the family had been baptized, we had no record of the children's having undergone the ceremony. Even if my grandfather had, he was still born a Jew descended from Jews, and the Nazis were more interested in race than theology. Therefore, if my grandfather were Jewish, my father was half-Jewish, which according to the chart meant that he was Mixed Ancestry 1st Grade, and while he could be a citizen of the Reich, was only a member of the German people's-community but not of German blood. Still more disturbing was something hinted at in the chart's Special Cases section. It said that a half-Jewish person not otherwise defined as Jewish would be so considered if he or she was a member of a Jewish religious community, thus indicating that religious practice as well as race did matter to the Nazis. While our neighbors in Trier had no specific knowledge of our family's genealogy, some of them might have noticed the lighted menorah in the attic window at Hanukkah or my grandmother building the flimsy hut in the garden on Sukkot and would have reason to wonder if she at least was Jewish. One could then imagine the day when Nazi officialdom would conclude that since both of my father's parents were Jewish, he was Jewish, too, and therefore could not be a Reich citizen.

My mother's argument that this worst-case scenario depended upon a very strained interpretation of the law failed to mollify my father. If German citizenship were taken away from him, he would have no legal protections and therefore no ability to maintain a business. The family would be ruined. He began talking about a move across the border into Alsace or Lorraine which had been part of Germany until not that many years before and where the language was still widely spoken. My mother told him if he wanted to move to Strasbourg or Metz, fine, but he would be going there alone. My grandmother undercut the idea from the other side, saying that it was obvious Hitler's plan to make Germany great again included the retrieval of all lost German lands, the crown jewels among those being Alsace and Lorraine. So for the time being, to my mother's relief, my father was carrying on as usual, though in a state of constant anxiety that had raised his blood pressure and caused him to become morose and withdrawn.

For several days after receiving my mother's letter, I was so preoccupied with the prospect of my parents moving to France, or worse, getting a divorce, that I failed to consider the new laws' implications for me personally. But one evening after work, eating dinner alone in my room and having nothing else readily at hand to read, I picked up the chart again and realized that if indeed my father were considered Jewish, that would make me a child of Mixed Ancestry 1st Grade, since I was born of a marriage solemnized before September 17, 1935. (Children born after that date would be considered Jews.) While I would be a citizen of the Reich, I would not belong to the German blood, and though the law did not indicate what particular handicaps this might impose, I could well imagine the stain of racial impurity jeopardizing my status as a scientist within a top secret Nazi weapons program. I must also acknowledge that feelings of guilt about my continuing furtive study of kabbalistic texts led me to wonder if it were unethical for me to continue in government service, and for the next week I agonized over whether or not I should say something to the Freiherr. I was concerned not only for my own well-being but also that of the rocket program, knowing that it might become suspect if it were seen, even marginally, as yet another product of Jewish science.

In the end I kept my own counsel, accepting my mother's view that my father was not legally Jewish, which meant that I could not be either. I was also influenced in this decision by the course of events, or rather, lack of them. The Führer followed what in retrospect can be seen as his usual pattern of doing something and then for a while not following up on it. Through mid-1936 the Nuremburg Laws were but sporadically enforced, in part because the upcoming Olympics were about to put Germany at the center of the world stage. Subsequent letters from home rarely mentioned the issue, though after German troops came marching through Trier on March 7th as part of the Führer's remilitarization of the Rhineland, my grandmother, who had earlier predicted this action, finalized her plans to emigrate, having decided upon Toledo as her refuge in exile.

•   •   •

Already by the time I came to work at Kummersdorf it was apparent that if we were going to launch the big rockets we were developing, we would have to relocate to a facility that was both much larger, and more sophisticated and secure, than one just a few miles from Berlin. "To enlarge the bounds of human empire into outer space we must probe with ruthless toughness the causes and secret motion of things," the Freiherr announced as he unrolled a set of blueprints on a conference table. "I'm imagining an idyllic combination of my twin alma maters — the intellectual firepower of Friedrich Wilhelm, wedded to the pragmatic zeal of the Technical University." In addition to laboratories there was to be a dormitory complex labeled "Solomon's Village" set in a forested landscape, and beyond this, warehouses, fabrication buildings, test stands, gantries, and of course, launch pads.

The Freiherr had scouted some locations along the North Sea but it was actually his mother who suggested a place on the Baltic near where she had grown up, and where her father used to go duck hunting. Peenemünde was a heavily wooded, thumb-shaped peninsula that, except for a few tourist cottages and a little trolley system we could use to connect our various facilities, was otherwise deserted, with unobstructed views up and down the coast.

Within days of Colonel D. passing up the Freiherr's recommendation to Berlin, things began to move. As soon as the Air Ministry got wind of it, they promised five million marks to the project. General Becker, Colonel D.'s superior, was outraged. "Just like that upstart Luftwaffe," he growled at one of our staff meetings. "No sooner do we come up with a promising development than they try to pinch it. But they'll find that they're the junior partners in the rocket business!" And with that he authorized an immediate expenditure of six million marks.

Construction proceeded rapidly and we officially took occupancy of our new quarters at Peenemünde on May 3rd, 1937, bringing up with us about 350 people, a third of them engineers, the rest shop workers. It was also the day that the Freiherr was formally promoted to Technical Director, East Works, Peenemünde Experimental Center.

I received the title of Chief Technical Counselor with an office just down the hall from him. Although in response to Colonel D.s directive to "hit the ground running" we were that same day already conducting engine tests, we also could not help indulging in the small pleasures of settling into our new home. Over lunch in the Hearth Room, the Technical Director asked me to help him select from among several options for lighting fixtures for the Aerodynamics Institute. We ultimately decided upon wall sconces with Ionic filigreeing since they put us in mind of the Greek myth of Icarus and Daedalus. They were also a nice contrast with the modernistic wall clock in the lobby whose two simple hands pointed to black marks rather than numbers, suggesting the unlimited possibilities that the future holds.

The opening of Peenemünde Experimental Center was obviously cause for celebration and so a big party was planned for that following Friday evening, May 7th. The highlight was to be a dramatic interlude composed by the Technical Director himself entitled, "Martian Rites of Spring," whose simple plot involved the arrival of the first Earth astronauts to the red planet which they find ruled over by a glamorous Queen (played in drag to hilarious comic effect by Colonel D.) and her court of green-haired, three-eyed ladies in waiting. Following Shakespeare's practice of reserving for himself a small but pivotal role, the Technical Director would appear toward the end as the white-bearded Vagrant Viking of Space, making a brief stopover on his way to Neptune, who prophesies that "before the youngest among you taste of death" Earthlings will have established colonies on every planet in the solar system. (Given that we assumed a moon landing in the 1950s and a Mars mission by 1980, this prediction seemed less far-fetched then than it does today.)

Our rehearsal was the evening of May 6th, and having stayed up well past midnight, I arose after nine the next morning and was surprised when I arrived at the office to find small groups of engineers standing around talking in hushed tones instead of working in their labs. "What's up?" I asked. My first thought was that something had happened to the Führer. One of the engineers handed me a newspaper with the banner headline, "Hindenburg Tragedy"; right beneath was the iconic photograph of the doomed Zeppelin half-consumed by a fireball. The disaster had taken place in New Jersey about 7:30 the night before, local time.

Engineers that we were, conversation immediately turned to possible causes. A spark created by an electrical short? A build-up of static electricity? (The article noted that there had been thunderstorms in the area.) Someone even suggested sabotage. We all agreed that this was a blow to German technological prestige since despite the inherent volatility of thousands of cubic feet of hydrogen gas, we had never lost a Zeppelin to this kind of explosion. It was about this time that the Technical Director arrived at his customary banker's hour. He had heard the news over the radio, but aside from expressing regret at the loss of life, was entirely unperturbed by the catastrophe. "Good riddance to those things. They were as much a dead end as the electric automobile. There are flying boats today that can cross the ocean in a third less time and without a ground crew that's like a cast of thousands."

"Yes, of course," I said, "I'm just concerned that this will kill off promising non-commercial development, like the way the Americans—"

"Good for the Americans, Arthur, but let me tell you, when you think about it, we should be thanking our lucky stars for this disaster. It is a blow to German prestige, but guess how we're going to climb back up to the top? The Zeppelin was always a Weimar albatross around the Führer's neck. What could he do? People were sentimental. Who wasn't moved the first time he saw one of those leviathans hanging up there in the sky like something out of a dream? But sentiment won't win wars or get us to the moon. The big rocket will. For that we need money and manpower and raw materials. And guess what? With Zeppelins out of the picture, there'll be more for us. There's another reason to celebrate. So everybody, back to work!"

While I supposed the rest of Germany was in mourning (we were so isolated up there it was hard to know), the mood at that evening's little theatrical performance was lighthearted and upbeat. That the Technical Director could play the role of the peripatetic Viking as such an utterly convincing buffoon was both the cause of much jollity and a reminder of just how talented the young man leading us was. I acquitted myself in the role of Lady-in-Waiting #2 serviceably well despite being unable to share in the festive mood.

After it was over, I returned to my quarters and pulled out the notebooks that contained my plans for the Zeppelin-launched missile system. My first impulse was to destroy them, but as I am not a rash or impulsive person, I held back. By Sunday afternoon, after further consideration, I changed my mind. From a purely technical standpoint, the wreck of the *Hindenburg* undoubtedly called into question the reliability of the Zeppelin as an airship, much less a mobile launch platform. Yet I knew that even if our latest gyroscopes could not yet control our smallest prototype vehicles, it would be hard to make the case that Zeppelins were the way through the impasse. And to be honest, once I had fallen in love with my Zeppelin idea, I simply stopped thinking about other alternatives, including ways of building better gyros. Then there was the Technical Director's definitive passing of judgment against the Zeppelin. What possible grounds could I have for doubting his wisdom on this? At the age of twenty five he was leader of the world's most advanced engineering project. I wasn't. The sooner I flushed my brain of these otiose plans, the sooner I could attune myself to direction from him that might actually result in something useful.

In the end my notebooks became as painful to me as the box of letters and mementos left over from the Greta episode that I once kept hidden in a dresser drawer. Of course, such artifacts must be exorcised as well as destroyed, and in the case of the Greta *billets doux* after dousing them with a mild solution of hydrochloric acid, I weighted the box and dropped it into the Mosel from the Roman Bridge that we used to cross on our way to looking at the stars. Having gone with water before, and there being no convenient bridges from which to drop things, I decided upon a fiery end to the notebooks. I gathered them up and walked from my room through the woods to the place the Technical Director had shown me once where his grandfather had a hunting camp. I gathered some brush and sticks on the lee side of a boulder and lit a match. After a few minutes, I had a good fire going and fed it the half dozen notebooks, one after another. I put the last one in at a forty-five degree angle so that for a few seconds it suggested (at least to my imagination) the configuration of the *Hindenburg* as it burned lower right to upper left.

•   •   •

That image of the sumptuous Martian court undoubtedly captured something of life at Peenemünde in the early years. Fritz Todt, Commissioner for the Regulation of the Construction Industry, who had to sign off on most of our projects, was forever complaining that we had built a paradise up there on the Baltic, not only in terms of facilities, but in its relation to the tumultuous world beyond its confines. We had newspapers, of course, but I often went weeks without reading one, both because I was too busy with work, and because nothing from the outside seemed to affect us anyway. As far as most of us were concerned, we were already inhabiting a future so technologically advanced that politics and history were irrelevant. I remember, for example, receiving a letter from my mother in the late spring of 1938 that made reference to the Anschluss and wondering to myself exactly what it was that had been annexed.

The specific character of our research no doubt contributed to our almost fatalistic detachment from the world-historical cyclone gathering beyond the Center's well-guarded perimeter. For example, although those of us who came to missile guidance from a background in pure rocketry hated to admit it, Colonel D. was correct when he reminded us that getting a rocket to its target was in principle no different than guiding an artillery shell. Where a shell landed depended entirely upon its speed and angle when it left the barrel of the gun. Gravity took care of the rest. Obviously, the missile wasn't fired from a gun — indeed, from a military standpoint, freeing it from that limitation was a major advantage — and so it required a powerful control mechanism consisting of gyros and jet vanes to guide it through its burn phase, the equivalent of the shell's travel through the gun barrel. But the rocket gained a life of its own and was totally out of our hands once it reached burnout--*Brennschluss*. (Like Raumschiffahrt the word has such mystical and incantatory power I cannot conceive of it other than in the original German, which I will retain here.) During test launches, I would listen intently to the Doppler telemetry through my headphones up to the moment of Brennschluss, about T-plus one minute, at which point I removed them and returned to my lab or just went for a walk since I now knew everything I needed to know, and nothing that I would do, or could do, would make any difference.

Like most scientific enterprises, our work proceeded by a series of fits and starts, of successes interspersed with what the Technical Director called "successful failures," since every explosion or dud that sent us back to the drawing board ultimately increased our knowledge of the causes and secret motion of things. One of the rare speed bumps in our royal road to Raumschiffahrt came several months after our move to the Baltic. Because we wanted to avoid interfering with construction of permanent facilities on the mainland for our projected larger rockets, the decision was made to launch some of our scaled-down prototypes from Greifswalder Oie, a small island a few kilometers to the north. Aside from a guesthouse that could accommodate the handful of summer visitors, the only thing on the island was an octagonal lighthouse constructed from red brick that somehow made it look much squatter than its sixty or seventy feet. The lighthouse was fully operational and maintained by an honest-to-goodness eccentric who within the last year had gained a measure of fame as the protagonist of the Propaganda Minister's illustrated children's book, *Lighthouse Keeper Hans Winziger and his Seventeen Dobermans*. Winziger was a few years older than the Technical Director and I, tall and thin, with prominent facial bones that seemed to stretch his weatherbeaten skin to its limit. His jet black hair, receding from his forehead, was combed straight back and slicked down with Bay Rum. He had earned a degree in chemical engineering and a commission as a lieutenant at the Reichswehr Akadamie in Potsdam where he had crossed paths with Colonel D., but resigned within a year on account of what he considered the Army's excessive pacifism. Soon thereafter he joined the Nazi Party.

Then in the dead of winter, February 1938, he took matters into his own hands. Basing his actions on Lübeck's possession of the Danish island of Bornholm in the middle of the sixteenth century, Winziger sailed a small boat loaded with weapons and ammunition, along with his Dobermans, and landed on the north end of the island where he ensconced himself in the ruins of the medieval castle of Hammerhus, displaying the Nazi flag from the top of its donjon. For several weeks, nobody paid him much attention, but as the castle was a destination for summer tourists, the Danish authorities eventually made the decision to intervene, and their increased presence in the sector compromised the security of our operations, which were necessarily curtailed. The Danes' polite entreaties to Winziger were ignored, and when police tried to approach the castle via its only ready access point, a stone bridge over a wide abandoned moat, they were confronted by a Doberman wearing a kind of saddlebag hurtling in their direction at full tilt. Then suddenly when the dog was about twenty feet away from them, there was an explosion that mostly obliterated the dog and slightly injured the two policeman in the lead. "The next one will be ten times that powerful!" Winziger shouted defiantly from the ramparts.

For the next several days, various attempts were made at surreptitious entries, but these were detected even in the middle of the night, and answered with the charge of yet another bomb-laden Doberman. Word of the siege gradually filtered out, and as the Führer wanted to avoid an international incident that might initiate hostilities before he was ready, besides being personally uncomfortable with the use of Dobermans as suicide bombers, he dispatched a delegation of Army officers to Bornholm, led by Colonel D., who was acquainted with Winziger and, of course, was familiar with the Baltic region. When a line of communication was finally opened, Winziger acknowledged that he was running out of supplies and was willing to surrender, but only as a prisoner of war to the Danish military. And so on March 1, 1938, an emaciated Winziger, carrying the folded Nazi flag and accompanied by his one surviving Doberman named Rolf, came marching down the path to the stone bridge where the formal surrender took place. Immediately afterward the Danes released Winziger on parole to Colonel D.

While the Führer was sentimental about dogs, not so his Propaganda Minister, who saw in Winziger and his Dobermans an obvious example of a true story that could inspire young people with the appropriate spirit of sacrifice. In the revised second edition of his children's book, each dog goes up in a colorful puff of smoke and on the next page is seen with Reichsadler wings in a sort of canine Valhalla benevolently looking down on Winziger and his remaining dogs. As for Winziger himself, he returned to his duties on Greifswalder where he and Rolf lived contentedly with the promise that whenever war came, they would be in the vanguard of the invasion force tasked with returning Bornholm to its rightful owner.

With the Winziger fiasco behind us we continued our march of steady progress in the key areas of propulsion, aerodynamics, and guidance through the end of the decade. When the war finally broke out in the fall of 1939, we did take notice, but were not especially perturbed. We accepted the government's account that the invasion of Poland was simple retaliation for territorial incursions into eastern Germany, and although I was not an ardent nationalist, I still couldn't help taking pride in a victory that began the erasure of the humiliation of November 1918. I was also convinced that the display of German technological superiority implicit in the performance of the Luftwaffe and our Panzer divisions would persuade England and France to seek a negotiated settlement, and thus avert another catastrophe on the scale of the Great War.

Ironically, our own fortunes in Peenemünde waxed and waned in inverse relation to Germany's battlefield successes. The gusher of Reichmarks flowed to a trickle after the collapse of France when it looked like the war might be over after the Luftwaffe's mopping up of the Royal Air Force, but the spigot was turned back on after the failure of The Blitz. The pattern was repeated during the initial victories in Russia in the summer of 1941 and then the subsequent stiffening of Red Army resistance through the fall and winter. During down times, the Technical Director became our cheerleader-in-chief. He often repeated one of his favorite maxims (which would later feature in the promotional brochures of the university he would help to found), "There's no such thing as Luck—Luck is what happens when Opportunity meets Preparation." While the rest of us were in the dumps as we learned about the imminent Russian defeat at Stalingrad in the late summer of 1942, the Technical Director behaved as if it were news of a winning lottery ticket. "With less pressure from the top for immediate results, now's our big chance to lay the foundations for what will come after the war," he announced one night in the Hearth Room where we had gathered around the radio to listen to the Propaganda Minister. "Let's let our imaginations run wild!" The next day he quietly reassigned some of our top people from their various labs to the Projects Office where they were already doodling designs for the next generation of vehicles. These included a winged version of our big rocket, the Aggregate-4, designated the A-9, as well as a massive 100-ton thrust rocket, the A-10. If we placed the A-9 atop the A-10, we were now getting close to something that could actually launch a satellite into orbit, but to cover our tracks, we would refer to it in all documentation as the "America Rocket," since a payload in the nose of an A-9 upper stage would just about reach the east coast of the United States after a long hypersonic glide.

Our spirits were also boosted by the advocacy of the Third Reich's premier rising star at the time, Albert Speer, who had been appointed successor to his boss Fritz Todt after the latter died in the mysterious crash of a plane that Speer had missed boarding by only a few minutes. While Todt had been critical of what he considered our lavish lifestyle and amenities, Speer, who was also the Führer's Chief Architect and a close personal confidante, appreciated the aesthetic dimensions of our enterprise. He had first come Peenemünde soon after his promotion in the Spring of 1942 and quickly established an excellent working relationship with us. As he would write in his postwar memoirs, "[rocket research] exerted a strange fascination upon me. It was like the planning of a miracle. I was impressed . . . by these technicians with their fantastic visions, these mathematical romantics. Whenever I visited Peenemünde, I also felt, quite spontaneously, quite akin to them."

While Speer was in love with technology, he was also a thoughtful and reflective personality, and something of an introvert, which is why, among the top people at Peenemünde, I was the one with whom he developed the closest rapport.

Speer and I also shared provincial middle-class backgrounds. He hailed from Mannheim in the neighboring state of Baden-Würtemberg. I had always believed that the Technical Director's sunny disposition had a lot to do with his sense of entitlement as an aristocrat. (Of course, he was the only German aristocrat I knew well, so my statistical sample was very small.) Men like Speer and I understood, however, that we owed our privileged positions to a combination of hard work and good fortune, with an emphasis on the latter. We took nothing for granted, and so over time our conversations ventured into areas of philosophy, religion, and even politics. While Speer never spoke to me directly about his relationship to the Führer, the fact that he belonged to his innermost circle went a long way toward dispelling my doubts about the regime. I came to see the crude and impulsive dictator as merely an intermediate stage in Germany's political maturation that would eventually give way to the more enlightened rule of men like Speer. Indeed, the fact that the Führer had chosen Speer as one of his intimates showed that he himself understood his world-historical role as a transitional figure. I further decided that the wisdom he demonstrated in this choice was likely manifest in his other actions as supreme leader, even if that was not always immediately apparent.

I think the Technical Director was bemused when he would wander into the Hearth Room for a midnight snack and find me, a notorious early bird, engaged in deep conversation with Speer. He was so used to being the leader of the organization that it was hard for him to imagine anyone, much less myself, hobnobbing with the big shots from Berlin. To his credit, however, there was never the slightest hint of jealousy, as he intuitively grasped the importance of all informal contacts to the success of our larger enterprise.

●   ●   ●

One unseasonably warm evening that summer I was working in my lab when I received a phone call from the Technical Director. "Can you come by my office now?" he asked. "Something's come up that I need to discuss." In an organization as complex as ours things were always "coming up," yet it was unusual for the Technical Director to summon me about a garden variety technical or administrative issue so late in the day.

"Another ultimatum from Colonel D.?" I asked, seating myself across the desk from him. I'd heard the rumors about setbacks in the east and assumed they were once again ratcheting up the pressure on us to produce.

The Technical Director shook his head. "If only it were that simple," he said. He reached for a manila folder atop one of the piles on either side of his desk and plopped it down between us.

"Colonel D. and I had a visit from a Gestapo major earlier today. Not a bad fellow, really. Turns out he was a few years ahead of me at the Lietz school I attended on Spiekeroog. Of course he didn't come all the way up here to make small talk, or even talk about rockets. It seems that in the wake of Udet's suicide note about Jews in the Air Ministry they're re-doing background checks on everyone who holds a supervisory position at a Reich research facility." He opened the folder and began sifting through several photostats. "Here's the sticky wicket," he said, using the English expression. "This is your paternal grandparents' marriage certificate. You see here where it says religion? And you see what's written there next to groom? Jew. Now since next to the bride it says Christian, that means your father was half-Jewish and that makes you one-quarter Jewish. So if we look at this"–and here he pulled out a copy of the Nuremburg Race Laws chart–"that makes you Mixed Ancestry 2nd Grade. So the good news is that you belong to the German People's Community, and can be a citizen of the Reich. And actually, there's more good news. Let's give the devil his due. The Gestapo are thorough if nothing else. Look at this. They actually found your great-grandfather's baptism certificate, dated September 19, 1817. Now it's true that this was a couple of years after your grandfather was born"–the Technical Director passed over to me his birth certificate–"but the Gestapo thinks that a father's conversion would apply retroactively to all minor children, in which case, regardless of what it says on the marriage certificate, your grandfather would not be Jewish, and so on and so on. They're just waiting for a clarification from the Reich Race Office on this."

"What's the bad news?"

"The Gestapo would prefer–and that's the word the major used–that all personnel in sensitive positions with top security clearances be of the German Blood and not just of the German People's Community. Seems it just looks bad to them."

I could feel my armpits becoming soaked with sweat, but I remained outwardly calm. As the Technical Director looked up at me, I felt I had to made a snap decision. This was the genealogical time bomb I had known was out there. Should I acknowledge that I knew something about this or just play dumb? Acknowledgment might be construed as confession, and at that moment I wasn't sure where the Technical Director stood on the matter. Should I risk assuming that I was indispensable and that he would protect me no matter what? Or would my continued presence at Peenemünde jeopardize the program? Saying that I knew something about this family history might allow me to control the story, whereas pleading total ignorance might arouse suspicion and invite further scrutiny. I also had to consider the safety of my parents in Trier. While my grandmother was now securely ensconced in Toledo's ancient *judería* (secure because in Franco's Spain there were officially no Jews), I was worried what the Gestapo might find out if they began snooping around back home — sukkahs and menorahs that the neighbors must have seen. For all I knew, maybe they had already collected this evidence. And if they were really thorough, they might learn about my friendship and collaboration with Korvo, who never made the slightest effort to hide his racial background. I wondered now who might have seen me that day I accompanied him to the synagogue on Oranienburgerstrasse.

"That marriage certificate is news to me," I began cautiously, "but I've always known about my ancestors' conversion and baptism. My father has a copy of the baptism certificate somewhere. I've seen it. Why my grandfather's marriage certificate lists him as a Jew is a total mystery. I never recall anything Jewish about him, though he died when I was six or seven years old. Neither can I imagine why he would have wanted to identify himself as Jewish if he wasn't. Maybe the notary who filled it out knew something about his family background. The only other thing I can think of is my grandmother who got senile and for some reason started thinking that maybe she was Jewish. She's still living but left Germany a few years ago. I admit I liked her and would try to humor her by lighting candles on Hanukkah and maybe a couple other things, but that was about it. As you know, I was raised pure Protestant, went to a Lutheran boarding school, and so on."

About midway through this little speech, I suddenly thought about Greta Marx. Would they find out about that? I remembered that when I reviewed the Race Laws after I received my mother's letter I noted the provision that if a Citizen of the Reich had sexual relations with a Jew he could be subject to prison or prison with hard labor. Could the 1935 law be applied retroactively to 1929? I presumed not, but who knew?

The Technical Director seemed to hang on my every word. He usually fidgeted when he had to listen to someone for more than thirty seconds, but he wasn't moving a muscle now.

"What happens next?" I asked.

"Frankly, I wouldn't care if you were a rabbi," he said looking me straight in the eye. "My family always had good relations with the Jews who lived on our estates in Silesia. Very clever people, you know. Hardworking. But that's not the world we live in right now. Let me level with you. Colonel D. thinks very highly of you, both as a person and a professional. Thinks you're brilliant and appreciates the fact that you don't bring your ego to the office like some of us." He raised his hand. "Yes, guilty as charged! But at the end of the day, he's all Army, pure old school. Lived through hell in the last war and knows that by definition every man on a mission is dispensable. I don't have the military chops to go against him on that. He knows that in the end our success depends on staying in the Führer's good graces, and he doesn't want to jeopardize that with a possible Jew coming out of the woodwork. So he wants to do something really nice, find a cushy job for you in private industry where you could make use of your talents, and get you out of here. For the sake of the rest of us, he says. Might even be doing you a favor if we help you drop off the Gestapo's radar screen."

"Should I go empty out my desk?"

"I'm not going to tell you that I slammed my fist down and said, 'If Waldmann goes, I go!' There's a part of me that wanted to, but what good would that do, really? It wouldn't be fair to the rest of our team, and besides, at this point, I don't think they'd let me leave. But I did tell him that although you might not be absolutely indispensable, without your pulling things together in guidance, we'd probably be two years behind where we are now. So I asked him to give me a little time to work my contacts in Berlin. I can't tell you how badly he wants a launch in the next few months. He tells me that he can almost taste it, but he knows that if we mess with the team right now, it might not happen. So he agreed to do nothing for the time being and keep our fingers crossed that the Gestapo snoops in Stettin have enough on their plate to distract them from Peenemünde for a while."

There wasn't much more for me to say beyond "thank you." I was now in limbo, totally dependent on the Technical Director's efforts on my behalf. It wasn't an enviable position to be in, and yet as it seemed to demonstrate his possession of almost transcendental powers, I found it oddly comforting, not because I was jealous of those powers, but quite the contrary, because knowing that I didn't have anything close to them confirmed his precedence over me in the metaphysical realm.

As we left his office and returned to the residence village, we were treated to an uncommon display of the auroras which dramatically backlit the girders and blast walls of the ten-story Test Stand I. We observed the show in silence for a few moments and then the Technical Director said, "You know, Arthur, if we could really push the A-10/A-9 thing, or even just the 9, and put a man up there, I could imagine that the shock to the human spirit would be such that the war would come to an immediate halt. The nations of the world would lay down their weapons and join in an expression of collective awe, which not incidentally would be a tacit acknowledgement of absolute German technological superiority. Just too bad it probably won't be in time to help out those poor bastards hunkered down in Russia."

The notion that a rocket launch would end World War II was absurd but wholly in keeping with the Technical Director's visionary turn of mind, which Colonel D. and many others constantly grumbled about but also recognized was woven into the peculiar fabric of his practical genius. Take that away, and we probably wouldn't be anywhere close to where we were now. But it was his next comment that practically froze my blood.

"Isn't it interesting that my chief lieutenant is a little bit Jewish? I mean regardless of whatever the Gestapo and the Reich Race Office say—and don't worry, Arthur, I'm sure we can get this fixed—you actually have Jewish blood flowing in your veins."

"But so do a lot of people, if you go back far enough," I said somewhat recklessly. "Hell, maybe even one of your ancestors back in Silesia took a shine to a pretty Jewess and married her."

"How I wish!" said the Technical Director. "But that's lost in the mists of history. I mean, not that long ago people in your family were speaking Hebrew and still waiting for the Messiah and whatever else it is that Jews are supposed to do. I know they don't eat pork."

For the Gestapo to think that I might be Jewish was not irrational—dangerous, but not irrational—and therefore something I could deal with. But once the Technical Director started down this path, who knew where it might lead?

"I'm not Jewish," I reiterated. "Anyway, what's your point?"

"It's just that the Jews are like a weathervane. Whenever something happens to them, big changes are on the horizon. The Romans try to stamp out Jewish agitation in Palestine, and the next thing you know God becomes man on Earth. Somewhere else in the Bible it says that when the Jews start moving back to Palestine, it's a sign that the messiah is returning to Earth. We know that since the Nazis took power a lot of Jews have done precisely that, and even if they're not going to Palestine, a lot more have been moved in that general direction. And here you are figuring out how to make the rocket go where we want it to. Okay, okay, I'll shut up about it. I just think it's interesting."

There were naturally more fits and starts through the summer and fall on the road to that world-historical day in October 1942 when we made the third attempt at a successful launch of our big rocket, the A-4. Speer, who had come up from Berlin, reported that with the slowing of the Stalingrad offensive, the Führer was again looking in our direction, though after several recent failures he had come to doubt that our guidance system could achieve anything close to the desired level of accuracy. The stakes for us were high, and throughout the preceding weeks Colonel D. had been like Ajax in the *Iliad*, tirelessly making the rounds of all the labs and production facilities at the Center exhorting us to ever more strenuous efforts to stave off what seemed like inevitable defeat. Finally on October 1st, two days before launch, he sent all of the top people handwritten notes whose text was a single line in Latin: "*Naviget haec summus est hic nostri nuntius esto.*" It came from Book 4 of Virgil's *Aeneid*, a work that virtually every early twentieth-century European schoolboy had been drilled in, and so we all recognized it as Jupiter's admonition to Aeneas that it was time quit dawdling in Carthage and get on with the business of founding Rome, regardless of the personal cost to him — and to us.

The morning of October 3rd the sun rose on the kind of perfect autumn day along the Baltic that I would always miss after our move to the American Southwest and South: deep blue skies, sunshine without glare, a fresh breeze coming off the water dotted with whitecaps. Some of us had been out at Test Stand VII since before dawn checking and double-checking all systems with an obsessive vigilance that bordered on the pathological. The rocket stood cradled in its gantry to which it was connected by various umbilical cords and hoses. While painted in the harlequin black-and-white pattern like its predecessors to facilitate analysis of roll issues, this one also sported a sort of logo between two of the tail fins designed by our resident artist (a position insisted upon by the Technical Director), Gerd de Beek. Captioned *Woman in the Moon*, it showed a female figure, naked except for stockings and high heels, who straddled a crescent moon surrounded by stars. Pin-up girls were, of course, a usual feature of military hardware, and the Technical Director felt that the inclusion of the image, apart from bringing good luck, would serve as an important morale booster to a team that had been under an excruciating amount of pressure lately. It had been added only two days before after Colonel D. had dropped his objections, based not on the frivolity inherent in the mildly prurient cartoon of a naked woman, but because the moon and stars hinted at a peaceful objective for a project that had been funded exclusively by a military establishment that wanted only the most destructive weapon imaginable. He was also concerned that the reference to *Woman in the Moon* would cause problems for us in some quarters because the film's director, Fritz Lang, now in exile in Hollywood, had been born of a Jewish mother.

Lift-off was scheduled for that afternoon but immediately after lunch in the Hearth Room, the Technical Director motioned for me to follow him to his office. I knew he was still concerned about excessive roll at launch and perhaps wanted to review settings for the roll-rate gyros one last time. When I arrived there, however, he picked up an envelope and waved it over his head. "Our buddy Speer came through for us!" he announced. "Your problem is all taken care of!"

"You talked to Speer about this?" I asked. I was annoyed that I hadn't been consulted by either the Technical Director or Speer himself, though given the latter's position in the highest echelons of the government I could understand his need for discretion.

"Not directly, of course. With Colonel D.'s approval, I initiated contact through channels which eventually found their way to the Armaments Minister, as I knew they would. We didn't hear anything for a long time, in fact, not until this morning when he asked for a private meeting. He told us that yours was not the first case of its type to arise and that the Nuremburg Laws were a major headache for him since so many key people in munitions production turned out to have a Jew squirreled up in their family trees. But he went on to say that the Führer himself knew the laws were a 'blunt instrument' and understood from the get-go that there might well be people of dubious ancestry doing critical work for the Reich whose cases would have to be dealt with on an individual basis." The Technical Director then handed me the envelope. "Take a look," he said. It contained a single sheet of rag paper folded in thirds. As I opened it, I first noticed the embossed swastika within a circle in the upper-left- hand corner and immediately beneath that the words in all capitals: DER FÜHRER. After the salutation to the Reich Minister of the Interior, it read as follows:

Please be advised that Dr. Arthur Waldmann of the Peenemünde East Development Center has been affirmed in the status of Citizen of the Reich and Member of the German Blood. This determination supersedes any and all previous statements about Dr. Waldmann's citizenship or race.

Beneath was the nearly illegible bolt and squiggle (except for the florid "H") that I recognized from other documents as the Führer's signature. Colonel D. had been cc'd. There was no reason to think the letter was anything but authentic, though it later crossed my mind that maybe the Technical Director had forged the document (but where would he have obtained the stationery?) to free me from any anxiety that might interfere with my ability to resolve our guidance problems, such was the pressure we were now under. I handed the letter back to him and offered my sincere and honest thanks. He took both it and the envelope, placed them in a manila folder which he then held up as if it were a prop in a magic show, and dropped it in a cabinet drawer of what I presumed were personnel files.

The Technical Director and I left his office and soon caught up with the procession of dignitaries headed by Speer walking to the viewing stand. The countdown was already in progress and proceeded smoothly until it was stopped at T-minus 28 minutes when a problem was discovered with a pair of cooling nozzles. It took about an hour for a team from the Propulsion Lab to make repairs, during which time I could almost feel the observers' skepticism melting into embarrassment for us. Finally the count was resumed about 3:30, and just before 4:00, the umbilicals dropped away and the rocket began its ascent on a blinding pillar of fire. It described a near perfect arc, heading out over the Baltic with Brennschluss occurring only one second prematurely. As it moved into the heights of the upper atmosphere, it left behind a jagged contrail which led some of our guests to believe that the rocket had come to an untimely end, but this was merely the effect of powerful high-level winds, as radio telemetry showed that it continued on course. When the signal stopped about five minutes later, we knew that the rocket had crashed into the sea 120 miles downrange after having achieved an altitude of 52 miles. Not only had the test been a complete success, but we had incidentally set the world records for the highest altitude ever achieved by a man-made object, as well as absolutely obliterating the record for speed, which had reached almost Mach 5 right after Brennschluss.

The Technical Director, Colonel D., myself and a few other of our top people were on the roof of the Guidance Laboratory's Measurement House when we received confirmation of these results. I can only describe the emotional release at that moment as volcanic. People were whooping like red Indians, hats were tossed in the air, and it was one of the few times in my life I've actually seen grown men cry. At one point the Technical Director and Colonel D. were rolling on the ground in a raucous fraternal embrace. It would become one of my later life's regrets that none of our subsequent collective accomplishments, not Explorer I or even Apollo 11, would equal the sheer joy of this occasion.

That evening over a meal of Wiener schnitzel and Sacher torte and in the presence of Speer and all the other dignitaries, Colonel D. waxed poetic. "We have successfully invaded the realm of outer space and shown that it can be a bridge between remote points of Earth. In the near future no place will be beyond the reach of the German eagle. Even the heavens will become a province of its domain. This day, the third of October 1942, is the beginning of a new age–the Space Age."

As I raised my glass with the rest of them, it occurred to me that this wasn't the first time I had heard the clarion announcement of a new epoch in world history, and that it probably wouldn't be the last.

CHAPTER 9
BROKEN DREAMS

Colonel D.'s biggest challenge after the October launch was maintaining the program's forward momentum so that the resources now available to us could be fully exploited. The problem was the inevitable letdown that came after achieving what not so long before had seemed impossible. This was especially the case for many of the top people like the Technical Director and myself who had been laboring on this project for most of our adult lives. We had worked a miracle; didn't we now deserve a little respite?

The answer, of course, was no, and at all events, the laurels that we were resting upon quickly lost their leaves. A prototype is one thing, an idiot-proof production model quite another, and to achieve those refinements, continued test launches were necessary. These did not go well. After a qualified success on October 21st (147 kilometers down range) the next four attempts through early January were "reluctant virgins" — complete duds. Then we were once again overtaken by events. In early February 1943 General Paulus surrendered what was left of the 300,000-man army that had been sent to capture Stalingrad but which instead found itself surrounded. The Führer was so distraught that we later learned he had asked Speer if it would be possible to fire the A-4 from the 80 centimeter siege mortar Dora which the Army had managed to withdraw before encirclement. The fact that he still thought of the missile as just a big artillery shell and that he might now really cancel the program if results were not forthcoming snapped us back to reality. Any hope of future ballistic missile research and development now depended on the mass production of the A-4, as boring to us as that might seem.

As for remaining in the Führer's good graces, we still had an ace-in-the-hole with the unconditional support of Armaments Minister

Speer who made increasingly frequent visits to Peenemünde throughout 1943. Of course he wanted to keep tabs on how quickly the A-4 was becoming operational, but it was also obvious how much he enjoyed the opportunity to socialize with men like himself who felt compelled toward creative expression on a grand scale. Germany's deteriorating military situation had put on hold the plans he had drawn up at the Führer's behest for the transformation of Berlin into an imposing world capital. The crown jewel of this new Germania was to be the People's Hall, a monstrous domed building almost 1,000 feet high that would accommodate an audience of 180,000. He confided to some of us that he now doubted his architectural dreams would ever be realized, but he took heart whenever he went out to inspect our test stands, which in his mind represented at least a partial fulfillment of the same German spirit that lay behind his own impossibly ambitious project.

One evening after such an inspection tour, we were all enjoying brandy and cigars in the Hearth Room when, following a brief lull in the conversation, Speer cleared his throat and said, "I've been going back and forth about this all day, but because I feel like we're brothers under the skin, I'm going to commit an indiscretion and tell you something that I think you need to know. Needless to say, never let it go beyond this room. If it does, there will be consequences for all of us."

"About a week ago the Führer and I were taking our usual evening walk around one of the small lakes near his headquarters. He needs to get away from people to collect and organize his thoughts, but he also likes someone there to bounce ideas off in case something comes into his head. I'm rather an introvert myself, so I don't mind the company of a person who might not say a word to me for hours and then expect me to listen to him with rapt attention. Anyway, we had been walking by this lake for some time in silence when the Führer turns to me and says, 'Speer, I had the most terrible nightmare earlier this week. Fräulein Braun and I were having a picnic on the seacoast near Peenemünde. Several children were playing around us. I was seated before an easel painting a picture of the scene across the water which was unmistakably the white cliffs of Dover, even though we were on the Baltic. Every time I touched my brush to the canvas, there was a roar behind me and a rocket flew over my head in the direction of the cliffs, but the first one got about halfway, turned into a gooney bird, and started flying in circles. The next rocket covered about half the distance of the first, then it, too, turned into a gooney bird and began circling. As I continued to touch brush to canvas, the rockets would cover shorter and shorter distances before becoming birds and going in circles. I was growing more and more frustrated. Finally, Hess came up behind me and started laughing uncontrollably at the picture, saying, "In England we use things like that to wrap bloaters." Fräulein Braun then handed me a paring knife, and I cut off Hess's fingers and toes. He put up no resistance, and there was blood all over the place, but he wouldn't stop laughing, and now in the sky overhead was a huge Zeppelin with hundreds of sea birds flying around it. I wanted to run away but was now standing on a tile floor that looked beautiful but was strewn about with dead and mangled bodies. I knew it would blow up as soon as I took one step on it. The Zeppelin then descended toward me and I could see that the man at the controls looked like one of those rocket scientists though I don't remember which one. Next thing I knew I was sitting up in bed in a cold sweat.'"

Speer came to the end of his narration, and none of us said a word because the implication was obvious: The Führer now believed that the rocket would never make it to England. On one level we all knew that it was absurd to base military strategy on a dream, but we also understood that this is how things worked under a system with a supreme leader. Although Speer was telling us this in confidence, I think our initial collective silence was based on the fear that any rationalist dismissal of the Führer's dream, if it did get back to him, would only work to our disadvantage. But it also occurred to me that maybe dreams were a perfectly sound basis for decision making. After all, with the admittedly notable exception of the debacle on the Volga, Germany had done rather well for itself these past ten years, whatever method the Führer was using.

Colonel D. was the first to speak but only to say that maybe it was something the Führer had eaten. Given that everyone knew he ate the same bland vegetarian food every day, and that each dish was sampled by at least two tasters before it ever passed his lips, this was not likely. Still, we all laughed heartily at this lame assertion. The Technical Director then took a different tack, saying he would be worried if the Führer's doubts about such a new and untried technology were not infiltrating his unconscious life. "I have bad dreams like that all the time," he said—this was news to me—"so please reassure him on the basis of what you've seen here that we're making heroic efforts to overcome the challenges that lay ahead which, you can tell him, are less formidable than those we've already overcome." The conversation continued on this cautious track for a few more minutes, and we were about to move on when my heart started to race. Something had occurred to me and I struggled to overcome my reticence about speaking up. The tension must have shown in my face as the Technical Director turned to me and said, "Is there something wrong, Arthur?" A switch now flipped.

"The Führer's dream is powerful, but the obvious interpretation is not the correct one," I asserted boldly. "The apparent failure of the rockets to reach England is an uncanny and accurate visual impression of how the vehicles vanish from sight around the time they reach the sound barrier, and their progressively earlier disappearance is a sign of the rocket's growing technical sophistication. The birds in the Führer's dream are actually pelagic doves representing the peace feelers that will come flying back in our direction as the rockets rain death and destruction upon London. The Zeppelin and exploding tile floor do allude to the destructive power inherent in this new technology, but the dead bodies strewn about are those of the Reich's enemies. The presence of a rocket scientist in the Zeppelin's control car looks forward to a postwar future when our talents will be directed to peaceful ends and the German people will once again travel the world in these graceful machines, now filled with non-flammable helium because we will have control over America's supply of the gas."

"What about Hess?" asked one of my colleagues.

"No toes means he will spend the rest of his life confined, whatever the war's outcome. No fingers means he will never write anything. He laughs because he's a fool. The children playing on the beach, I forgot to mention, are of course the German people."

The rush of mental clarity that overwhelmed me as I spoke these words was such that I could have offered a solution to Fermat's Last Theorem right then and there if someone had asked me to do so. But in the next instant the power was gone, and although it would be false modesty on my part to say that I was a person of merely average intelligence, compared to what I had just experienced, I now felt like a dunce. Had some supernatural agency taken possession of me? You would think that someone who had long envied the spiritual gifts conferred upon others would have welcomed the moment as a vindication of all the time and effort devoted to this end, a kind of down payment on the ultimate prize of free access to the Heavenly Academy, but instead I felt cheated. The mastering of Moses de Leon's synthetic Aramaic, the hours spent wrestling with the tedious homilies of the Zohar, the decision to become an engineer so as to reach Heaven by mechanical means when my real loves were philosophy and art— all this so that I could break open a dictator's dream?

Colonel D. looked at me as if I had just walked on water, while the Technical Director broke into one of his trademark sunny smiles. Speer took another sip of brandy and nodded judiciously. "A most interesting interpretation," he said.

While we recognized the signal importance of Speer's advocacy, we also knew that we could not mortgage our future to a tissue of personal relationships. Palace intrigue was a feature of the regime, and we wanted to avoid becoming collateral damage to a forced resignation or unexpected suicide that would lead to our fall from the Führer's grace. In an autocratic state, there is ultimately an audience of one, and the Technical Director understood the importance of playing directly to him. In early 1939 when Colonel D. had arranged for the Führer to witness a couple of static test firings at Kummersdorf, the Technical Director had explained how a liquid fuel rocket worked, using a cutaway model, but the demonstration made little impression. About all that it elicited from the Führer was a bored, "Well, it was grand!" over his vegetarian lunch. For months afterward, the Technical Director fumed about the lost opportunity. "Colonel D. is a mechanical engineer who thinks like a mechanical engineer," he told me, "but it will require the touch of an artist to reach into the mind of an artist, or at least, the mind of a former art student."

Toward that end the Technical Director proposed that we produce a feature film highlighting our accomplishments that might be shown to the Führer at the appropriate psychological moment. There was already a good deal of material in our archives to work with. The Technical Director and I spent several days in the projection room reviewing footage that extended from his earliest experiments at Kummersdorf through the construction of the Center, and on to recent developments that included spectacular images of the October A-4 flight, captured by a dozen strategically placed cameras loaded with high-resolution color film, a rare and expensive commodity in the early 1940s. Much of this material, however, had been produced with purely technical aims in mind—close-ups of nozzles to check for exhaust gas flow, scale models buffeted around in dimly lit wind tunnels—exactly the sort of thing that was immensely fascinating to mechanical engineers but almost no one else.

We both recognized that the first thing we needed was a script with a compelling story line. What would move our audience? It wouldn't exactly be the story we wanted to tell, the tale of a visionary team of young and talented engineers who struggled inside a hidebound military bureaucracy to realize their dream of Raumschiffahrt. A story of David and Goliath would hold no purchase on an autocrat whose hero was Goliath. Indeed, the overarching theme would have to be one of brute force, pure and simple.

Our search for inspiration almost inevitably led us to *Triumph of the Will*. (Like all major military installations, a print had been deposited in the film library of our on-base cinema.) We ultimately decided that our narrative would be structured around a movement from a few small things to multitudinous large ones. There would be a scene of an engineer working on a particular component, the camera then pulling back to reveal a lab full of engineers. We would show the process of setting up a rocket for launch followed by a montage of a dozen successful launches. With the aid of time-lapse photography, a patch of virgin forest would be transformed into the site of the ten-story Test Stand I. The main characters in our film would be the machines themselves which as much as possible would dwarf the human beings around them.

Recognizing the importance of the project, Colonel D. allowed the Technical Director and me to take time off from our usual round of meetings to work on the film, although whenever a question as to our whereabouts was answered with "They're in the projection room," Colonel D. would grumble about "paying the ransom" or "the high price of genius." There were quite a number of scenes that had to be shot. The Technical Director went at this task with the zeal of an *auteur*. Although he had never made a movie before, he had written a number of playlets for our entertainments, and had had some contact with the film industry about a decade earlier when he worked on publicity for *Woman in the Moon*. Indeed, to put himself in the right frame of mind, he acquired a folding director's chair and a megaphone, and accoutered himself with Fritz Lang's signature monocle and high-crowned Borsalino. He also began to employ movie jargon in rocket work, saying things like "That's a wrap!" at the conclusion of a successful static test.

We were blessed with an unusual number of warm days that winter, and within a month or so had the new material we needed. After some debate we had decided to include scenes of our "successful failures" as reassurance to an audience, now reeling from a string of military defeats, that sometimes the darkest hour really is just before the dawn, which for us was the October launch. At that point in a deliberate allusion to *The Wizard of Oz*, one of the Führer's favorite movies, the film switched from black and white to color, and showed the triumphant lift-off of our big rocket. As the missile disappeared into the stratosphere the scene dissolved into a map of Flanders and northern France with dozens of cartoon A-4s poised on their launchers. As the Technical Director's voice counted down to zero, the rockets lifted off, white lines tracing their paths as they reached their apogees above the Channel before arcing down toward cities and military bases in England. We closed the film with images of springtime at Peenemünde—wildflowers, seabirds, sand, and surf, with the ten-story Test Stand I rising up from among the spruces. This bucolic scene then shifted to another more recent A-4 launch, the roar of the engine accompanied by Wagner's "Flight of the Valkyries."

Although the Technical Director wanted to remain with the project to the end, the demands of running the Center eventually called him back to his usual duties. Most of the editing, therefore, fell to me and after several more weeks, I had distilled dozens of hours down to what I considered a very tight and artistically satisfying twenty minutes, with narration and musical score. When the Technical Director saw it, he declared me a cinematic genius and went right to Colonel D., asking him to set up a showing for the Führer as soon as possible. Colonel D. was also impressed with the film but said with the Russian front yet to be stabilized, the time was not ripe. This was our best shot, he said, and he didn't want to waste it.

The psychological moment arrived in early July when it became clear that to the Army High Command that Operation Citadel in western Russia was not going to blunt the Red Army's summer offensive. At eight o'clock one morning an excited Colonel D. poked his head into our offices and told us pack up a print of our film and meet him at the airfield in an hour. We boarded an He 111 bomber-transport and before noon were being greeted at the entrance to the Wolfschanze, the Führer's East Prussian headquarters, by Armaments Minister Speer. He conducted us to the complex's cinema where he reviewed the details of our presentation and made a few minor suggestions in the interest of concision. We then waited there for an hour before the Führer arrived with his entourage. He greeted each of us by name and after exchanging brief reminiscences with Colonel D. and the Technical Director about his visit to Kummersdorf, we sat down to watch the film.

Twenty minutes later when the lights came back on the Führer jumped out of his seat and applauded, his aides quickly following his example. He went to a table in the back and, for lack of a better term, began playing with the models we had set up there of the rockets and their support equipment. It was obvious that he had no particular idea of what he was doing, so the Technical Director walked over and began explaining how the mobile launchers would work. The Führer listened impatiently and asked him how soon it would be before we achieved production of 2,000 missiles a month each carrying a ten-ton warhead. Of course, production of even a few hundred missiles with only a one-ton warhead was still several months away. Colonel D. intervened at this point to finesse the gap between expectation and reality, but the Führer cut him off, shouting, "What I want is annihilation—annihilating effect!" Colonel D. seemed taken aback by a vehemence more appropriate to a Party rally than a high-level strategy session, but he quickly regained his composure and said, "Yes, that's what we all want, and we are well on our way there, my Führer!" I tried to catch the Technical Director's eye for a reality check, but he had become intensely interested in the light fixtures on the ceiling.

The following morning just before leaving the guest bunker for the airfield, we received a summons to go next door to the conference room. When we arrived, we found it unoccupied except for an aide who was carefully arranging some papers and pens on the table. Within seconds of him finishing the task a door at the opposite end of the room opened and in walked the Führer, along with Speer and his usual entourage. The first order of business was the formal conferring of Colonel D.'s promotion to brigadier general which had come through a few weeks earlier. After the completion of that ceremony, Speer picked up one of the documents on the table and began reading. I could hardly believe my ears: It was a resolution granting the Technical Director the title of Professor. Although I believed I had steeled myself against every possible humiliation that might be a consequence of my second-tier status in both the realms of the scientific bureaucracy I inhabited in my mortal life and the sacred hierarchy of my spiritual one, here was a blow I could never have foreseen. It must be understood that the title "Professor" in pre-war Germany was not simply a rank that one advanced to by hard work on a well-defined career track but rather was granted by the state only on the rarest occasions to men of extraordinary talent and accomplishment. The only equivalent for someone today would be receiving the Nobel Prize. Moreover, by longstanding custom it was never given to a man under the age of fifty-five. I doubted that with all the other things on his mind it would have occurred to the Führer on his own to do this. It must have been on the recommendation of either General D. or Speer himself. The former I could live with since all of General D.'s machinations were directed toward the goal of protecting his own organization. The thought that this was the doing of the Armaments Minister, with whom I felt I had a special relationship, was infinitely more painful.

As Speer finished reading the citation, the Führer stepped up to the table. He was smiling as he leaned over, took one of the fountain pens, and signed the document. "How can anyone so young have accomplished so much?" he said, shaking his head in wonderment. "At the age of thirty I was still blindly groping my way toward my destiny, and have spent my middle age trying to achieve it. You found yours as a schoolboy and haven't wasted a moment since. I envy you your youth."

Salutes! Dismissal! It was all over in less than five minutes. But as I was walking out of the conference room, I heard Speer call my name. When I turned to go back, I saw that the Führer was extending his arm for a handshake. "Herr Waldmann," he began, "as you may know, the Armaments Minister has apprised me of your special circumstances, and I want to reassure you that I continue to stand by the endorsement of your loyalty that I forwarded to the Reich Minister of the Interior. I also want to thank you personally for the correct interpretation of my dream a year ago last March. I have had to apologize to only two people in my life. The first is Field Marshal von Brauchitsch. I did not listen to him when he told me again and again how important your group's research was. The second was General D. I never dreamed that your work would be successful. Neither of these wrongs would have been righted without your shining a light into the darkness."

● ● ●

It was exactly six weeks between our trip to the Wolfsschanze July 7th and August 18th. If I remember my first summer at Kummersdorf as a spring-like season of relative freedom and infinite possibility, then the summer of 1943 possessed the corresponding autumnal glow of peaceful, well-deserved fulfillment. Certainly the Führer's kind words had made a profound impact on me. While I initially thought of the interview as a sort of consolation prize, I began to think of it as actually something more valuable than a piece of paper attesting to a mainly ceremonial honor. As far as I knew, the Technical Director had never had a one-on-one exchange with the Master of Europe and putative future Leader of the Western World. Really, what would make the better story for one's grandchildren half a century from now?

On the material level, construction of facilities at the Research Center was now basically complete, and my personal living situation could hardly have been more comfortable. I lived in my own bachelor apartment, with private bath, nestled amid the spruce trees not far from a small pond where I used to row a boat sometimes. It was only a few steps to the officers' mess hall where one could order up a full breakfast of eggs, sausage, orange juice, pancakes, whatever one wanted. A short walk in the opposite direction led to the Guidance Laboratory, where as a senior scientist no one expected me to show up at any particular time, though in fact I always made it a point to be there by 8:00 a.m. One of my assistants would then brief me on the outstanding issues of the day, and I would have the luxury of choosing which one of them would benefit from my personal attention. Lunch would usually be taken in the Hearth Room's Weinstube where General D. and the Technical Director would preside over a convivial hour during which conversation would ricochet from Center gossip to leisure time activities to the most arcane technical conundrums.

While the Technical Director himself was now at the top of his game when it came to engineering and project management (a level of performance he never descended from until those last years after he was kicked upstairs to Washington), he was also devoting time to the production of yet another film. It seems that when the Propaganda Minister saw the movie we had shown at the Wolfsschanze, he was so impressed that he wanted something of a similar nature but for a mass audience. This dovetailed perfectly with the Technical Director's idea that now was the time to prepare the groundwork for the sacrifices in blood and treasure from the German people that would be necessary to build the big rockets that would finally get us into space after the war. Of course, the film would have to meet the Propaganda Minister's immediate requirement of bucking up morale at a time when Allied bombers were operating with impunity over German cities and re-enforce the official theme for all German films to be released in 1943, "Sticking It Out." But the Technical Director figured he could smuggle his larger agenda into the movie by subtle visual touches, for example, including an animation of the America Rocket's trajectory en route to the destruction of New York that showed in the background an astronomically unrealistic conjunction of the moon, Mars, Jupiter, and Saturn. The goal was to aim for a Christmas release, around the time that the Führer would be announcing the first mass A-4 attacks against England.

Of course, I was still hoping for a miracle that would forestall the A-4's ever going into battle. Perhaps our stubborn resistance in the face of new Allied offensives in both Russia and Italy would lead to a negotiated end to the fighting on not unfavorable terms. As the A-4 moved closer to operational status, I came to realize that it was qualitatively more horrific than any other weapon in the history of warfare. A rock or a bullet or a Tiger tank shell will make you just as dead, but at least you might know they're coming toward you and offer a chance of escape. Not so the A-4. Because it descends at supersonic speed, you're dead before you ever hear it. I shuddered with perhaps misplaced empathy for our enemies when I tried to imagine what it would be like to live where death could rain down upon you without the slightest warning. The A-4 brought terror to a whole new level, its rather puny one-ton warhead notwithstanding, although naturally the bigger rockets on our drawing boards would carry bigger bombs.

Although there's no way for me to prove it to you, let me say in my defense that sometimes I acted in small ways to retard the development process. For example, when presented with a certain technical problem, I might not pursue solutions that I knew would be unlikely to occur to others not gifted with my peculiar genius. On numerous occasions I resorted to the Jesuitical doctrine of mental reservation, beginning a response to a question from one of my colleagues orally but only completing it in my head. "Would it be possible to increase the effective range of the guide beam by adjusting the internal antennae?" I was asked one day, and I responded, "No, such a change would make little difference" — and then added silently — "without altering the configuration of other components in that module."

The Technical Director's work on his movie, and my wrestling with these moral qualms, were interrupted in mid-August by a visit from one last VIP — the Aviatrix. Her main purpose in coming to Peenemünde was to consult on a new jet-powered vehicle being developed at the Luftwaffe Center on the west side of the peninsula, but she was also going to be guest of honor at an A-4 launch scheduled the same week.

The Aviatrix had by now become a larger-than-life figure in our national consciousness. Although our ideology was staunchly patriarchal, with the ideal woman a homemaker and breeder of racially pure children, there was something appealing in the notion of the random female who surpassed men in a traditionally masculine domain like warfare. It was as though we were saying to our enemies in the decadent West, if we allowed it, even an army of our women could defeat you! The effect was only heightened by the Aviatrix's small stature, barely five feet tall and a hundred pounds. Her exploits, often featured in newsreels, included piloting bombers on night raids over England. With goggles pushed atop her leather aviator's cap she was the very picture of a Teutonic Nike.

I paid close attention to the demeanor of the Technical Director when the Aviatrix joined us on the roof of the Measurement Building to observe the launch. I wondered if he still bore the torch for her from their long ago platonic relationship at the glider school in Grunau. While the demands of rocket work for me had entailed a monkish, celibate existence, not so the Technical Director, whose more frequent travels to Berlin allowed him some measure of what General D. euphemistically referred to as his personal life. This had lately taken a domestic turn as he had become engaged to a physical education teacher who lived in the capital. I never met the woman, but I assumed there was a deep attachment, even bordering on love, as the Technical Director had gone to some pains to secure the right to marry. It seems that there were Jewish ancestors in her family tree and the initial request for permission had been turned down because of the Technical Director's top secret security clearances. At this point he decided to use his rank as a major in the SS to pull strings for a reversal of the decision. The matter was eventually referred to the Reichsführer-SS himself, which was another reason the Technical Director had to bite the bullet and put on the uniform during his visit in July. Permission was eventually granted, though a date was never set, and indeed, the wedding never took place.

It was immediately apparent to me, however, that the flame was not completely snuffed out. As the rocket lifted off the pad, everyone on the roof shielded their eyes against the glare of the sun except the Technical Director whose eyes darted back and forth between the A-4 and the Aviatrix. When the demonstration was over (it was a "reluctant virgin," a rocket that didn't quite achieve its intended apogee), the Technical Director begged off joining the group escorting the Aviatrix to the Luftwaffe Center for her test flight of the new jet, insisting that a stack of paperwork awaited him back at the office.

At the formal dinner that evening, he still seemed uncharacteristically diffident. Perhaps when you have always been the star of the show, you simply don't know how to take your spot back in the chorus line. We were standing at our places around the table when she walked in, a nearly invisible vortex of conviviality, surrounded as she was by the colonels and generals who towered over her. As we took our seats, I could see she was wearing the dress blue uniform of a Luftwaffe Flight Captain, with the diamond-encrusted Iron Cross First Class awarded to her by the Führer himself pinned to her tunic just above the heart.

After the meal, a smaller group consisting of General D. and the Center's top people adjourned to the Hearth Room for the usual brandy and cigars. (The Aviatrix partook of neither.) As the party became more relaxed, the Aviatrix slipped off her shoes and curled up cat-like in a huge leather armchair. The conversation moved from Army and Air Force gossip to the two topics that really engaged the passions of those present, technology and war. Unlike most everyone at Peenemünde, she had extensive combat experience in the present conflict, including a recent stint on the Eastern Front at the invitation of General von Greim, widely rumored to be her lover. Although her tour there was intended mainly as a morale booster, she naturally insisted on more substantive assignments, and so flew her single-engine Fieseler Storch on numerous reconnaissance flights over Red Army formations. When someone cautiously noted that even with success in the current offensive it would be a long time before we could recover from the "debacle on the Volga," the Aviatrix snapped, "Go ahead, say it—Stalingrad. Do you feel better now? Two hundred thousand of our brave men dead. But we're a nation of soldiers, not shopkeepers. We live not for life but for sacrifice, and the spiritual abundance created by that sacrifice will far outweigh whatever temporary tactical advantage was gained by the Russians. Let me tell you, every time I climbed into my Storch, I was inspired by those beautiful deaths to fly a little more boldly than before."

Her optimism was infective and now the Technical Director re-entered the conversation. He noted that despite all the problems moving the A-4 into production, it was still nothing short of amazing to think that only ten years ago the biggest liquid fuel rocket could still be carried about on a man's shoulder. Now they had a machine that could carry a payload equal to the weight of a man and his life-support system to the edge of space. From there the conversation drifted back to flying and the Technical Director spoke with nostalgia about the time he and the Aviatrix were students at Wolf Hirth's glider school in the Riesengebirge in Silesia. She was staring off into space when he asked her about someone they both once knew, and instead of responding to the question, said, "I would be the perfect candidate for the first human in space, wouldn't I? I mean, besides being one of the few test pilots who's actually flown a rocket-powered vehicle, I'm also one of the smallest. Right?" Heads around the room nodded in general agreement and then turned toward the Technical Director. He seemed caught off guard. "Well, when the time comes, we'll see," he said, and when this answer seemed unsatisfactory, added, "Getting the A-4 onto the battlefield now denies me the luxury of thinking about such pleasant questions."

The room was blue with cigar smoke by the time General D. excused himself around eleven. An hour or so later there was a small explosion that rattled the windows, and someone remarked that it must be Stölzel who was testing detonators for anti-aircraft tracers over on the Luftwaffe side. This first explosion was followed by a few others, and then like the onset of a downpour the number seemed to increase exponentially. Shattered glass came flying at us from all directions, someone shouted "air raid!" and we all ran outside to find everything backlit by the eerie red glow of flares and incendiaries. My natural instinct was to seek shelter in one of the many bunkers located about the installation, but instead I stayed with the Technical Director who, oblivious to the whistling of falling bombs, was already trying to assess the damage and organize fire brigades. Soot and sand filled the air, and absurdly, all I could think about was when I'd be able to take my next shower. He directed me to check out the Measurement House while he and the Aviatrix headed north to the test stands.

When I arrived at my destination, I found General D. in pajamas and riding boots overseeing the distribution of extinguishers. "Take this and come with me around back. I think we can save this one if we work fast." There was a small fire on the roof, and covering our faces with handkerchiefs against the thick smoke, we climbed up the stairs until we were close enough to put out the flames. Only now did I become aware of the drone of hundreds of bombers already beginning to fade in the distance. It was all over in less than an hour. I spent the rest of that long night running around with an extinguisher and alternately fascinated with the unearthly beauty of the flames and despairing at the thought of how much work there would be to get the place up and running again. Toward dawn I found General D. sitting on the ground next to a bicycle rendered useless by the badly cratered road leading up to the test stands. His head was in his hands, and when I called his name he looked up at me and with tears streaming down his grimy face cried out in perfect agony, "My beautiful Peenemünde, my beautiful Peenemünde!" I had never thought of the man as having a soul any larger than was minimally required to be an artillery officer, but it now occurred to me that for some people the love of mere things could be as profound as the scientist's love of truth or the mystic's love for an ineffable God—the *Ein Sof*. I put my arm around him and said we could take hope from the fact that there was no smoke coming from the north end of the island. We started walking up the road, and the further we went, the more intact its condition. As the woods parted on our approach to the beach, we could see the test stands backlit against the morning sky, seemingly unhurt. From the top of Test Stand I, I could see the red, black, and white flag snapping in the breeze, and on closer view see the Aviatrix holding the pole and waving it back and forth. A moment later the Technical Director came running toward us from its base. "God be praised!" he shouted. "Our mighty test stands have been spared!"

CHAPTER 10
BLIZNA

By noon of the following day, it was obvious that the destruction was less catastrophic than initially feared. Assuming the British bombardiers knew their targets, the planes seem to have come in half a mile south of their intended runs. Our crown jewels—the test stands that would have been eerily illuminated by the full moon—were completely unscathed. There was some damage to the still unfinished Production Works, and a few of the residences had taken direct hits, including that of our Chief of Propulsion who was tragically killed along with his wife and three small children. My private quarters were now marked by a bomb crater. Ironically (and war is nothing if not ironic) the heaviest casualties were recorded in the Guest Labor Camp, where dozens of conscripted Poles died along with a handful of Frenchmen.

Within days the painful decision was made to dramatically scale back our operations since we knew that eventually an overflight by a British reconnaissance plane would show Bomber Command that their work here wasn't done. Only limited reconstruction was undertaken so as to leave the impression that the site was no longer operational. Damaged and minor buildings were blown up and fake bomb craters were dug near remaining essential facilities like the wind tunnel. We climbed up on roofs and painted black and white lines to simulate charred beams. Some research and development activities would continue here as long as the test stands remained intact, but all production would now be concentrated in a gigantic underground factory being carved out beneath one of the Harz Mountains in Thuringia. Primary testing would be moved to an SS facility at Blizna in southern Poland which was well beyond the reach of Allied bombers.

While these changes would not sever my connection with Peenemünde—I would still be based there at the Guidance Laboratory—all of our top people would now be dividing their time among the three locations. Control of the rocket program was also shifting from the Army to a consortium that included the Armaments Ministry, which would set standards and objectives, and the SS, which would run the factories and supply the labor. It all left me feeling like a child whose parents had died and who was now being sent off to live with distant and probably unsympathetic relatives.

On the other hand, the air raid and its aftermath also brought an end to my feelings of guilt about living in Todt's "paradise." Our protracted phony war was over, and the real war had found us with a vengeance. My house had been bombed! My co-workers had been killed! It wasn't the same as losing an arm fighting a tank battle in Libya or Bessarabia, but I could now lay claim to at least second-class citizenship in the war's empire of suffering. The literal baptism by fire also awoke latent sentiments of German patriotism. We landsmen of the Palatinate had always looked west to France and England as much as we looked east to Prussia, but hundreds of English airmen had just tried to murder me. In fact, General D. was convinced that the test stands which could have been rebuilt in six or eight weeks were never the primary target of the raid; rather, it was planned to kill as many scientists and engineers as possible. In that respect, it was a tactical failure.

Losing the home at Peenemünde also recalled to me my real home in Trier. While I hadn't been back there in almost four years, I continued to exchange letters with my parents on a monthly basis. I'd had no direct communication with my grandmother, however, since she moved to Toledo, Spain, just before the war, but then none of us had because she had decided that any contact with "the Jews" (of which collectivity she considered herself representative) would jeopardize our safety and security. Instead, she irregularly placed classified ads in one of three Spanish newspapers to which she had instructed my parents to subscribe. These ads would contain some word or phrase that would be familiar to any of us in the family, for example, "the mole," a nickname I had acquired because of my introverted habits. Of course, the ads were all in Spanish, so identifying the relevant ones was a formidable though not impossible challenge, at least for my father, who was fluent in French and actually enjoyed now having an excuse to broaden his linguistic repertoire. Once an ad was located, there was still work to be done, however, because she would never say anything direct, like "I have the flu" or "send me a pair of good walking shoes"; rather, everything was cloaked in wordplay. The request for shoes might be "Missing, two old Weimeraners, last seen barking near Santa Maria de la Blanca." "Weimaraners" were of course German, "barking dogs" were how she described sore feet, and "Santa Maria de la Blanca" was a church that had originally been a synagogue (an obscure reference I recognized but that would have escaped anyone else).

My father would always identify and decipher at least a few of these messages, though what percentage of the overall total these represented there was no way to know for sure. At all events, we assumed that my grandmother wasn't desperate because she never took the risk (which was hardly a risk at all) of sending a normal letter. These Spanish newspapers would be sent on to me in batches, and occasionally I would spot a few messages that my father had missed, which wasn't surprising given my excellent reading knowledge of Ladino. As far as I could tell, these were mostly bland status reports on the order of "Eating well, gained a few pounds" or "Unusually hot here for Pentecost week" (by which I knew she really meant the underlying Jewish holiday of Shavuot). Every now and then I would see something that looked like it might be significant but didn't obviously connect with anything in family lore. One such notice in the Lost and Found section read "Lost this past Thursday outside Sr. Simon's shop two umbrellas, one blue, one red. Blue and red." The name Simon caught my attention because she and I had once talked about the various Sephardic surnames that could be both Jewish and non-Jewish. The repetition of "blue" and "red" also looked like code though I didn't know what to make of the umbrellas. It was always more likely than not, of course, that the ad was exactly as it appeared to be, a notice put in the paper by someone who had lost a couple of umbrellas.

It was around that time that I had one of those recurring dreams common to people who possess more than average competence in their chosen fields. I was back in school taking a test for which I had somehow forgotten to prepare. As I was puzzling over the exam paper, the words that were there dissolved and in their place appeared a familiar passage from the Zohar: "From within the sealed secret a *zohar* ["splendid artifact"] flashed, shining as a mirror, embracing two colors blended together. One will fly, one will die." I awoke from this dream as from a nightmare and in my conscious mind immediately connected it with the odd repetition of the two colors in the classified ad which I was now certain had been placed there by my grandmother. On the one hand I was understandably terrified by the implications of the phrase, "One will fly, one will die." How could it not be a reference to my longstanding and spiritually tortuous relationship with the Technical Director and the question of which one of us would lead humanity into outer space? Assuming that "fly-die" was co-ordinate with the ad's "blue-red" sequence, I began ransacking my stored images of our respective mundane and symbolic lives to see if there was anything that might specify each of us as red or blue but could come up with nothing definitive. (Neither of us wore clothes of that color much; the Technical Director's sports cars were always dark green; the coat of arms of Trier included the color red, but so, too, did that of Wirsitz where the Technical Director was born.) But although I couldn't solve the riddle, I did find solace in believing that for the very first time something prophetic had been revealed to me in a dream. I was no longer just a mere interpreter as I had been with the Führer but was now myself the portal of the divine. The Zohar presupposes that dreams of this nature come only as the result of the soul's upward movement toward (if not necessarily attaining) the Heavenly Academy: "In a dream, a vision of the night when people are lying in their beds asleep, the soul leaves them, as it is written: 'as they sleep upon their bed, He uncovers human ears.' Then the Blessed Holy One reveals to the soul, through that level presiding over their dreams, things that are destined to come about in the world, or things corresponding to the mind's reflections, so that the dreamer will respond to the warning" (Tractate *Joseph's Dream*).

Although my prophetic dream (if that's what it was) didn't necessarily alleviate my fears about the future, it at least provided a kind of simplifying rubric. While the binary structure of "fly/die" hypersensitized me to anything connected with flight or death, it also afforded me the luxury of indifference to vast swaths of personal experience. There were even certain practical benefits. Given the decentralization of our operations, I would now be unable to avoid frequent air travel to Thuringia and Poland, but whenever I flew, especially when the Technical Director did not, I reasoned that I was probably immune to death. Of course, when the situation was reversed, I was theoretically the one more at risk, and yet sitting in my office at Peenemünde on a quiet October morning while the Technical Director was up in his Heinkel in skies increasingly inhabited by marauding P-51s, the notion that I was the one more likely to die was sufficiently absurd as to dissolve my fear. Indeed, my biggest worry now was that the Technical Director might be killed in a plane crash since meeting death while flying would completely discredit the prophecy, if that's what it ever was in the first place.

So it was that I almost enjoyed looking down upon the Earth from 20,000 feet as we approached Blizna on my first trip there. The Waffen-SS facility, codenamed "Heather Camp," encompassed thousands of acres near the confluence of the San and Vistula Rivers, about 90 miles northeast of Krakow. The landscape was mostly flat and swampy, with scattered villages occupying the intermittent stretches of dry land.

The primary task of our new testing program was to figure out why over half the missiles launched were disintegrating on their way back down to Earth. Direct observation seemed a good way to start, and so we selected an abandoned village whose gutted synagogue had a sort of turret that made an excellent platform from which to scan the skies. Indeed, the Technical Director fixed the location of the synagogue as ground zero, figuring that given the current state of the missile's accuracy, the precise target would be the least likely place for it to land. When I pointed out that it was nonetheless tempting the gods to deliberately aim a ten-ton rocket at our exact position, he just shrugged and said that he always preferred controlled irony to accidental tragedy.

Just before noon on the first day of testing (the Technical Director disliked mornings in Poland even more than early hours in Germany), the two of us arrived at our observation post. The interior of the synagogue was a shambles, all upended pews and broken light fixtures. Everything of value to a German soldier or Polish peasant had obviously been looted from the place. I noticed a Torah scroll unrolled for several feet atop a pile of bricks and masonry and unthinkingly began to read the Hebrew. From behind me the Technical Director said, "What a waste. It's easy to imagine what an architectural gem this once was. One of the more beautiful small synagogues I've ever been in."

"You've been in synagogues, plural?"

"As a boy I'd sometimes go around with my grandfather to collect rents. A lot of these tenants were Jews, most of them descendants of the several hundred my family brought in to repopulate our estates after the Black Death. I even went to their services a few times. Very primitive and disorderly but you had to admire their tenacity, clinging to their old ways in a sea of hostile Christians. It's too bad the jig is finally up for them now."

Our test procedure was simple. We communicated with the launch site by means of two-way radio. From launch to target was five minutes and thirty-five seconds, assuming we had a nominal Brennschluss at fifty-five seconds. At around four minutes, we positioned ourselves on opposite sides of the turret, and wearing specially designed Zeiss polarized sunglasses to reduce glare, began peering into the sky. Because the rocket would be traveling faster than sound, nothing would announce its presence. We simply had to be lucky enough to catch a glimpse of it on its final plunge, note the precise sequence of disintegration if it was in fact breaking up, and of course hope that the rocket would never achieve pinpoint accuracy as there was absolutely nothing we could do to take cover.

The Technical Director radioed the launch team that he and I were ready for the first missile, and a few minutes later he received confirmation that the launch sequence had been initiated. We both checked our watches. I tried to busy myself with preparations, but aside from putting on the sunglasses there weren't any.

The Technical Director seemed completely at ease. He began talking about how it's a shame that small villages like this one couldn't be lived in by one-tenth of their usual inhabitants. Even in its semi-ruined state, it seemed like a nice place to live, if you had the right group of about fifty people. He said that when he was at the Lietz School in Spiekeroog, he stayed on the island one Easter vacation when almost everyone else went home, and how wonderful it was to have all the grounds and buildings to yourself. Maybe that's how it would be for the first settlers on Mars. Of course, it would be really important to quickly develop hyper-propulsion systems to put the planets of other stars within easy reach lest those within our own solar system soon become overcrowded.

As well as I knew the Technical Director I couldn't believe how blasé he was as the clock ticked down to the four-minute mark. The deeper he went into his reverie about exoplanets, the more nervous and fidgety I became. I suppose he thought his idle chatter would distract me from the gravity of our situation because this was his usual tactic in trying to put me at ease on an airplane. I, on the other hand, thought that only to the degree I could remain absolutely focused on both the real and imagined danger of our circumstances would I have a chance of survival, and that as soon as I "blinked" by being lulled into a momentarily false sense of security, I was doomed. But as often as I told him that his good intentions were making my condition worse, he was convinced that next time around his palliative musings would cure me. Why should now be any different?

Finally at the three minute and forty-five second mark the Technical Director glanced at his watch, smiled at me, and said, "Well, let's see if there's anything happening in the sky this afternoon." We took up our positions on the turret and fixed our eyes upward. At least we were doing something now. Surely death cannot come to one so full of anticipation of it, I thought. At five minutes and five seconds the Technical Director began counting down from thirty. The pounding in my chest reached a level where I began to consider the irony of the missile falling harmlessly away from us while I died from a heart attack, though another twist might be that I would die from heart failure and then be annihilated by the missile. But would that matter? And who would ever know? All this while I was trying to carry out my task, straining to see a black dot in the sky. Though since none of us had as of yet actually seen a disintegrating missile come down on top of us, I wasn't exactly sure what I should be looking for.

"Five-four-three-two-one-zero!" Muscles I never knew I had flinched. Nothing happened. Amazingly, the Technical Director had immediately begun an upward count after reaching zero. Thirty seconds — nothing. Sixty seconds — nothing. After another minute we contacted the launch team. They said that everything had been nominal at least through Brennschluss plus two minutes and nine seconds at which point there had been a telemetry failure and they lost track of it.

By now it was obvious that wherever the rocket (or parts of it) landed, it wasn't here. The Technical Director made a joke about how the cost of the new Gestapo headquarters in Krakow would come out of our salaries. Relieved beyond measure, I laughed hysterically at this lame attempt at gallows humor, but his very next words into the microphone were like a punch to the gut: "How soon can you set up the next launch?" While I knew perfectly well that we were supposed to be out here observing a series of missile tests, deep down I thought that showing a willingness to face certain death once would earn us enough credit to be released from the obligation to ever do it again. War, of course, doesn't work that way, and neither does the advancement of science. The Technical Director wouldn't think of calling it quits without collecting the data. "There's one on a second launcher ready to go? Well, by all means, fire when ready, Gridley!"

I had thought perhaps the second time wouldn't be as bad as the first because now I had advanced further into the domain of the known, but it quickly dawned on me that this very notion was exactly the sort of rationalization that would distract me from focusing on the horror which was the only thing that might keep it at bay. And now adding to my fear was the realization that with each successive launch, it was a statistical certainty that the odds of being hit by the missile increased, although of course the odds for any single launch might be no more than a thousand to one. Still, one had to be careful not to be seduced by the notion that improbability was tantamount to impossibility, another one of those mental "blinks" that would positively foredoom one's doom.

Once again the Technical Director counted down the last thirty seconds, but around nine seconds (I think) there was a flash of light, a wave of heat passed through my body, as though I had just experienced an intense embarrassment, and I was thrown hard against the wall of our turret. I may or may not have been out for a few seconds, which might account for why I have no memory of sound from an explosion, but the next thing I knew I was leaning against the balustrade beside the Technical Director who was looking toward a column of smoke rising from another village two or three kilometers to the southwest. "I totally missed it coming down. Did you get a look at it?" he asked excitedly. When I told him no, he said, "Damn!" and without missing a beat radioed the launch team who said it would be at least an hour before they'd be ready to go again. Another mild expletive and his annoyance evaporated. "Well, nothing to be done," he said. "Let me see those binoculars." He looked through them for some seconds then handed them over to me. "Amazing how much damage even an unarmed A-4 can do. The old artillerist in General D. would be pleased." I could see what looked like a few cottages on fire, but between the smoke and the trees I couldn't tell if the place was inhabited. The SS had told us that any civilian casualties would be our problem, but honestly, what were they going to do, sue us?

"Might as well take our lunch break," announced the Technical Director. I unwrapped the thick brisket sandwich I had brought and began wolfing it down like a man who hadn't eaten in a week. The Technical Director removed from a paper sack his usual lunch of an apple, a few slices of Munster cheese, and a thermos of coffee. To this day it remains a mystery to me how he maintained such a large and robust physique on such a meager diet–he either had an incredibly low metabolism or secretly binged on Bratwurst and Pfannkuchen in the middle of the night.

"That last one was rather a close shave, wasn't it, old bean?" he said after he had taken a few bites. I was relieved to hear him express a normal human response to the situation and saw an opening.

"A close shave? By all rights we should be drinking schnapps in the underworld with Thiel now. You know I'm a coward. Tell me the worst place in the world today, and I swear whatever it is I'd rather be there."

"A tank battle in Russia?"

"Sign me up. But here's the thing I don't get. True, I probably know more about missile guidance than anyone on the planet, but Thiel knew more about propulsion and he got whacked in the air raid, but we pushed on, and the same thing would probably happen if I got blown to kingdom come later this afternoon. But what are you doing out here? Hard as it is for me to imagine, I know that when it comes to physical danger, you're basically fearless. Just wired up that way. But you're the heart and soul of the whole program. If you get it, the whole thing goes up in smoke. Probably push Raumschiffahrt back twenty or thirty years, maybe longer. There are a dozen non-essential people in the organization who could be out here doing this. Why did you talk General D. into believing that only your trained eye could resolve this re-entry problem?"

The Technical Director considered the question seriously. He looked out over the landscape, featureless except for the shadows of cumulus clouds passing overhead, and took a bite of his apple.

"You know, Arthur, how absurdly fortunate we have been, and I don't just mean that we have been living like gods in Peenemünde, enjoying its natural beauty, and eating good food and drinking fine wine, now four years into a world war. But even if the Lancasters and Halifaxes were to take that completely away, it would hardly matter because our real blessing has been the freedom to pursue our dreams. There are what, maybe two billion people on the planet? Four-fifths of them are Hottentots and Chinamen living in huts, while most of the Europeans and Americans are dead-end farmers or factory workers, not to mention the fact that thousands of them are getting slaughtered on battlefields as we speak. I can't bear the thought that one of them might take a look at us and say, those big shots with their titles and their fancy degrees and all the perks, what gives them the right to such pampered lives while the rest of us grub around like moles? Well, the answer is that we're out here risking our necks to create superweapons that won't just kill a few dozen bomber pilots but will have the power to wipe out whole countries. You're right, it's crazy, but that's precisely what shows we're worthy of everything we've got. Anything less and they'd be right in calling us leeches or drones. It also justifies how a hundred years from now when ninety-nine percent of all humans living today will be utterly forgotten the names Thiel and Waldmann will be there in the history books."

The radio cackled to life with word that the launch team was now ready for the next test firing. The Technical Director took a last sip of coffee and put his half-eaten apple back in the paper bag. "Ah, my friend, if we could escape these present circumstances and live in paradise where we would never die and never grow old, I wouldn't be getting on that radio again to tell the launch boys to aim another rocket at us, nor expect you to be here assisting me. But knowing that death awaits us one day no matter what, an eternity of annihilation, we might as well take our chances here, advance the technical knowledge of the species, and if it comes to that, know in the split second before our fiery obliteration that by surrendering our lives to the first operational ballistic missile, we will be winning glory, a hollow immortality I admit, but better than none at all."

I knew how I was going to respond, but the speech was so eloquent I felt obliged to let the words hang there in the air for a few seconds. "I'm all for glory," I said, "I just have a bigger problem than you do with the process of getting there."

Seventeen seconds before impact of the next missile, I caught a glint of sunlight in the sky and called out to the Technical Director. We both reached for binoculars but, unable to hold the object in my field of view, I followed it with the naked eye. It was above and in front of us and seemed to be coming in our direction, but I nonetheless found it difficult to make a connection between the silvery speck in the sky and anything that might happen on the ground. At nine seconds–the Technical Director was calmly proceeding with the countdown–I thought I could make out the harlequin markings on the missile's skin, though its descent at almost Mach 2 should have precluded this degree of visual acuity. What I am certain about is that at four seconds, I could see the missile somersault and then explode in a shower of sparkles that gently fell to Earth like the burnt embers from a fireworks display.

"Excellent!" shouted the Technical Director. "We got one! Did you note the wobble as the skin peeled off nose to tail?"

"I didn't see the skin come off, and wasn't it more of a somersault than a wobble?"

"Somersault? No, I didn't see that, though I guess you could see a big enough wobble as a somersault."

"And wasn't it more of a starburst than an unpeeling?"

We went back and forth like this for several minutes, neither of us wanting to admit that our observations were basically inconclusive.

The Technical Director ordered another launch. At this point there was a new temptation to resist: the idea that as long as I could see the rocket coming in my direction, it would always veer off or explode at the last instant. (This was, of course, a corollary to the false belief that death will never take the exact form one expects.) Despite my determination not to be seduced by this false I hope, I channeled every ounce of physical strength into my eyeballs, which strained to the point of aching as they attempted to resolve a tiny dot in the late afternoon glare. And behold, my efforts were rewarded with another sighting! I locked my gaze onto the rocket and followed it down as if my line of vision were the very guide beam. Together we watched its immolation as it descended straight-arrow, nose-first into a stand of birch trees less than half a mile away, sending up an almost perfectly spherical ball of smoke and fire. Of course, the successful flight of this A-4 was a waste of time and effort as far as we were concerned because it would tell us nothing about the sixty percent of missiles that were failing. The Technical Director immediately ordered another firing, but the launch team said it would be dark before they could ready the next missile, and so, having accomplished virtually nothing on our first day out, we left the synagogue and returned to our base.

When we arrived back there, we learned the resolution of the day's one outstanding mystery. It turned out the missile that seemed to have vanished had gone rogue and scored a direct hit on an SS R&R facility, killing several officers who were there in the courtyard for mid-day calisthenics and axe practice. So the Technical Director's joke about destroying Gestapo headquarters was not so far off the mark, though since it was merely an SS recreational facility, its destruction had no immediate effect on our testing program. The next day the Technical Director and I were out there again observing rockets, but when news of the accident reached Speer later in the week, he ordered our immediate withdrawal from the site and, as we learned subsequently, gave General D. a thorough dressing down for putting two of his top people in harm's way. We were replaced by several highly competent but non-essential personnel who over the next two months were able to collect for us a wealth of useful data, while suffering only a handful of fatalities.

CHAPTER 11
THE GOLEM

Sometime during the summer of 1944, the Technical Director returned from a reconnaissance mission he had undertaken in hopes of identifying prisoners—"detainees" we called them—who might possess skills we could put to good use on the A-4 production line at the Mittelwerk, our vast underground factory in Thuringia. We were especially keen to find mechanical engineers, electricians, metal workers, and chemists. Within an hour of landing at the Peenemünde West airfield, he called me to his office to discuss his findings. We reviewed the files of a couple dozen promising candidates until the Technical Director picked up one folder, set it down on the desk, and walked to the door to make sure it was locked. When he came back, he handed it to me and, lowering his voice to a hoarse whisper, said, "Here's one from a batch of detainees just arrived from a camp in the east on the verge of being overrun." The notation on the tab was a letter followed by a long number, but when I flipped it open, I read the name "Jakob Shlomo Korvo." My first thought was, what an ugly middle name, no wonder I never heard him say it. My second was, Korvo? My Korvo? I looked up at the Technical Director. "Yes. I'm certain it's the same man. You knew he was a Jew, of course. Seems he was teaching mathematics at a private school in Katowice when he was arrested, though as you can see he also has some experience working in industry, and we both know that once upon a time he dabbled in amateur rocketry. He could be a real asset to us down there. I'm going to see if I can get him some special treatment, maybe a job that lets him come up for a breath of fresh air every now and then."

The news that Korvo was in the Mittelwerk induced a momentary feeling of nausea. Since the beginning of the year, I had made two or three trips there to troubleshoot problems with components for the guidance system which continued to be the Achilles heel of the whole program. As much as I tried to focus on the technical aspects of the task at hand, I could not help but be aware of the sub-optimal working conditions in the tunnels, which were damp, chilly, and dimly lit. Because work continued round the clock on two twelve-hour shifts, there was the constant din of heavy machinery. The skilled German workers could at least leave at the end of their shifts, but most of the detainees were housed, if that's the word, in underground barracks furnished the wooden bunks four levels high with straw for mattresses. Latrines were oil drums cut in half with a two-by-four across the top and despite the chlorine dumped on them every so often, dysentery, typhus, and tuberculosis were rampant, carrying off several hundred men a month.

Conditions had improved somewhat on my last visit in late spring — there was even a movie house for the Kapos and block captains — but the daily lives and demeanor of the general population were basically unchanged. Despite the constant harangues and death threats from the guards, the detainees moved about their tasks like robots at speeds several rpms below the human norm. Worst of all were the slack expressions on their faces, like death itself gazing objectively back at life, which I went out of my way to avoid looking at, despite the perverse temptation to satisfy my curiosity about the nature of absolute suffering.

In the end, although both of us wanted to do something for Korvo, I urged the Technical Director to proceed with the utmost caution. We agreed that at this juncture the Technical Director should ask only that Korvo be allowed to wear civilian clothes instead of the standard issue striped uniform so that his motivation for high quality workmanship might be enhanced.

In early November I had to make another trip down to Thuringia to sort out problems with the gyro accelerometer, the device that controlled Brennschluss and thus the missile's glide path to its target. When I arrived at the factory, the Kommandant was not in his office but his batman had instructions to take me to where he'd been called to deal with an issue on the main production line. It was shut down and the prisoners were standing in neat rows three deep beside the unfinished rockets. Before one of these stood a tall thin man in an SS colonel's uniform looking down at a detainee who lay crumpled at his feet. In his right hand he held a revolver, and there was the faint odor of gunpowder in the air. Three other detainees were next to him standing at attention. He walked over to the first one, placed the barrel of the gun against the man's temple, and then, turning to address his audience, shouted out, "I like to see a few corpses lying about, it makes the rest of you deadbeats seem almost alive!" I flinched, expecting to hear the report of the gun, but then the Kommandant dropped his arm and called, "Dismissed!" at which point everyone, including the three detainees with him, hustled to their workstations.

I accompanied the Kommandant back to his office, which was furnished with the usual gray metal desk and chairs except for a loveseat of embroidered damask upholstery angled into a corner. He tossed his hat on the desk and fell onto the loveseat, throwing his arms and legs apart in an exaggerated gesture of exhaustion. "'That takes more out of a man than you might think!"

"I admit I wouldn't have the stomach for it myself," I said cautiously, "though, given the prevalence of sabotage, I can understand the practical necessity of maintaining —"

"Practical my ass!" he said. "Do you think I could live with myself popping them off like that just to keep this factory in tune? What do you think I am, some kind of monster?" He glared at me just long enough to cause me to reflect on the vulnerability of my own immediate situation, and then started to laugh.

"I only meant," I continued, "that any man might do the same in your position, I mean wanting to run things efficiently and to support the war effort."

He slowly arose from the loveseat and went back to his desk. "Even for the sake of victory, that little display I just put on to frighten the bourgeoisie of this place might get me a free pass to Hell. Or perhaps not."

I politely cleared my throat and suggested it was about time I turned to the business at hand, resolving issues in the mass production of guidance system components. Requesting permission to move about the factory at will, I explained that solutions were more likely to be forthcoming if I could study the guidance problem within the broader context of the entire manufacturing process. He agreed wholeheartedly and arranged for a member of his staff to escort me.

I returned to the shop floor. The chassis of a long line of A-4s sat on wheeled carts that followed a track from deep within the mountain toward the tunnel entrance. More than anything else what struck me as I walked the length of the assembly line was the unrelenting noise. I had spent a fair amount of time in factories and foundries during the past decade, but had never heard anything like this. Even if everyone spoke the same language, they would be hard pressed to conspire to make much mischief. It was as though the sound were a living force that, when it realized there was no escape from the rock walls, would return to its origin angry and vindictive.

I continued my walk down the assembly line until I came to a sign indicating the cross tunnel that housed the Guidance Section. As I entered I noticed that the noise level dropped considerably, though it was also darker and colder. The rock walls were lined with wooden workbenches strewn with wires and tools and all kinds of metal parts. Bundles of electrical cables snaked along the ceiling, and illumination was provided mainly by goose-necked lamps clamped to the benches. A dozen or so men were hunched over their work, some of them looking through magnifying lenses set on stands as they manipulated tiny components with tweezers and needle-nosed pliers. Most were civilians though there were a few detainees among them, and all seemed intent on their work. Eerily, hardly a word was spoken.

This was a far cry from the clean, modern production facility that we had been setting up in Peenemünde before the British air raid. As I walked around, I thought it was a miracle that any of the rockets coming out of this place would ever get off the ground, much less come down within twenty miles of their targets. Even a millimeter's misalignment can turn a gyro accelerometer into a worthless piece of junk. Although I was obliged by the situation to project an attitude of ruthless toughness, I couldn't help feeling a terrible empathy for these men and found myself offering gentle words of encouragement despite the fact that most of them probably didn't understand much German.

As I continued my inspection, I noticed one civilian employee who I took to be a section leader moving from bench to bench, occasionally picking up subassemblies to scrutinize the work. He was rather pasty-faced with what looked like once fat cheeks now hanging loosely on their bones. When he turned to me to answer a question about calibration tolerances, I had a not altogether unexpected shock of recognition: It was Korvo. In the back of my mind, I knew he must be down here somewhere, but to be honest, there was a part of me that was always hoping that I would never quite find him. But now I had. Of course, I had the presence of mind not to say a word, and evidently, so did he. In fact, he remained so poker-faced, conveying the same utter submissiveness to me as he would any Nazi official on a VIP tour of the operation, that I began to doubt whether or not it really was Korvo. Something about conditions in the tunnels homogenized the appearance of the workers. He looked neither happy nor sad, like a man who was content to be alive and not in any immediate discomfort right now, though that could always change. His responses to my questions were factual but not mechanical as he continued to give no hint that he had ever seen me before. After several minutes, I was forced to conclude that this was man was not Korvo, that I had deluded myself, perhaps out of a misplaced sense of guilt. I turned away, but as I did I felt a small object drop into my back pocket as a more familiar voice now croaked into me ear, "Count your dead, Arthur, they are alive!" But when I looked back at the man, my eyes were met with the same indifferent stare.

I continued with the tour and made careful notes, which I reviewed at a meeting with top managers toward the end of the day. I then settled in to the rear seat of the staff car for the all-night drive back across Germany, even ground travel by daylight now being considered too risky for our top people. Only now did I reach into my pocket and remove the object that Korvo had slipped into it. I recognized it as a piece of aluminum electrical conduit, about three inches long and perhaps half an inch in diameter. When I looked into the end, I could see paper rolled up inside. I was torn between a desire to read the contents right then and there or to throw the whole thing out the window; either action would draw the attention of my driver who I had no reason to think was not a Gestapo agent, so I casually unzipped my overnight bag and dropped it in.

After numerous delays, I returned to Peenemünde around noon the following day, Wednesday, November 8th. As I walked to my residence, I noticed that it was unusually quiet except for what sounded like loud music coming from the direction of the Hearth Room. I left my bag in my room and headed over to investigate. When I arrived there, I found a raucous celebration in progress. Champagne was flowing freely; there were platters with fancy hors d'oeuvres, and some of my colleagues had formed a chorus line and were dancing the can-can. Had the Allies capitulated overnight? Were our missiles the determining factor in the victory? Before I could figure out what was going on, someone shouted for quiet. "He's on the radio again!" It was the voice of the Propaganda Minister: "Brutal and cynical attacks of the Anglo-American air forces on the German population . . . . let not the world forget that our V-1 attacks were already for revenge . . . . today I announce that our newest and most impressive revenge weapon has come into use . . . . the brilliance of our German scientists . . . . together morale and technology will lead us to final victory!"

I spotted General D. circulating among the crowd, a drink in one hand, but seeming more subdued than the rest. When he came up to me, he said, "I'm as surprised as you are that he chose today to make the announcement. I wish we could have kept this under wraps a bit longer. We had intelligence that panic levels in London from these mysterious explosions were reaching the breaking point but now that people know what they are, even if they can't do anything to stop them, they'll go back to their keeping calm and carrying on just like during the Blitz. I suspect the Allies have already figured out the A-4's range, and now there'll be even more pressure to push the offensive in the Netherlands. Not the psychological moment I would have chosen but such decisions are above even my pay grade. Still, we're national heroes now, so we might as well savor the moment, eh?" He raised his glass and downed the contents.

Notably absent was the Technical Director. When I inquired after him, I was told that he had left early, saying that he had work he needed to do back at the office. I went over to the building whose exterior had deliberately been left unrepaired after the air raid and went inside. My footsteps echoed in the empty hallways. The Technical Director was not in his office, but I heard sounds coming from the nearby Projection Room. Light was flickering under the door, and when I pushed it open, I saw the scene in *Woman in the Moon* where the big rocket is wheeled from its assembly building to the launch site. Slouched down in a chair, arms folded across his chest sat the Technical Director. Without looking around he said, "Come on in, Arthur. I figured you'd be as thrilled by the announcement as I was."

"It's a culmination, a kind of success, no matter how you slice it," I said. "After all these years, finally some recognition. So what if we both know that a one-ton bomb that misses its target nine out of ten times isn't going to make any difference in the end, no matter how fancy the package."

"I stopped caring about the war even before Normandy." He looked over his shoulder into the darkness and then shouted at the top of his lungs, "Did you hear that, Gestapo spy, wherever you are? The war is over!" He turned back to the screen, which now showed final preparations for the moon shot. "You know what really gets me, Arthur? The presumptuousness of that bug-eyed toad taking our creation's name away. I admit, 'Aggregate-4' didn't have the ring of *Golden Hind* or *Half Moon* or even *Santa Maria*, but it was concise and to the point, and expressed the scientific spirit that we brought to the work."

I admitted that I, too, had become attached to the designation.

"Now it's Vengeance Weapon Two—V-2. A big stick in a grudge match. Plus it will always be mixed up with the V-1. They'll think we invented the jet bomb and then naturally progressed to the rocket bomb. What an insult to be associated with that piece of crap."

We continued to sit in silence. The film now showed the lunar travelers strapping themselves into their cots prior to lift-off. "I wonder if we even have the right to call ourselves scientists now, Arthur. We're Avengers. The A-4 has gone into space, all right, but it's landed on the wrong planet."

We watched the countdown and launch, followed by a technically primitive animated sequence of the rocket's translation to the moon, but concurred in switching it off after the landing, having noted in previous viewings both the unscientific representation of a moon with a breathable atmosphere and the absurd conflation of the romantic and espionage plot lines.

I accompanied the Technical Director back to his office. It turned out that having pressing business to attend to was not merely an excuse. He shuffled through the pile of papers on his desk and picked up a set of orders. "These came in this morning from Speer. He's the only clear-headed one down there. The brilliance of us German scientists notwithstanding, he knows that while we gave Montgomery a bloody nose in September, we can't keep him out of the Netherlands forever, so if we want to continue the terror campaign against London, we'll have to extend the range of the A-4. Excuse me, the V-2.'"

"The A-9," I said, "our bastardized A-4 with wings stuck on. That would give us more than enough range to launch from inside the Reich. But it's been two years since General D. yanked everybody off that one so that we could go all in on the A-4."

The Technical Director pointed to a stack of thick manila folders. "I've gone through the notes and drawings of the boys in the Special Projects Office and was reminded just how far along they'd gotten. Sure there were problems with aerodynamics and guidance, but in the past two years we've resolved a lot of those issues. Just ask London. You know, I think we've still got the capacity here to cobble together a working prototype in the next couple of months. We don't even have to start from scratch. I'll just have an A-4 pulled off the Mittelwerk assembly line and shipped up here."

"Maybe, but then there's testing and God knows how much time to re-tool for mass production. We're probably talking six months, minimum. Montgomery could be in Berlin by then. Anyway, we already know that the war is over for Germany."

And here, although I know it could not literally have happened, I saw a physical sparkle in the Technical Director's eye. "Over for Germany, perhaps, but not necessarily for us." He passed me a folder. "Recall that there were two concepts for the glider missile, unmanned and manned. A pilot reduces payload by 37% but yields a tenfold increase in accuracy. His approach to the target is subsonic and an ejection seat throws him clear of the missile before the final nosedive."

"He then parachutes into captivity in Kent or drowns in the Channel."

"Yes, and even that's sugarcoating it. His chances of surviving the ejection are probably no better than 50/50. But Arthur, you're missing my point. The war is over. The A-9 will never go into production. We know that, but they don't. All we have to do is tell them that we're working on the prototype of a piloted V-2 that will keep terrorizing London no matter what happens in the Low Countries, while what we're really building is the first vehicle that will carry a man to the edge of space. In fact, it won't be much different from a weaponized A-9—basically just a hardened crew compartment to handle the aerodynamic pressures encountered at higher altitudes."

"The Red Army now sits on the border of East Prussia. They could well make a beeline for us in the next few weeks."

"Of course, and we would be captured and sentenced to hard labor in Siberia. At best. Or maybe the Russians will head straight to Berlin and it will be worse than Stalingrad and this thing will drag on into the summer. My point, Arthur, is that this might be our last best chance at Raumschiffahrt. If we fail, we fail, but if we succeed, who knows? The mission might even turn out to be the redemption of the Reich, not that sending someone into space will defeat the Allies, but that such an accomplishment might begin atone for the A-4's reign of terror on our soon-to-be erstwhile enemies."

Leave it to a Christian, I thought, even one as theologically muddled as the Technical Director, to come up with a doctrine of manned space flight as substitutionary sacrifice. "Or at least such a demonstration of technological superiority," I offered, "combined perhaps with another bloody nose or two, might yield more favorable terms in a negotiated surrender."

For the next few hours, the Technical Director and I pored over the documentation, like two castaway pirates studying a map of buried treasure. The more we looked at it, the more we convinced ourselves that it was doable. Short of a precipitous collapse, the deteriorating military and political situation could even work to our advantage, as with the breakdown of command structures it would become easier to channel resources in our direction. So it was decided then and there that under cover of developing a manned V-2, we would actually aim for a manned sub-orbital space flight in early 1945.

My only demur was the name. "Given our limited time frame, this won't really be a new missile, but a bastardized version of the A-4. So let's call a spade a spade, and instead of A-9, designate it A-4b, the 'b' for bastard."

The Technical Director was charmed by the idea. "Yes, I like the sound of that: The Bastard."

•   •   •

It was late afternoon by the time I returned to my quarters and unpacked my bag. There once again was the piece of electrical conduit that Korvo had slipped into my pocket. I looked inside, hoping that somehow that's all it was now, an empty pipe, but I could still see paper rolled up inside. I stuck my finger in and slid it out. I then unrolled two sheets of onion skin, every square inch of which, front and back, had been covered with what I recognized as Korvo's cramped but surprisingly precise and legible handwriting. For several minutes I stared at the sheets without reading a word, paralyzed with fear. I knew that the penalty for a prisoner attempting to communicate with the outside world was summary execution; I assumed something not much better for his correspondent. I also knew that the proper thing to have done was to have immediately reported it to the Kommandant. I could perhaps now claim that the pipe had been surreptitiously slipped into my pocket (true) without my realizing it (false), and that I only discovered the object when I returned home (also false), but since I found this account somewhat implausible, I assumed the Gestapo would, too.

From an ethical perspective, not looking at the contents was tantamount to ignoring the cries for help of a drowning man. But if no one else were around, and the man drowned, who would ever know? Yes, but going that route would require a certain ruthless toughness that some of my colleagues might possess, but not I. As a spiritual weakling, my fear of everlasting guilt nearly equaled my fear of punishment by the authorities. If we were to lose the war, as I expected, what if against all odds Korvo survived his time in the Mittelwerk and we were to cross paths again in Germany or whatever strange country (Bolivia? New Zealand?) the gods, who like nothing more than irony, would have us both emigrate to? That would be an awkward reunion. Moreover, helping Korvo now might earn me a powerful character witness in the event that my colleagues and I were hauled up before some Allied kangaroo court after our surrender.

So it was that out of a blend of cowardice and self-interest, I allowed my eyes to focus on the page. As I considered anew Korvo's desperate situation, I now felt like an acolyte of some dark rite who doubted that he was worthy to read the words of a man who, even if through no intentional acts of his own, was living an intensity of human experience that made my own relatively comfortable existence seem a kind of death-in-life. Nothing connected with my pursuit of the heavens by mechanical means had ever made me feel like such a worm. Knowing that its contents could bring me no peace, I began to read:

"So many preliminaries to attend to! Of course, I don't want to leave anyone out. Let me begin, then, with a few words addressed to the little shit of an SS private or corporal who finds this letter despite my best efforts to keep it hidden. Don't turn your head to look around! Yes, it's you I'm talking to. I know all about you, Hans or Franz or Fritz or Helmut. You were the fellow who struggled with the school lessons that I breezed through, and for whom I was foolish enough to feel embarrassment as you stammered through the recitation. Normally you would have gone on to some dull factory job, gotten into an occasional brawl at the local tavern, and more or less accidentally bred a couple of ugly children, but unfortunately for me, these have not been normal times. It seems that Mr. Zeitgeist has thrown up a big nobody who has decided that if all the little nobodies like yourself could be banded together they might give the illusion of adding up to a somebody! Imagine that! The life of somebody like you could have meaning! Do you know what that is? Of course not. But it's fun to wear a uniform and go marching with your buddies, and

whenever the smallest unhappy feeling comes into that vacuity that, in someone like me, is where the soul resides, you get to lash out in as violent a manner as you could wish. Yes, you would have to think twice about killing me, but no more than that!

Well, enough time spent on Hans and Franz. (Would you believe that it took me five days to write the preceding paragraph? In some ways, what a waste of effort for someone in my position, having to steal every moment from watchful eyes even to scratch down a word, and all on penalty of death! But as I say, the preliminaries must be attended to in any good treatise.) Now I should move on to the intermediate echelons: the junior and senior officers whose eyes might read this as it moves up the chain of command. But I won't, for the reason that you differ in degree but not in kind from your front line subordinate. Which is to say you are also shits, a little bigger, yes, but still compounded out of the same brownish-black smelly offal. Nothing personal here; you'll agree that a man in my position would be technically remiss if he described his tormentors as anything more than the absolute lowest order of biological existence. No, I think the time (time: in some ways I have more of that now than I could ever have imagined, I feel practically immortal. For example, it's now six days since I began this parenthesis, so relentless has been the surveillance. But I am infinitely patient, (I'm not going anywhere, so what's the rush?) the time has arrived to say greetings to Herr Kommandant himself. We've never been formally introduced, though you've certainly seen my number on a roll call or two, and you know about me, or at least, about workers like me who have passed a few of your tests to move up to 'advanced' positions on the line. My name is blah, blah, blah, you don't have time for such finer points, and frankly, neither do I. I have listened to some of your harangues, and along with what I've heard through the camp grapevine, know you to be a man of finer sensibilities. Last week when you fired a Luger into the side of a detainee's head (don't you appreciate my use of the correct administrative term for the likes of me?) you said that sabotage was giving lie to the absolute truth of German power. I always like a rationale for summary execution that includes something of a philosophical edge. Though I wonder, if German power is absolute, how could sabotage even be possible? In fact, how could I even have the will to write the absurd letter to you (well, not to you per se, but as I said, the preliminaries must be attended to!). Well, you're a smart fellow, you could explain it to me, I suppose if you wanted to bother, though I doubt you'd even let me live that long. (You might start explaining, and then I might look at you the wrong way, and you'd kill me on the spot, and then regret that you'd even wasted that much time.) In some ways, you are the biggest shit of all, but I suspect that you might be, as it were, only papered over with shit, that underneath there might be something, if not like me, at least more than the pack of automata that you command. When you read these words, and realize how hyperconscious I am of my and your situation, you won't just ball the paper up, and throw it away and say 'just kill the bastard,' but you'll want to think carefully about my demise. Maybe you'll see this as some kind of battle of wills between us; perhaps given your formidable intellect, you will see this as an opportunity for instruction, of myself, and certainly of my fellow inmates. At all events, with each sentence I eke out, I am making your life a little more complex. I want you to know that I fully appreciate even the small additional burden I am adding to your, well, existence (I know how problematic that word 'life' is for you!).

But let me now turn to my intended audience. (Don't get too excited here, Kommandant, I'm not going to be revealing any names.) I intend to speak to: the outside world. Is there still an outside? Once every two weeks myself and many of my surviving colleagues are marched out one end of the tunnel to a building where we are sprayed with cold water and disinfectant. Sometimes it is day, sometimes night. I mention this only because inside we seem to have slipped onto some 25 or 26 hour cycle, and whenever I go out I am always completely surprised by the position of the relevant heavenly bodies. Anyway, though the grounds of a Konzentrationslager are no royal park, there is fresh air, a breeze, the occasional scent of wildflowers. I dream about these things underground, and to be honest, I find that the fictional rendering in my head is actually superior to what I experience outside. So lately I have come to the point of wanting to skip these excursions altogether. (Note to Kommandant: the anonymity you impose on the detainees is such that after a while we appear interchangeable to even the most conscientious of guards, and so it has been fairly easy for me to barter my exit pass to other men for things I consider more important. A little individual identity in camp, even though it undermines somewhat the dystopian vision you've created here, would promote tighter security.) My sense of the world beyond Germany has become similarly fictionalized. I am sure that if this moment I could be transported to London or New York to meet actual human beings working for the Allied cause I would become completely disillusioned with their moral and ethical characters. I would discover that the most high-minded among them has some very mercenary reasons for 'doing good,' I mean in the sense of satisfying one ego drive or another. But down here in the tunnels, I certainly have no reason not to believe that an ideal reader of this missive might actually be moved by this rather oblique personal testimony, and led to do something that could shorten the reign of all this evil by even a second. (Yes, indeed, life as a slave has taught me that there's no such thing as 'the long run' or 'the big picture.' Those boil down to excuses to do nothing.)

Speaking of doing something or nothing. In the midst of all this moralizing I almost forgot the real purpose of my death-defying (or less melodramatically) death-deferring missive. It's to let you know that I've been up to something these last several months. I can tell you about it now because even if the Germans don't kill me, I feel that I'm reaching the end of my endurance, and am still vain enough to wish that someone somewhere might remember me, or failing that, Herr Kommandant, at least that I could forever haunt the consciousness of my tormentor. (For the record, I do believe in an immortal soul, dividual or otherwise, so when I say 'forever', I mean it in an old-fashioned picturesque sort of way, like you down in the seventh or eighth circle of Hell, up to your neck in a lake of fire, with a little unappeased fragment of my spirit [most of which sits contentedly contemplating the big rose in the Paradiso], lacerating your exposed flesh like an angry hornet equipped with a cat 'o nine tails on each of his appendages. Or something of that order, as my library at present doesn't include Dante's text.) Funny, but isolated as I am down here,

I feel less and less dividual every day. In fact, I'm getting unbelievably connected in both space and time, in ways I never would have thought. Judaism, for example. It's what got me into the lager system, but to be honest, it's been a much bigger deal to my keepers than it has been to me, until recently anyway. But somehow working on these big death machines I got to thinking about the old story of the medieval Prague Rabbi, and how he saved the Jews of that town from a pogrom. In retrospect, the salvational aspect of the story seems a bit droll to someone in my circumstances, as you might well imagine. (An ancestor was saved so that one day I might be born and made to suffer extermination with most of my co-religionists? That was a good deal?) But the method of defense was both ingenious and prescient. He fashioned an artificial man out of clay who was impervious to whatever weaponry was brought against him. To put this in contemporary terms, the creature, who was named Golem, was a one man Panzer, and unleashed on the heathen (I mean Christians; slip of the tongue there), he destroyed their forces in no time. Unfortunately, this Semitic Berserker went a little out of control afterward, and the rabbi had a devil of a time getting him to behave again. I don't think it ended happily for Golem, as neither would it for Dr. Frankenstein's creature, who was compounded out of the Jewish predecessor some centuries later. Anyway, for months I had been working on these rockets, feeling pretty bad about how I was making a weapon that could only delay my liberation (this was back when I could still believe in such a thing), and always trying to find some way or another to sabotage them. I got quite good at this, at least, I was never caught. Probably half the rockets that passed under my hands had some flaw sufficient to insure that they would probably never come within ten miles of their intended targets. But this was still merely a defensive strategy, and one that I knew others were also pursuing, if the frequent executions of saboteurs less clever than I was any evidence. I really understood these mechanisms, having worked with rockets in the early days with the Technical Director and his associates when the Technical Director was hardly more than a school boy. (Hello, TD! Hope life is treating you well!) I realized that if I were patient enough, slowly and incrementally I could re-work these guidance mechanisms so that they would not only fail to reach their intended targets, but instead hit targets that I intended for them. Of course, my success rate has probably been small, but for the past several weeks, a number of rockets have left here that I have re-programmed as 'Golems.' A few seconds after launch my Golem program will take command of the rocket, and instead of going off to London, it will turn tail and head to Berlin, or one of several other choice destinations inside the Reich.

Well, it's time for me to bid my audiences, intended and otherwise, a fond farewell. To the big and little shits who may have intercepted this note, I want to thank you for expanding the range of what I thought humanly possible. Were my imagination as an individual suddenly projected to that of an entire culture, I admit that never in a million years would I have come up with a place like the Mittelwerk. Herr Kommandant, you and your colleagues have realized the vision that I suppose was latent in Descartes, that nightmarer of modernity. At this point, I may indeed only exist because I think; there's really not much else left to me of existence. Working under present conditions it seems that every day another body part falls off or fails (I lost an ear lobe just this morning); yes, it's only so much protoplasm, yet I feel spiritually diminished. Isn't that odd? But there you have it. My will lingers on, though, like a patient with a debilitating, but non-fatal disease. Honest to God, I wasn't thinking about this at all when I was creating the Golems, but it occurs to me now that even after I am dead (which even now I hope will be very soon) these monsters of my imagination and technical ingenuity will lend my will a certain immortality, don't you think? It will be utterly destructive, yes. Who knows how many innocent children will be murdered by one of my rogue missiles crashing into some Berlin neighborhood. But you can take some solace in knowing that I learned this kind of bloodthirsty indifference from you Nazis, so in that respect I remain a subject to your conquest. My warmest congratulations.

And now to the reader on the outside for whom I have scratched this out in blood, both figuratively and literally (though certain parts of the text have benefitted from the admixture of some graphite which

I managed to steal). First, Eli, Eli lama, etc., etc. Let's set aside for the moment the fact that dozens of us die horrible deaths every day in this hellhole. My suffering alone has been enough to fill two or three universes with pain, and you have gone on about your business instead of throwing everything aside to come and rescue me. Yes, I'm sure your life has been disrupted by the war, too, and no doubt even the most ambitious plan would probably have been doomed to failure, but everywhere up and down the camp grapevine the word is that nothing, nothing, nothing was ever done to help us, not even a lousy stray bomb. I don't know how you could live with yourself all this time; for me a suicide mission ending in a futile death charging the electrified razor wire that surrounds the camp would have been welcome relief from the pain of guilt. But it's easy for me to say that, and I'm sure that were I in your position I would have done the same hand-wringing and felt the same pity. You shit. Second, I do ask that you let the world know that the occasional missile that developed a mind of its own and decided to head home to Germany instead of popping over to England was not an accident. I gave it that mind, and let me tell you, it wasn't easy. This may not be as simple a request as it sounds, because of course there will be no official account of such a happening. One way or another such random acts of destruction will be blamed on Allied bombing. But somebody somewhere will have caught a glimpse of the rocket on its free fall, and a set of tail fins from a missile whose warhead failed to detonate will end up in a backyard in Charlottenburg or wherever, and a soldier home on leave will recognize it for what it is and the rumors will circulate. I expect you will have to do some travelling around to collect and document these happenings, but you may have a good deal of time on your hands in the postwar years, if not sooner, then later, and you will do this for me. Third, an observation and a prophecy. Neither Hitler's A-4s nor my Golems will have a significant impact on the outcome of the war. When you've been forced to live and breathe rocket for as long as I have, you come to know your machine as, if not a friend, at least a next door neighbor, maybe the quiet widower who scowls at you when he comes out to pick up his newspaper and who you suspect of having murdered his wife. The rocket has consumed the best technical minds in Germany and many of her scarce materials to the point that after the war, rocket men may actually claim to have been helping the Allied cause by denying these resources to tank or aircraft production. I wouldn't put it past them. But as a weapon, take my word for it, in its current form, it's a complete abortion. Millions of man hours to do with a ton of dynamite what even an inexperienced bomber crew can do ten times over in a few minutes. Given another five or ten years of development, it will be a different story. My Golems will demonstrate a significant improvement over the accuracy achieved by the garden variety A-4s, and I'm a malnourished slave working alone in a tunnel. Imagine what I might have been able to do working in a proper facility under peacetime conditions. Either America or Russia will eventually be heir to all that Germany has done. Who knows which one will get to Mittelwerk first, but if nothing else, the war has taught them complete amorality, and the winner of this prize will soon figure out that an improved rocket with a more powerful bomb like the one Heisenberg proposed back in the thirties will mean the extermination of all opposition. I am convinced of such an Armegeddon. And then (oh, why can't I just accept the complete depravity of the human species?) people will be so horrified at the result that no one for generations will even want to think about rockets. So ironically, my adolescent dream of rockets into space will actually have been retarded by efforts to push development at all cost, which meant involving the military forces of a dictatorship during the most brutal war in history.

How strange to be alive thinking about how your words will still be talking after you've been annihilated. Morituri te salutant! Residually yours, B385620."

In the encroaching Baltic darkness, I found myself staring blankly out a window at a laboratory building that had been deliberately left in ruins after the British air raid. I was struggling to suppress an impulse to order a car and driver and head straight back to the Mittelwerk where I would probably have enough sway with the Kommandant to have him order Korvo's immediate release from the tunnels on the grounds that it has just been discovered he possessed highly specialized skills that could be better put to use here in

Peenemünde. Or would I? Whatever his growing cynicism about the war effort, he had not likely been promoted to his position by bending the rules on personnel matters involving enemy aliens. What if he called my bluff? Korvo would not be freed and I might end up down there working beside him.

I next considered approaching the Technical Director. I trusted him absolutely, so there was no concern about showing him the letter, but the Technical Director could be an effective agent for good only as long as his loyalty to the regime remained above suspicion. Was the good intention of one man really an effective expenditure of his moral capital? Even if the Technical Director agreed to some kind of Korvo rescue, in good conscience I would probably end up counseling against it, lest this second intervention on his behalf (after asking that he be allowed to wear civilian clothes) begin to attract the attention of the Gestapo. Again, Korvo would not be released and now the whole rocket program might come tumbling down around us, including the proposed Raumschiffahrt, which I sincerely believed to be a much greater good.

Indeed, while I was haunted by the thought that something truly awful might happen to Korvo in the next hour or minute as I sat there in my room, I also wondered if it was fair to me to be expected to worry about him all the time. Hadn't we already stuck our necks out for him? He could have been shivering in a ragged, lice-infested prison uniform but instead he was dressed as well, or better than, his German co-workers. I'm only a human being. Didn't God owe it to me (if not to Korvo) to let Korvo endure to the almost imminent Allied victory? As I reconsidered it, maybe that hypothetical postwar meeting in Berlin or La Paz or Auckland should not be so awkward after all. It was as likely as not that Korvo knew through the prison grapevine that his "friends" at Peenemünde had intervened on his behalf. The wholly uncharacteristic embrace that he would give me when the fates brought us together on a city street in the southern hemisphere would be an expression of his deepest gratitude. Of course I would make heartfelt apologies for not having done more, but Korvo would cut me off, telling me that in the last analysis, war was all about survival, and he had survived.

But really, now, was it reasonable to think that the Korvo I knew would show such generosity of spirit? I switched on a lamp and carefully re-read the letter a dozen times and began to feel irritated by its alternating pathetic and presumptuous tone. It occurred to me that Korvo was not entirely blameless in this affair. He could have just walked away from rocketry circa 1931 if he had any inkling that even his independent research might contribute to the re-armament of a genocidal nation-state. He was educated, his family was solidly bourgeois, he had options. Yes, being a Jew might have eventually tripped him up, but that alone probably would not have gotten him sent to the Mittelwerk. He might have just been shipped east in an ordinary transport of Jews to what *in November 1944* [emphasis mine] I had little reason to believe was anything other than a straightforward resettlement program.

The more I reflected on the letter's contents, the more I could see the same old selfish, self-absorbed Korvo coming through. I grant that there was an element of altruism in his convincing amnesia act. Had he left it at that, I would have been saved from the horns of my current moral dilemma, not to mention my feelings of guilt seeing a former friend down there rotting away in the tunnels. But no, he had to throw it all away with a gesture as melodramatic as it was ineffectual. Did he think that now because he was suffering he was supposed to become a writer? It all showed a serious defect of character.

A final consideration was this: I knew that Korvo had an impish side. The last time I had encountered him living underground, he was prepared to risk his life being shot off in a rocket to mock the Christian holiday of Pentecost. What if Korvo, after delivering his little treatise to me, had decided to free himself via suicide which given all the toxic compounds he worked around would be relatively easy. How highly amused would the dead Korvo be at the thought of his erstwhile rocket companions tying themselves in knots and risking their lives to animate the machinery of a brutal and disintegrating bureaucracy to save a man who, by the time all the paperwork had been signed off on, no longer even existed.

I now began to feel more at peace as I realized that the best course of action for all parties concerned was also the most sensible, which was for the time being to do nothing, nor to mention a word of it to anyone. I again looked down at the letter in the circle of light created by the goose-necked desk lamp that had followed me since my days as a schoolboy in Koblenz. The document was quite a work of art. I had never seen a piece of paper so thoroughly covered with text from edge to edge such that at arm's length it looked like a monochromatic arabesque carved in wood rather than scratched out on paper. I could imagine hiding it away and giving it back to him on that future day in Auckland — what a surprise! — or in the more likely event of his death donating to one of the inevitable museums built to commemorate the heroism of the war's many victims. But these prospective good deeds didn't come close to balancing out the risk associated with holding on to it. No place on person or property was safe from the prying eyes of the Gestapo, not even the most remote and deserted stretch of Usedom's beaches. Besides, after reading it over and over I had committed it to memory, an autonomic process in the amygdala of someone who as a boy had memorized whole tractates of the Zohar. There was also no denying that like the Zohar itself, Korvo's text had the fervid quality of a spiritual cri de coeur, words inscribed in black fire upon white fire. I despaired that I would never be able to forget a single tittle.

There was no reason to agonize further about what to do. I shredded the letter into a coffee mug and dropped a match in. The contents were so combustible that all was reduced to ash in ten seconds. I ran a little water in and poured it down the drain.

CHAPTER 12
IN THE CATHEDRAL

With the exception of some junior colleagues working on the Wasserfall anti-aircraft missile, by late December 1944 nearly everyone at Peenemünde, and certainly all of the top people, had been mobilized to bring the A-4b project to fulfillment as soon as possible. We were proceeding on two tracks simultaneously, the unmanned and manned versions, possible because about 90% of the components were common to both, the main difference, of course, being the cramped crew compartment in the latter. But as far as I knew, only the Technical Director and I understood that the manned A-4b—which in our private conversations we invariably referred to as The Bastard—was being readied for Raumschiffahrt and not merely a piloted test flight to assess its effectiveness as a cruise missile, essentially a rocket-powered V-1.

A few days after Christmas around 11:00 p.m., I received a call from the Technical Director summoning me to his office. There was nothing unusual about this as he customarily kept late hours and thought these were the times when his best ideas came to him. When I arrived, I was resigned to hearing some elegant solution to one of the many technical problems with The Bastard still bedeviling us, but instead I found him in a pensive mood, seated at his desk, upon which were two Bibles and what I immediately recognized as a Hebrew dictionary. He gestured for me to sit as he continued scribbling some notes, and then, setting down his pencil, asked me, "Have you ever read the Book of Daniel?"

Although my grandmother considered Daniel a generically incoherent agglomeration of late Second Temple writings of inferior literary quality, and therefore canonically suspect, she also recognized the book's place of honor in later kabbalistic tradition on account of its hero's extraordinary powers of dream interpretation. Because Daniel was more a visionary than a prophet, and therefore not obligated by God to publicize the content of his divine inspirations, he was allowed to perceive his visions with greater clarity and intensity than even Ezekiel. In addition, the Zohar explains that "Son of Man," the honorific title given Daniel in the book, presents him as an amalgam of both human and divine attributes—another embodiment of Adam Kadmon and the Twelve *Sephirot*—and in that respect a physical interface between God and Man. Given my grandmother's easy commerce across this divide, I always felt that she had the luxury of indifference to a text that admittedly the rabbis had sound aesthetic and theological reasons for consigning to what she called the "remainder bin" at the back of the Bible. But to the extent that Daniel was a portrait of the spiritually defective soul who nonetheless achieves divine insight, the book absorbed my attention from an early age. Later on, as I began to reflect more and more on my role in Raumschiffahrt, I also began to value the book for its many pronouncements on messiahship.

"I must have read it in one of the mandatory religion classes in boarding school," I said, which was probably true. "The lion's den, the handwriting on the wall. That's about it."

"I believe in God, that goes without saying, but as a scientist, it's obvious that a lot of what's in the Bible is childish superstition," the Technical Director continued. "Still, considering what we're going through in the world today, we can't dismiss any possible source of wisdom, and going back to the Bible now, I'm amazed at what I'm finding. Not the fairy tale stuff we remember from our school days but the prophecies about kingdoms and empires in the later chapters. Here, take a look at this," he said, turning the German Bible toward me and pointing to some verses in chapter eleven:

"And the king shall do according to his will; and he shall exalt himself, and magnify himself above every god, and shall speak marvellous things against the God of gods, and shall prosper till the indignation be accomplished: for that which is determined shall be done. Neither shall he regard the God of his fathers, nor the desire of women, nor regard any god: for

he shall magnify himself above all. But in his estate shall he honour the God of forces."

"A ruler who worships only the God of forces. Remember our last meeting at the Wolfsschanze? 'What I want is annihilation-annihilating effect!' Then there's this," he said indicating another passage:

"And at the time of the end shall the king of the south push at him: and the king of the north shall come against him like a whirlwind, with chariots, and with horsemen, and with many ships; and he shall enter into the countries, and shall overflow and pass over. He shall enter also into the glorious land, and many countries shall be overthrown: but these shall escape out of his hand, even Edom, and Moab, and the chief of the children of Ammon. He shall stretch forth his hand also upon the countries: and the land of Egypt shall not escape. But he shall have power over the treasures of gold and of silver, and over all the precious things of Egypt: and the Libyans and the Ethiopians shall be at his steps. But tidings out of the east and out of the north shall trouble him: therefore he shall go forth with great fury to destroy, and utterly to make away many. And he shall plant the tabernacles of his palace between the seas in the glorious holy mountain; yet he shall come to his end, and none shall help him."

"The Führer invaded many countries and now may be coming to his end," I said with as much conviction as I could muster, "but this is all about countries in the Middle East hundreds of years ago. It's hard to see the relevance to today,".

"Arthur, you're not getting it. It's all prophetic and allegorical. Egypt could be France; Edom and Moab might be Sweden and Finland. I'm wrestling with the numerology now to try to get clarity on this which is why I've also consulted the Hebrew Bible. You know, in Hebrew the letters represent numbers, so every word has a numerical value. The main thing is that with the collapse of the mightiest empire the world has ever known, I think we're living through the pageant of cosmic events foretold by Daniel–'the time of the end.' We may be on the cusp of some kind of fundamental change in the relationship between the human and the divine. Naturally, there are messianic expectations. And here we are perhaps just weeks away from sending the first human being into space. Do you think that's a coincidence? I don't, Arthur, and I could never forgive myself if we failed to acknowledge the signs that God has presented to us. Raumschiffahrt may well be tantamount to Jacob wrestling with the angel, or Jesus rising from his tomb."

"Assuming that's true, what difference does that make to The Bastard's development program? Do we need to put some kind of radar on it that can pick up angels?"

The Technical Director either ignored or was oblivious to my attempt at mild sarcasm. "If I thought we could come up with such a device in the next few weeks I would," he replied. "No, the reason I called you over here is that my growing awareness of the theological dimension of Raumschiffahrt has put me on the horns of a dilemma. Who shall ride The Bastard?"

At that moment all I could think of was how my years of seeking personal fulfillment by attaining the Heavenly Academy through unconventional means, and of struggling with doubts about whether or not I had the leading role in this radical transformation of relations between the human and the divine, now came down to this. Messianic expectations, indeed. Who had been more deeply committed to the life of the spirit than I? By the age of eight I was being conducted into the mysteries of the Zohar and later had mastered the new discipline of aerospace engineering only as means to achieve a metaphysical end. The Technical Director, as far as I could tell, was a boy like so many others, whose interest in machines had never extended much beyond the operations of the mechanisms themselves. Like an heir who could trace his spiritual origins from princes of the blood, did not I have a better purchase on the throne than some claimant descended from the minor nobility? Yet perhaps the Technical Director's unexpected and burgeoning interest in theology was the salient fact here. For a brilliant yet spoiled and superficial young engineer to have grown spiritually in such a short time—might that not be the sign of divine election in this case?

"Why yourself, of course." The words just popped out. It was over. Done. I drowned in the wave of enforced relief that washes over anyone who runs up the white flag of unconditional surrender.

"I am the logical choice, aren't I," observed the Technical Director matter-of-factly. "We've known one another a long time, so you understand that I speak without egoism when I say that nobody understands the soul of the rocket in all its manifolds more intimately than I. And although I fear death as much or more than the next man, being killed in the rocket bothers me even less than the prospect of being killed by the rocket back at Blizna. I would be much happier to die in an A-4 than to rot away from cancer in some hospital ward at the end of the twentieth century. I'm almost 33 — not much older than Alexander, the same age as Jesus. I would become an instant legend, not that I care, because when you come from a family like mine, you realize how cheap human fame is. Arthur, if I were a purely selfish man, I would not hesitate to throw someone from the top of a test stand to make sure I got on the first flight. But the signs are ambiguous. Is the launch of The Bastard the fulfillment of man's messianic dream, or only the first stage in a long process? God may be up there at 70 miles above the surface with a message for us, but what if He's on the moon or Mars or Alpha Centauri? What I'm trying to get at, Arthur, is that because I possess, by whatever fluke of history, the world's most comprehensive understanding of these new technologies, I am simply too valuable to risk on this first step. The chances of success under present conditions are uncertain, and it's only the prospect of contact with the divine that could justify such a quixotic venture. But we mortgage too many future projects to this one if I am the pilot."

The Technical Director reached over to a stack of manila folders. "For the past several days I have been going through Wehrmacht and Luftwaffe personnel files looking for just the right combination of physical, technical, intellectual, and spiritual attributes. Unfortunately, as you might imagine, dispositions in one of these areas tend to cancel out those in another. How many priests do you think there are who can fix their own radio sets? But after wrestling with this question in both my waking and sleeping hours, I've narrowed it down to two." He passed me a folder.

""The Aviatrix?" I was incredulous. "Let me say the obvious: She's a woman."

"And now I'll say the obvious: I've thought this all the way through. The fact of the matter is that she's unquestionably the best and most experienced test pilot in Germany. Although there will in fact be very little piloting involved in flying The Bastard, she has a photographic memory for everything from visual detail to physical sensation. And then there's another thing: She's already dead."

"Excuse me?"

"Not in the literal sense, of course. But since the assassination attempt back in the summer, she and a few others have been trying to organize a corps of suicide pilots to crash V-1s into heavily defended British targets. The Führer is apparently flattered at the idea, but wants to hold off until the last desperate moments of the regime for fear that it will actually boost Allied morale, knowing that we've exhausted all other expedients. As one of the originators of the idea she's somewhat in my position with regard to our own program: She's more valuable as an administrator than as a worker. There's precious little administering to do, actually, but she accepts that a figurehead is required. Nonetheless, she has thoroughly mortified herself to be in spiritual solidarity with her pilot corps. In fact, she carries a capsule of cyanide around her neck and has told me that she will swallow it the exact instant she hears news of the Führer's death. This is what I mean when I say she's already dead. Riding The Bastard may be suicidal, but from her standpoint the potential reward here is worth the risk: an heroic and symbolic act that might so awe our enemies as to preserve the Reich. The fact that she is ignorant of the potential theological dimension is irrelevant; indeed, it may actually be an advantage, since a passionate Nazi's testimony about an unexpected religious experience would be more convincing than a Christian's."

"Well, in that case I guess she's ideal," I said. It now seemed that being superseded in the attainment of Heaven by a female jet jockey might almost be bearable on the grounds that it was something no man, but only God, could have contrived.

"To be honest, my soul-searching on this matter has been less about her technical qualifications than about—" He stopped and looked away for a moment. "This is a bit awkward, you know, old bean," he continued, using the English expression. "Ever since we met ten years ago at Grunau, I've carried a torch for her. Never got very far, though. I think by now I've accepted the fact that she is like one of those warrior virgins in Wagner, a Valkyrie dedicated to the cult of flying, and how can one be jealous of that? So I don't think I am trying to kill her. Yet there's this little part of me that worries whether allowing her to climb aboard that rocket fulfills some unbelievably subconscious wish I have to get back at her for spurning me. Still, The Bastard isn't one of her buzz bombs. There's a very decent chance that whoever goes up in it might well make it back to Earth alive; a very decent chance, indeed."

I was incredulous that he did not know about the Aviatrix's barely clandestine affair with General von Greim; either that, or he knew but did not want me to know that he did.

"Anyway," the Technical Director went on, reaching for another pile, "we now come to the other candidate. He rather nonchalantly tossed me a folder. I looked at the name and broke into spontaneous laughter. "This is the funniest thing I've seen since the war started," I said. "The Bastard and The Coward. You practically have to put me in a straitjacket to board your Heinkel. I'd be utterly useless up there even if I wanted to go."

The Technical Director drew a long breath. "I know it seems odd at first, yet everything about this project is so outlandish that I'm not surprised the two top candidates for Raumschiffahrt are near polar opposites. In some ways, it actually reassures me that I'm on the right track. Of course I would never make you do this if you didn't want to, but if you need reasons I can provide them.

"I'm listening."

"First, from a purely technical standpoint, 'pilot' is a complete misnomer. The occupant of that capsule represents a totally passive element as far as flight operations are concerned. This is strictly man-in-a-can. We strap you in, and all you do is sit there for the next twenty minutes. The rocket lifts off, Brennschluss is pre-programmed, you hit the eject button, a parachute opens automatically, you drift back down to Earth. What we need is someone who understands what is going on, and who can accurately monitor his own consciousness. Given the limited state of our telemetry, there is no substitute for a human observer.

"Second, psycho-spiritual considerations weigh as heavily in this decision as do scientific ones. This is where someone like you has a real edge over the Aviatrix. You're right, when it comes to flying, you're a coward. The Aviatrix is fearless. From the time she flew a glider straight into a thunderstorm back at Grunau, to when she almost got killed testing that crappy Luftwaffe rocket plane, she always keeps her wits about her. She is always the Aviatrix. You, on the other hand, can barely maintain bladder control during a routine flight on a calm day. Imagine then how you will feel when you're accelerated past Mach 4 and vaulted so high above the Earth that you will see the stars come out at noon. Your fear will be unbelievably intense; it will be transcendental. As a practical matter, you will be so taken out of yourself that it will be as though you're still here on Earth observing a simulacrum of yourself in space, so you will have no problem maintaining control over bodily functions. Your body will simply be motoring along on its own, oblivious to 'your' fears. Trust me on this. The Aviatrix's suicide project research group has some very good human factors data here. In this condition, like high speed photographic film, your soul will be hypersensitive to even the faintest supernatural presence that might be in the vicinity. Or in more theological terms, you will be the perfect candidate for grace, having been scared shitless to the point that there will be nothing other than God to rely upon. So if God is to be encountered during Raumschiffahrt, it's as likely to happen to you as anyone."

"All the same, I still think I should wear a diaper," I said.

"Finally, there's the ethnic consideration. You're Jewish."

I began to sputter inarticulately, but the Technical Director held out the palm of his hand to my face before I could get out a word.

"As a Christian I cannot get excited about these fine genealogical distinctions that seem to obsess your people."

"My people? *My* people?"

"Arthur, let's be honest here. The Gestapo said you were a Jew, it caused a problem, we fixed it, but you're still a Jew. Nothing in the Führer's letter says you're not a Jew; he merely elects to overlook the fact given your value to the Reich. Besides, even if you're not a legally correct Jew in the mind of some rabbi, relative to anyone else working in the upper echelons of a German weapons program, you're so incredibly Jewish that you might as well go home every night, take your shoes off, and talk theology with a burning bush into the wee hours."

"You know as well as I do that I'm never going up in a rocket. Are you out of your mind? I know humor is the best medicine for stress, so is it that you find the idea of an anti-Semitic regime on the verge of collapse turning to a Jew for salvation so terribly amusing?"

The Technical Director seemed taken aback at my vehemence. "Maybe that's part of it. I remember the day at Friedrich Wilhelm when a group of Brownshirts stormed into the physics lecture where I was graduate assistant and dragged out the Jewish professor conducting the class. They held him upside down by a trouser leg over a stairwell meaning to give him a good scare when the fabric ripped and the poor devil fell four stories to his death. For several minutes afterward, you could hear his groans echoing back up the stairs. I was outraged as much at my own impotence as at the professor's murder. Of course, his tormentors walked away laughing and joking, and nothing ever happened to them. I hadn't thought about this until now, but yes, I suppose there is a kind of justice in a German rocket having a Jew as its first passenger. But to be honest, Arthur, that's not what I had in mind. I was thinking more that when mankind sent its first emissary to God, it would be appropriate if he was numbered among God's original chosen people. Also, and I hope you take this the right way, I see this mission as preliminary to a much greater project. Instead of assuming that God was going to establish Heaven on Earth, maybe we should be thinking in terms of mankind bringing Earth up to Heaven—building space stations in Earth orbit and establishing colonies on other planets. You, then, would be the forerunner, just as John the Baptist was to Jesus, and Judaism was to Christianity."

I knew the Technical Director well enough to know that when he slipped into this visionary mode, there was no point to further discussion. I told him if he wanted to keep me in the running that was his business, but that there was no way I was going up in The Bastard.

In any case, I was certain the question was moot. The light flashes on the eastern horizon grew brighter by the week, and given even the most optimistic timetable for The Bastard's development, the Russians would surely arrive long before the manned mission ever got off the ground.

The first launch of a Bastard test vehicle took place on December 27th. It began to spin on its vertical axis out of control and crashed only seconds after lift-off, flopping over on its side like a harpooned whale. By now none of our group was particularly concerned as we all subscribed to the Technical Director's philosophy of the "successful failure." A second Bastard in January came through the launch phase with flying colors though it lost a wing during re-entry, no doubt due to an easily addressed welding issue. Work also continued on a crew compartment though knowledge of this was closely held among the top people, and only the Technical Director and I knew that the goal was to send the manned Bastard into the highest possible trajectory rather than the more shallow track that would be used for the test of a glider missile weapon.

Because throughout January the Technical Director remained undecided who would go up with The Bastard — I believe he was secretly awaiting a sign from God — he undertook to prepare both the Aviatrix and me for the mission. My "training" consisted of a fitting for a pressure suit (our cover story being that my height and weight approximated that of an actual test pilot), and learning how to use a highly sophisticated Handkammer HK 12.5 cm 7.9 aerial surveillance camera. Since this was "man in a can," there wasn't much I could be trained for, although in theory a few of the systems had manual overrides. Indeed, through Brennschluss we estimated that the G-forces would basically have me pinned and immobilized in my seat. But while there was limited practical preparation, the Technical Director also provided me with a syllabus of religious books on topics like angelology and the afterlife that he strongly encouraged me to read. Most of this was pious Christian nonsense, but I did take notice of some mystical works by Balthasar Walther, an early seventeenth-century Silesian physician and distant relative of the Technical Director. Walther made several trips to Palestine where he met with followers of the renown rabbi and kabbalist, Isaac Luria. Although Walther published no works, he left behind an extensive collection of manuscripts which had been bequeathed to the Technical Director from his father's side of the family and was now in their private collection.

Although I assumed the Aviatrix was not undergoing similar religious instruction for the reasons noted earlier, she was now regularly spending two or three days a week at Peenemünde. Perhaps there was a regimen of flight training for the mission that the Technical Director had simply decided would be wasted on me. Of course, all aspects of the A-4b program, both unmanned and manned, were classified top secret, but as the Aviatrix moved around the facility, she displayed a certain prissy swagger as if to let people know that whatever she was doing here, it was of the utmost importance. She also knew as well as anyone the Reich's desperate military situation and took it upon herself to boost our morale, and so perhaps bring about the miracle that ardent supporters of the regime totally believed in, the *Endsieg*-Final Victory.

One day in mid-January I saw her, resplendent in a black acetate SS uniform, walking the hallways of the propulsion laboratory and pulling old flyers and announcements off the walls. "Have you ever seen such a mess? Look at this," she said, shoving a yellowed piece of paper under my nose, "this announcement for a chamber music concert is almost two years old! And this–a notice about new hours in the commissary that was destroyed in that awful raid! How can men be expected to focus on the *Endsieg* with all these reminders of a spurious past flapping around them every day." I politely agreed, offering the admittedly lame excuse that the hodge-podge of flyers lent the otherwise sterile environment a collegiate atmosphere that reminded the men of their university days.

"Well," she replied, tearing down a flyer announcing last month's Christmas pantomime with the disgust of a commander ripping the insignia from the uniform of a deserter before the firing squad, "this is no time for sentimentality. Germany has given us her heart and soul, and now the time has come to give it all back, and more. The only question that matters is, do our actions make a contribution to the

Endsieg? Needless clutter does not make a contribution; an orderly display of news and information does. When I informed your boss about this situation, he immediately issued an order that effective next week all announcements would have to be cleared through his office and then posted in designated areas of each building, according to their purpose, official or unofficial. I offered to begin the clean-up process in my spare time, though at the moment, I have precious little of that."

Around the 20th of January, we received official word that the Ardennes offensive had ended in failure. We were both elated and concerned: elated because we could expect that the Reich's diminishing resources would now be showered upon wonder weapons like jet planes and rockets, concerned because our success hinged on how soon the Russians, who seem to have taken a breather on the border of East Prussia, would continue their march along the Baltic. We also had the problem of increased pressure on us to improve the accuracy of the A-4s coming off the production lines at the Mittelwerk. Of the eighty percent of those making it to Brennschluss, about a third were breaking up upon re-entry and another third were landing more than a mile from their intended targets. Naturally the SS managers assumed sabotage and were becoming ever more draconian in their punishment of detainees, but every engineer in Peenemünde knew perfectly well that this is what you got when you rushed the development process.

It was in response to a Kommandant outraged at this failure rate that the Technical Director had planned to send our own Production Works chief down to Thuringia, but since he had contracted a serious case of the flu, he asked me to go instead. "I don't have to tell you that it's pretty much a charade at this point, but go through the motions and leave them with a list of technical-sounding recommendations. You know the drill."

After three nights on the road dodging rogue P-47s and P-51s hungry for targets, I arrived exhausted at the Mittelwerk, but instead of being conducted to the Kommandant's office, I was taken just down the hall to his private screening room where I found him watching an American gangster film. "Please have a seat," he called to me without turning around, "this will be over in a few more minutes." When the lights came up, he greeted me warmly and we chatted about movies for a few moments. "I tend to be an early riser and find that a good movie helps facilitate the transition between dreaming and waking life," he said. "I can usually get one in before the rest of my staff arrives in the morning. By the way, did you know the guy in that movie, Edward G. Robinson, is actually a Jew? Someone told me that just the other day. Born in Romania. It's amazing how those people turn up in places where you'd least expect it."

The Kommandant then asked me if I'd like to accompany him on his morning rounds. Although I was thoroughly sleep deprived and wanted nothing more than to lie down somewhere, it was hard not to interpret the request of an SS colonel as a direct order.

We passed along a series of metal catwalks and stairways until we reached the main factory floor. As we approached the side tunnel that housed the guidance sub-assembly section, I asked to take a look. While the lighting had improved not much else had changed. There were the same rudely made wooden tables and workbenches impossibly strewn with wires and small metal parts. I walked slowly among the workers, hands behind my back, stopping every now and then to feign interest in what they were doing. I kept an eye out for Korvo, but he was nowhere to be seen. I had a terrible sinking feeling about his absence until I remembered that there were two shifts and thus only a fifty percent chance of finding any one detainee on such a random inspection.

We returned to the main tunnel, and in another 200 yards or so entered the largest chamber in the factory. Here the ceiling rose to a height of more than fifty feet so that the rocket could be set upright in its launch position. Indeed, only in this vertical attitude could certain final calibrations be made to the guidance system. The last time I had visited here, strings of bare light bulbs dangled from jagged rock outcroppings. Now the contours of the tunnel had been smoothed so that as the walls rose up they converged concentrically to form a great domed chamber. In the cupola at the top was what looked like a small roseate window, illuminated from behind. About halfway up the sides of the dome, the tracks of two huge overhead cranes used to raise and lower the missiles were visible. Apse-like recesses on opposite sides of the tunnel provided additional space for various fabrication and testing activities.

The Kommandant beamed. "It's quite remarkable, isn't it? Quotations of Gothic architecture here in an underground rocket factory run by slaves in the midst of a war. Immediately after renovations in this section were completed, everyone began referring to it as The Cathedral. Of course, it's not only the space that's awe-inspiring but what it contains. As you can see, when one of your rockets is set up, people can hardly restrain themselves from sneaking furtive looks. We used to beat the prisoners for slacking off until we realized how effective a tool for discipline it was, impressing these people, especially the Jews, with a sense of their own insignificance, relative to the accomplishments of the Reich. Of course, it's still technically a violation of the rules to stop and look, but the punishment now is rarely more than a slap or a kick.

I pointed toward the cupola. "Is that sunlight up there coming through the window?" The Kommandant laughed. "The detainees have been led to think so, but it's another 200 feet through solid rock to reach the surface. That's actually a special floodlight with a visual spectrum very similar to that of—" His explanation was broken off by the arrival of an officer who saluted and asked to speak with him. They stepped aside for a few moments and when the Kommandant returned, he explained that our inspection tour would have to be interrupted briefly for a mass execution, though of course he did not use those words, calling it instead a "collective judicial action." That very morning his internal security team had completed an investigation of suspected troublemakers and were bringing them in for punishment. He was apologetic and even a bit sheepish. "Although conditions have improved here in recent months, I do not want to give you a false impression. This is no paradise, and occasional displays of brute force are still necessary to maintain order."

As he said this, guards began barking orders at the detainees who now formed themselves into phalanxes several rows deep on all sides of the rocket. When they were in place, other guards marched in a line of twelve men, hands tied behind their backs, burlap bags over their heads. Cardboard signs hung around their necks indicating their respective crimes: "slacker," "saboteur," "thief," and so on. The eerie silence was now broken by the whirr of a powerful electric motor as one of the track cranes lowered a pair of steel cables with hooks on the end. To these were attached a long wooden beam supporting a dozen nooses which were then fitted snugly around each prisoner's neck.

The Kommandant confided to me, "I don't hate these men. We probably would have done some of these same things were we in their position. I'm not anxious to rob these men of their remaining years, but we really don't have a choice, do we?"

The question seemed oddly sincere, and I realized he expected an answer. All I could think at that moment was how, as far as the Gestapo was concerned, I was still a Jew.

"The operative term here is not choice but necessity," I said cautiously. "Germany is in a struggle for its survival, and toward that end, it needs the rocket. You and I know that, and I dare say the twelve men on the scaffold know it. They will die believing, falsely, that they died as heroes. Most of us will die with no such palliative illusions. They should consider themselves lucky. In fact, I almost envy them."

The Kommandant broke into a weary smile. "I'm afraid you caught me at a weak moment, Professor, but your words have brought me back to my senses. Perhaps I have underestimated you."

An officer now handed the Kommandant a folder containing the various indictments. He quickly flipped through them, but after pausing to read one, walked over to the man labelled "Thief": "Well, we are honored today to have among us a budding artist!" he announced. The Kommandant tucked the folder under his arm and began applauding, then gestured for the whole assembly, both detainees and guards, to join him. When the applause died down, he continued: "Some weeks ago, a foremen noticed that a few cans of paint had mysteriously disappeared. Not a large amount, but such an unusual item to be pilfered. Food, clothing, tools, sharp metal objects, such thievery is to be expected. But paint? What good would that do somebody? Then one afternoon during a routine inspection, a guard makes a most remarkable discovery. Upon the ceiling in a dark corner of one of the dormitories he notices an unusual pattern of lines and circles. He calls his superior who has never seen anything quite like it. Believing it to be some kind of map or code, he shines a bright light on it, and what does he see? A yellow sun framed in a silvery corona and surrounded by the nine planets showing features like the Martian ice caps, Jupiter's great red spot, and the rings of Saturn. The whole thing was quite amazing, and I might almost excuse the defacing of Reich property on aesthetic grounds, but the theft of critical materials to execute the work indicates subversion of a most ingenious and dangerous order, and so is rightly a capital offense. I can only wonder what led you to do such a thing. Don't the weekly visits above ground provide sufficient opportunities for light and air? Your few hours a week up there are hardly more than mine, and I don't feel the need to paint an artificial heaven on the ceiling of my office. Or do you dream that the rockets you're helping to build will take men to other planets instead of helping Germany reshape the Earth into a more pure and orderly one? An intriguing question, but one that you and I–especially you–do not have the luxury to pursue today."

The prisoner remained impassive throughout this harangue.

The Kommandant then gestured for me to join him near the crane operator's booth located in one of the apses. The crane operator himself stood apart from the controls, head bowed in the detainee standard submissive pose. "The crane operator is French as are some of the condemned men," the Kommandant explained to me, "and we have a rule here that no one can be forced to execute members of his own nationality. Normally I'd just attend to it myself at this point— there's really nothing more to it than pulling a lever—but since you, Professor Waldmann, are one of the creators of this wonderful weapon, I will give you the honor of destroying its would-be destroyers."

There is, of course, no photographic record of this event, but I doubt that my face at that moment showed any incriminating emotions of empathy or remorse. For as long as I can remember, I've possessed the ability to bracket my feelings—to put them in a parenthesis, as it were, or maybe even squirrel them away into a footnote—for examination at some later and more propitious time. This is not to say that there were no emotions, though what I mainly remember is an overplus of pragmatic considerations. Was this trip to the Mittelwerk some kind of loyalty test, the Reichsführer-SS himself having come up with this plot which included having me present at an execution? The fact that I had been ordered to make the trip by the Technical Director on account of the Production Chief's illness raised disturbing questions about their possible involvement, but I considered it more than likely that they were merely unwitting accomplices.

Whatever was going on, I knew that even the appearance of hesitation could be fatal, so I quickly reckoned the counterfactual. What would happen if I refused to pull the lever? Regardless of my fate, the Kommandant would step over and carry out the execution himself, unless of course all the condemned were SS men just pretending to be prisoners as part of the ruse, in which case nobody would die except for me. In sum, if I didn't pull the lever, at least one person would die, but if I did, it was possible that no one would die.

Another thing holding me back was a certain sadness over lost innocence. Even if this was totally justifiable homicide, I had never killed anyone before. In that respect I had been so much luckier than the millions of front-line soldiers in this war. But as soon as that thought crossed my mind, I realized how fatuous it was. How many people does a good infantryman kill in a week? Ten? A hundred? Two hundred? Yet just a few weeks earlier, one of our A-4s came crashing down into a movie theater in Antwerp killing almost 600 people and injuring hundreds more. A soldier just uses a gun that someone else made for him. But I myself was a maker of something many times more deadly than a gun. By January 1945, I had already killed thousands of people, many of them civilians. Really, what difference would a dozen more make?

All of this mental churning took place within the few seconds it took me to walk over to the lever, and without further ado, I pulled it down, very convincingly I might add. The high-pitched whir filled the Cathedral as the cables began to go taut. Slowly the wooden beam ascended taking with it the dozen nooses. As the ropes tightened, a few of the men began to move their heads, as if trying to shoo away a fly. Only as they began to be lifted off the ground did the unpleasant involuntary twitches and convulsions begin. I think everyone there, probably even the prisoners, was grateful for the practice of covering the condemned men's heads in burlap bags. Then suddenly a voice, hoarse but plainly audible, and coming from the "Thief," cried out, "Count your dead, they are alive!" It was unmistakably Korvo's, and it occurred to me at that instant that of course he was the artist who painted the stars and planets on the ceiling. I noticed some of the guards instinctively raising their rifles, but as the echo of his words died away, the Cathedral was again filled with the white noise of the crane's electric motor.

By design, the whole process was not swift, but I'm sure it seemed much longer than it really was, and I'd estimate that from the time the nooses tightened until the twitchings ended was no more than three or four minutes. The dozen bodies swayed gently in the breeze of the ventilation system six or eight feet high, the urine that had quickly soaked their pants now dripping from their toes onto the ground.

CHAPTER 13
BASTARD IN SPACE

Because the act of executing several men including one former friend seemed so out of character for me, it was relatively easy to carry on with my work as if nothing had happened, because on some level I believed it had not happened, for the reason that it could not have happened. For the next couple of days I was able to lose myself in the minutiae of the missile, but I knew that the inevitable feelings of guilt and self-loathing could not be kept at bay indefinitely, and they began to gnaw at me on the tedious three-day drive back to Peenemünde. I countered these with a variety of rationalizations, including pinning the blame for the whole affair on Korvo himself. For a slave in an underground rocket factory, he really wasn't so bad off, thanks in part to our intervention. How stupid could he be to steal paint and redecorate the ceiling? Who did he think he was, Michelangelo? (The Kommandant was right–it did point to a dangerous subversiveness.) Alternatively, maybe he wanted to be caught and executed, even a pampered slave's life in a tunnel being no picnic, and decided that he might as well go out with a bang. In that case, my killing him was actually doing him a favor, and if he was aware that it was me running the crane (because in all honesty I can't remember if the Kommandant addressed me as "Professor Waldmann" or just "Professor"), I could take solace knowing that he left this life with a possible expression of silent gratitude on his lips.

But however potent rationalizations might be in waking life, they're paper tigers once we go to sleep. My chronically impoverished unconscious life now became more animated, though when I considered my dreams objectively, despite the impressive level of technical detail, their overall quality struck me as rather banal, pretty much what you'd expect under the circumstances. In one recurring nightmare, I am the twelfth man on the beam, and it's Korvo in an SS uniform, with a badly bruised neck and pupil-less eyes, who pulls the lever on the crane. In another I'm alone on the parapet of the ruined synagogue near Blizna looking up at an A-4 coming down directly at me with Korvo riding it like a bucking bronco. In a third, somewhat more original, Korvo, lounging on a subtropical Pluto, waves good-bye to me as I drift off into the exoplanetary void beyond, lashed to the tail fin of an A-4.

My conscious mind wasn't doing much better. I obsessively rehearsed dozens of scenarios that might have led to different outcomes. Some involved alternate paths in the labyrinths of everyday life, like how back in the summer of 1930 I decide not to attend the Oberth lecture where I met the Technical Director, or I happen not to read the issue of *The Rocket* that carried the announcement of the lecture, or I never see the issue because it gets lost in the mail. Other scenarios imagine heroic actions undertaken by a bolder version of myself, like the one in which I grab a ceremonial sword from the Kommandant's belt, cut Korvo's noose from the beam, and then follow him in a madcap, Keystone Cops escape through the tunnels and ventilation system of the Mittelwerk which Korvo has scoped out during his months of internment. Of course, this mental exercise is a complete vanity of vanities: Nothing in my brain will make the reality of what's happened budge an inch.

Yet the human psyche is such a peculiar rag bag of surprises and contradictions, isn't it? Over the next several days, the intensity of my nightmares began to fade until one morning I woke up from a mostly dreamless sleep feeling as refreshed as if my soul had been taken up to Heaven and returned by the angels in its original pristine condition. It was only after having been awake for several minutes that the memory of what happened came back to me and how I was supposed to be miserable. The effect was liberating, if unexpected. I decided it must be the consequence of a profound awareness deep within my soul that no God worthy of the name would let me go unpunished, and that since the only punishment commensurate with my crime was death, I had without realizing it developed the outlook of a man with a terminal disease. I worried less about the future now. The rage for petty order in every aspect of daily life, right down to making sure that my watch ran exactly two minutes and thirty seconds fast so that I would never be late to staff meetings, relaxed, and I even began to enjoy the company of my colleagues more since I knew I wouldn't have to put up with their insufferable human foibles much longer.

Curiously, while my dream life now returned to its usual moribund state, my ability to interpret others' dreams — or at least, the dreams of one other person — remained undiminished. For the past year and a half since my brief interview with the Führer at the Wolfsschanze I would occasionally receive letters from Speer giving detailed summaries of dreams the Führer wanted me to break open. While I was reluctant to become the in-house Daniel to the Führer's Nebuchadnezzar if only because I worried what might happen if my powers ever deserted me, both General D. and the Technical Director encouraged me in these endeavors, seeing it as a way to check the ever-increasing influence of the SS over the rocket program. What struck me about these dreams was how both grandiose and trite they were. The imagery was of planets hurtling at one another and gigantic ghostly visages materializing out of the void, much of it seemingly cribbed from the Book of Revelation. Either his subconscious was reaching back to the security of an infantile state (the piety that I learned much later characterized his mother's household), or he had taken up Bible study as his world crumbled around him. The problem for me was that the meaning of these dreams was so obvious: The dreamer was going to Hell. How to communicate that back to him? He was now so moody and impulsive that he might react with violence to such an interpretation, yet he was not so stupid as to miss the insincerity of any attempt to mollify him. So at a time when I would have preferred to focus on my own psychodynamics, I was obliged to expend mental energy coming up with creative ways to finesse the truth of his nightmare visions.

Despite such distractions, my overarching concern at this time remained my candidacy for Raumschiffahrt. I was now convinced that larger forces were at work. Despite my poor qualifications, I decided that the Technical Director had been moved to consider me for the mission because God foreknew that I would fail the test of saving

Korvo in Thuringia, and so had already made arrangements for an act of retributive justice. As a solace to me, however, I would be allowed to exit this life in a rather spectacular way and thus make a contribution to knowledge that would undoubtedly stand the test of time.

Of course, it was entirely possible–more likely, even–that the Technical Director would give the nod to the Aviatrix instead of me. This in turn led to the problem of what, if anything, I should do to lobby for my cause. Should I go straight to his office and simply tell him that I wanted to ride The Bastard for all the reasons (mainly theological) that he had enumerated before? But might not that raise in his mind the question of why a man who was pathologically afraid of air travel, and who had previously dismissed the prospect of his going into space as ludicrous, would have suddenly experienced a change of heart?

Even if I said nothing, I worried that certain details of my last trip to the Mittelwerk might filter back to Peenemünde. While I doubted that the Technical Director would ever learn of Korvo's fate–in the tunnels he was known only as a number and not a name–it was conceivable that my starring role in a mass execution might be reported up the chain of command by a well-intentioned Gestapo agent thinking that he was doing me a favor. Yet I could easily imagine the Technical Director taking a dim view of my actions. It was one thing to build weapons of mass destruction to advance the interests of a militaristic authoritarian regime, quite another to personally execute several men, less for their specific offenses (though that was not irrelevant) than as a crude act of terrorism. Whatever else could be said about the Technical Director, he was a man of high standards who might well see my moral weakness on this occasion as a sign that I was unworthy of the mission.

He was also a man who always took the long view. What if the full story of what I did in the Mittlewerk were to come out, even many years later? Would this not forever taint the glory of the first manned space flight in a way more damning even than how the Saturn V's roots in V-2 development soured many people on the whole Apollo program? My competition, the Aviatrix, was an ardent Nazi, to be sure, but the first Raumschiffahrt would carry the Nazi label no matter what, and at least her crimes were more of the political or ideological than criminal sort.

A few days weeks into the new year the Technical Director set the date for Raumschiffahrt: February 13, 1945. Of course, except for the Technical Director and me, and a very small subset of our top people, everyone believed that the manned Bastard would be launched in a shallow trajectory to test for both range and survivability, and that the one-man crew would be either the Aviatrix or some other experienced test pilot. In actuality The Bastard would be launched in a more or less vertical attitude with the goal of reaching a maximum altitude of about 120 miles. Back in December, we worried that we would be prisoners of the Russians by now, but in late January it became apparent that instead of marching across Pomerania, the Red Army was turning southwest to make a beeline for Berlin. (Only in May did the Russians finally occupy the Usedom area.) This change in the military situation had obvious practical benefits, but we also took it as a good omen for a successful outcome.

On Thursday, February 7th, I was puttering around in the Guidance Lab when the Technical Director walked in, closed the door and, putting both hands on my shoulders as he looked me right in the eyes, said, "Arthur, you're it." A wave of relief passed through me, but since I had been so adamant about the absurdity of my going into space, I did not want to make the Technical Director suspicious by readily embracing the commission.

"Do you honestly believe that I'm a better choice than an ace test pilot who, although a woman, is a veritable icon of German—"

But the Technical Director waved his hand impatiently to cut me off. "Arthur, I hope you don't take this the wrong way, but in the end, I really had no choice. The Aviatrix came to my office yesterday and withdrew from consideration. "

"How come?"

"She said that she feels an obligation to devote herself full time to the pilots she's training for the V-1 suicide missions. But it was more complicated than that. I think she was afraid of either dying or not dying on The Bastard."

"Well, that doesn't make a lot of sense, does it?" I said.

The Technical Director sighed. "Not a lot does these days. But there was a kind of logic to it. On the one hand, she genuinely loves her V-1 boys—and most of them are hardly more than that since it would be a waste to put a real pilot in a suicide plane—and has come to see herself as their surrogate mother. They're the children that, ah, she never had. In her mind, to die in pursuit of a purely scientific objective would be a form of abandonment, and she can't stand the prospect of that weighing on her conscience. Also, if she's going to die in this war, she only wants a death accompanied by annihilating effect. She told me that either upon the Führer's order, or the moment some lily-livered general signs an unconditional surrender, if it comes to that, she will climb into her specially designed turbocharged V-1 packed with twice the usual amount of high explosives, plot a course for London, and dive bomb the thing directly into the Houses of Parliament."

"So that covers dying. What about not dying?"

"For Raumschiffahrt to be a success, the pilot must come back alive. This was something I don't think she ever fully understood."

"So no successful failures, then. I appreciate that."

"Believe me, Arthur, I've spent hours and hours trying to figure out how to build maximum redundancy into this vehicle. But the more the Aviatrix learned about the various safety and escape features, the less enthusiastic she became about the project, though her personal loyalty to me was such that she would never openly express disenchantment. She would say things like, 'I wonder how much a ten-minute flight like this during wartime can really make a contribution to knowledge' and 'Do you think such a hastily conceived and executed project will really stand the test of time?' Merely going up a hundred miles to take a quick peek and then come right back down—what was the big deal? The stakes here were too low, and because I've made The Bastard as safe as a Heinkel, so was the risk. If there's little or no chance of dying, where's the incentive for someone like her? I could tell her heart was no longer in it. She was dedicated to the awful necessity that was being imposed upon her to instruct young men and perhaps young women in the ways of a fiery death, a tragedy of

Wagnerian proportions that must necessarily be capped by her own annihilation on the banks of the Thames. But of course, her loss will be your gain. Besides, although she was obviously more suited to the mission physically, in spiritual terms, you always had it all over her."

I was in equal parts delighted and depressed to know that someone had rejected The Bastard because it was too safe. "Safe as a Heinkel": That would make it a lot easier to climb into the thing, but my survival would seriously undermine the deeper satisfaction I was feeling knowing that my extinction would be proof positive of divine justice operating within a broader cosmic structure. I had assumed that, were I selected for the mission, it would be as though my death were a scheduled event. Now the Technical Director was making me have my doubts.

Later that afternoon when I walked to the north end of the island to look at the pad from which The Bastard would be launched, I was reminded how primitive this technology really was. By the early 1960s there was a kind of structural (and even visual) seamlessness to the vehicles we were producing, but there were parts of The Bastard that looked like they had been cut out with tin snips (because they were) and a lot of it was held together by rivets probably no better than those that popped when the *Titanic* struck the iceberg. No, I was never going to climb out of that thing alive, and this restored my previous feelings of stoical contentment. Upon reflection, it was better than the diagnosis of a terminal illness, because even the most painless of diseases will eventually bring about the diminution of one's mental and physical capacities, but as the world's first spaceman, I would be fit as a fiddle right up to the moment when the Technical Director hit the firing button and launched me into *le grand peut-être*.

Never before had I inhabited such an unadulterated state of infinite resignation, and even today I looked back upon those days in early February with a certain poignancy. I was free at last from the temptation of believing that mine was a case of greatness deferred, not denied, and so also free of all future humiliations of being thirty-five or forty or fifty and still clinging to the notion that I might be a late bloomer. Also, as one about to cross over from being to non-being, I was released from any possible competition with the living. I had become a veritable Oedipus at Colonus, alive in name only. Between the Technical Director and myself, for example, the contest was over. Once I had committed to The Bastard, we were like apples and oranges, Jacob and Esau.

Oddly, in this liberated state over the next few days, I felt like I was doing some of the most creative work of my career. Adjustments I was making to A-4 guidance were dramatically improving the accuracy of our rockets. (Too bad for Germany, and of course, the Allied victims, that those casualties were pointless and would have no impact on the outcome of the war.) What a shame I hadn't arranged for my death ten years earlier! Had I been solving problems at this level back then, I might be the one dispatching a friend and colleague on a probable suicide mission to fulfill my technological and theological ambitions, not the other way around.

The emotional roller-coaster of the past few weeks now took me to new heights such that I often had to suppress my feelings of euphoria for fear that I might do something to jeopardize my chances of actually going through with Raumschiffahrt. For instance, because nothing really frightened me anymore, I had become extremely cavalier about air raid warnings, rarely bothering to go into the basement of the Guidance Laboratory when the sirens went off. Then one day a bomb exploded a couple hundred yards from the building, shattering a window and sending a shower of glass in my direction. I suffered only a few scratches, and while the incident in no way made me more fearful, it occurred to me that it would be just like an ironical God to let a nugget of British shrapnel kill me and thus deprive me of a more meaningful demise atop The Bastard. Henceforth, I followed mandated safety procedures to the letter.

There then emerged another kind of challenge. I began to wonder if my total commitment to die for my complicity in Korvo's murder might by some miracle release me from the obligation to actually do so–that surrendering all prospects for survival would earn me so many spiritual credits with God that he would reward me with life. He had done something on that order with Abraham–why not then with me? Such musings that there might be hope for me after all began to chip away at my penitential armor plate. Maybe the Russians would change their minds, overrun Peenemünde tomorrow, and so put an end to plans for Raumschiffahrt. I found myself keeping an ear cocked at all hours to hear if the sounds of their artillery were drawing closer.

I also made efforts to shore up my underlying mental fortitude. In the Center's library there was a copy of the *Spiritual Exercises* of St. Ignatius of Loyola (we had a substantial Catholic contingent), but while I appreciated the methods I couldn't stomach the theology. Reading Loyola did, however, put me in mind of *Tzimtzum*, the concept that his younger contemporary, Rabbi Isaac Luria, teased out of the Zohar's exposition of the *Sephirot*. *Tzimtzum* describes God's creation of the world as the omnipresent *Ein Sof's* contracting just enough to open up an empty space that both allowed for the existence of other entities and made a place from which for the first time *Ein Sof* could perceive itself. *Tzimtzum's* lesson for me was that only by emptying myself of myself would I gain sufficient self-awareness and self-control to achieve my objective. The good news here was that I had always been well-suited temperamentally to such ontological evacuation. For someone with a substantial ego like the Technical Director, this would have been nearly impossible, but while the vices of most men run toward aggrandizement, mine fell to asceticism, which is why I had rarely chafed at my monkish existence these past several years.

Of course I would have to go farther now, and so I did. I arose every morning at four to eat a simple but nutritionally balanced breakfast of canned sardines, black bread, and honey. (This was the pre-launch breakfast we recommended in the early days of the Mercury Program but there was no way the flyboys of the astronaut corps would ever give up their all-American feasting on steak and eggs.) I would then pass the hours until sunrise blanking out my mind by meditating upon the individual letters of the Hebrew alphabet, each one an avatar of particular qualities of perception and insight. I also practiced a form of Bibliomancy with the text. Although I obviously did not have in my possession a copy of the Zohar (which runs to over twenty bound volumes), I would draw sets of random numbers from a hat keyed to the various tractates of the Zohar from which since my earliest days of study with my grandmother I had memorized selected passages. I still recall the very first one drawn when I began this regimen: "There are colors disclosed and undisclosed, but humanity neither knows nor reflects on these matters." Earth was painted in colors of red and green, blue and yellow, but who knew what hues awaited the perceptive and unencumbered eye translated directly to the heavens? Answering this question had now become my responsibility or, at least, that is how I interpreted the text.

But although I would travel toward Heaven an evacuated self, I would not be empty. Whole universes might come to occupy the space created by *Tzimtzum*. It occurred to me that Earth's curiosity about Heaven might be mirrored in Heaven's curiosity about Earth, and so I decided that I would fill the mental bilges pumped dry of ego with precise information about the natural world. After breakfast each day, I would go for long walks through the spruce forests and along the shore, employing my considerable mnemonic powers to record details about every single plant and animal that I encountered. In the afternoon I worked in the Guidance Laboratory, mainly out of habit, before another simple dinner of sardines, bread, and honey, followed by more meditation exercises. Originally I had thought to use the few hours before bed to record entries in a journal, because surely the last thoughts of the first man to be launched into space would be of interest to posterity, but I ultimately decided against this, believing that a man like myself deserved as little posterity as possible, the loss to history notwithstanding.

On February 12th, the winds shifted around to the south and the temperature rose to sixty degrees. The launch crew, most of whom were still unaware of the mission's real purpose, worked in shirt-sleeves and sang folk songs. It was Shrove Tuesday Eve, and despite the relative impoverishment of living conditions compared to previous years, the Technical Director had decided to go ahead with the annual masquerade ball in the Hearth Room. Since even the Gestapo had melted away by now, the Technical Director, thinly veiling his hopes for the near future, had come up with a script based loosely on the American tale of Captain John Smith's rescue by the Indian princess, Pocohantas. The action had been transposed to

Saturn's moon, Titan, the Indians becoming blue-faced aliens with antennae sticking out from the tops of their heads. At the end of the Technical Director's version, Smith (played by the Technical Director himself) marries Pocohantas (played by Wangermann, our baby-faced Propulsion Lab Associate Director, in drag), who then set sail across a sea of methane for the western hemisphere of Titan, which they had been granted as part of her dowry. I let myself be cast in a non-speaking role as one of the Titanians. It seemed wholly fitting that I spend what might be my last night on Earth playing an alien, since whether dead or alive, by the same time next night I would be a different order of being.

When the festivities were over, I walked back to my room alone. Just before leaving, the Technical Director had asked if he could make any "special arrangements" for the night, hinting that he knew one or two patriotic young women in the village who might be willing to sacrifice their virtue for the cause of space exploration. Though I might be a monk, I'm not a saint, and gave the offer serious consideration, but ultimately declined, feeling that any break from my usual routine would mock the disciplined life I had been living for so long. So after washing my face and brushing my teeth, and checking twice to see that the heat was turned off and the doors locked, I simply climbed into bed. I read an article in a technical journal and, just before turning out the light, made up my to-do list for the next day, which consisted of only one item: "Ride The Bastard to Heaven." Then I lay there waiting for sleep to overtake me, but instead of losing consciousness, my mind raced and my pores tingled. Within minutes I was convinced that I had developed feeling even in those most remote inner organs, the spleen and pancreas. It finally occurred to me that while it might be heroic to live out my last day on Earth no differently than any other, it was also completely foolish. Not only was I neither a genius nor a saint, I was also not a superman.

I climbed out of bed, got dressed, and decided to walk down to the beach. As it was a new moon and mostly cloudy, the night was almost pitch black. Tall firs waved gently in the preternaturally warm breeze. I stopped every few minutes to listen for small animals and birds rustling in the understory. An owl flew by and landed on a branch a few feet away. I wondered what it would be like to be an owl, to be completely comfortable in the dark, and without awareness (I presumed) of death. It occurred to me that my earlier walks, where I was gathering impressions to take up with me, were incomplete, and I now literally began thanking every bird, tree, and rock for the pleasure they had given me during my years at Peenemünde, and apologizing on behalf of the Technical Director and all our top people for the inconvenience that their rockets had caused them–the loss of habitat, the noise pollution. When I finally arrived at the water, I had the illusion that I could hear every bubble of spume burst as it crawled up the shore, and I thanked each of them, too.

When I returned to my room, I was still not ready for sleep, so I sat down at my desk and began writing out as much of the text of the Zohar as I could remember. I worked at lightning speed, and although I knew I was leaving out big chunks, I nonetheless had the distinct sense that I was producing a comprehensive copy, a work of genius. When I finally set down my pen, I noticed the pale light of dawn in my room. I put my head down and began to dream about Spain in the days of Moses de Leon. The two of us were walking through the labyrinthine streets of Toledo, probing the intricacies of the text we both knew de Leon had been counterfeiting for years, though out of respect for an old man's life's work, I said nothing about this. Our peripatetic symposium seemed to go on for days until we came to the *quebrado* in the main town square, where carpenters were hammering together the high scaffold that would be used by the Inquisition. The sound was actually that of someone knocking. The ambient light was still pale. I had slept only a few minutes, but felt more refreshed than I had in weeks. I opened the door. It was the Technical Director.

"Is it time already?" I asked.

The Technical Director looked down and shook his head. I noticed that he was still wearing pajamas underneath his trench coat.

"Let's not go through with this," he said, "not now, anyway. It's taken us almost five years to get to a serviceable A-4, and here we are trying to make The Bastard operational in less than five months."

I was dumbstruck. It wasn't like the Technical Director to change his mind at the last minute, and something about this early morning embassy made me suspicious. "But going from nothing to something is harder than going from something to something better," I countered. "Besides, the test flights went off without a hitch, more or less."

"We got lucky," said the Technical Director.

"'Luck is what happens when opportunity meets preparation.' How many times have I heard you say that? We've done our homework. And the Russians are giving us the opening."

"If it were like the old days, Arthur, when we oversaw every solder, every weld, that would be one thing, but the junk that's getting sent up here to us from Mittelwerk . . . . The Kommandant tells me he's popping off a dozen saboteurs a day, and still I can't promise you that The Bastard out there isn't a bucket of bolts. Who knows what it might do."

"I know the missiles off the assembly lines are junk, but our people have gone over this one with a fine-toothed comb."

The Technical Director stood there silent for a moment, then looked away.

"What's really going on here?" I asked.

He shook his head and sighed. "Arthur, we have to be careful. The Führer is doomed, but he's not dead yet. '*He shall go out with great fury to bring ruin and destruction to many.*' Remember? I'm convinced he has spies among our top people, and if word about this rogue operation gets out, we're goners." He lowered his voice. "Then there's this. Within the last forty-eight hours, I've exchanged coded messages with an Allied power, and it's not the Russians. If we turn over all the documentation behind our research of the past decade, they promise that no harm will come to us. In fact, they will give all those I identify as critical personnel contracts to work at a new facility they're building that will make this place look like that clown town we had at Foggy's Rocket Center. Imagine, Arthur, the money, the resources! In a year or two we can do a Raumschiffahrt that will be far better than this roll of the dice."

Although I had a professional obligation to argue with my boss about questions of technique, this did not usually extend to matters of policy. Yet I had now arrived at a place to which I might never again have the courage to return. I would have to die some day, and would spend the rest of my life fearing that moment, unless I could die today, an eventuality for which I was wholly prepared. If by some bizarre happenstance I did not die on the The Bastard, then there's a chance that I might be witness to the most spectacular theophany since Ezekiel saw the angelic chariot of fire, and there was a kind of genius in that, wasn't there?

"Have you accepted their terms?" I asked.

"I can't see any reason not to, but no, I haven't yet. We're a team and I wanted to run it by you, Wangermann, and a few others I know I can trust."

The thought now occurred to me that maybe the Technical Director was thinking that if we could build a sufficiently reliable vehicle a few years down the road in the United States — and I was certain it was the Americans he was talking to — then perhaps despite his indispensable role in our organization he might secure the honor of being the first man in space. Like Moses he was leading humanity toward a new promised land, but he would surpass Moses by crossing over into that land himself. I wasn't going to let him get away with it.

"One last rocket won't make any difference," I said. "We launch this morning, and this afternoon you tell them we'll take the deal. But here's the thing. Once we go over to them, we'll just be hired hands. We'll live in big houses and drive big cars, but it will be their show. It sure as hell won't be one of us Germans doing Raumschiffahrt. It'll be some bone-headed farm boy turned fly boy from Iowa or wherever they grow all that corn. Comic books, not the Book of Daniel."

The image of a big dumb American riding to Heaven made him wince. He knew I was right. It was we Germans who had labored in the trenches all these years. Almost ex nihilo we created the Kegeldeuse, the Miraks, the Repulsors, the A-3, the A-4, and now The Bastard. The German military was on the verge of defeat, but German science had one last chance to triumph. It was clearly now or never.

After going back and forth about it for the next several minutes, the Technical Director finally concurred and agreed to let the mission go forward with the proviso that we continue to operate in secrecy since we could not predict the consequences of either success or failure on the reactions of our present or future masters. He left me, promising to return at the originally appointed hour.

During the interim, I attended to one final task, the composition of my will. Since I had little money and few possessions, this mainly consisted of expressions of gratitude to friends and mentors. In a postscript to my grandmother, I offered my thoughts on certain passages in the Zohar that had only become clear to me in recent days. I hardly knew what to say to my parents, whose ambition for their son was a comfortable business career back home in Trier. There had never been the slightest chance of that, but I still felt that I was letting them down, if only because it seemed ungracious for a child not to survive at least until his parents had passed on, given all the time and expense of raising him. Nor were they the sort of people for whom the triumph of an idea, even one with such world-historical ramifications as Raumschiffahrt, would ever make up for the loss of an only son.

When the Technical Director came back an hour later, he was dressed in his usual semi-formal attire for launch days, including his trademark high-crowned tweed hat, but minus the trench coat, given the balmy, spring-like weather. He escorted me over to the Hearth Room where the team was enjoying their standard launch day breakfast of black bread, cheeses, liverwurst, Schlackwurst, boiled eggs, smoked fish, and (my favorite) Pfannkuchen. My normal inhibitions about eating before air travel were nowhere in evidence today and I ate heartily. Brightening up the room was a large bouquet of tulips from the commander of a mobile A-4 launch unit who had just been forced to evacuate a position in northern Holland. Lack of sleep seemed not to have affected my appetite, and I had second generous helpings of everything.

Although a staff car was waiting outside the Hearth Room for the half-mile trip to the launch site, I asked the Technical Director if we might walk instead. He checked his watch and nodded his approval. With him in the lead, a dozen of us then set out on foot toward the north end of the island, enjoying the rare February sunshine and a light southerly breeze. I said very little as I was unsure who among us was fully informed about what was really going on. Indeed, it was clear from the conversation that several of them expected today's pilot would be the Aviatrix, another Luftwaffe test pilot, or even Hans Winziger's dog, Rolf.

When we arrived at the pad, most of the group proceeded to their stations to supervise technicians who had been working there since dawn. Only the Technical Director, Wangermann, and I stepped into the metal shed that served as an improvised "ready-room," where, after I emptied my bladder and bowels, they helped me into a set of thermal underwear (with a sort of built-in diaper in case of emergency) and then the specially designed high-altitude pressure suit. As soon as the helmet was fastened in place, the only sounds I could hear were the white noise from the portable ventilator and the thumping of my own heartbeat. Through my visor, the world looked like the scene inside an aquarium. My only means of communication now was through hand signals and facial expressions.

Though normally terrified to ascend the rickety gantry elevator fifty feet to the top of the rocket, today I found myself thoroughly enjoying the view of the surrounding countryside and the sea beyond, which I gestured toward with my heavily gloved hand. The Technical Director responded with an obviously forced smile. Did he feel sadness knowing that he might never see me again? Or was he wrestling with jealousy, having always believed that he would not only design the first functioning spaceship, but fly it, too? Or did his expression belie a guilty wish that the mission would fail, and that he, the Technical Director, might get his chance to be the one after all? Perhaps it was just as well that we could no longer speak to one another.

With Wangermann's help, the Technical Director shoe-horned me into my contoured seat. It was so cramped that I could barely move my head side to side. This truly was man-in-a- can — a sardine can. The hatch, pierced by a small eye-shaped window, was then screwed into place. There was just enough room between the visor of my helmet and the window to hold up the camera that the Technical Director had provided me with, specially modified to hold enough film for 128 high-resolution color photographs. Taking pictures was my only assigned task, assuming I retained consciousness. After tapping all around the hatch with a rubber mallet to insure the tightness of the seal, I saw the Technical Director's face one last time. He mouthed a sentence that I interpreted as "See you in the Hearth Room for lunch."

I was now alone atop The Bastard. I reflected upon the irony that, for a man about to see more of his home planet than any other human being in history, my visual world at the moment had been reduced to a few square inches of sky criss-crossed by the gantry's girders. Rather than being about to ascend to Heaven, I felt more like a man in a diving bell at the bottom of the sea. Over the next several minutes, I was aware of various rumblings and groanings of the rocket as it was fueled and readied. Each one unnerved me. Never before had I realized how many noises it made, but why shouldn't it? It was probably the most complex machine ever created, containing dozens of exotic materials, each with its own peculiar tuning. Locked into a tiny chamber atop a column of thousands of pounds of volatile liquids and gases about to ignite, there was no human precedent for my experience. The situation was, strictly speaking, surreal. The only thing that preserved my sanity at this point was my former mystical research. When an ominous ping somewhere beneath me was not followed by the explosion I expected, I was granted a heterodox vision of myself as one of the early Christian Desert Fathers, St. Simon or St. Daniel, who ventured up onto tall pillars and stayed there for years to affirm that men were spiritual beings condescending to a mortal existence, not the other way around, and thus by their sacrifice reminding everyone else that they were more than miserable gobs of flesh temporarily smeared across the ether. Buckets attached to pulleys brought the ancient stylites food and water, and took away their wastes. Pneumatic tubes could perform these same functions now. Wouldn't such an arrangement today make the same point about the transcendent quality of the human experience, that we could be as much at home in Heaven as on Earth, without all the fuss involved in actual Raumschiffahrt, I wondered?

Launch was scheduled for ten o'clock. At five minutes to ten the rocket's intermittent rumblings became continuous. I knew that I could stop the whole proceeding just by pressing the red "chicken" button on the instrument panel, but whenever I felt myself on the verge of a loss of nerve, I pictured the scene of the Technical Director donning the space suit he had had secretly made for himself and rushing out to the pad before any of his military superiors could stop him.

As the clock counted down the final seconds, I could hear electric motors pumping fuel and oxidant into the combustion chamber. Then I felt the wave of sound moving up from beneath my seat, followed by a shuddering far beyond anything I had expected. I had just enough presence of mind to know that this was caused by the rocket pulling against clamps holding it in place so that when it was finally released, it would literally jump off its pad. When the clamps did let go, I was pushed violently backward into the contours of my seat. I sensed motion, but couldn't tell in what direction. My suppressed fears now assaulted me with a vengeance, and I screamed out for God to save me, while a not unpleasant warmth spread down my thighs and across my buttocks as I lost both bladder and bowel control. Out the window, there was nothing but steam and smoke. Was I plunging back to Earth? But in a few seconds, though the shuddering continued, the smoke out the window cleared, revealing a uniform patch of pale blue. As the rocket accelerated, G forces almost suffocated me. Though I tried to imagine that the Gs were squeezing the fear out of me, I was almost at the point of passing out when suddenly everything relaxed and the rocket was enveloped in total silence.

Brennschluss. The motor had cut off, exactly as planned. The mission clock marked 59 seconds. I was now weightless.

Until now the previous high altitude record had been held by the Italian mountaineer turned aeronautical adventurer, Dante Caroma, who ascended in a balloon to a height of 70,000 feet. Frozen to the bone and nearly delirious from insufficient oxygen, Caroma claimed that he had observed a darkening of the sky from blue to violet. But for me, riding The Bastard through the 200,000 foot mark, there was no question about it. It reminded me of the one solar eclipse I had observed, only much faster, as if the hand of God had lifted the luminous blue shade that diurnally hides from us a creation so vast that our souls would be torn between awe and despair if we could gaze upon it twenty-four hours a day. I could see a slice of the Baltic and pick out what looked like the island Borhnolm, though its shape seemed a little distorted. I also noted the curvature of the Earth, thus becoming the first person to be able to visually confirm that the Earth was indeed round.

I had now gone higher and faster than any human being in history, and had reached the place that the most brilliant minds of past ages had believed to be the actual location of Heaven. Could they all have been wrong? As The Bastard approached apogee, I looked intensely into the blackness to see if there was anything that might provide a rationalist basis for revealed religion—some gaseous cloud of heretofore invisible spirit-stuff, for example, that might account for the visions recorded in the Bible.

But I observed nothing of the sort. I was totally alone up there. My estrangement, both physical and cognitive, was absolute. And now, just as an infantile warmth had spread across my thighs and buttocks when I had lost sphincter control during the boost phase, there was a parallel sensation of a spiritual nature as the self that contained my soul let go, and I felt myself pouring out the window of the cockpit and filling up all the blackness between myself and the Earth and the blinding spike of light that was the sun and the innumerable points of lights that were the stars and galaxies. I knew that an observer on Earth was seeing the light that had departed some of those remoter heavenly bodies millions of years ago, but it occurred to me as my expanding soul now reached those places that The Bastard had not only catapulted me upward in space but also backward in time. It was entirely possible, then, that The Bastard's bright contrail was being seen not only by the good neutral Swede lingering over a late breakfast of herring and eggs, but by his prehistoric, even preliterate, ancestor whose barely articulate gruntings of fear and trembling at the sight would someday evolve into the myths of Thor and Ygdrasil. Perhaps somewhere among those hundred thousand intervening generations a Neolithic tribe was worshiping The Bastard at this very moment.

I picked up the Handkammer, then set it aside. There was no point in taking photographs, I thought, because they could never do justice to my ecstatic experience. When I got back to Earth, if I ever did, I would simply open my eyes and the spectacular images stored in my brain would be projected onto any readily available surface. Such miraculous powers would confirm the Technical Director's intuition that the heavens were more than mere metaphor. While I found this new datum both curious and exciting, I also felt a tinge of sadness, oddly enough, that it was not the Technical Director himself making this discovery. For myself, it was perhaps a case of pearls before swine: Only the true genius, who lives life almost within reach of the divine, and thus suffers more cruelly from the fact of mortality, can fully appreciate what it might mean to be godlike.

Although I had the sensation that I'd been living in space for weeks, months, even years, it had only been five minutes since liftoff. The Bastard would soon be entering the descent phase. I pressed my visored face against the tiny window looking east toward the Pomeranian coast but was surprised not to see the sun. In fact, light seemed to be coming from the opposite side of The Bastard. Where the hell was I? Was the Technical Director sending me and The Bastard to England, à la Rudolf Hess? Was this intended as a dramatic gesture to show the Allies that we were really switching sides? It couldn't be. Even at maximum range, the rocket would never make it across the North Sea. Only at that moment for the first time in all the weeks leading up to Raumschiffahrt did the word resurface in consciousness: Golem.

Of course! The purpose of the note that Korvo had painstakingly composed was to let the world know that there might be a reason if any of the rockets that came off the Mittelwerk assembly line had gone rogue. So where was I headed? Kiel? Hamburg? Berlin? The rocket was basically a cannonball now, its destination irrevocably fixed at Brennschluss. I supposed that I still had a chance of survival, assuming that guidance was the only thing Korvo had hijacked, and that he had not, for example, installed a barometric fuse in the fuel tank that would cause the rocket to airburst at a certain altitude for maximum annihilating effect.

Out the window I noticed that the heavens were taking on a faint purplish hue. Minutes earlier, ascending through the upper reaches of the atmosphere at a speed of more than 2,000 miles per hour, I had been unable to mark the transition of the sky from blue to black. It just happened: Earth, then Heaven, perhaps the way a body goes from life to death. But the descent was necessarily more gradual. If reentry were too steep, the friction of the air molecules against The Bastard's metal skin would cause the rocket to incinerate. The Technical Director had told me to expect the cockpit to warm up, though he was confident that the bakelite tiles glued to the underside of the crew compartment would protect me. I was wholly unprepared, however, for what I now saw. The purplish hue was being replaced by the red glow of superheated gases punctuated by an intermittent stream of fiery embers. Although I recognized these as minute chips of tile that were supposed to fleck off and thus conduct heat away from The Bastard, I was completely unnerved at the prospect of the rocket disintegrating. Also, what to this point had been an almost preternaturally smooth flight became terribly bumpy. It felt as though The Bastard were being lifted up and thrown back down again, and it reminded me of a particularly awful flight to Berlin in the Heinkel. The Technical Director, who was at the controls, had underestimated the ferocity of a thunderstorm which he had said wasn't worth the extra fifteen minutes to avoid. But even he was so shaken up upon arrival that it was several minutes before he could bring himself to speak again.

The cockpit thermometer now rose to 135 degrees, and the turbulence was so severe that I had no idea of which way was up or down. A terrible, hellish odor rose to my nostrils—the smell of my own shit starting to cook. My body would be next. In desperation, I pushed against the window thinking that maybe I could open it and get some fresh air. It was at that point that I saw something outside.

Indistinct at first, slowing emerging from the cloud of enveloping gases, it took the form of a hand extended in my direction. No, not a hand, but a fist, holding tightly to something. Was this the Left Hand of the incarnate *Ein Sof*, the divine presence, which according to the Zohar was to be identified with the *Sephirot* of *Chesed*, or lovingkindness? I had been too delirious even to pray, but surely God does not need man to summon Him, and perhaps He felt sorry for me, who, after all, had volunteered for The Bastard as a means to atone for his involvement with a weapon so devilish that it killed not only the free men against whom it was launched, but the slaves who were condemned to build it. As the hand grew larger, however, it became clear that it was not one of the *Sephirot*, but a more garden-variety sort of hallucination. The hand belonged to one of the twelve men I had executed back in the Cathedral. It held a noose. A hooded head now accompanied the face, chanting words through the burlap that I couldn't quite understand but thought might be Aramaic. Soon there was a second fist, a second rope, a second head, then a third, fourth, and so on, until twelve disembodied hands and heads were arranged in a semi-circle around The Bastard. Was this an invitation to join them?

Alas, this was exactly the sort of melodramatic confection that I would have expected my guilty unconscious to have come up with. *Ein Sof* would have done better. My fear was now tinged with disappointment.

In the midst of all this, I noticed that space was gradually turning blue. The sky! The temperature had fallen to 110 degrees. Still, the annoying hallucination persisted, and if anything, the chanting had only grown louder. I felt that I was supposed to remember something, but what? The ejection sequence, of course. When the altimeter reached 50,000 feet, I had to pull back on a stick that would adjust the control surfaces to put The Bastard into a shallower dive and slow it down. As I did so, I recalled that this was when a wing of our first test vehicle had broken off, but now The Bastard responded perfectly. I next had to watch both altitude and air speed. When I reached 25,000 feet and a speed of 289 miles per hour, I had to hit the eject button, since at that point aerodynamic forces would push the nose of The Bastard down and it would begin to accelerate again.

I looked at the fading chorus of corpses out the window and considered what to do. It seemed like the fiery reentry had refined my fears out of existence, and I knew that it would never be easier to die than right now and that I would be in good company. What good would it do me to go back to Peenemünde anyway? Despite the Technical Director's optimism, I doubted that we would ever really end up in America building rockets to the moon and Mars, and on weekends mowing the backyards of our suburban bungalows, and getting together on the Fourth of July to feast on knackwursts and schnitzels. America was a moral nation, at least more moral than

Germany, and as soon as they figured out what had been going on down in Thuringia, all the top people would be tried as war criminals, even those who had never directly pulled a lever to kill someone, like I had. And if they turned out to be a bunch of hypocrites, as drunk on power and violence and empire as every other victor in history, and were prepared to make the Technical Director and me and all our top people rich as Croesuses if we would build the rockets that would let them cow not only every nation on Earth but every planet in the solar system—well, if some men could live with their own perfidy, I could not. The needle on the altimeter passed below 35,000 feet. I folded my hands in my lap and smiled. This would be so easy, I thought.

But as The Bastard continued its descent and broke through a deck of clouds, I had my first sight of the Earth below. The sea! Not the color-enhanced blue fantasy of the now all too familiar Apollo 8 photograph but the wrinkly gray-green sheet that made even sunny days on the Baltic feel overcast. Most people complained about it, but for some reason it made me feel secure. I would miss that, along with the distinctive smell of the fir trees and the sound of the wind whistling around my ears. Of course, I did not deserve these small pleasures, but who on Earth did? The Technical Director? In a few minutes I would be annihilated. No doubt the Technical Director and a few of the top people would arrange a memorial service, maybe even if the weather was favorable, go out in the Technical Director's little sailboat, the *Orion*, to cast a wreath into the ocean, and on the way back, maybe feel against their cheeks the first hint of spring in the southerly breeze. And the Technical Director would be thinking about all the useful telemetry that The Bastard had sent back and how the flight had been another successful failure whose lessons would be put to good use in a few years when maybe he'd be building rockets in America without the pressures of war, and this time, he'd get it right and there would be some real margins of safety, and he'd finagle himself a spot on what history would record as the first manned flight.

But as I continued looking down, I realized it was neither the Baltic nor the North Sea, but an expanse of forest, and that given the position of the sun, I was clearly headed southwest rather than northeast. On the horizon I could see what looked like snow-capped mountains. The

Alps? It reminded me of the view from the Zeppelin when I was twelve and my grandmother and I were flying over the Harz Mountains. Suddenly I felt it would be an act of betrayal to allow myself to pass seamlessly into oblivion by the machinations of either Korvo or the Technical Director. The altimeter read 23,900 feet with a speed of 297 miles per hour. Right on schedule The Bastard was going into its terminal dive.

There was outrage, then panic, and I hit the ejection button so hard that my hand literally smashed through the instrument panel.

CHAPTER 14
IN THE CAVE

The available light filled the space around me like a luminous white fog, comforting but featureless. Naturally I wondered if this were the afterlife, and I was seized with the fear not of Hell, which this didn't feel like at all, but of Heaven and that I had backed the wrong horse, as it were, because Heaven was turning out to be something on the static Christian model, where you sit in a gallery contemplating a big white rose all day, rather than an eternal April in Andalucia, featuring Moorish courtyards where sages in striped linen djellabas stroll beneath the orange blossoms gesticulating passionately but without rancor as they probe the intracacies of our sacred texts. Gradually, however, the light began to fade and familiar objects emerged from the haze: a lamp, a table with a pitcher of water on it, a chair in the corner of the room, a tall man sitting in the chair, who now stood up and approached me as I lay in bed. I recognized the broad smile even before I was able to assemble the disparate features into a face.

"First we land rockets on the wrong planet, now you bring them down on the wrong country," said the Technical Director. With the words "rockets" and "wrong country," I recalled my thinking toward the end of Raumschiffahrt, that maybe I was being launched toward the Allies.

"Are we in England? France? Is the war over?"

The Technical Director, whose manner had seemed uncharacteristically subdued to this point, let out a big laugh. "That's a good one, Arthur. Oh, how we might wish it so, but for better and worse we're still here and the war rages on, though not particularly for us."

"Am I back at Peenemünde? Where did I come down?" Although I now realized my body was soaked in sweat, I nonetheless felt refreshed, purified, the way one does after a high fever breaks.

The Technical Director shook his head. "Try Thuringia, and believe me, no one is more surprised at your endpoint than myself, though I suppose you might really have the best claim to astonishment."

"I'm not dead," I said. It seemed appropriate to establish this just for the record.

"The rocket came down the worst possible place, actually. An Area Leadership School for Youth not far from the Mittelwerk. Dozens of casualties, many dead. The impact seems to have ruptured a gas line, which in combination with the unused fuel ignited a huge fireball. The only good thing is that since The Bastard crashed at just over Mach 1, nobody heard or saw what hit them and so it's being reported as a gas explosion, just a garden variety act of God. Luftwaffe radar tracked the final descent and knows it was a rocket, but they don't know where it came from. Given the current military situation, a mobile launcher somewhere along the Rhine front is their most logical surmise. Of course, we've denied any knowledge of it and will continue to do so."

"So what does everyone think happened to me?"

"Another place we got lucky. The day after the launch, we heard rumors the Russians were advancing and then got the order to evacuate. Everything was thrown into confusion and nobody was surprised when you didn't return from your supposedly being on assignment in Berlin. There's a scuttling crew finishing its job in Peenemünde now. We've been relocated to an old agricultural school near here, but of course it's all a joke. The Kommandant and his SS goons are the ones in charge, and for their sake I'm going through the motions, chairing meetings, doing design work on paper, but nobody's bending any metal, and never will. We're just trying to run out the clock."

As the Technical Director was talking, a nurse came in the room to check on me. It was now plain to me that I was in a hospital room. "Captain Schulenberg, you're awake! God be praised!" She took my vital signs and was highly solicitous of my well-being. When she left,

I turned back to the Technical Director. "What was that about?" I asked.

"Assuming you survived ejection, I knew about where you would have landed, so I began calling the local hospitals. I found out that this place had an airman who had been discovered hanging from his parachute in an oak tree. He had no I.D. on him, but when I made further inquiries, they told me that when they cut him down he was in a state of delirium, raving about how he had been up to Heaven and seen the stars at noon, before going into a coma. I knew then that I had my man. I put on my SS uniform and flew down here, identifying you as Captain Walter Schulenberg, Waffen-SS Air Arm. Aside from the mild concussion, it seems that you came through almost without a scratch, though of course we'll monitor you closely over the next few weeks, just in case there are some lingering aftereffects."

I listened attentively throughout the Technical Director's explanation of all that had happened, but the whole time my silent inner voice repeated one word over and over: Golem, Golem, Golem, Golem . . . . So our Bastard–my Bastard–had been one of Korvo's Golems. Under the most impossible conditions, he had succeeded in turning a Revenge Weapon V-2 into Revenge Weapon V-3, and I had ridden it into outer space, the first human being to go there. (Note: My own postwar technical analysis suggested that of the 18 V-2s that landed in Germany during the war, perhaps as many as seven were the products of Korvo's sabotage.)

I spent another few days in the hospital before rejoining the Technical Director and the rest of our team at our makeshift headquarters in Bleichrode where our operations were a complete farce. We dutifully checked into our cramped offices each morning and tried to look busy at our drafting tables or blackboards whenever the SS were around, but a lot of our time was just spent playing cards, studying English (and sometimes Russian), and doodling all manner of spacecraft on paper napkins which we would then incinerate in ashtrays. (The word was that I was recovering from pneumonia which I'd contracted on my drive down from Berlin.) During that time, I mentally reviewed my experience of Raumschiffahrt and tried to commit it to memory in granular detail, since although I'm sure I would have been given writing materials if I'd asked, I was reluctant to put anything on paper. To be honest, I was disappointed that the neurological quality of my recollections about Raumschiffahrt were no better than those that I might have abstracted from a long weekend in Paris or a vigorous hike through the Black Forest. There was no opening of the eyes followed by the literal projection of images onto the surrounding walls, either the scenes of extraterrestrial splendor I'd witnessed or my own hallucinatory demons. I couldn't escape the nagging feeling that the Aviatrix or the Technical Director himself might have done better — no doubt he would have returned from space with an updated version of the Ten Commandments, etched in tablets of lucite. On the one occasion I did ask him about a technical debriefing session, he waved me off.

"Arthur, I think we need to get into the habit of never talking about any of this. Ever. We launch a rogue rocket that ends up killing 127 teachers and students — 127 German teachers and students, some of them mere children. Children, Arthur! The regime is dying, yes, but it's not dead yet, and while in the next few weeks someone will have the misfortune of being the last person executed by the Gestapo for treason and insubordination, I don't want that last person to be me, or you. And when we fall into the hands of the Allies, I wouldn't put it past them to use this as an excuse to go after us, especially the Russians. The reality, Arthur, is that, because your rocket veered so far off course, we got almost no telemetry from it, and so we can't even justify it on scientific or engineering grounds. It might just as well have never happened, and because of that and because here's a chance to save our skins, we should go forward from this point as if it never did. Wangermann, you, and I are the only ones who know the whole story here. A few more know it was manned, but they don't know where the rocket ended up, and I've put out the word that it crashed harmlessly in the Harz Mountains after our Luftwaffe test pilot successfully bailed out and was rescued by some shepherds. Please, let this be the last time we even think about February 13th, 1945. As far as the world is concerned Raumschiffahrt must be a dream still awaiting its realization."

So after all of our successful failures, I had managed to bring about a failed success. The Bastard and I had fulfilled all our objectives, even the now militarily irrelevant one of showing that a piloted glider missile could achieve a range of over 300 miles (with the survival of the pilot), but our accomplishment had to be disqualified on what to my mind seemed, with the exception of the guidance issue, purely non-technical grounds. I considered telling the Technical Director about Korvo and his Golems, thinking that in some ways that might take us off the hook for the Leadership School tragedy, but given the possibility that other Golems we didn't know about had already brought death and destruction inside Germany, it occurred to me that I might be held accountable for knowing about what Korvo was doing but saying nothing.

I also couldn't help thinking that there were selfish motivations in the Technical Director's erasure of Raumschiffahrt. Looking back over the history of the project, I know there must have been times when he was simultaneously excited at the prospect of being the genius behind the first manned spaceflight and yet frustrated by the fact that there was no way he could be that first man himself. Certainly Goal #1 outweighed Goal #2, which is why he proceeded with it, but as he had hinted to me back in the hospital room, there was a part of him that didn't want this mission to succeed. But it did succeed, and now the Technical Director would have to live with the fact that his subordinate, Arthur Waldmann, the man-in-the-can, would until the end of time be remembered as the trailblazer into space. But with Raumschiffahrt now expunged from the historical record, he might have another shot at it some brilliant late winter day in, who knows, 1947, himself riding a perfected A-4 high over the deserts of the American West. He would be the chosen one after all, returning to Earth with news about the phenomenology of the space-time continuum, or whatever. Well, genius always finds its own luck, doesn't it?

Around the middle of March, we heard rumors of another move to what was being called the "Alpine Redoubt" in Bavaria where deep underground bunkers were being stocked with food and ammunition that would allow the regime to conduct a protracted resistance in the likely event that the rest of the country was overrun. In preparation for this, the Technical Director and I spent an afternoon going through several cartons of personal items that had come down from Peenemünde, including one that contained a number of photographs and other mementos. I pulled out a picture of the Technical Director and I in our black SS uniforms on the day we hosted a visit by the Reichsführer-SS. "Do you think pictures of us parading around with the top brass is going to help our case with the Americans?" I asked.

"I've told you, Arthur, they know about this already, and besides, it's in our past now, there's nothing we can do about it, or could have done about it. We wanted to build rockets; this was the only way to do it. Any one of them would have done exactly the same, and I'm prepared to tell them that until I'm blue in the face. In fact, I'm making a point of keeping all my awards and commendations, and every scrap of paper that had the Führer's autograph just to prove to them that I have nothing to hide or be ashamed of. Anyway, that reminds me of something. Let me show you."

We left the former classroom building where we had set up our offices and walked over to what had been the school's cattle barn. We climbed a ladder into the hay loft, and there in a corner the Technical Director pulled back a tarpaulin covering several stacks of wooden crates. "I'm still waiting for a couple more of these to arrive from up north. These are the crown jewels that I began collecting as soon as I got word that we were evacuating Peenemünde — our laboratory notes, technical drawings, telemetry records, the whole shebang. You know as well as I do that without these any captured hardware will be just a bucket of bolts. Whoever ends up with this will shave years off their development program, and nothing personal as far as you or anyone else is concerned, but to make sure our ace in the hole stays top secret, I'm going to be the only one who knows where it's buried. If the Americans or the Russians or whoever we end up with don't give us a fair deal, they don't get the treasure. Simple as that. Might also come in handy if the Kommandant and his boys try to pull anything on us last minute. Tomorrow I have one last dash and dodge up to Berlin, but as soon as I return I'll be taking care of this."

A few days later, however–in fact it was the Technical Director's theologically noteworthy thirty-third birthday–I received a phone call from him in the same hospital where I had emerged from my coma. On the late night drive back down to Thuringia, his driver had fallen asleep at the wheel and sent the car careening into a ditch. The injuries were not life threatening but the Technical Director had broken his arm. Could I come to see him at the hospital as soon as possible?

When I arrived, I found him in good spirits, joking with the nurses, of course, despite the unappetizing plate of food on the bed tray in front of him. While I expected to see his arm in a cast, I was not prepared for the monstrosity that dominated the left side of his body. Not only was the arm encased in plaster from above his elbow to the tips of his fingers, but it was thrust out in front of him, the forearm parallel to his chest at about the level of the sternum. He looked like a man permanently frozen in the position of a referee indicating an offside penalty in a ball game. "Not so good for driving a truck, either," he noted, "which is why if you'd do us the favor of checking to see if the coast is clear, we need to talk."

He explained that since the order to evacuate to the Alpine Redoubt could come at any moment, and he was now incapacitated, the responsibility of interring the archive would now fall to me. The last boxes from Peenemünde had arrived and were in storage with the others in the hayloft of the cattle barn. The Technical Director had offered substantial financial incentives (I assumed from his own personal funds) to a sergeant and two corporals in the SS platoon assigned to "protect" us to load this material, which they had been told were weapons and ammunition being cached for future guerilla operations, onto two trucks and then accompany me to the internment site. This was actually part of the Mittelwerk complex, but as the main entrance had now been sealed off by an explosion, the route would take us on a roundabout path to the back of the mountain where the Technical Director had identified an airshaft that was still open. We would be leaving at around midnight that very evening, and because we would be traveling back roads in poor condition, the drive would probably take us most of the night.

As I scurried around that afternoon making final preparations for my mission, I ran into Wangermann who asked me if I'd heard anything about how the Technical Director was doing. I told him that just recently I'd visited him in the hospital and, except for the fact that his arm was in traction, he was doing fine and should be released shortly. Wangermann was much relieved to hear this and went on to tell me that "the natives were getting restless" in his absence; that in fact, even among some of the top people rumors were circulating that there would be no removal to the Alpine Redoubt and that the Technical Director had cut his own deal with the Allies, toward whom he was now fleeing in one of his own personal airplanes. I was happy to quash these rumors but also shocked that my colleagues would have so little faith in the man who over the past ten years had led them to such world-historical achievements.

Sometime after midnight, I met up with the three soldiers who loaded the trucks in about 45 minutes. The route to the internment site was scarred by potholes both from lack of maintenance and Allied air attacks, and because of that and only being able to use the trucks' parking lights for illumination, rarely could we go over ten or fifteen miles per hour.

As the sky lightened in the east, we turned onto a gravel road that traversed a densely wooded area and then continued on for another half hour or so until rather suddenly the trees gave way to a barren plain dusted in white and punctuated by many piles of loose rock. Rising up to a height of about 1,000 feet above this plain was the lumpy summit of the Kohnstein which, until being selected as the site for the Mittelwerk, had been intensively mined for gypsum. Those operations had been headquartered on this side of the mountain, opposite from what was now the main entrance. The place was deserted, literally a desert. Although it was the first week of spring, apart from a few weeds there was no sign of plant or animal life. Almost twenty years of gypsum mining had completely despoiled the environment. The utterly useless thought occurred to me that this would be a good place for a launch pad.

The soldiers began anxiously scouring the hillside for the airshaft. The sun was coming up over the horizon, and the trucks would stand out against the white ground like bulls-eyes for any passing P-47 pilot. Within a couple of minutes, the sergeant found the entrance and the others went back to the trucks to drive them in closer. We shoveled away some loose rock, and then the sergeant and I went in to inspect. The passageway, just tall and wide enough for men of average height to walk single file, was supported by heavy oak beams, some of them cracked and splintered. After about a hundred yards, our flashlights illuminated a chamber about the size of the Hearth Room back at Peenemünde that was empty except for some rusty pickaxes. Despite the cool air of the mine, the sergeant was sweating profusely. "Here?" he asked, barely being able to squeak the word out. I nodded and he ran quickly back toward the entrance.

Feeling no claustrophobia of my own, I continued past the room down the passageway for another few hundred yards until I came to a much larger chamber that I recognized as one of the cross tunnels of the Mittelwerk. The floor was covered with twisted metal, rat's nests of copper wire, jet vanes, broken work benches, all products, I assumed, of the last-minute efforts to scuttle the factory. Whenever the Russians or Americans finally broke into the place, they weren't going to recover much in usable condition.

Back down the passageway, I could hear the grunting and cursing of the soldiers bringing in the cartons containing our archive, which I knew could well be our ticket to a better life after the war. While they were obviously anxious to finish the job and get out of there, I was in no hurry at all. In fact, I felt an uncanny sense of belonging to the place and began playing the flashlight on the walls and ceiling like a potential buyer checking out the basement of a house he is thinking about purchasing. At one point I noticed a wooden hatch on the floor. Pulling on the heavy iron ring, I lifted it up and discovered a narrow vertical shaft one of whose walls showed vestiges of a rope and pulley system. A not unpleasant smell like that of acetone wafted up; perhaps it had been a place to dispose of toxic chemicals. Leaning into it I could just barely make out the bottom about ten or twelve feet down. I closed the door and sat down on top of it. In the distance I could hear the crunch of gravel and the calling of the soldiers as they went about their work.

After a few more minutes, I lifted up the door again and looked down. It occurred to me that a pit like that would be good training for Raumschiffahrt: silent, surrounded by blackness, utterly alone. Such a condition would plunge most men into despair, but I now felt as though my flight had made me a specialist in this area, like a yogi who can sleep comfortably on a bed of nails. Maybe I would be better off in the long run just staying down there. Of course, that would entail a premature death. I rather doubted that the sergeant would conduct an extensive search for a malingering egghead rocket scientist. Assuming that I survived the drop, I could take the same semi-fetal position that I adopted during Raumschiffahrt. Given the low level of oxygen in the tunnels combined with fumes from toxic compounds, I would most likely soon enter a semi-conscious state, passing in and out of hallucinations. Death would occur within hours, certainly no more than three days (the outer limit of life without water), but mentally and spiritually I would again be at one with the immensity of space-time and be able to recapitulate an infinity of possible lives in a way that, at least as far as my unconscious mind was concerned, would make me immortal. Contrasted with my prospects in the outer world, with its marauding P-47s, and the uncertainty of my treatment at the hands of my Allied captors, an abbreviated life there in the tunnel made a lot of sense. A couple of times I caught myself dozing off, not surprising since I hadn't slept the night before. At one point I dreamed that I was again experiencing weightlessness in The Bastard during those two or three minutes after Brenschluss. I pulled myself back to wakefulness, and looking up, saw Korvo sitting on a mangled piece of sheet metal opposite me.

"I wondered how long I would have to sit here before you took notice." He had the bemused expression of the perpetrator of a relatively harmless practical joke. His clothes were the same ones he wore when I knew him as a student, black pants and a white shirt with the cuffs rolled up to the middle of his forearms, though now he also had a noose around his neck whose thick coiled knot hung over his breastbone like the medallion of a Levitical priest. There was no color to his face except for a few bruise marks, but otherwise he looked like his natural self.

He continued: "I appreciate the visit. I wanted to come up and see you in The Bastard, but that's easier said than done. We dead are no longer limited by constraints of time and space, but you see that's exactly the problem. It's too easy to be anywhere and everywhere, and the concentration required to coalesce in any one place is almost herculean."

"Well, what about now?" I asked, genuinely curious.

"We can exploit the memories of the living to some degree," he replied. "But Raumschiffahrt! Jesus! Not only did your brain lack any specific associations between space flight and yours truly, but since no human being had ever been in space before, I couldn't even draw from some stockpile in the collective unconscious. No, those twelve guys chanting in Aramaic up there were just your imagination, pure Waldmann. Down here, of course, it's different. I'm as real as these walls of gypsum. The underground has truly become my *metier* — Magdeburg, the Nazis, and now you! Not that I hold my tragically premature demise against you in the least. I was growing rather tired of the world, and had toyed with the idea of suicide long before I was shipped off to the Mittelwerk. But I didn't want to have self-annihilation on the conscience of my eternal soul, so when I got to the tunnels I figured I'd just leave it up to my tormentors. When you showed up in the Cathedral, I was not at all unpleased. It's a shame to have such an intimate business as one's death presided over by strangers, and I felt lucky to have an old friend play such an important role in my translation to this next order of being, or rather, non-being. So it's not my execution per se that I'm here to talk with you about."

"It's vaguely re-assuring to know that you can be just as exasperating in death as in life," I responded, "though I suppose at least you're providing me with evidence of the immortality of the soul. But really, Korvo, I murdered you. You had your head in a noose, the other end of the rope was attached to a crane, and I pushed the button that raised it. On top or that, you were humiliated in your final moments of Earthly existence. For a prisoner fed gruel, it was amazing how much shit dropped out of you as your body wrenched in its final paroxysm."

"Point well taken. But if it makes you feel better, I can assure that my lack of tidiness on that occasion was the least of my concerns. Dying was a pain, yes, and if I had to do it all over again, I'm not sure I would sign up, but on the other hand, I love being dead. No clocks, no obligations, every day like the Sabbath, Saturday, or Sunday for Christians. It's like decades-early retirement."

"So you've forgiven me? Wonderful. Now I can go on with my life. I'll be sure to mention this conversation when the Allies interrogate me about your murder."

"Jesus, Waldmann, nobody said anything about forgiveness. Now who's being exasperating? We dead, by definition, could not care less about all that. No, I've intruded upon this bathetic moment in your life less for your sake than for mine. Basically, I'm here to request that you not die in this pit because as far as you're concerned the Mittelwerk belongs to me and I would prefer not to have your company. I know I talked earlier about anywhere and everywhere, but it's more complicated than that. Your allotted chance for suicide was not hitting the eject button in The Bastard, and you didn't take it. No *kiddushim ha shem* for you Sephardic guys! Your people would have eaten a plate of pork chops, drunk the baptismal font dry, whatever it took to keep living the good life under blue Andalucian skies. Well, all right, there were the flames of the occasional auto-de-fé—but I'm getting off the subject. Anyway, in another decade or so, there will for sure be a few human souls haunting the thermosphere—by the way, guess which nationality?"

"Not German. Russian?"

"Bingo. Russians to begin with. Anyway, as the first dead man in space you would have had a certain prestige that de facto would have allowed you the right to tell those guys in their ghost Vostoks which orbits they could, and could not, haunt. True, by the end of the twenty-first century, especially on account of the first two disastrous Mars missions, there would be too many casualties for even the long-accumulated noetic energy of a long dead Marrano to keep control of, but for a while you would have had things pretty much your own way. Lucky bastard. But no, you got all resentful at the thought of the Technical Director surviving you and ejected. Although I've already told you more than I should have (please forget what I just said about the Mars missions), I will prophesy" —and here Korvo momentarily looked upward and spread out his hands in the pose of Old Testament prophets as represented in medieval art—"Arthur Waldmann shall not pass away either above the Earth or below it."

He slid over next to me. "Look, to be honest, there are no actual rules on this. At first, I thought I might just spook you a little into going on with your admittedly dreadful life, maybe just some voices in your head, I don't know, I'm still new at this stuff, but I figured that after surviving Raumschiffahrt you weren't going to scare easily, so I'm giving you the full supernatural treatment. So do me a favor right now and get the hell out of here before Sergeant Meat Cleaver gets any more antsy and detonates the charges that his men have just finished setting." He stood up to go away but looked back once more before heading deeper into the tunnels. "Okay, one last thing. There are a couple scraps of meaning still clinging to your sorry future life and they involve the Technical Director who now awaits you in the Alpine Redoubt. But please, I don't need any more roommates down here than the few thousand I already have."

While I was obviously surprised to have just conversed with a dead man, I was also struck by the reasonableness of everything he had said, and so taking his words to heart, I calmly headed back toward the entrance where the soldiers were finishing up their work. I stepped back in for one last look around, nodded approvingly, and then gave the order to run the wires from the dynamite at the entrance to a spot behind a slag heap about 200 yards away. When we were all hunkered down, I myself pressed the detonator. (Execution, ejection, explosion—I was clearly developing expertise in pushing consequential buttons.) When the dust settled and I was satisfied that the cave was sealed, I called the men to attention and delivered a short speech about how the Führer's strategy of phased retreat was even at that very moment drawing the Allies into a trap from which they would never escape, yielding a German victory that would be as unimaginably sweet as it was incontestably total. With seeming reluctance, they climbed into one of the trucks and drove away. I had been so convincing that I think they almost believed me.

CHAPTER 15
PASSION PLAY

When I returned around dawn to our makeshift headquarters at Bleichrode, I learned that just after midnight the Kommandant had given the order to evacuate and that all of our top people had departed for Oberammergau aboard a deluxe train, complete with dining car, that had been named the "Vengeance Express." Although I wasn't surprised at the news, I was also miffed that no one had left me any orders or instructions. Perhaps they assumed it was obvious: get myself to the Alpine Redoubt by whatever means at my disposal. So I climbed back into my truck and started driving south. Aside from having to dodge a couple of P-51s outside of Ingolstadt, the trip was uneventful, and by late in the afternoon I could see snow-capped mountains in the middle distance. The sweetish smell of fir trees filled the air, and as the peaks along the former border between Germany and Austria came into sharper focus, the Moselander in me couldn't help feeling a certain uneasiness at just the thought of such vertiginous terrain.

The route to Oberammergau continued through the gentle valley of the Loisach, and after crossing one modest ridge (with an admittedly dicey hairpin turn) separating it from the valley of the Ammer, I arrived at the famous village. It looked just the way I'd always imagined places in the Alps, with its brightly painted half-timbered houses and gingerbread roofs, the whole scene presided over by an imposing mountain, the Kolben, whose shape approximated that of a Tyrolean hat.

When I reached the town square I parked the truck in front of a half-timbered building displaying a huge swastika banner from an upper balcony and a sign over the entrance identifying it as the Hotel Jesus. I walked in and found the lobby crowded with many of my colleagues but was surprised to see them strangely attired in robes, tunics, togas, and sandals. Several were wearing fake beards. My first thought was that these were disguises donned in response to some security crisis. Were these outfits ancillary to an escape attempt undertaken after discovery of the Technical Director's contacts with the Americans? Was it a result of intelligence that we might fall into the hands of the French instead of the Americans? Yet what good would it do us to go into hiding dressed like Moses or Julius Caesar?

At that moment I felt a meaty hand settling upon my shoulder. "Waldmann, you're just in time!" It was General D. but unlike the others he was wearing lederhosen and a green felt hat. "We need a new John."

"My apologies, General, but I've just arrived and literally have no idea what's going on here."

"What's going on is that we Seppels really know how to throw a party, war or no war! Our first night here we were sitting in the bar already bored out of our minds when Alois came over–Alois Lang, he owns the Jesus and always plays Christ, though of course there's been a long dry spell, they haven't put it on since the big one in '34 when I think even the Führer came. Anyway, we got to talking and when he found out that the Technical Director usually organized a theatrical for Fasching, he said, 'Who knows what the world will look like at the next scheduled performance in 1950? Since we have enough men and it's still close to Easter, why don't we stage a little impromptu Passion Play?' As soon as the Technical Director heard that, we were off and running."

"But General," I said, "how come you're not in costume? I'm sure you'd make a good-a good–" but although I didn't have an ending for this sentence, General D. burst out laughing before he realized my embarrassment.

"Are you kidding? You know I have no talent for anything but slapstick. You want me to remember what Matthew says to Mark after they see Jesus rise from the dead? No way! But listen, I just found out that our John is out of action—some Preissn, I'm sure, who was no match for our local Saufspiele, still hung over at noon the next day. They're starting the dress rehearsal in about ten minutes. Your part is easy, just a few lines in a couple of early scenes, then you can go somewhere and rest up until this evening's performance. That's an order!" he shouted, looking sternly at me and then laughing again. Since technically I wasn't a soldier in the Army, I didn't have to take orders, and certainly not mock orders, from him, but at this point I found it frankly a relief for someone to tell me what to do.

When I arrived at the theater across the way, I found small groups of a dozen or so scattered around different parts of the stage, some obviously actors, others adjusting costumes or make-up or helping the actors go over their lines. The biggest group was at center stage clustered around a man who seemed oddly larger than life. When he turned in my direction, I could see that it was the Technical Director, his enhanced size the result of loose-fitting robes that had been draped over the massive cast that held his broken arm in a horizontal position.

"Waldmann, thank God you've made it here safely. I've been worried sick. I'm sorry we didn't have the chance to speak before the evacuation. Did you — did everything go all right?"

It was strange but until that moment I had completely dismissed all recollection of burying the archive and my encounter with Korvo. It now came back to me. Had it gone all right? Well, I had been turned from my purpose of burying myself alive, but I knew that's not what he was talking about. On the spur of the moment I came up with an appropriately cryptic and memorable phrase. "The cat's in its cradle," I said. He breathed an audible sigh of relief.

"What's your role, Simon of Cyrene?" I asked him, tapping the diagonal wooden beam that supported his outstretched arm.

"That would have made sense, now that you mention it. I would have preferred a much smaller part. But since Alois is really the only one here competent to direct and so can't play Jesus himself like he usually does, they all insisted that I have the place of honor, especially since with this cast it seems like I'm already bearing a cross."

"John! Where's our new John the Baptist?" an assistant director called out from the other side of the stage.

My role, if pivotal, was not demanding. In the first scene, dressed in a camel hair shirt and ragged loin cloth, I would be baptizing people in dumb show at the Jordan. In my other scene I would have a non-speaking role. In fact, I would be dead. This was the occasion where Salome, played in drag by a junior engineer in our aeronautics division, would request of Herod the head of John the Baptist brought in upon a platter. This would be staged by wheeling me in on a table with curtained sides and a hole cut in the middle for my head to fit through. The only real acting challenge here was to maintain the admonitory expression that was presumably frozen into my face at the moment of death.

Performances of the Passion Play began as the fulfillment of a vow by the good burghers of Oberammergau that if God saved the town from a visitation of the Black Death in 1633, they would produce a play about the life and death of Jesus every ten years from then until the Second Coming. Originally performed in the church graveyard, by the twentieth century the play had moved into a permanent theater building that could hold thousands. On this occasion, however, there was an audience of only a few hundred, mostly townspeople and some off-duty Waffen-SS.

After I baptized the Technical Director and my disembodied head sat there on its silver platter, I was free to go out into the audience and enjoy the rest of the play. While our people were up to their usual standards of amateur excellence, the real bravura performance was that of the Kommandant in the role of Pontius Pilate. In his white toga, purple stole, and gilt laurel wreath atop crew-cut hair, he looked every inch the Roman governor of a rebellious province where a new Messiah popped up every week, a role wholly appropriate to someone who until just a few weeks before had been overseer of a slave labor camp. When Jesus is brought before him the first time, he listens to the complaints of the Sanhedrin (dressed in their traditional horn-shaped hats and speaking in recognizable Yiddish accents) with growing irritation etched into his face until, in one of the production's not-so-subtle anachronisms, he reaches beneath his throne for his MP 40 submachine gun and fires a long burst into the air to disperse them. He then orders a Centurion to scourge Jesus but dissatisfied with the sluggish pace of the punishment, he kicks the soldier aside and begins whipping Jesus himself with sadistic brio. (I later heard that this was an improvisation on the Kommandant's part.)

From a purely creative standpoint, however, the final scene of the production demonstrated the most consummate artistry in its weaving together of both ancient religious and contemporary historical themes. It is now Easter Sunday as the hooded figures of the two Marys approach the tomb where Jesus has been buried. Suddenly the Earth rumbles (a howitzer fired behind the building), lights flash, and a papier-mâché stone rolls away from the entrance. In the opening stands an androgynous angel all in white, upon whom the spotlight focuses, illuminating a bird-like face that registers an expression of barely concealed annoyance. It is the Aviatrix. She extends her arms, which have been fitted with wings, and ascends by a system of invisible ropes and pulleys to a platform about ten feet above the stage. From here she looks down at the Marys and then out at the audience: "You fools, why do you look for the living among the dead? Do you not remember what He told you while He was still in Galilee?"

She turns her head toward the back of the stage, and there on an otherwise invisible scrim is projected several times larger than life a sequence of images showing the Technical Director driving the money changers from the Temple, distributing loaves of bread to the crowd, healing a sick child, and walking on water. The Aviatrix pauses as the audience gasps its approval at the visual effect, and then continues, "Did He not make clear what must happen; that the Son of Man would be handed over to sinners—abandoned by His disciples—and condemned to death on the Cross?"

But instead of these events appearing on the screen behind her, we now see images of bombed-out cities and wounded soldiers and civilians concluding, for only an instant, with a photograph of the Führer awarding medals to a line of young boys in Volksturm uniforms. Raising her voice to a higher pitch, the Aviatrix goes on:

"He will be the man for all eternity, who was sure of Himself despite terrible pain and suffering, and who will show the way to victory. He is the only one who remained true to Himself, who did not cheaply sell His faith and His ideals, who always and without doubt followed His straight path toward His goal. That goal may today be hidden behind the piles of rubble that our hate-filled enemies have wrought across our once-proud continent, but which will shine again before our burning eyes when the rubble has been cleared.

"Once more the armies of the enemy powers storm against our defensive fronts. Behind them is the slavering force of Jewry that wants no peace until it has reached its satanic goal of world destruction. But its hopes are in vain! As He has done so often before, God will throw Lucifer back into the abyss even as he stands before the gates of power over all the peoples. A man of truly timeless greatness, of unique courage, of a steadfastness that elevates the hearts of some and shakes those of others, will be His tool!"

The spotlight now shifts to another elevated platform above and to the right where stands the Technical Director in shining cloth-of-gold robes. Smoke and flames seem to billow out around his feet and as the audience sees the nose of an A-4 gradually ascending behind him, I recognize a clip of the color film we shot of an early successful launch that we later screened at the Wolfsschanze. The Aviatrix turns to the audience one last time, and I see spittle flying from her mouth as she barks out: "He is gone ahead of you back to Galilee. Go, now, tell the others what you have seen and heard, for only such truths as these will stand the test of time."

•   •   •

Because it was well after midnight when I finally extricated myself from the Passion Play cast party, I'd had only a few hours of sleep when an orderly knocked on my door and summoned me to the Kommandant's office around 5:00 a.m. I arrived to find General D., the Technical Director, and most of our other top people, all looking seriously hung over, arranged in a semi-circle around the desk where the Kommandant stood, smartly attired in his full dress SS uniform, including leather gloves and riding crop. To his right was the Aviatrix in a crisp, close-fitting blue serge jacket, her Iron Cross First Class with Diamonds prominently displayed beside her left lapel.

"I will keep this short," he announced. "Early this morning I received word that I have been appointed Plenipotentiary of the Führer for Jet Aircraft. I must leave for Berlin within the hour. The

Aviatrix has bravely volunteered to fly me there in a Storch that is waiting for us at the Garmisch-Partenkirchen airfield. I expect that my new duties may keep me away from the Redoubt for an indefinite length of time. In my absence Colonel Wagner will be in command. Long live Germany! Long live the Führer! Dismissed!"

Shuffling out of the Kommandant's office, the Aviatrix buttonholed the Technical Director, but before she could get a word out he waved her away. "You know as well as I do that nothing worthwhile has ever been accomplished before 10:30 or 11:00 in the morning, and especially a morning after a late night like the one we just had. I'm headed straight back to bed. Talk to Waldmann. Whatever it is, he probably knows as much about it as I do," and with that he was off. Clearly annoyed but resigned to her lack of options, the Aviatrix turned to me and said, "Let's go outside. I need to have a word with you."

As we walked down a side street off the main square, she began by telling me what I already knew, that the situation in Berlin was becoming desperate. "The Russians have already taken up positions in the eastern suburbs."

"We've heard the rumors. Despite the heroic efforts of our armies, it seems as though defeat may now be inevitable."

"Defeat?" she said with extreme condescension, the veins bulging out around her temples. "No one has said anything about defeat. The enemy can bomb our cities and pillage our countryside, but as long as the spirit of the nation remains strong, Final Victory is within reach. I am, however, concerned about the immediate safety of the Führer and that is the only purpose of this interview. Am I correct in understanding that you were involved in the planning and development of the manned V-2?"

While I had always known that the Technical Director was considering the Aviatrix as a prime candidate for Raumschiffahrt, he had led me to believe that she was unaware I was her main competition. Now I was uncertain exactly how much she knew about my role in the project and felt the need to proceed with extreme caution.

"If you mean the proposed winged version of the missile, the A-4b, yes, I did some work on it. It was highly experimental."

"I also understand that you once launched a dog and brought it safely back to Earth."

"Yes, that's correct," I lied, "we had a successful launch and recovery of an animal."

"And I know the next step was to launch a human being, so let me get right to the point. A unit of the Waffen-SS has secured an improvised airstrip in the Tiergarten where I'm reasonably confident I'll be able to land the Storch, but as the Russians advance I'm less sure about getting out again. While it's imperative for Final Victory that the Führer be able to lead us from the Alpine Redoubt, he has made it clear that he will not leave Berlin until the last possible moment. We still have overland access to the city from the west and north. Assuming that we could arrange transport, and assuming that you have such a vehicle, would it be possible to bring a crew capsule down from Peenemünde, substitute it for a warhead on a currently operational V-2, and then fire it from a mobile launcher located in central Berlin?"

I was so taken aback at this proposal that for a few seconds I just stared blankly. On account of my own experience which of course I would never share with her, I could only think about her inquiry in terms of Raumschiffahrt. Why would anyone want to launch the Führer into outer space? Was it possible that she imagined some divine being, some angel or Adam Kadmon himself, might reach down and lift him up to Heaven where he would remain in a state of suspended animation until the military situation on the ground improved?

"Launch the Führer into space?" I said finally.

"Space?" she said uncomprehendingly as if I had just been speaking Aramaic. "Why no, launch him to the Alpine Redoubt."

The idea was so preposterous, not to mention technically infeasible, that I wanted to burst out laughing, but instead I scratched my earlobe as if giving the matter further thought.

"Well, to be honest, I think we got lucky with the dog, since we had calculated the odds at less than fifty-fifty. A man would be more challenging, especially a middle-aged man who might not be in top physical condition. But the real problem is that the A4-b's long range was enabled by the addition of wings. Now while theoretically it might be possible to weld a pair onto an existing V-2 already in the field" — the thought crossed my mind that such a missile might be one of Korvo's Golems — "I don't know that we'd have the capability to carry out such a fabrication anywhere except —"

"So the answer is no," she said, cutting me off. She looked at me with the transcendental hatred of a member of a race that had long owned certain prerogatives denied other mortals which now seemed unjustly snatched away. When it came to the *Endsieg*, she obviously had no patience for a Doubting Thomas like myself. Would she just take out her Luger and shoot me? At this point the act would have no legal consequences. The thought crossed my mind that maybe the Technical Director had mentioned in passing once my status vis-à-vis the Nuremburg Laws, but in retrospect I doubt that even her reservoir of tyrannical self control would have been enough to allow her to suffer my very presence if she thought I was even Mixed Ancestry, Second Grade.

In the end, she simply turned her back on me and walked away.

The next day the timely appearance of a P-47 allowed the Technical Director to persuade the nervous Colonel Wagner that our top people should be dispersed in small groups throughout the area lest we all be killed in a single bombing raid. With the Technical Director, General D. and a dozen others, I was transferred about eighty kilometers to a ski hotel atop the Oberjoch where the Alpine skies were pure azure and the hotel service was excellent. The location suited us well as we'd heard that the Americans were entering Austria to our south. For a few days we just lounged on the terrace soaking in the sun and gazing up at the glittering snow-capped peaks of the Allgau. "How infinitely peaceful it all seems!" remarked General D., over drinks late one afternoon. "Is it possible we've just suffered through six long years of war? Maybe it's all been a bad dream!"

The false news report on May 1st that the Führer had died in street fighting against the Russians allowed the Technical Director to broach the subject of surrendering to the Americans with General D. If we'd had any anxieties about how he might react to the proposal, they were unfounded. He readily agreed, adding that the time had now come to put our baby — the A-4 — in the right hands.

We sent one of our group down into the valley on a sort of reconnaissance mission to try to make contact with the U. S. Army. The effort was successful, and the next day all of us made the trip to the Counter Intelligence Corps headquarters in the small Austrian town of Reutte. Although the Technical Director wasn't the least bit worried about turning ourselves in — "if they've done their homework, they know we've got something that they want," he said — I was prepared to be locked in a cell like a common prisoner of war. In fact, once again, the Technical Director was right on the mark. As soon as they confirmed that we were indeed the Peenemünde rocket scientists, we were treated like visiting dignitaries. As the Technical Director would tell interviewers for years afterwards, "I wasn't kicked in the teeth or anything. They immediately fried us some eggs."

CHAPTER 16
AUTO - DE - FÉ

At this point I have only two incidents to add since the story of the Technical Director and his rocket team following their removal to the United States, from the earliest launches of captured A-4s at White Sands, New Mexico through the conclusion of the Apollo Program, has been thoroughly documented elsewhere, at least as far as I'm concerned. If this narrative were a movie, the camera would now pull away from the scene of us chatting and joking with American soldiers in Reutte to a long shot of the Allgau at sunset, while a sequence of titles rolled informing you, the audience, about later events in the principals' lives:

The **Technical Director** went to work for the U. S. Army where he developed intercontinental ballistic missiles, including the Redstone which launched America's first satellite and astronauts into space. Later on as the director of a major NASA field center, he oversaw the development of the mighty Saturn V, which carried American astronauts to the moon. He died in 1977.

After being briefly detained by the Allies, the **Aviatrix** took up a career of competitive gliding and stunt flying until being recruited by the Technical Director as a Human Factors Specialist. She was later appointed a lecturer in our local university's Department of Psychology and Aeronautics, and rose through the academic ranks becoming a Full Professor, Dean, and University Provost.

General D., after being held by the British as a prisoner of war for two years, moved to the United States where he worked for the U. S. Air Force and later a major defense contractor, rising to the position of vice president. He was involved in the creation of the world's first guided nuclear air-to-surface missile and also NASA's X-15 rocket plane.

Hans Winziger escaped to Sweden at the end of the war where he earned a doctorate in chemistry at the Royal Institute of Technology, specializing in volatile organic compounds. Under the Technical Director's sponsorship, he emigrated to the United States and later became Professor of Chemistry, Vice President for Faculty Management, and University Provost.

Arthur Waldmann continued to work on guidance issues during a long career with both the Army and NASA until his retirement in 1978.

I know that seems a bit skimpy, but the brevity does reflect something of how the next thirty years felt. In one's natural life there's a density to the first couple of decades which then attenuates with the advance of maturity. We have rich memories of life at nine or twelve or seventeen, but quick, tell me what you were doing when you were forty-three. My vocational life had somewhat the same trajectory. I could date it from the evening I met the Technical Director at the Oberth lecture, and it reached a climax that day in February 1945 when I was shot into space. Already by the following spring, I felt the onset of a long denouement, confirmed in our translation to America. After extensive debriefings and interrogations, the Technical Director was flown to the United States in September, while most of the rest of our team endured two weeks of seasickness crossing the Atlantic in the cattle car of an old Liberty Ship, the *U.S.S. Central Falls Victory*, toward the end of 1945.

While I would never describe our subsequent relationship in terms of estrangement, the Technical Director's ever-increasing administrative duties simply meant that I spent less time around him. There was also the fact that while in Germany our work was invisible to people outside a small circle of military leaders and technical experts, in democratic America a lot of what we did was out in the open. As interest in rocketry increased during the 1950s, so did the celebrity of the Technical Director, who became the face of the space program until he was eclipsed by the Mercury astronauts. He published books and magazine articles; he was featured in a series of Disney television programs about space; there was a movie made about his life, though even he would acknowledge its many gross misrepresentations. With fame came wealth (mainly from speaking fees—his government salary remained modest) and with that the ability to do things that the rich do. He pursued expensive hobbies like scuba diving and reindeer hunting, and went on vacations to exotic places like Nepal. Except for the occasional cocktail party to celebrate a holiday or welcome a visiting dignitary, we never socialized.

I, on the other hand, adopted a more ascetic mode of life, at least for those first few years out in the desert, whose barrenness my colleagues hated because, oddly enough, it so resembled the moon. But because I was still feeling guilt for some of my wartime actions, the treeless and boulder-strewn landscape of New Mexico offered spiritual comfort as it seemed a step in the right direction toward Hell, or at least Purgatory, where I probably belonged. (Furtively, I practiced various kinds of mortification, like walking barefoot through rattlesnake country on dark, moonless nights). The intensity of my remorse had faded, however, by the time of our move east in 1950. For the next twenty or so years, I would go to my office in the morning and come home in the evening to the small house that I had built on the mountain overlooking our town, and relax in the handmade furniture that I had crafted. I was married briefly and then divorced. My parents came over from Germany to live here for a few years and then, growing nostalgic, returned home to die. Like stained glass windows, the Zohar seemed something from another time and even if I'd had a copy, I probably never would have cracked it open. Needless to say, I had nothing to do with the local Jewish community, who wouldn't have considered me Jewish anyway.

The philosopher Kierkegaard said that the specific character of despair was precisely being unaware of despair, in other words, feeling a kind of benumbed contentment. Contentment, indeed. I liked the mental challenge of figuring out how to get a nuclear warhead or an astronaut from point A to point B. The views from the back deck of my house were not as spectacular as those from Oberjoch, but arguably more picturesque. I thought very little about my past. Because I had always accepted the Technical Director's argument that my Raumschiffahrt must remain secret lest the stink of Nazism infect the future prospects of manned space flight, the whole experience became less and less real to me, and there were days when I genuinely wondered if it had really happened. If it did, I simply recognized that while some trailblazers are famous, others, usually the forerunners, are not. Everyone has heard of Vasco da Gama who rounded the Cape of Good Hope and sailed to India, but who knows about Alfonso de Paiva, who scoped out possible routes to the East some ten years before?

I think it was a picture in our in-house newsletter about 1968 that cracked the protective shell I had built up around myself and led me to again reflect upon those momentous years in the 1930s and 1940s, and my relationship with the Technical Director. The occasion was a flight of the "Vomit Comet," a KC-135 aircraft that would execute a parabolic dive allowing astronauts in training to experience twenty seconds of weightlessness. The Technical Director had somehow finagled a ride on one and a photograph showed him floating in the padded fuselage, arms and legs extended like a skydiver (another of his hobbies, by the way), with a big boyish grin on his face. Yet despite his evident enjoyment, I was suddenly overwhelmed with feelings of the most profound pity for him because I knew that as a man now approaching sixty, this was as close as he would ever come to going into space while I had actually done it. For years I used to wonder if in the domain of Raumschiffahrt I was forerunner or messiah, and now the answer seemed obvious: I was both. I had, however, undergone an occultation, like the sages of the Zohar who for decades during the Roman persecutions after the destruction of the Temple hid out in caves, or perhaps like the Messiah himself, who was said to have been born at the very moment the Centurions desecrated the Holy of Holies and to this day wanders the world unrecognized until the morning of the Last Day.

Moreover, I knew that for the Technical Director there was not just a sense of personal loss behind that smile, but also an awareness that the enterprise to which he'd dedicated his life was now crumbling before his eyes. Of course, to those on the outside, the late 1960s looked like the glory days of the space program. Yet as it became increasingly apparent that the Russians were dropping out of the race to the moon, funding for the program began to be cut. The success of Apollo 11 was the final nail in the coffin. Except for the near disaster of Apollo 13, nobody paid much attention to the remaining missions.

It was against this backdrop that I received a call from the Technical Director in early December 1969. We had just completed our second successful lunar landing with Apollo 12, and I figured that he wanted to warn me about more cutbacks to the budget for the Guidance Lab. Instead of asking me up to his office, however, he suggested that we meet at When Pigs Fly, his favorite local barbecue joint. I agreed, though of course like all good Marranos, I disdain pork, and instead would order a plate of their overcooked vegetables.

"It's been too long, hasn't it, Arthur?" he said, standing up to greet me when I arrived. In fact, I literally could not remember that last time we had spoken in a non-professional setting. As expected he did begin with bad news about our budget. We commiserated on the sorry state of things until our food came and then he said, "I want to show you something." He handed me a letter-sized envelope. "This came in the mail the other day. A local postmark, but no return address." Inside was the clipping of a recent article from the *New York Times Magazine* entitled "The Devil's Architect," and on the first page was a picture of Albert Speer and the Führer at the latter's Obersalzburg country house examining architectural plans for postwar Berlin. "Flip ahead to page 110," said the Technical Director. The article included photographs of all the major Third Reich figures, and there on page 110 was one of the Technical Director with the caption, "Well, we've solved the take-off problem." Scanning the text I saw that it was extracted from Speer's account to the *Times* interviewer of the June 1942 launch of the A-4 that reached Mach 1 but then came suddenly crashing back to Earth less than a mile off shore. In the column above and below his picture, someone had highlighted the following lines:

"The order to go into mass production was still premature, but we went ahead anyway, at the Mittelwerk, an abandoned salt mine in the Harz mountains. . . . When I first inspected it, in December, 1943, I met the first slave laborers. They were gaunt, badly cared for, wretchedly fed and laboring under frightful conditions. . . . I gave orders on the spot, and more when I got back to my ministry in Berlin, to improve working conditions in these plants. I did not act on compassionate grounds. We were in the middle of what had become total war, and I was willing to exploit this labor—and, of course, that was a crime. I argued for better treatment on the grounds a technocrat invariably invokes—you just do not increase production by starving and murdering your labor force."

In addition to the highlighting, the words "that was a crime" had been underlined. I shrugged. "This is basically old news," I said. "I think by now everyone knows that the A-4 wasn't made by union workers on a sparkling assembly line in Detroit. I heard that Speer had written his memoirs. He's obviously trying to sell books. There'll be some turbulence, but trust me, it will all blow over."

"I'm not so sure, Arthur. The day after Apollo 11 lifted off, Drew Pearson wrote a story about what a brilliant engineer I was but also about how I had been in the SS. I have no idea how he found out about that, unless someone who's seen our Army files tipped him off. And here's something almost no one in town knows about. Late last year I got a subpoena to testify at the trial of some old Mittelwerk guards in Essen. After going back and forth about it for some weeks, the NASA lawyers up at headquarters talked them down to having me give a deposition at the German consulate in New Orleans. I told them the place was run by the SS and that we had nothing to do with the workers. They asked me about sabotage—I told them I had never received an official word about it. Afterwards there were a couple reporters out front and I repeated that I had nothing to hide and that I had never colluded in the mistreatment of detainees."

"Okay. No collusion. I still don't see the problem."

"The problem, Arthur, is that we both know it's not true. I never received an official report of sabotage, but we knew it went on all the time and how the SS dealt with it. You and I may never have witnessed any hangings, but some of our people did. Besides, even when the operation worked smoothly, things were bad for the workers. Remember when we found out that guy Korvo was down there, and we tried to do something to make his life a little better? I wonder what ever happened to him."

Another line of Kierkegaard's came back to me from that long-ago undergraduate philosophy course at Friedrich-Wilhelm: "If a man cannot forget, he will never amount to much."

"Imagine if we had been born in America instead of Germany," I said. "There's a good chance that everything we did there in the 1930s and 1940s we would have done here, minus the use of slave labor. But even if we did, we would have been on the winning side. Do you think now a quarter century later they'd be dragging you into court to defend your actions in the line of patriotic duty? Like Speer said, it was total war. What choice did any of us have?"

"Arthur, do you believe in God?"

Not this again, I thought. "Why yes, of course, don't we all?"

"I'm more convinced than ever that there must have been divine intervention when I decided at the end of the war that the secrets of rocketry should go to the Americans, a people who read the Bible. For the past several years I've been attending weekly Bible study, and the other day we were reading the Book of Jonah. Everyone knows about Jonah being swallowed by the whale, but the real point of the story is about how he goes to prophesy against the Ninevites who were the most immoral people in the world at that time and how they listened to Jonah and put on sackcloth and covered themselves with ashes and how God saw them turn from their evil ways and so did not destroy them. Did you know that the Jews have one day of the year when they repent their sins, kind of like what Catholics do when they go to confession, and on that day they read the whole Book of Jonah aloud?"

Yom Kippur. My grandmother and I used to observe it secretly when I was a boy by trying to stay away from home all day so my parents wouldn't realize we were fasting. "No," I lied, "I didn't know that."

"Sometimes I envy the Catholics and even the Jews for having a system to flush out the gunk in your soul. I tell you, Arthur, even if all this Speer stuff blows over, between that and NASA on the chopping block, it's got me pretty damned depressed."

I believed in God also and had long ago decided that punishment for my crimes must not be death since He could so easily have arranged that during Raumschiffahrt but elected not to. For a while I thought maybe the punishment was being denied fame for Raumschiffahrt, but over time I realized that my remarkable experience was like a golden chalice that precisely because it remained secret could never be tarnished and so it didn't feel like punishment at all. Unlike the Technical Director, I was not blessed with a beautiful wife and family, but that was true for a lot of people, and I don't think the mere absence of good fortune counts as punishment. As I noted earlier, for many years now I had inhabited a state of spiritual and emotional numbness. Perhaps that was punishment enough, or maybe it was simply not knowing if at some time in the future, including a possible afterlife, the hammer might really come down on me. Only God knew, literally.

In sum I considered myself a lost cause, but as had happened many times before, whenever the Technical Director was down in the dumps, I couldn't help feeling sorry for him. It seemed wrong that someone so richly endowed with everything from intelligence to good luck should be in a state of despair. Although flawed like every human being, he nonetheless showed what the human species was capable of, at least in the scientific and technical fields. He was a man in full whose existence might give the rest of us hope. If only for selfish reasons, I wanted him to be content with his lot. Then out of nowhere, the homeland of all brilliant ideas, something occurred to me.

"I can't make the Mittelwerk go away or get you on a spaceship to Mars, but there's something I think I can do to help you flush the gunk out, as you say. Are you busy Saturday morning?" I asked him.

"How early?"

"Nine o'clock."

"Can you make it a little later?"

"Remember back in the early fifties when we were working on RS-1, and we didn't even have enough money to build a proper static test stand?"

"Of course I do," said the Technical Director, his face lighting up. "I went on a scavenger hunt just like Foggy used to do in Berlin, and we cobbled it together for a few thousand bucks. I loved that pile of junk. We did some of our best work with it. Haven't been out there in ages."

"Well, that's the place," I said. "Meet me there this Saturday at ten."

"Can you tell me why?"

"No."

· · ·

Redstone Test Stand, also known as Interim Test Stand, was located in an isolated area near the river, several miles from our closest residential subdivisions. The site actually included two components, the stand itself, a sixty-foot-tall structure fabricated mainly from scrap steel that looked like two fire towers pushed together, one with and one without the observer's shed atop it. The other some three hundred feet away was the command and control bunker, three old railroad tank cars side by side with passageways cut between them, and periscopes sticking out through the several feet of soil and turf they were buried under. While the facility would eventually be restored and declared a National Historic Landmark, in late 1969 it was rusty and falling apart.

That Saturday morning the place was completely deserted as I expected. The weather was seasonally cool and sunny with a light westerly wind. I had completed all my preparations and was sitting on the first flight of the metal steps leading up to the top of the gantry when about a quarter after ten the Technical Director pulled up in his white Mercedes-Benz. (It was sign of how comfortable we had become in our adopted country that we no longer felt obliged to drive American automobiles.) When he got out, he was wearing the outfit that he had always favored for launches going back to the early days on Griefswalder Oie, a gray trench coat with a high-crowned tweed hat. I was somewhat surprised by this; perhaps he expected that I was going to fire off a small rocket.

We chatted for a few minutes about the glory days working on Redstone and Jupiter, and then I opened up the small suitcase I had brought and handed him a card which read:

AUTO

SINGULAR

DE FÉ

CELEBRADO EN REDSTONE
TEST STAND

SÁBADO 6 DE DECIEMBRE 1969

He studied it earnestly for a few moments and said, "You're coming at me from totally out in left field. I have no idea what a 'unique automobile' has to do with anything and why this is in Spanish."

"Do you remember back during the war when General D. wanted to let me go from Peenemünde because the Gestapo discovered that I had some Jewish ancestry?" I asked him.

"Of course I do. I think Speer intervened and took care of it despite the fact you quibbled the whole time and said you weren't really Jewish to begin with."

"Well, I wasn't and still am not as far as the Jews are concerned, but the Gestapo were closer to the mark than they realized. What I never told you or anyone else for that matter is that I was raised in a household where my eccentric grandmother, who had only married into a family that had once been Jewish but who herself had barely a drop of Jewish blood, passionately embraced the faith and inducted me into its mysteries. Not the mysteries of the Orthodox or Reform Judaism of modern Europe but those of the Spanish Jews of the late

Middle Ages just before and after their expulsion from Spain in 1492. It was a strange and mystical faith that most real Jews would look upon as fantastical, but above all it was a faith that we held in secret, just like the Marranos, the Jews who had converted to Christianity but continued to observe Jewish beliefs and practices in secret."

"This doesn't completely surprise me, Waldmann. With me everything is right there on the surface, but you've always played it close to the vest. We complemented each other, which is one reason I think we made a good team. But what does any of this have to do with a Spanish car?"

"I know you know your languages. It's the Latin '*auto*,' not the Greek one, from '*actus*,' an act or a proceeding. It was an 'act of faith,' a public proceeding where those accused of heresy were examined by the Inquisition and punished accordingly by everything from penitential prayer to burning at the stake. Because on this occasion there is only one defendant instead of many, it will be an *auto singular* rather than an *auto general*. A lot of those caught up in the Inquisition's dragnet were recent converts charged with backsliding into Judaism—Marranos. But no matter how horrific the punishment, as the Inquisition saw it, they had only the best interests of the accused at heart because the goal of the process was the purification of his or her soul even if that sometimes meant the destruction of the body. When you said the other day that you wanted to flush the gunk out of your soul, the idea of an auto-de-fé immediately popped into my head. Of course, the original ones were aimed at former Jews whose actions harmed Christians. This one is aimed at a born-again Christian—yourself—whose actions harmed Jews. Don't take that too personally. I was up there atop the same pyramid as you, beneath which a hundred thousand slaves groaned and sweated blood. Besides, this is a fake auto and I'm a fake Jew. Still, I feel an uncanny kinship with that distant time and my remote co-religionists such that my knowledge of how to conduct these proceedings seems almost intuitive as if I were tapping into a Marrano collective unconscious."

"Okay, how do we get started?" I could see that the Technical Director was becoming bored and restless with my lengthy exposition.

"I will take the role of the *Promotor Fiscal*, in effect, the prosecuting attorney and judge. Often the Inquisition would spend days or weeks in the preliminary examination of the accused, and in cases of resistance, would employ enhanced means of interrogation to draw out the confession of guilt. But since you have come here willingly, I think we can dispense with the *toca, cordeles, garrotes*, and *strappado*."

"Thank you for that," said the Technical Director.

"To begin, you can remove your hat and coat and put these on." From my suitcase I removed the *coraza*, a tall, conical hat like a schoolboy's dunce cap, and a *sambenito*. This latter was a sort of tunic traditionally made of goat hair. That being unavailable in our mid-sized provincial American city, I fashioned one out of a burlap sack I obtained from a grocery store. While the medieval originals typically featured images of devils and the flames of Hell, I elected to decorate the Technical Director's *corazo* and *sambenito* with the more relevant images of swastikas and rockets.

As the Technical Director pulled the *sambenito* over his head, he said, "Scratchy, like sackcloth. Jonah, right?"

"Exactly."

While he was doing that, I put on the cheap black acetate robe that I wore to graduation ceremonies as an Adjunct Professor of Aeronautics when some bigwig defense contractor (and potential donor) was receiving an honorary degree and the Vice President for Faculty Management threatened to take away our Tier 1 parking privileges if we failed to attend. The Technical Director completed his wardrobe by jauntily placing the tall cap upon his head. "Neat costume," he said. "I'm ready to take direction."

A concrete pad spread out in a radius of about thirty feet from the base of the stand. "If you would, please take a position on the edge of the pad in a direct line with the command bunker and facing the stand."

"Right-o!" he said.

This part of the proceeding wasn't so strange as the Technical Director and I had been involved in many amateur theatricals. While he was taking his place, I walked up the steps to the first steel platform where I could look down upon him from an elevation of about a dozen feet. This roughly corresponded to the spatial arrangement of prosecutor and penitent at the typical sixteenth-century Spanish auto. Next to where I stood was a steel crossbeam upon which I had earlier placed a small silver menorah where it was sheltered from the wind.

"The auto commenced with the saying of Mass. That would obviously be inappropriate here, but in the interest of retaining a religious ritual at the start of our proceedings I will now light the candles of this menorah and recite the blessing as today happens to be the second day of Hanukkah." I struck a match and lit the *shamus* with which I then lit the two candles, moving from left to right according to custom. *"Barukh atah Adonai, Eloheinu Melekh ha'olam, asher kid'shanu b'mitzvotav, v'tzivanu l'hadlik ner shel Hanukkah.* Blessed are you Adonai our God, Ruler of the universe, who has made us holy through God's commandments, and commanded us to light the Hanukkah candles."

The Technical Director mimed applause. "For a fake Jew you speak pretty good Hebrew," he said. I ignored his attempt at humor.

"I will now read the brief condemnatory sermon I have prepared which by custom is intended as much to edify as to convict:

"Before you were formed in the womb, God decreed for you endowments beyond those of ordinary mortals. You have a robust physique, a magnetic personality, movie star good looks, and the courage of ten men. Above all, however, there was that dynamic and incisive brain.

"In addition to these natural gifts, you were destined to be born into a *Junker* family that gave you all the social and economic advantages that Germany had to offer. You attended the finest private schools, enjoyed good food, fine clothes, your own car. You had money to pursue your favorite hobbies. Being a Freiherr opened doors for you, and if that wasn't enough, your father was a high government official.

"You developed a passion for astronomy and dreamed about reaching the stars. You matured when the groundwork was being laid by others to accomplish this task and you were presented with opportunities to participate. While still a teenager, you knew that your vocation was to build the machines that would take humankind into space. Over time, nothing else mattered to you.

"So began your fall from grace.

"You soon realized how terribly expensive it would be to fulfill your dreams and only wanted, as you used to say, a rich uncle to provide the funds. In 1932 that rich uncle showed up in the person of Captain D. He wanted you to build rockets for the Army and made you an offer you felt you could not refuse, and really, why should you have turned him down? Every nation has the right to defend itself, and generations of your *Junker* forebears had committed themselves to that enterprise. You were following family tradition.

"The next year, 1933, the Nazis came to power. Of course you saw them as vulgarians and disapproved their methods. On the other hand, what was wrong with wanting to make Germany great once again? The Versailles Treaty limited big guns; it said nothing about rockets. The Führer loosened the nation's the purse strings. So what if he couldn't see the A-4 as more than just a glorified artillery shell? One day it might take men into space, and even if there were a war, maybe it would end before an A-4 were ever launched in anger. But the war did come and when the rockets rained down on Paris, Antwerp, and London, all you could do was shake your head and say they landed on the wrong planet.

"Worse still was the building of those rockets by slave laborers working under horrific conditions. Thousands died. You knew it was bad but did nothing except obtaining for one prisoner the privilege of wearing civilian clothes. Your conviction that these machines would one day take us to the moon and Mars justified their continued development no matter what the human cost.

"One might think that the experience of defeat would produce remorse and contrition, but you took up with the Americans right where you left off with the Nazis. Although you did not foresee that the real wonder weapon of the twentieth century would be the rocket wedded to the atomic bomb, as soon as the Americans wanted a missile to carry one, you were happy to oblige.

"I could go on. In short, your whole adult life you have never passed up a chance to sell your soul to the Devil. How do you answer these charges?"

"Innocent by reason of mental defect," replied the Technical Director in a calm, clear voice. "My brain was dynamic and incisive but not holistic and integrative. I failed to see that science had been subjugated by politics. I was also constitutionally unable to feel empathy for those outside my immediate circle of friends and colleagues. I have donated my brain to science upon my death, and I predict that when autopsied it will be discovered that it was missing some essential cortex, lobe, or limbic structure. In sum, despite being a genius, I am also a fool."

"That is a self-serving exculpation that avoids the question of moral responsibility."

"Yes it is, and thus another proof of mental defect."

"Do you have anything else to say in your defense?"

"No."

"The court therefore finds you guilty of mass murder and crimes against the human spirit. At this point the *Promotor Fiscal* would normally pronounce sentence, but there is an extenuating circumstance that must be taken into account."

"What extenuating circumstance?"

"A confession. My own."

"Once upon a time, I thought that I would be the one to lead mankind to the stars. I had always taken somewhat literally the notion that Heaven was up above, and while like most of us I lacked a talent for spiritual travel, I aimed to translate the inchoate ideas of men like Oberth into machines that could actually take us there. Then I met you and saw your notebooks and your drawings, and my whole world came crashing down. I could see that, creatively speaking, compared to you, I was a flatworm. I had thought I was the Messiah; now at best I was the precursor, or just one of the bottom tier disciples. I decided to become your flunkey, yet I could never quite leave it there. I would dabble in the number symbolism of the Zohar, for example, and discover some sign that my subordinate status was only a temporary occultation, but then nothing would happen and I would return to my condition of quiet despair, still hoping, I'm ashamed to admit, that the blunt instrument of fate would intervene, and that maybe you would die in a plane crash, just as Todt did, and like Speer I would take over as your successor and finally prove to the world my brilliance.

"That is one reason I was willing to undergo Raumschiffahrt. If I actually made it to outer space in The Bastard, then I would be the hundred-to-one shot that at the last moment beats the favorite in a photo finish. And if I died in the attempt, well, then, I would be released from my sufferings.

"Of course, against the odds I did go into space and live to tell about it, but then you took away whatever glory there was for me in that first stab at the heavens with your perfectly well-reasoned argument for secrecy. Only lately has that wound somewhat healed when I saw your picture in the Vomit Comet and started feeling sorry for you knowing that you'd never get closer to outer space than a padded fuselage while I, Arthur Waldmann, had actually made it there. Yet entertaining such sentiments only shows how petty I am and leaves you as the Noble Tragic Hero of the story—your story, not mine.

"For your crimes you will be relaxed from this ecclesiastical court to the civil government which alone has the authority to carry out the ultimate penalty of burning at the stake. But because your judge and jury today is as deeply a flawed human being as yourself, if not more so, I am reducing the sentence to one of being burned in effigy. Please remain in place while I step down from the dais to accompany you to the *quemadero*."

(In the minute or two that it takes me to descend, the reader might wish to reflect on how my "confession" was grossly incomplete, having made no mention of my role in Korvo's execution. My motive for this deletion was simple self-preservation: There is no statute of limitations on murder and I did not completely trust the Technical Director.)

When I came to where he was standing, I instructed him to turn about face and accompany me the hundred or so yards back to the command and control bunker. We walked around to the far side of it, and there suspended from a section of electrical conduit that ran above the entry way was a crude, scarecrow-looking effigy of the Technical Director that I had fashioned from an old pair of trousers, a shirt, and a throw pillow. To personalize it I had enlarged a head shot of the Technical Director that NASA used in its promotional materials and pinned it to the pillow. Also earlier that morning I had soaked the whole thing in lighter fluid.

"Burning in effigy was the usual punishment for someone condemned to be burned alive but who had run away," I explained. "While I genuinely believe that it might really take the refining fire of the *quemadero* to redeem your soul, such barbaric measures can hardly be countenanced in our more civilized atomic age, and so this vicarious act will have to suffice."

With that I lit a match and touched it to the foot of the effigy. In retrospect I realized that I had gone somewhat overboard with the lighter fluid as the effigy practically exploded in a ball of flame—like the ignition of a rocket?—and singed both of our garments. When it had completely burned to ashes, the Technical Director took a deep breath and volunteered that although the immolation had been merely symbolic he did feel oddly cleansed and refreshed.

"Are we done?" he asked.

I replied that there was only one more element and told him to accompany me back to the Test Stand. "All that's left is the *verguenza*— the shaming. You may now remove your *coraza* and *sambenito*." I took them back up the stairs to the lower platform and using duct tape attached them to a metal crossbeam. "During the period of the Marrano persecutions, your ritual garments would have been hung up in the parish church you attended so that even though you were technically back in the fold as a Christian in good standing, everyone would see the reminder of your heresy, bringing shame not only to you but to your descendants, generation after generation. This cap and vest will probably blow away after a few winter storms, and hardly anyone ever comes out here anymore, yet if someone does happen to see it, I'm sure the images of intertwined rockets and swastikas will give them pause."

We chatted for a few moments more, the Technical Director again thanking me for my "intervention," as he called it, and then, as he was about to climb into his Mercedes, he dropped this bombshell.

"I just got back from Washington last night. I'm not telling you any tales out of school when I say that for a long time I've been feeling burned out in the bad sort of way running the center here. We gave the Americans want they wanted, beating the Russians to the moon. There are still five missions scheduled, but now it's like, been there, done that. Glorified carpentry, just doing the same thing over and over again, but with a lot more anxiety. You know as well as I do that, good as we are, the odds of fifteen men making it to the moon and back alive cannot possibly be one hundred percent. My life has had more disappointments that you realize, Arthur. You're right, it looks like I'll probably never make it into space. For a time I thought maybe as a consolation prize I'd be allowed to run the whole shop up there, but it's a big political appointment, and they're never going to let one of us Germans become head honcho. The Jewish vote, I suppose. But the number four slot has been open for a while—the Associate Administrator's Deputy. We haven't completely defined the parameters of my bailiwick yet, but I'll mainly be a strategic planner, a big ideas guy who'll come up with projects for the future and then try to sell them. I even got them to change the name to Deputy Associate Administrator. Anyway, on Monday morning I'm convening a meeting with all the top people to announce it; there'll be a press release later in the day. I'd appreciate it if you'd keep this under your hat till then."

"Secrecy is my middle name," I said.

As might well be expected, the atmosphere in the conference room on Monday was funereal even before the Technical Director walked in as rumors of his impending departure had been circulating in some quarters over the weekend. While acknowledging that it had been a difficult decision and that he would miss the day-to-day interaction with team members here, some of whom he'd been working with since the early days at Peenemünde, he tried to put the best face on the matter. He shifted into his old Sunny Boy mode and joked that we would finally have the rich uncle up at headquarters we had always wanted who would make sure that Houston didn't get all the goodies. But there were also tears at the end of the meeting, and not just for ourselves. Despite his talk about strategic planning, there was the feeling that, now that NASA had gotten out of him what they wanted, he was more a liability than an asset and was being kicked upstairs to a well-paid sinecure.

Immediately after the meeting, he left on an extended family vacation and did not return until February when our city threw him a big farewell party which culminated in the unveiling of a granite marker honoring him in the center of town. As the crowd cheered, he flashed his infectious smile and raised both arms, giving the V for victory sign. That was the last time I would ever see him.

• • •

The predictions about the Technical Director being kicked upstairs turned out to be accurate. As the Apollo program wound down, the country was in no mood to spend billions more on pie-in-the-sky outer space projects. Between that and the Vietnam War, the nation's reserves of treasure and blood were nearly tapped out. About a year and a half after his move, one of our people ran into him wandering the halls at headquarters, complaining that he really had nothing important to do there and speaking nostalgically of the days when he used to bend metal or, at least, tell people how to do it. Not long after that he cashed in his chips and took a plum job with a defense contractor that paid many times what he had earned during his years in government service. He never returned to our town, and for the next several years I heard little about him, save an occasional anecdote when someone I was acquainted with ran into him at a conference or a trade show.

Then in early 1977 I received the following letter:

"Dear Arthur,

"When I sat down to write, it seemed like we hadn't touched base in two or three years but looking at the calendar today I realize it's been more like seven. I'd always meant to at least drop you a line again expressing my appreciation for your 'unique car.' I know it was offered in the same spirit of good humor and comradeship as our little holiday theatricals in the old days, and although it may not have cleared my conscience, it has helped to open my eyes.

"The calendar also tells me that today, February 13th, is the anniversary of that amazing journey you once took, which is a nice bit of kismet because it reminds me that despite your protestations to the contrary, you possess immense reserves of personal courage, and are thus the right man of whom to ask this huge favor.

"I don't know if word has travelled down the grapevine to you, but about a year ago I was diagnosed with colon cancer. As you can imagine I was determined to fight this with every fiber of my being, and so I have, but lately the cancer has spread and I can see the handwriting on the wall. Under the circumstances, it was right and proper that I update my will, and I have done so. It turns out there is quite a lot of money involved. Between speaking fees and royalties from books, it runs into the high seven figures. Naturally, I have first looked to my family's needs, but I also wanted to leave a legacy to the community where I worked so many years and included a substantial bequest (along with most of my papers) to the Center for Space Exploration and Technology we all helped found a few years ago.

"I now realize that I have made a serious error of omission in my bequest to them and see that it would be a grave injustice if future generations hear the story of modern rocketry without a complete picture of how it was brought into being. That picture must include a dramatic representation of its terrible human cost.

"The enclosed codicil seeks to correct that error by reapportioning my bequest. However, I have thus far revealed its terms to no one, and I am placing in your possession the unique copy, as I know how upsetting this will be to many old friends who I fear would try to dissuade me from my intentions, and in my weakening state, they might well succeed. Also, upon my passing, I do not want to burden my family with the carrying out of its terms, and so I have named you as executor. I won't pretend that this will be easy. It will take someone of courage and fortitude, someone who has lived a life like yours, to complete the task, which is precisely why I'm asking you.

"You need not reply with an answer. In fact, I'd prefer that you not. As you might imagine, I'm feeling a bit fatalistic these days, and I know that you either will or will not accede to this request. In any case, only a fool would think that he can control what happens from beyond the grave, and I am no longer a fool."

The text of the enclosed codicil read as follows:

"Whereas, I now desire to make certain changes in my last will and testament:

"Now therefore, I do hereby make, publish and declare this as a first codicil to my said last will and testament to be annexed to and taken and allowed as part thereof:

"I hereby amend my last will by adding thereto a new section:

"Of the sum total that I give, devise, and bequeath to the Center for Space Exploration and Technology, the amount of $2,600,000 shall be used solely and exclusively for the following purpose: The Trustees shall acquire one of the caves at the base of Mont Vert near the city limits containing not less than 5,000 square feet of usable space. When this cave has been modified to meet all applicable state and federal safety standards, the remaining funds shall be used to construct therein a re-creation of the main V-2 assembly area at the Mittelwerk in Thuringia as it was in 1944 and 1945. The primary focus of this educational exhibit shall not be on technical matters but rather the lives and working conditions of the slave laborers who were confined there. A professional staff with appropriate credentials in research and pedagogy should be employed to curate this permanent exhibit which will be known as The Jakob Korvo Museum of the Mittelwerk. I furthermore designate Arthur Waldmann as executor of this codicil to whom I also grant final authority to approve the exhibit's design and execution."

In the hours after my initial shock upon reading this, my emotions oscillated between two extremes. On the one hand I was honored to know that my actions had evidently helped to enable a profound transformation in the moral life of another human being. How often are we so blessed? While I personally do not believe in a Christian afterlife divided between Heaven and Hell, the Technical Director clearly did, and so in that respect I could be seen as an agent of redemption, a kind of Angel of Mercy (a familiar figure to readers of the Zohar).

Alternatively, however, I could also see this as a supremely self-serving attempt to secure his posthumous reputation at no expense to himself. With only weeks or months left, he had now lived the life that he had wanted, single-mindedly pursuing his dreams of space, regardless of their effect upon others. While he remained a local hero, however, I'm sure he was also smart enough to realize that as memories of the Cold War and the heroic age of the space program faded, he would come into sharper historical focus as the Faustian character that he really was. But by bequeathing the world The Jakob Korvo Museum of the Mittelwerk, in one stroke he would demonstrate both his humility by acknowledging a forgotten forebear and his remorse in having been complicit in one of the worst episodes of twentieth-century barbarism. Not only would he thus preemptively rehabilitate himself, he would also once again claim a place of primacy that might well have been mine. Often in recent years had I contemplated the possibility of belatedly becoming the Albert Speer of the German rocket program, the quintessential insider who in a very public way (as Speer did at Nuremburg) admits to the evil nature of the enterprise with which he had been so closely associated. Now with The Jakob Korvo Museum of the Mittelwerk, any mea culpa on my part would be seen as a half-hearted gesture, too little, too late. Another lost opportunity.

Unless, of course, I chose to do nothing. The Technical Director had asked that I not communicate my willingness to him, no doubt to save himself the anxiety of wondering if I was just saying this to make a dying man happy, and if I would carry through with the project after he was gone. I looked at the codicil again and remembered how, after returning to Peenemünde from the Mittelwerk, I had burned Korvo's missive. I could set a match to the codicil now and no one would ever know. I agonized for some time about this and in the end stuffed the Technical Director's letter and codicil into a drawer. The future was unpredictable. At all events, I could always burn it later.

The following June I read the notice of the Technical Director's passing in our local paper. As was to be expected, accolades to the "Father of Modern Rocketry" came pouring in from around the country and around the world. But the last moon landing was by now almost five years in the past and except for a few Skylab missions that attracted almost no attention, and one Apollo/Soyuz that drew only a little, not much had happened in space lately, nor would until the first Shuttle mission four years hence. While feelings of resentment toward the Technical Director preyed on me for a time, I saw that within a few days the news cycle had digested and excreted him. Despite his singular accomplishments, the world really didn't care that much about him. A month later he had dropped out of conversations I had with colleagues at the Guidance Lab and the university. Later that summer Elvis Presley and Groucho Marx would pass away. Some people become larger than life in death, but this German rocket scientist would not be among them.

I tried to put it all out of mind but inevitably the other shoe dropped. In early 1978 the Center for Space Exploration and Technology announced that thanks to a substantial bequest from the Technical Director's estate, they would soon begin construction of a facility to house the Saturn V Dynamic Test Vehicle, a fully operational prototype that was used to evaluate the hundreds of components and subassemblies in each of the rocket's three stages. Thanks to the efforts of the Technical Director, the Test Vehicle had been transferred to the site of the still to be completed Center just a few weeks before the first moon landing. Since then it had been displayed as an outdoor exhibit, and now, after nearly a decade exposed to the elements it was showing significant damage from both weather and pest infestations. Unless the Test Vehicle were moved to an enclosed space, it was very possible that this particular engineering marvel, one of only two surviving complete Saturn Vs, would be lost to posterity.

Preservation of the Test Vehicle, with whose design and fabrication I was intimately involved, was certainly a worthy goal, though I wondered about the wisdom of spending two and a half million dollars to build what was essentially a garage for an old rocket booster. Of course, such a question evaded the whole issue of any responsibility I might bear in the expenditure of this substantial sum. I pulled out the Technical Director's letter and codicil. Clearly his final wish for the money was the development of The Jakob Korvo Museum of the Mittelwerk. I knew this, and presumably the witnesses (whose names were unknown to me) who signed the codicil also knew it. But if what the Technical Director had said were true and I possessed the sole copy of the document, I would now be the only one with the power to redirect the funds. Should I take action or just set a match to the thing and be done with it?

My grandmother was always a bit suspicious of the Bible on the grounds that it had been so easily co-opted by Christians and turned into the "Old Testament," but there was one verse from Deuteronomy that she liked because she said it fortified her in the eccentric path she had chosen: "I call heaven and earth to witness against you this day: I have put before you life and death, blessing and curse. Choose life, by loving the Lord your God, heeding His commands, and holding fast to Him." To choose life—wasn't this the real purpose behind all the esoteric study and fidelity to the religion of the Marranos? The Technical Director was dead. Korvo was even deader. I had drifted into a comfortable sort of death-in-life, a man with nothing to look forward to except his own real death.

The Center's news release came out on Friday. The following Monday I arranged to meet with our local newspaper's science and technology reporter who had interviewed me a few times in the past and to whom I now handed over a copy of the codicil. The story broke in the paper the next day. Predictably, reaction was swift and pointed. The Center Director produced his copy of the will (minus the codicil, of course) and said that the bequest to preserve the Test Vehicle reflected the Technical Director's sentiments as expressed to him personally many times. Local civic and political leaders weighed in with concerns about the impact on our tourism industry. A splashy new exhibit was just what was needed for the Center to keep up with competing technology museums, especially the Kennedy Space Center in Florida, which had its own Saturn V on display. It was hard to imagine, observed the mayor, that families travelling through town on their way to the beach or Disney World would want to spend time here in a dank, smelly cave looking at old photographs of emaciated prisoners.

Among the top people who had known the Technical Director for thirty or forty years, a consensus developed that if the codicil were authentic, it was probably the result of dementia that had developed as his overall condition deteriorated. One of our lab directors who had visited him in the hospital reported that at times he seemed overwhelmed with remorse and uncertainty: "He would go off on tangents about how there was so much misery in the world and how all the money to send a few dozen men into space could have been better spent elsewhere. I told him, no, that building rockets was his destiny, a force stronger than he or any other man could have controlled. 'Think of all the technical innovations that owed their development to the space program—computers, microelectronics— not to mention the spiritual uplift that you brought to millions of people around the world when they watched our moon landings!' 'Do you think that's really true?' he asked, and I said, 'Yes, absolutely,' and I'm almost certain I saw a faint smile spread across his face."

Legal challenges to the will kept it in probate for almost two years but were ultimately resolved in favor of the codicil's authenticity. (It should be noted that neither the family nor any of my former colleagues joined the Center as parties to the dispute. Indeed, the only one who spoke out publicly against the codicil was the Aviatrix, who was then serving on the Center's governing board.) During that period I remained confident of a positive outcome and began preliminary work on The Jakob Korvo Museum of the Mittelwerk. I identified a former limestone mine that had been expanded from a natural cave at the base of Mont Vert as a promising site and began looking for historical artifacts with which to furnish it, discovering, for example, that several V-2s were still held in storage at our former New Mexico test range. Dr. Dick Lumpkin, an Assistant Professor of French at the university, alerted me to a recent memoir about the Mittelwerk published in France, and with the assistance of that former prisoner, I assembled a database of other survivors and began collecting their testimonies. Dr. Lumpkin, who himself had recently finished a book on Holocaust memorials in France, also had many helpful suggestions about creating a meaningful experience for visitors to the museum. It was he who came up with the idea of giving everyone an identification card with a photo and personal history of an individual prisoner to personalize their visit, a protocol, incidentally, that was later adopted by the United States Holocaust Museum in Washington. He also deserves credit for Camp Mittelwerk, a set of week-long programs for young people ages 9-14 and 15-18 that allows them the opportunity to learn what it was really like to work in a Nazi slave labor camp. (Campers divide their time equally between playing the roles of slaves and guards; there is now also a program for adults.)

The Jakob Korvo Museum of the Mittelwerk opened in 1982 with a ceremony that included members of the Technical Director's family and a delegation of Mittlewerk survivors. Despite the fact that it remains unaffiliated with the Center for Space Exploration and Technology across town and is not included in the Tourism Bureau's promotional materials, it has enjoyed a steadily increasing stream of visitors since its opening and just two years later won the prestigious Leonard David Obler Award for Experiential Exhibitions from the Council of American Museums of the History of Technology.

EPILOGUE:
SEPHARAD

Despite the success of The Jakob Korvo Museum of the Mittelwerk, or perhaps rather because of it, I did indeed become *persona non grata* in many quarters of our community, just as the Technical Director anticipated. Although two or three of my former colleagues privately told me that they sympathized with my actions, none came out with public statements in my favor, and I don't hold it against them, especially those who still had families to support. It was mainly the locals who launched the personal attacks, accusing me of everything from tricking the Technical Director into changing his will to redirecting funds from the bequest into offshore bank accounts. At one point I even caught wind of a whispering campaign that claimed I was actually Jewish or half-Jewish and that a deep-rooted ethnic antipathy accounted for my having become the Judas of the rocket team. Of course, there was actually a smidgen of truth to this calumny and I wondered if somehow awareness of my brush with the Nuremburg Laws was more widely disseminated than I realized.

It's perhaps fitting that after the museum opened I lived more and more an underground sort of life. Having retired from both NASA and the university, I spent most of my time at home, going out only to purchase necessities and to take early morning walks in the cemetery, not that I had ever been much of a social butterfly. I came to see this isolation as a kind of mild martyrdom, a lenient prison sentence like that of Speer's twenty years in Spandau. I even adopted his means of passing the time by meticulously measuring out the cemetery as a scale model of the world and then going on walking tours of all six continents using guidebooks from my local branch library.

Whatever the personal cost to me, however, I have absolutely no regrets about my actions in the matter of the will. "Why deny the people of our city a 'hero' in the personage of the Technical Director?" wrote one correspondent to our local paper, expressing a commonly held view. "We do not have a German like Dietrich Bonhoeffer or Colonel Claus Schenk von Stauffenberg in our midst. The Technical Director is as close as we get, remembering that heroes come in many varieties and there are few in this world who have perfect credentials." I could not agree more! But those who want to preserve an image of the Technical Director as a man who was merely self-satisfied with his accomplishments and felt no misgivings about the negative consequences of his life's work, whatever its world-historical significance, actually rob him of his heroic credentials and will bequeath to future generations not a hero but a hollow man, the spoiled aristocrat and opportunist of his present-day detractors. His supposed defenders sell him short, for how could such a genius not be sufficiently self aware to come to terms with his own failings, even if only on his deathbed. In short, if I have betrayed him, my betrayal, like that of Judas, has put into motion the process that will ultimately redeem him for all time.

• • •

On that rather dramatic note I had originally concluded my narrative, but felt that readers might be curious about the author's later circumstances, and so I append this epilogue.

While I had been content living my monkish life, I became increasingly troubled at the thought of dying and being buried here, and so began casting about for alternatives. Retirement to Florida seemed an obvious move, but the prospect of ending up in assisted living and being obliged to eat meals with strangers from Ohio and New Jersey made Speer's almost ten years alone in Spandau with von Schirach and Hess look like a family vacation. Germany held a certain appeal. I had not been back since leaving in 1945 initially because until the 1960s there was concern that as one of the top people in the rocket program I might be the object of a kidnapping attempt by Soviet agents. By the time it was safe to travel there, my parents had passed on and I otherwise had no reason to go. Lately, however, I had developed powerful feelings of nostalgia for my home in Trier, and I fantasized about the streets and woodland paths that I had long ago walked with my grandmother, but it was precisely the fear that these *in situ* reveries would seem pale in comparison with the original experiences and would only leave me disappointed and depressed that led me to rule it out.

Israel seemed promising for a short time. So much of my inner and outer life had been directed by my eccentric relationship with Judaism; and Israel was the ancient and now modern homeland of the Jews, so why not? But there were complications. Under the amended Law of Return (1970), the right to immigrate to Israel had been extended from individual Jews to the children and grandchildren of Jews, and their spouses. In theory I could claim the right through my grandmother, but to do so I would have to produce some kind of document proving her Jewish connection, such as a letter from a rabbi or rabbinic court, conversion certificate, or birth, marriage, or death certificate. None of these existed, of course, because while my grandmother was strongly attracted to certain aspects of Jewish belief and practice, she had always identified less as a Jew than as a Marrano. I did have the letter from the Führer stating that despite my status as Mixed Ancestry, Second Grade, I would be allowed to continue my work with the rocket program, but even if that level of Jewish connection were satisfactory, I could imagine the uproar if it ever became known that Israeli citizenship had been granted upon the Führer's word. Outside the Law of Return I would have to emigrate as a U. S. citizen with a very checkered past that included membership in the SS. This also did not appear very promising, and I soon abandoned the idea.

But the aborted attempt did lead to the insight that the critical operative term for my future was not Jew but Marrano, and this directed me to the place from which I now write these closing words: Spain, the Book of Jonah's Sepharad.

Our coded communications with my grandmother were cut off after the liberation of France, and it was only in the winter of 1946 that my parents received a letter from a lawyer in Toledo informing them that she had passed away the preceding spring, just a few days short of her 88th birthday. Accompanying the letter were several cartons containing books, manuscripts, and a small number of personal mementos. In accordance with her will she had been cremated and her ashes scattered in the Tagus. The will also directed that the small house she owned in Toledo be rented out after her death with the proceeds sent to my parents until such time as they might decide to occupy or dispose of the property.

Upon my parents' deaths all of my grandmother's possessions, including the house in Toledo, passed down to me. I rummaged around in a closet where I had stashed the cartons and fished out the deed, which ran to several pages, composed in opaque Spanish legalese and written in a nearly indecipherable script. I sent off a letter to the real estate company managing the property and received back word that the house was currently unoccupied. This seemed an obvious sign. I then called a travel agent and booked a plane ticket to Madrid.

As the plane broke through a thin deck of clouds at the end of the nine-hour flight and I looked down, I realized that while I had been imbued with a language and spirituality rooted here, I had never given much thought to the physical appearance of the place. What images I had must have come from *Don Quixote*, because I couldn't remember ever reading anything else about Spain (except very obliquely the Zohar), and not even reading the book myself but only hearing a children's version of the famous windmill episode read by my teacher in one of the lower grades. Naturally I pictured windmills that looked like the ones in Holland, minus the tulips or any sort of greenery, but instead surrounded by a desert landscape like what I had seen in Hollywood movies about the American West—an arid emptiness where there was nothing to compete with the florid speeches of the crazy old knight and the harsh rejoinders of his hard-headed squire.

While hot, dry Spain does exist, that happened not to be the initiatory experience I was to have arriving in late December. The bus ride down from Madrid to Toledo was made through heavy rain, with reports of flooding throughout the country coming in over the radio. The storied plains of La Mancha were barely visible through the mist, and what little I saw was in varying shades of coral and aquamarine.

Happily, the rain stopped by the time I disembarked at the bus station in Toledo. At three o'clock on the afternoon of Christmas Eve the place was nearly deserted. I picked up my small suitcase and began walking up the hill, past the walls built by King Wamba who, like most of the feckless Visigothic kings in the last decades before Muslim rule, was no friend to the Jews.

After a good fifteen-minute hike I reached the old town center, the Zocodover, a charming Romance corruption of the original Arabic which meant cattle market. Christmas lights were strung overhead, a crèche was in one corner of the plaza, and a rather Nordic-, even Aryan looking fir tree occupied the center. From here two or three main streets plunged into the dark mazes that I would soon discover I had faultless instincts for navigating. I entered one and passed a waiter who was folding up umbrellas in front of an outdoor café. In my stilted, Ladino-inflected Spanish, I asked him if there were any *hostales* nearby, and he was kind enough to walk me a few doors down the street to one whose tiled walls were decorated with Toledo's ubiquitous arabesques and six-pointed stars.

The next morning I could see by the shaft of light coming into the tiny courtyard below my window that the famous Spanish sun had elected to put in an appearance. I dressed and went out into a medieval cityscape of juxtaposed lozenges of glare and deep shadow. It was Christmas morning and the only people on the streets were small groups of Japanese and Korean tourists who moved about tentatively, like archaeologists who had stumbled into the well-preserved imperial capital of some lost civilization. On a hunch I followed Calle Comercio south out of the Zocodover. It headed slightly uphill and then down to another plaza which fronted the Cathedral. I bore to the right toward the Mudejar church of St. Thomas and just beyond that point saw a sign indicating that I had reached the entrance to the *judería*.

I wish I could say that at this instant a wave of recognition overcame me, and that, as I followed the arrows pointing toward the Transito and Santa Maria Blanca synagogues, I experienced an uncanny sense of homecoming, as though certain molecules of DNA inherited from remote ancestors and now using my body as temporary housing reacted with other molecules in the air and remembered, in whatever way chemical compounds can be said to remember, that they had been here before. I was happy, yes, but I had been happy all morning, having the town mostly to myself, me and the northeast Asian bourgeoisie, for whom Christmas was merely a touristic curiosity. The *judería* didn't look very different from the rest of the town. I peered down twisting alleys and tried to imagine Medieval people in their coarse clothing going about their daily business buying, selling, and gossiping, but in fact I was unable to visualize them. Imagination fared better when I put my hands on a brick, and I thought about the moment, as particular as the one I was in now, when the mason had slapped that brick into place. It was, let us say, 1097, a few years after the transfer of the city from Moor to Christian, the Jewish community flourishing in their role as economic and cultural mediators between old and new regimes, the very height of the *Convivencia*, though of course they didn't know they were living at the height of an epoch any more than we do now. What they did know was the weather, a warm breeze or chilly blast on the mason's face at the moment that brick went down, a black fly buzzing around his ear, a sore on his left hand that seemed not to be healing properly (the melanoma that would kill him in a year or two), the overheard conversation of two women walking in the street behind him, and then of course all the invisible thoughts in the man's head, his daydreams, sexual fantasies, worries about his daughter's marriage prospects. Something of all that must have entered the brick as he slapped it into place, else why would I think of it now almost a millennium later?

The guidebook had warned me about the unprepossessing exterior of the Transito and so I was on the watch for it, but I still managed to walk past three times before recognizing it. The issue was moot, however, because when I pulled on the door, it was locked. A sign on the wall next to it gave the closing dates as 1 and 6 January, 1 May, and 24, 25, and 31 December. It seemed to me that of all days, a proper memorial to ten centuries of Jewish life in Spain ought to go out of its way to be open on Christmas, but there was nothing to be done. I retreated to a small plaza across the street and sat down on a bench with a view across the Tagus of olive groves stretching to the horizon.

The groves put me in mind of my main purpose in coming to Toledo. I now unzipped my waist pack and pulled out a small box made of olive wood. I cracked it open and inside on a velvet cushion was a heavy iron skeleton key about six inches long. The bow of the key was in the shape of a flower; the teeth sticking down from the shaft at the other end looked like four miniature two- and three-tined forks. This was the key to the house that my grandmother lived in from sometime in 1937 until her death in 1945. While she did not keep a complete diary, notes she had left behind told the story. She had originally been attracted to Toledo because of its associations with the Zohar and Moses de Leon, but genealogical research showed that some of her distant Graetz (originally Garcia) ancestors had lived in the city and had been in the service of Samuel ha-Levi Abulafia, the royal treasurer, who had built the Transito as a private chapel for his family and his retainers. Eventually she was able to identify a house in the *judería* that she believed had been owned by a great-great-great-great-great-great-great-great-grandfather, and because, before its emergence as cultural attraction in post-Franco Spain, Toledo's *judería* was a shabby, undesirable part of town, she had been able to purchase it with her modest savings.

The key had a satisfying heft to it, suggesting an instrument that would unlock not just a door but a world. In the years immediately following the death of Franco, there were occasional stories in the paper about American Jews showing up in Spanish cities with keys that their families had kept or had by other means reacquired and re-entering homes their ancestors had occupied before the Expulsion. I was now on the verge of doing the same. All I had to do was find the place. I had the address, a *callejon* or alleyway, which unfortunately was not indicated on my map. As the realtor's office was closed, I would have to search it out on my own, and was sure that somehow race memory would lead me to it, but after an hour of crisscrossing the *judería*, I had come up empty. There was nothing for it but to find someone from the neighborhood to ask.

Of course, the only people on the streets were Japanese and Korean. Spaniards stay home on Christmas day and most businesses are closed. As I walked past one place, Julián Simón (Hijo) Artesania, a shop that sold damascene ware and ceramics, I looked through the window and saw a man moving around inside wearing pajamas, slippers and a nightcap. When he noticed me he smiled, and evidently thinking that I wanted to buy something or at least inquire about hours, approached the door and opened it.

"Please come in, come in!" he said.

"I didn't mean to disturb you, I know it's Christmas and you're closed—"

"If you're here, I'm open. Look around if you want and let me know if you have any questions."

He was a man in his late sixties or early seventies. A few clumps of thick, white hair seemed pasted in an irregular pattern around the equatorial regions of his head, which hung lantern-like just forward of his shoulders. He had the kindly eyes of someone who had perhaps learned long ago that unexpected visitors might be gods from Olympus or other divine precincts. The shop itself evoked the whimsy of one of those untrained folk artists who become the darlings of big city collectors. The walls were lined with shelves upon which sat dozens of multicolored plates and bowls, along with large and small pieces of damascene ware. There were the inevitable representations of the Knight and his Squire and lots of six-pointed stars, but most were original abstract designs. The light reflected from black, red, and gold enamel and metal bathed the interior in a kind of autumnal radiance.

"Do you do all your own work?" I asked him, examining a large damascene plate whose nodes and intersecting lines reminded me, inevitably, of the *Sephirot*.

"Most of it," he said, "though as the sign says, I am the son. My father has a shop on the other side of town, and we sell one another's goods."

Now that I thought of it, I had seen his father's place on my walk into town the day before.

"Simón," I asked, "is that a common name in Toledo?"

"It is a little unusual here," he said, "but not unknown. Oddly enough, it's a name that I've run into on my travels for business and pleasure all over the world—Brazil, Singapore, South Africa. A couple of years ago I was in Israel and when I opened the Tel Aviv phone book there was a whole page of them. Of course, it's a name that goes back to the Bible."

"Yes, it sounded a little Sephardic," I ventured. "I wonder if perhaps your family might be descended from the Jews who lived here a long time ago."

Sr. Simón laughed and said, "Jewish, Arab, whatever, it's all mixed up here. Who really knows? I'm always having this discussion with my uncle who looks more Jewish than Maimonides but is convinced that we're direct descendants of King Wamba himself!"

This seemed like a good moment to tell him about my errand here and show him my key. I placed the wooden box on the table and opened it slowly as though I was letting a genie out. He put on a pair of reading glasses and leaned down to inspect it.

"A very nice specimen," Sr. Simón said. "Hardly a spot of rust. Definitely forged in Toledo, mid- to late-eighteenth century."

"I had the impression it was more like mid- to late-fifteenth century."

"Even in this dry climate, iron rusts and though it's possible that a small artifact handled as often as a key might survive five centuries, we almost never see one. Besides, you see this shape in the bow? It's a stylized *fleur-de-lis* that came in with the Bourbons. Let me show you." He gestured me over to a chest of drawers near his work table and opened one that contained a hodge-podge of metal artifacts, old tools, fasteners, clamps and the like. After rummaging around for a moment he pulled out a metal ring with about a dozen keys that looked very similar to mine. "People would be cleaning out their houses and just throw these things away, but in recent years they've come to be prized as antiques. I'm not saying that this is the case with your grandmother, but sometimes a real estate agent is only too happy to tell a willing buyer that a derelict old house in town is the family castle."

"I believe that she did her research," I said. "For various reasons she was no stranger to ancient and obscure documents."

"No doubt," he said, "and it may well be that her house really was once owned by your great-great, etc. grandfather in just the same way that we Simóns might be the heirs to Visigothic kings. Or maybe we're the Jews and you're the Visigoths. I wouldn't lose sleep over it, Sr.

Waldmann. It is, after all, we the living, who get to decide these things."

We chatted for a few more minutes about the vagaries of family history and he gave me directions to the house, but as soon as I left I knew that I no longer had any reason to go there. It was just as likely as not that our family had no connection with the place and I worried that some tell-tale sign, now that I had been tipped off to the possibility, would confirm the lack of authenticity. All that really mattered was the image I had formed of my grandmother sitting there at her desk patiently reading her ancient texts with a look of quiet contentment on her face, and why spoil that? Besides, I had never intended to move there myself, having made other plans. The next day I visited the real estate office and completed the sale of the property as had been my intention.

I stayed in Toledo a few more days, then went on to Córdoba where I toured the Great Mosque of Abd al-Rahman and managed to eat the twelve grapes before the stroke of midnight on New Year's Eve. Late in the evening of New Year's Day after a long train ride, I arrived at my final destination: Granada. Certainly as a Marrano the city where the Catholic Monarchs had issued the Edict of Expulsion that for better and worse had created the strange hybridized cultural matrix to which I was a distant heir held an undeniable appeal, but I confess my motives for moving here were more practical and professional. In the months when I was casting about for a place to go into self-imposed exile, I was reading one of the aerospace journals I still subscribed to and ran across an article about a number of small start-up companies that were working on new designs for Zeppelins. It seems that up until 1937 the Zeppelin Company had been immensely profitable and that following the unfortunate *Hindenburg* accident and attendant closure of its primary operations those funds had been moved to an endowment under the trusteeship of the mayor of Friedrichshaven. A stipulation limited use of the funds to airship development, and now after half a century the endowment had grown to the point where the trustees had decided that the time was ripe for a Zeppelin revival. Market research indicated possible sales of upward of 80 Zeppelins for tourism, cargo transport, and scientific research, and technological innovations in avionics and power plants could easily overcome earlier limitations. (Needless to say, these new airships would be filled with helium, not hydrogen.) One of the companies that had received funding from the endowment was looking for engineers who had experience in the design of non-conventional aircraft. It was based in Granada, whose arid climate and diverse topography makes it a good location for testing purposes. I sent them my resumé along with some drawings that I had done for the Zeppelin-based rocket launch system back in the 1930s. They hired me sight unseen. No doubt my willingness to work for free until the company turned a profit (thanks to my generous NASA pension) made their decision a relatively easy one.

●　　　●　　　●

Everyone's story, once told, becomes an obelisk, a sort of gravestone, but only Moses in the Book of Deuteronomy was actually able to bring the narrative of his life to its close by including the report of his own death. (Leave it to that proto-Marrano, Isaac the Blunderer, to raise doubts about its authenticity, thus opening up the can of worms called skepticism that six centuries later Spinoza would finally turn upside down and scatter all over the place.) So even here in my eighth decade my story remains unfinished. Just this week I met for the first time with my new youthful colleagues whose passion and excitement for their work is something I haven't seen since my days back at the Rocket Center in Berlin. By the time he was forty, the Technical Director was too old ride the rockets he had spent his whole life building, but the gentle Zeppelin imposes no such age restrictions. In a couple years I'll be part of the crew putting one of our prototype airships through its paces, looking up at the snow-capped peaks of the Sierra Nevada to our port side or out across the seemingly endless plains to starboard. To be suspended almost motionless between Heaven and Earth, it's perhaps the place I always wanted to be.

ACKNOWLEDGEMENTS

Although *Confessions of a Marrano Rocketeer* is a work of fiction I have drawn on a number of sources for historical details. These include the following:

Dornberger, Walter. *V-2*. New York: Viking, 1954.

Laney, Monique. *German Rocketeers in the Heart of Dixie*. New Haven, Yale UP, 2015.

Michel, Jean. *Dora*. Trans. Jennifer Kidd. New York: Holt, Rinehart, Winston, 1979.

Neufeld, Michael J. *The Rocket and the Reich*. Cambridge: Harvard UP, 1995.

—-. *Von Braun: Dreamer of Space, Engineer of War*. New York: Vintage, 2007.

Reitsch, Hanna. *The Sky My Kingdom*. London: Greenhill Books, 1997.

Speer, Albert. *Inside the Third Reich*. New York: Simon and Schuster, 1997.

Stuhlinger, Ernst and Frederick I. Ordway III. *Wernher von Braun, Crusader for Space: A Biographical Memoir*. Malabar, FL: Krieger Publishing, 1996.

—-. *Wernher von Braun, Crusader for Space: An Illustrated Memoir*. Malabar, FL: Krieger Publishing, 1996.

I am also indebted to Robert Luther and the late Ernst Nathan for their personal reminiscences. Special thanks to AnneMarie Martin for an early edit of the manuscript, and to Allen Wier for encouragement and advice at a critical juncture.

ABOUT THE AUTHOR

Daniel Schenker divides his time between Lacey's Spring, Alabama and Lenox, Massachusetts, where he lives with his wife, their teenage son, and their two dogs.

NOTE FROM THE AUTHOR

Word-of-mouth is crucial for any author to succeed. If you enjoyed *Confessions of a Marrano Rocketeer*, please leave a review online—anywhere you are able. Even if it's just a sentence or two. It would make all the difference and would be very much appreciated.

Thanks!
Daniel Schenker

We hope you enjoyed reading this title from:

www.blackrosewriting.com

Subscribe to our mailing list – *The Rosevine* – and receive **FREE** books, daily deals, and stay current with news about upcoming releases and our hottest authors.
Scan the QR code below to sign up.

Already a subscriber? Please accept a sincere thank you for being a fan of Black Rose Writing authors.

View other Black Rose Writing titles at
www.blackrosewriting.com/books and use promo code
PRINT to receive a **20% discount** when purchasing.